# *Mafiella*

## WELCOME TO THE FAMILY

## VALENTINA'S ACADEMY - YEAR 1

## ROSALINDA DIAZ

<u>**Mafiella**</u>
<u>**Welcome to The Family**</u>
By RosaLinda Diaz



<u>Mafiella</u>
<u>Welcome to The Family</u>
Paperback ISBN: 978-1737550952
E-Book ISBN: 978-1737550921
Copyright © 2024 Rosalinda Diaz
Gumption & Grace Publishing

TO: _______________

AN HONORARY VALENTINA

*For my mom who would make an excellent Don.*
*Thank you for the inspiration.*

# *Chapter One*

I n her cramped and narrow bedroom, which had probably been used as a butler's pantry by the past residents, given its odd rhombus shape and proximity to the kitchen, Stella sat on the frigid stone floor clutching a yellowed envelope. The oppressive stillness closed in on her along with the darkness. *Piccolo Angelo* was scrawled across the front of the envelope in fading script. She kept this treasure hidden between the pages of an atlas under her bed, away from prying eyes, never telling a soul that it existed, anticipating this moment for the last three and a half years. She'd clung to the promise of the envelope's contents when life became unbearable. It might only be a simple letter from her mother or grandfather, some shred of love to get her through the next few years until she'd be free from this place.

The envelope's contents wouldn't be a mystery for long. Stella traced her nickname with the tip of her finger. She wondered if maybe she should wait and savor the anticipation a little while longer. Once she opened it, the thrill would be over, and she'd know whatever Nonnu had wanted kept secret. She was more than a bit nervous if it contained anything close to the life-changing information of the other envelope. Maybe she'd wait. What was the harm in delaying another year?

Stella brought the paper to her nose and imagined she could still smell Nonnu's cologne and feel the touch of his callused and leathery hands as he pressed the two envelopes against her palm on his deathbed and made her promise to protect them with her life. He instructed her to open the first when he died. Stella had protested, but Nonnu said he could feel the end nearing, and the first envelope would keep her safe. The second, he said, was not to be touched until her sixteenth birthday, and she was never to show it to anyone. Ever.

Growing up in the suburbs of the Mile-High city, it was just the four of them: Mom, Granny, Nonnu, and herself. Stella had never met or even heard of any other living family. There weren't any photo albums or framed images adorning the walls of their five-room red brick ranch-style house. When she'd asked about the missing pictures, Granny said all their mementos had been lost in a fire. As far as Stella knew, she was the end of the family line. A line that kept getting shorter. Mom had died before Stella turned five, leaving her with vague, hazy memories. The kind that didn't feel entirely her own. They were pieced together from Granny's stories and her daydreams. But it hadn't been a bad life. She'd adored her grandparents, who were loving and affectionate, if a bit quirky.

Nonnu would get a far-off look in his eye and tell her about the "good old days" back in Brooklyn, New York. But before he went into too much detail, Granny would prod him out of the easy chair and remind him the grass could use a mow, leaves needed raking, or the driveway was mounded with snow and due for shoveling. That would be the end of storytime. But Stella had been fascinated by his tales of righting wrongs and looking out for the little guy.

When Granny died four years ago, Nonnu retreated into his special world more and more. It was just the two of them, with an occasional visit from a home nurse when he started going downhill. Stella did all the cooking and cleaning while still attending school. She'd offered to quit or do remote learning, but

Nonnu insisted she go in person. He was old-fashioned that way. It was a lot of responsibility for a twelve-year-old. Still, being an only child, constantly surrounded by adults, Stella had always been mature for her age. Being raised by her grandparents, having strict rules, and emphasizing self-sufficiency had helped. They'd had no friends or people over to the house, but Stella assumed they were private people. Granny always said that home was for family, and family was them. On special days when Nonnu was fully present and aware, they'd take the light rail down to the Italian district and go through the market, selecting items for dinner. At the same time, Nonnu quizzed Stella on the Italian names for the produce. If she got them all correct, he'd buy her a gelato. For some reason, he always told the same story on these trips. The story of their rebirth, he called it. And he always started the same.

*Not so long ago, in the slim set of years between the Before and After Times, the world was on fire. Everything was in turmoil. Countries in crisis. Riots in the streets. There was disquiet in every city as people demanded radical change. The pendulum always swings back; you must be ready when it does, he'd say, wagging his finger in her face. The lucky cities were amicably carved up, neighborhood by neighborhood, family by family. Some streets were bisected, leaving your neighbor suddenly in an entirely different domain. Then, there were boundaries no one could agree on, and cities went to war. Eventually, one family emerged victorious. They grew in power and territory—oozing from the city centers into the suburbs as law enforcement lost more power, officers, and ambition. Who could blame them? They were fighting the citizens, the mafia, the gangs, the drug cartels, and anyone else who wanted a piece. It was only a matter of time before they stepped back entirely and became figureheads.*

*Sure, there were places they hadn't reached—yet. Places with wholesome names and even more wholesome people who had never heard of us or the need for protection. Places where people were good neighbors and took policing into their own non-corrupt hands, but that didn't mean they weren't on the hit list. Somebody would get them—eventually. This was our renaissance. If only I could have finished what I started. When she asked what he meant, Nonnu would sigh wistfully and reply that someday she'd understand.*

STELLA REMEMBERED CLUTCHING both envelopes to her chest as she sat in the living room while paramedics worked on Nonnu, who was slumped in his favorite chair. After fifteen minutes, he still wasn't moving, so she pushed the secret envelope down the front of her tucked-in shirt and ripped open the other letter. She stared at the page until the paramedic touched her shoulder.

"Is there someone we can call for you, honey?" the woman asked. Stella handed her the sheet of paper containing a single name and a phone number.

Standing in front of a two-story mini-mansion popular in the early twenty-first century, gripping one suitcase in her right hand and shielding her face from the sun with the other, Stella looked up at the man bounding down the driveway. She hadn't even known her father existed until she opened the first letter Nonnu had given her. He was a mass of frenetic energy, jingling the coins in his pocket or gesturing wildly with his hands. He was vastly different from herself and her reserved mother. Other than their identical emerald green eyes, Stella had wondered what else she'd inherited from him. She didn't have enough time to discover their similarities. Shortly after she'd arrived, he was back in jail. Stella was left to the tender mercies of his wife, her new stepmother, Margaux, and her half-brother Oliver.

At first, Stella had been excited to have a mother again. Margaux put on a good act when Stella showed up, fussing over her and making promises to shop for new clothes. Nonnu had taught Stella how to read people's motives, and she could tell Margaux was not pleased. Stella's arrival had disrupted the image of her otherwise perfect life. Perception trumped reality every time. Pristine and polished, Margaux was the quintessential suburban homemaker, even if her husband regularly spent time in federal prison; she covered it easily by saying he was away on business. But that was just a facade. At home, she had another side, cruel and dismissive. After finishing her daily chores, Stella often skipped dinner to hide in her room. It was a stark contrast and adjustment from the loving home she'd just left.

When she'd reflected on the uncertainty of a letter to provide for her wellbeing, Stella would become angry. How did Nonnu even know her father would take her in? She could be in foster care or on the street. Life was uncertain. People died all the time, at least they did around her. She turned the soft envelope over in her hands. Maybe this letter contained the code to a safety deposit box full of cash, allowing her to escape the drudgery of suburbia and start over. Stella touched the locket on a chain dangling mid-chest. There was no longer a digital picture that would flicker in the darkness and keep her company, the battery having died years ago. Still, she remembered the image of her mother's broad smile and her at two laughing into the camera. She rubbed the worn, smooth metal until it warmed under her touch. All this anticipation was overwhelming. Her emotions felt like an overinflated balloon. Just one more inhale, and she'd pop. She felt the sobs waiting to escape at the back of her throat, a bubble of fear rising with her increased anxiety, but she didn't cry. Not anymore. Stella forced out a quick breath to steady her nerves. Whatever it was, she could handle it.

*"You're a star, my Stella, and stars are built by pressure,"* Granny had told her whenever tears threatened after a scraped knee or when her mother had died.

There was no clock in her room, digital or otherwise. Per her stepmother's rules, she and her half-brother Oliver's devices were kept in an automatic locking box on the kitchen island to charge overnight. She dared not flick on a light to draw Margaux's attention from upstairs. Stella preferred to pretend she was invisible. In this house, it usually worked. Instead of a lamp, Stella relied on the full moon cascading through the transom window onto a slim patch on the floor to provide enough brightness to see.

Finally, the grandfather clock in the entry began to chime. Stella counted 1, 2, 3…10, 11… She took a deep breath as the twelfth chime clanged, then slid her finger under the fold in the envelope, loosening the seal. It lifted free with ease. The envelope was old, much older than the three and a half years she'd had it. Stella could have "accidentally" opened it many times, but she had promised to wait. And a promise was sacred. She pulled the contents free and unfolded the paper.

A typed letter with a note affixed to the top of the page by a rusty paper clip obscured the letter's contents. The note was in Nonnu's cramped scrawl and must have been written near the end of his life, as the lines of text drifted downward on several occasions, displaying his fading motor skills.

*Mi Piccolo Angelo, this is to secure your future.*
*Remember where you come from and who you can become.*
*They will make you ready to take your rightful place in our*
*world.*

*All my love,*
*Nonnu*

*Where do I come from? You never told me, Nonnu.* Stella shook her head, confused but not surprised by these ramblings. Toward the end of his life, her grandfather often said strange things, but she'd written it off as his progressing disease. Now Stella wondered if she should have probed further. With trembling fingers, she removed the small piece of paper to reveal the letter underneath. It was dated the year of her birth.

• • •

*Gentile Signor D'Angelo,*

*We are honored to place your granddaughter, Stella D'Angelo, on our roster. Thank you for selecting Miss Valentina's Finishing School, where we continue to provide an irreproachable education for all aspects of social etiquette. Prominent Sicilian families have been placing their daughters in our care since 1939. Your family will not be disappointed.*

*This is fortuitous timing, as when Miss D'Angelo reaches sixteen, we will have matriculated the previous group and begun initiating a new congregation of young ladies into our program. I am aware your daughter was not of age within our enrollment window. My apologies.*

*However, Valentina's Academy receives one set of students every four years in order to produce ladies who will be a credit to whichever family they join in marriage, as you well know. Spots fill up quickly but rest assured, Miss D'Angelo's place in our school is secured. As requested, your granddaughter's enrollment and identity will be confidential.*

*Thank you for the advanced tuition payment. We look forward to her arrival.*

*Sincerely,*

*Velia Valentina Oscuro*

*p.s. If permitted, I would like to express my deepest sympathy for your unfortunate current circumstances.*

Stella stared at the letter. D'Angelo? Their last name was Dallas; she'd always been told that. Was that why Nonnu had given her the nickname *Picolo Angelo*, Italian for little angel. She thought it was a sweet nickname, but was it a clue to their real identity?

"Nonnu, what did you do?" she whispered, lying against the cold stone floor.

Clouds passed over the moon, leaving her in complete darkness. Why did her identity need to be concealed? Disappointment and confusion washed over her. This was it. There were no more surprises or letters. She had been left, as she feared, with more questions. All this time, her magical envelope was an acceptance letter to an old-fashioned girls' school. What was she supposed to learn there anyway if the goal was to marry her off by graduation? Did Mom know about this plan? The letter stated that she'd never attended, so why enroll Stella? And why was it such a secret? Ugh! She turned onto her stomach, trying to make out the inscription under the school seal at the top of the page.

"Didn't you know me at all, Nonnu?" she asked aloud to the darkness.

How much money had he wasted on this place by paying her full tuition upfront? She could have used that money to make a new life away from here in two years. What did Nonnu expect her to become, a homemaker? In the *Before Times*, that was certainly a possibility for women. Not in the *After Times*, with the economy fluctuating like the tide, only some families could enjoy the luxury of a single income. Even Margaux, homemaker extraordinaire, ran an online business that kept the money flowing, albeit in secret. Margaux enjoyed the pretense of pretending to be a lady of complete leisure. Plus, finishing school was not Stella's style at all. Maybe she could get his money back instead of attending. Now, that was an idea.

If only she had access to her phone, she could verify this school's existence. It was sixteen years ago, after all. The whole world had been taken apart and rebuilt in that time. What if they weren't even operating anymore? Of all the scenarios she'd dreamed up over the last three years, finishing school never entered into any of them. As the clouds shifted and the moonlight flooded her room again, Stella studied the letterhead and return address to glean as much information as possible until tomorrow morning when she could retrieve her phone. The address was 1200

Bluff Road, Monterey, California. Although only up the coast, she'd never been. In fact, the most she'd seen of the state was when she arrived from Denver by train and her monthly visits to the desert to see Dad in prison.

She ran her finger over the raised emblem at the top of the page. It was a crest, but too small to decipher the images, although was that a rose crossed by a knife? No, that would be too weird for a school, she decided. Stella folded the page, but before slipping it back into the atlas, she flipped open the book to the page where she had been hiding the envelope all these years. The book had been Nonnu's, and it fell open to a detailed map of Monterey. The moonlight was too dim to decipher details, except for the circle Nonnu had placed around a piece of land that curved back from the sea like a crescent. All this time, the clue to what was in the envelope had been right there, and she'd never noticed. Stella slipped it back inside the atlas before replacing it in its hiding spot and crawling into bed. She pulled a threadbare bunny rabbit to her chest.

Nonnu had single-handedly signed away her entire future.

# Chapter Two

It was the fourteenth of August. The day before Margaux and Oliver generally visited Dad in prison. Stella hadn't been able to sleep. She was up all night thinking up a way to convince Margaux to allow her to take their planned visit with Dad on Thursday instead. Her birthday wouldn't be a big enough reason. She'd tried that once before. They only had four hours a month, and Margaux kept most of it for herself and Oliver, allowing Stella half an hour to twenty minutes by herself on the last visiting day of the month. Margaux explained that it had just been herself, Dad, and Oliver for nine years. Their family unit needed nurturing without her interference. It was an arrangement that suited Stella fine. Stella figured Margaux had made up some lie because Dad had started encouraging her to be more involved with the family. She had tried to tell him the truth initially, but it was easier this way.

Instead of being greeted by the smells of breakfast, as Stella expected when she emerged from her bedroom, the kitchen was as pristine as she had left it last night. Panicked, she checked the SmrtChefPro's progress, realizing with horror that the failsafe power generator had not kicked on during an overnight electrical outage. Stella smashed her finger against the SmrtChefPro screen. The prompt asked if she wanted to proceed with the last programmed meal; Stella selected cancel and quickly chose the express breakfast: soft-boiled eggs and toast. So much for the gourmet meal she had planned. Everything was state of the art but a few seasons old and didn't always work perfectly. The appliances started, and the aroma of coffee soon filled the kitchen. As an afterthought, she sliced some fresh strawberries, knowing how Margaux loved them, before pouring herself a bowl of cereal. She would have had the SmrtChefPro do it, but interrupting an already in-progress meal increased the chances of crashing the entire system, which she had learned the hard way. Stella perched on the stool beside the sink to monitor breakfast's progress, then reached for her phone.

Oliver's Augmented Reality glasses were charging in their case. Knowing how expensive they were, she was careful not to bump or disturb them. He'd received them last Christmas and had already been through two pairs. No one used phones anymore except Stella. Once, she'd slipped on the AR glasses when everyone had gone to bed. Suddenly, a buff military man was pointing a machine gun directly at her. She'd whipped off the glasses, almost dropping them on the floor, before realizing Oliver had left the video game he had been playing paused on the screen. She'd never touched them again. AR glasses were disconcerting. They had a screen facing out that showed the person's eyes, so it wasn't possible to tell if the person wearing them was watching a show or paying attention to anyone around them. They could also be programmed how the users wanted other people's AR glasses to see them. Instead of looking at someone's actual face, appearances could be changed to anything from a celebrity, a wood nymph, an animal head, or a design of the user's imaginings. Some programs let the viewer change other people's appearances.

Stella especially disliked this feature when Oliver let it slip that he had permanently set her to field mouse. She wondered what his setting for Margaux was. Of course, these devices were supposed to be switched to "learn mode" in class. Kids who could afford the AR contacts were blissfully zoned out all day. She preferred her old smartphone, even if she was teased mercilessly for it. Stella didn't mind seeing the world as it was. There were fewer surprises that way. However, there were days she thought it would be helpful to project her inner turmoil for the world to see; that way, people might be kinder. Of course, that would fly in the face of Granny's teaching to always hide her true feelings. It didn't matter. She was never getting a pair; best not to dwell on it.

Every bit of her was dying to search for Valentina's school. Still, she knew better than to do anything personal out in the open. Nothing of hers was sacred. After breakfast, if Margaux allowed, she'd go down to the coffee shop, jump on their Wi-Fi, and do her research. There was universal WIFI, but it was painfully slow because of all the government regulations and tracking software. She'd use it in a pinch but preferred to jump on a business, like Java Lava's offered internet connection. Of course, it would all be in vain if she didn't get to the prison to see her dad.

"Ugh, I'm so bloated this morning," Margaux said, entering the kitchen.

"Morning," Stella said, slipping the phone into her back pocket.

"Fix me that juice that makes me go poop," she said.

"But breakfast is almost ready," Stella replied.

"I don't want that anymore," she snapped. "I got a flood of new orders last night. Pack them up, Ella."

Margaux began calling her Ella after Dad had been sent back to prison. She seemed to especially enjoy using the nickname when ordering Stella to clean and scrub the house immaculately or pack and ship her online business orders. It was a name Stella had come to despise.

"Of course," Stella said, placing her half-eaten bowl of cereal on the counter. "I sliced some strawberries already." She offered Margaux the plate, which she ignored. Stella searched the fridge inventory on the kitchen tablet and selected the smoothie variety most likely to get Margaux regular. In a few moments, the fruit had been transferred from the fridge through a washing tube and into the juicer. It whirred loudly before draining into a tall, clear glass. Stella retrieved it from the appliance and set it before Margaux, who did not acknowledge the gesture.

The timer dinged, signifying breakfast was ready. Margaux shuffled out of the kitchen as Stella set out the items on the island, knowing they would grow cold and end up in the trash. She snuck a thinly sliced strawberry into her mouth. The tart sweetness made her cheeks tingle and her mouth water. She desperately wanted another, to feel the red juice gush between her teeth, but she didn't dare.

This was not the morning to piss off her stepmother. She decided to ask about the visit after the juice did its job. For the moment, she had to find out more about this school. Stella placed the eggs and toast in the warming tray, just in case, and slipped down the hall to the office. It was in shambles, as usual.

Stella switched on the virtual assistant and tidied up the clothing and costume jewelry littering the floor; when her foot hit something hard, she lifted a rhinestone-covered shirt to find an empty bottle of wine. She kicked it across the room toward the trash, dark droplets of red making a trail across the carpet. She hated it when Margaux did one of her midnight live sessions. There was always a ton for her to do the next day.

"Hello, Stella. What can I help you with?"

"Bring up open orders from the last twelve hours," she replied to the computer.

"Sure thing. Here are all the open orders."

"How many are there?"

"There are fifty-two open orders."

Stella blew out a frustrated breath so much for getting to her birthday celebration early.

"Print packing labels for all new orders," she said, grasping a pile of shipping bags.

An hour later, she had all the new orders packaged. She filled two tote bags and tiptoed to the patio door. It was quieter than the front door, and she usually snuck out this way. For some reason, if Margaux knew she was leaving, she'd forbid it, but if Stella was missing for a few hours, that didn't bother her. Maybe she didn't even notice she was missing. Out of sight, out of mind.

Stella shimmied through the bushes, dumping the packages into the outgoing mail bin, before stepping onto the sidewalk. The sun sliced through the thin layer of clouds, stinging her bare arms. So much for the marine layer, she thought, hurrying down the sidewalk. Since the library wasn't open yet, she set off through the cul-de-sac maze for the nearest coffee shop with free Wi-Fi, which wasn't exactly close, but Stella didn't mind. Finding new excuses to be out of the house during summer break became a hobby. The prefab suburban jungle wasn't exciting, but it did have a quaint shopping district. On days like today, it would attract visitors from the nearby subdivisions.

The long shadow of the high school perched on the hill blocked the sun for a few moments. When she was directly in front of the two-story cement monstrosity, she stopped. It had been two hellish years in those halls. She'd been resigned to going there for the next two years. Oliver, of course, was already at the fancy prep school one town over. She knew Margaux would never allow her to go anywhere but the free public school. Now, maybe she didn't have to. Although, a finishing school might be a bit more extreme than she was willing to endure to get away from that woman.

Stella continued past the school, a row of empty storefronts, the big box store turned library, and the grocery store until she reached Java Lava. Stella rarely had enough money to buy a drink and sit inside, so she usually sat against the mural on the side of the building to do her internet searches. But not today. She'd been saving up. She walked by the brightly colored mural of a smiling volcano spewing coffee with the caption: "We lava our customers a latte!" painted above and stepped inside.

The cafe was moderately busy, with only a few tables and two available armchairs.

"Well, howdy, haven't seen you in an age, but that's summer vacation, isn't it?" Jorge, the former pro-skater turned coffee shop owner, said as she reached the counter. "Did you and the family go someplace fun?"

She liked him because he never talked down to her. Plus, he always had on-point Chucks and funny cautionary stories about drinking too much caffeine.

Stella shook her head. Margaux sent her in quite often to pick up drinks for Oliver and herself, not Stella, of course. But since she usually bought two, it appeared she was getting them for her and her brother. She never had the heart to tell Jorge otherwise. Besides, who would believe Margaux was that horrid? Probably no one.

"The usual?" he asked.

She shook her head emphatically. She did not want Margaux's usual skinny cold brew vanilla latte.

"It's my birthday," she replied shyly.

"A birthday, well, that is something to celebrate," Jorge said, winking. "What'll it be?"

Stella had dreamed of this drink all year after Oliver had declared it too sweet and left it on the kitchen counter. She had taken a sip before dutifully tossing it in the trash.

"Could I get a white chocolate cinnamon chai latte?"

"Of course, you can. Quick, grab that last comfy chair, and Holly will be over with your birthday brew in no time."

Stella handed over several crumpled bills, then dropped the few cents of change into the tip jar before heeding Jorge's advice. It had been over six months since she'd sat inside. During the rainy winter, she could only stay huddled against the mural for a few minutes until the slim roof overhand wasn't enough shelter from the driving rain, and she was soaked, her keyboard touchscreen unresponsive to her wet fingers. She plopped on the faded seat facing the window, her whole body sinking into the worn cushions.

The pervasive scent of roasting coffee brought her back to Granny's kitchen. She would freshly grind coffee beans each morning and brew a large pot that she and Nonnu would drink throughout the day. Not a fan of coffee herself, Stella never wanted to drink it but was comforted by the scent. This was the perfect place to celebrate her birthday, surrounded by the familiar scents that brought her grandparents back to life, at least through her memories.

Holly placed an oversized white coffee mug on the table before Stella. "Happy birthday," she whispered, sliding a cupcake with a single lit candle on the top next to the latte. "A little gift from Jorge and me."

Stella looked up at Holly's pixie face. She had an upturned nose and gray hair that she kept tucked behind her slightly pointed ears. This was one person who did not need AR enhancement. Stella suspected Holly was actually a fairy.

"Thank you," Stella said, grinning.

The lights flickered, then went out. Holly cursed and rushed back to the counter.

"I'll flip the generator, don't freak," Jorge said.

Glancing around the cafe to see if anyone was watching, Stella picked up the purple and pink frosted cupcake. The flame glowed brightly in the dimness of the room, sending shimmering light spilling down the waves of frosting. Stella closed her eyes and made a wish.

· · ·

IT DIDN'T TAKE LONG to find Valentina's online. They had a simple one-page website with an image of an expansive institutional compound, their crest, and a simple motto stating their commitment to producing ladies of quality. No email, no address, no "contact us here" button. Further searches provided no more information. There were no reviews, tagged photos, or anything about Valentina's Finishing School online, which raised her suspicions. Stella sipped the last syrupy remains of the latte and dropped back into the comforting softness of the chair. What if this was a scam? And if it wasn't, highly unlikely, how was she supposed to know when to show up? Or even if she was, in fact, still on the roster for this year. How could she possibly decide between attending this school when she knew literally nothing about it. Maybe there were more clues in the letter. Regretfully, she realized there was nothing more she could do today, and it was time to head back to the house.

The entire way home, she tried to come up with a good reason to supplant the 'family' visit to see her father the next day. She hadn't contrived anything Margaux would likely agree to. With a heavy heart, Stella noiselessly opened the patio door with practiced stealth and slipped back inside.

"Uh, hi Margaux. I processed all the new orders this morning," she said, startled to find her stepmother in the kitchen this late in the day.

"Honey, thank you for helping me out this one time. I was so busy this morning preparing for my meeting. And how many times do I have to remind you to call me Mama?" she replied with saccharine sweetness.

Uh, none, Stella thought. But as she rounded the corner and realized the headmaster of Oliver's school was seated in the breakfast nook, she took the hint.

"I'm sorry, of course, Mama," she said. The word left a disgusting aftertaste in her mouth. "Hi, Mr. Phan. How are you?"

He nodded curtly at her but did not reply.

"Would you fix us some crudités, honey?" Margaux asked. "With that yummy hummus."

"Of course," Stella replied, retrieving the kitchen tablet. Her mind was still whirling about possible ways to acquire the visitation pass.

"This one is gonna be a chef. I can't get her out of the kitchen," Margaux said. "Now, what are we going to do about these boys' uniforms? They are positively outdated," she said, holding up a navy blazer with a gold patch on the pocket. "I have some sketches here from reputable distributors if you'd like to take a look."

"This has been our uniform for decades. I don't know if we need to change it now," Mr. Phan replied.

"It all comes down to excellence," Margaux said, tugging at his polo sleeve before allowing her hand to graze his bicep. Dave, I know you want these young men to stand out and be the best, but just look at this sad, basic blazer. We can do better for Chesterfield's reputation, don't you think?"

Mr. Phan took the bait and began swiping through Margaux's sketches. Stella figured they would be purchased through Margaux's company, thus giving her a tidy profit.

As the veggies were being washed, Stella seized the momentary silence. "Mama…I was wondering if I could go visit Dad tomorrow."

Margaux flicked her eyes up, her eyebrows straining against the monthly stay-young serum injected between them. "Honey, you know Ollie and I were planning something for tomorrow."

"I know, but Ollie was telling me about having to skip his first video game tournament of the season. Since he is the best player on the team, it would be a shame for him to miss it." Stella shot a meaningful glance at Mr. Phan.

In-person sports had never fully recovered from the *Before*

*Times*, but video game sports had taken off. One of the main reasons Oliver was even attending Chesterfield was for his gaming skills.

"Yes, our tournament," Mr. Phan said. "The first one of the season is extremely important. We need our team captain aboard."

"Is that tomorrow?" Margaux said, feigning surprise. "I've been so consumed with redesigning the uniforms, I plumb forgot."

Her stepmother disapproved of Oliver's gaming but begrudgingly allowed the hobby since it was the only way to get him into the elite prep school.

"And since it's my birthday, I was kinda hoping to see Daddy early," Stella said.

"A birthday visit, now that is special," Mr. Phan chimed in. "Where is your husband away on business at the moment?"

"Not far, a short train ride," Margaux replied, steel in her voice.

She'd never reveal where Dad was or why. Rather than press the issue, Stella swirled a dollop of hummus in the center of the plate before adding the vegetables and setting it between Margaux and Mr. Phan.

"Thank you. This looks delicious," Mr. Phan said. Now, I think this uniform exquisitely represents Chesterfield."

"May I go, Mama?" Stella asked.

"Yes, fine," Margaux said, returning her attention to the tablet with the sketch of the new, improved blazer.

"Thank you," Stella said, skipping out of the kitchen to her room.

Before Margaux could take back her promise, Stella logged in to the Federal Bureau of Prisons website, clicked the visitation registration link, entered their family ID, and replaced the names for tomorrow's visit with her own. Now, there was nothing Margaux could do about it. Visits were only allowed to be modified once. She was going to see her father tomorrow. Margaux couldn't stop her. A rush of excitement filled her chest.

While Mr. Phan was still mulling over the uniform redesign, a process that would clearly take a while, Stella retrieved her letter and looked for more clues. The single sheet didn't contain a phone number, as she had hoped, only their mailing address. Stella wrote it down along with the headmistress's name on a scrap of paper so she could search for it on the train tomorrow. Maybe that would lead to more clues, she thought. If anyone had answers for her, it would, she hoped, be her father.

# Chapter Three

The metal doors slid shut with a resolute clang. Stella stepped down the hall, shoes squeaking against the linoleum. The train had been late, which meant so was she, but the guard took pity on her when she mentioned her birthday and granted her entrance.

"There she is," Dad said as she was shown into the crowded visitation room.

It always reminded her of the elementary school cafeteria. That same stale, greasy food smell hung in the air. Stark overhead lighting cast a gray pallor on everyone's face. And it was all surrounded by disquieting motivational posters lining the walls. The inmates were seated inside a circle of tables while the families were on the outside.

Stella knew better than to run to him and held back her excitement, eager to find out the truth about her past. Instead, she calmly walked around the circle until she reached her father.

"There's the birthday girl," he said, reaching out.

Stella fell into his arms, the edge of the table cutting into her thighs. She was always so surprised by his solidness. Even after all this time, he felt like an invention. Something fatherless children do to create a sense of normalcy, but he was right here. The guard coughed, and he let go. They sat opposite one another.

"I was happily surprised to see you were visiting today. I hoped to be able to say happy birthday in person," he said.

He looked mostly the same as when she had arrived three years ago. Except now, most of his face was obscured behind a dark beard sprinkled with an ever-increasing number of gray hairs. He said it was his prison look, but Stella knew it was his break from Margaux look. She didn't like facial hair.

Stella looked into his bright green eyes, which were so similar to hers. "You remembered," she said, surprised.

"How could I forget?" He broke eye contact to pick at a piece of skin along his thumbnail. "You're my baby girl."

"We only met three and a half years ago," she said, not meaning to ruin the moment. Sometimes, she couldn't help an accusatory jab, although she always regretted it.

"Deep down, I knew," he whispered, reaching for her hand. "Did you do anything special yesterday?"

Even his sincerity felt forced. She never could tell if he exaggerated to make her or himself feel better. Maybe she just didn't know him well enough. If he was lying to make her feel better, it worked; a warmness blossomed in her chest despite her skepticism.

"Um … yeah, I did," she said, unsure if she should reveal the letter's contents. Instead, she decided to skirt the absolute truth to cherry-pick the details she wanted answers to, mainly her name.

"You found out about that, huh?" he said, giving her a smile that did not reach his eyes.

"It's true! Why didn't Mom give me your last name?" she asked, eager to understand.

Dad nodded almost imperceptibly. "I'm not sure this is the place to discuss it." He glanced around the open visitation room.

"Why didn't Mom give me your last name?" she asked again.

"Why did I grow up in Denver as Stella Dal—" Dad held up his hand, silencing her instantly.

"There are people that hold grudges," he said, dropping his voice. "Even against innocents like yourself. The code, the honorable code in your Nonnu's stories, is fiction now. They won't hesitate to hurt you. Please, for your own good, drop it."

Stella stared at the blue and white speckled table. A prickly sensation coursed through her entire body, and her breath quickened. She was sure he'd have the answers. "But this can't wait until you're out of here. I need to know now, please."

"All I can tell you is it was a tumultuous time. It's best if you don't know anymore."

"But Nonnu wanted me to know," she persisted.

"Your grandfather was a good man when I knew him, even if he didn't quite approve of me, but from what you've told me, his mental health was not tip top at the end. He never would have said a thing if he'd been in his right mind."

Stella knew that to be untrue. The letter was dated only a month after her birth. Nonnu knew precisely what he was doing. Dad was hiding the truth.

"I can't keep you safe from here," he said, grasping her hand. Their identical green eyes met, and she knew the conversation was over. Stella nodded and took several measured breaths. "If you want to connect to your roots, you could always change your last name to mine."

Stella was taken aback. She hadn't even known her father until recently. The idea of taking his last name made her heart race. She didn't want to hurt his feelings, but she didn't have any connection to his side of the family. Going from Stella Dallas to D'Angelo was enough of a mind trip for the moment.

"That's an idea, but Stella Candella? I think I'm gonna have to pass, *Papi*," she said, trying out the Spanish word for daddy. He cracked a smile, but the fold between his eyes deepened. "I mean, I love you, but that's too rhymed even for me."

He nodded, then pushed his hand through his wavy black hair. "Why don't you ever come with your stepmother and brother?"

Stella froze. She couldn't just say it was because Margaux forbade her from coming, so she remained silent.

"I want you to make more of an effort with your stepmother. She just doesn't understand why you create this distance between the two of you."

Her mind couldn't compute the words he was saying fast enough.

"She paid for your corrective eye surgery and got you all those school clothes—not because she had to, but because she loves you."

Stella had to use all her self-control not to roll her eyes or laugh. Margaux had finally agreed to the doctor's appointment because Stella's kid-sized glasses had broken, and she couldn't read purchase orders anymore. Then the doctor said she'd aged out of glasses, and the only solution was corrective surgery. Her school clothes were a joke. They were from the dingy second-hand shop in town, or Margaux gave her damaged items from her online store. Never anything new. Never anything of value. Ever. How was her father this clueless?

"Make an effort. I want you all to come together next time. Like a family."

"Sure," she replied. "That would be so much fun," she deadpanned. It had become second nature to agree and lie rather than try to explain how his version of their home life was so far from reality.

"What have you been up to since last month?"

Stella's shoulders relaxed. She was relieved to be changing the subject.

"Not much. What about you?" she asked, knowing it was always better if he talked about himself. Dad launched into an elaborate description of his kitchen duty. Then they exchanged recipes and talked about what they would make together when he, hopefully, got released early in six months.

"Time's up, say your goodbyes," the guard shouted before a brief bell trilled deafeningly through the space.

"Already," her dad said. "Time flies."

"Yeah, sorry I was late. Train issues."

"There's something for you ... a present, back home," he said suddenly.

She eyed him skeptically. "Why didn't you tell me about it last month?"

"It's something I was saving for a big birthday. I hoped to be there to give it to you in person, but you're a big girl now. I think the time is right."

"Thanks," she said.

"In my desk valet, the one with my ID bracelet and saints medal on the dresser. Do you know it?"

Stella nodded. She'd looked through it several times when Margaux had been out of the house.

"There's a small compartment at the bottom. Inside is a ring. I want you to have it. I know ladies don't usually wear things like that, but your mother got it for me, and it would feel wrong to pass it down to Ollie, not that he'd wear it."

"Wrap it up, one more minute," the guard shouted. Children began crying as their mothers pried them from their fathers' arms.

Dad pulled her in for one last hug, then whispered, "Just remember to make an effort with Margaux."

Her heart dropped. Always Margaux. Nothing for herself, not even an I love you. "Um, okay, Dad."

Then, the inmates were being escorted out as the family members watched, some sniffling and holding back tears, others openly crying. That familiar ache in the pit of her stomach grew, eventually encompassing her heart as Dad disappeared through the doorway and out of her life once again. At the end of each visit, it felt like it would be less painful to just never come back. She clutched her stomach and filed out to the visitor's exit with everyone else.

The one-hundred-twenty-five-degree mid-day heat hit her like a sledgehammer as she stepped out of CIM Mojave. Stella followed the slow-moving line of visitors onto the prison-to-train shuttle, her mind preoccupied with questions. The engine rattled to life, and they began the slow two-mile drive back to the station. She wiped a stream of sweat from her neck and rested her face against a metal pole. The AC coughed out spurts of cool air, but it was no match for the desert heat pressing in on them through the metal bus roof. She checked the time. A train would be arriving soon, so they wouldn't be waiting in the hot sun for long.

When the Los Angeles to Vegas train went bankrupt a few years into construction, the state combined its overcrowded correctional facilities and created a mega-prison in the desert with door-to-door train service. Why rip out perfectly good train tracks? Besides, it made the sting of wasting a billion dollars less painful if the politicians could spin this colossal mistake into a service for inmates and their families. This meant they were treated to a streamlined bullet train, not that it had stayed pristine for long, but it was ice cold. Stella watched as the compound receded into the distance, wondering about the secrets her father had chosen to keep.

# *Chapter Four*

The two-hour journey back to Irvine felt too short for the questions circling her thoughts. If anything, this visit made her more confused. Why would anyone want to hurt her? She hadn't done anything and didn't know anything. The chasm of sorrow that had only grown with each loss since her mother died felt large enough to engulf the world. Why did not knowing make her feel more alone than she had the afternoon Nonnu had died.

Instead of turning right and heading for home, Stella turned left and went down Main Street. After her unfruitful conversation with Dad, she needed answers; this was the only way she figured she'd get them. Stella pushed open the door of the library. A blast of frigid air and the smell of old books washed over her. She slipped inside and tiptoed to the computer corner, not wanting the librarian, who was busy behind the circulation desk, to see her. She took a sheet of paper from the dusty printer and one of the tiny golf pencils they still kept in squat cups alongside the computer catalog.

Then she wrote to Ms. Oscura. If Dad wasn't going to tell her anything, and these people didn't have a phone number, she could at least contact them in the only way she knew how. Well, almost. She'd never sent a letter to anyone, but she knew who to ask. Once she was finished, Stella approached the circulation desk. Ethan had become her best friend and more over the past year. When things had been too heavy to handle at home, Stella escaped here, and Ethan had noticed. He'd helped Stella get a library card and showed her how to search for books.

"Can I help you?" Ethan asked, his short, springy dreads bobbing above the monitor as he scanned the screen. He was still concentrating on the computer, preoccupied with his latest antique book search. The whine of the fluorescent lights echoed through the cavernous space.

"Gee, I don't know," Stella said, disguising her voice. "Is there a grown-up around?"

It had been a source of complete annoyance for Ethan that the elderly patrons did not take him seriously. The librarian glanced up. Seeing it was Stella, his frown melted into a smile that dimpled his smooth cheeks.

"I know I can't help you," he said, rising. "You know this library almost as well as I do."

It was true. When she'd first arrived, half of the former big-box store was still in the process of becoming the new library. It was a project spearheaded by Ethan's father, the newly elected mayor. It had been a campaign promise to transform the empty big-box stores that had become blights into functional community spaces. However, there had been little money for running the library once the building had been purchased. Land in California was always at a premium. Instead of watching the library turn back into a dream, Ethan and a small but dedicated group of bibliophiles volunteered to organize and operate the library. He had only been fourteen, but Ethan never gave up when he believed in something. When Stella discovered the library, it was still mostly filled with the dusty remnants of the former store's shelving. She'd helped Ethan transform the space into an oasis of reading. When she had extra time, they'd meet out back and transform discarded pallets into brightly painted benches. Her favorites were the galaxy ones she created for the kid's reading section.

Ethan walked around the circulation desk and pulled her into a hug. Stella allowed herself to relax against his solid chest. "How'd things go with your dad today?" he asked, releasing her.

Stella shrugged. "Not too bad. At least he remembered my birthday."

"I'm sorry I couldn't have been here to celebrate with you at Java Lava."

"You had family stuff to do. It's totally fine. I mean, it's just a birthday."

"But it's *your* birthday. This actually worked out better because your present didn't arrive until today," he replied, smiling brightly. He reached under the circulation desk counter and produced a brown paper-wrapped parcel.

"I told you before not to get me presents."

"I know, but I had to," he replied.

Stella tore through the wrapping, secretly thrilled. There was a peek of turquoise. She removed the paper and marveled at the first volume of Julia Child's *The Art of French Cooking*. Stella looked up wide-eyed.

"I know Margaux makes you do the cooking, but I think you enjoy some of it, right?" Stella nodded, flipping through the pages. "I thought you might enjoy learning a bit more from a true master."

"Thank you!" she exclaimed, studying the first few pages. Ethan was correct; there were detailed culinary instructions. "It's perfect."

"The future's just around the corner, as my dad says. Maybe it'll help you find a path worth pursuing."

"Step-monster told Oliver's headmaster that I'd end up being a cook," she replied.

"Maybe she's not as clueless as she appears,"

"Or maybe she just wanted me to make them a snack."

"Sorry, I forget how horrible she can be. Tell me more about your visit," he pressed.

Stella shrugged. "It was good, I guess."

"If it went well, why do you have that worry crease between your eyes?"

"Just didn't go as I hoped. Not a big deal."

"It is if you are upset," he said, reaching for her.

"I have a problem," she confessed.

"Anything I can help with?"

"I don't know how to mail a letter," Stella admitted, holding up the note she'd just scrawled.

Ethan smiled. "Even after all those orders you process for Margaux?"

"The computer generates the label, and the printer spits it out. I just stick them on the box. But if you can't help…"

"You're in luck because I know everything." He leaned over the counter, fished out an envelope from the desk, and handed it over. Stella folded the paper several times and stuffed it into the too-small envelope. Then, Ethan instructed her on how to write the address and gave her a stamp. He called it another belated birthday gift. Stella was grateful for the present since a single stamp cost as much as her birthday latte.

"Whoa, not so fast. Put your address there in the top left corner. That way if it can't be delivered the post office can send it back to you."

Stella bit her bottom lip. "I don't…want Margaux to know. Can I put the library's address instead?"

"Of course," he replied, eyeing her skeptically. "Stella, is something going on?"

"No. But you know how Margaux is."

"Good point. I usually get the mail during the summer anyway. Thankfully, forgetful Mrs. Gretchen gets in too late, or she'd probably misplace it somewhere in the stacks."

"Thanks," Stella said, relieved. She'd asked for replies to be sent as a text message, but sometimes people did not follow instructions the way it might be hoped. She felt terrible lying to Ethan but wasn't ready to share, not even with him.

"Hey, we just got in a box of vintage 1980s magazines. Want to help me catalog them?"

"You know it," Stella said, "but another day. I need to get home and make dinner. Margaux will already be furious because I managed to snag her visitation day. I don't want to piss her off further. Plus, I got an outage alert when I was on the train, so my perfect plan for dinner to be ready is shot."

Ethan pushed out his bottom lip in a childish pout, knowing Stella couldn't miss mealtime. "Yeah, power was out all over town. I had to cancel the senior mid-day movie. Mr. Jeffries was so bummed. He already had on his brown fedora and leather jacket."

"That's sad, but you'll reschedule, and he can pretend to be Indy another day."

"Yeah. You better get home. I don't want you to get in trouble."

Thankfully, she had a frozen lasagna dinner as a backup. She kissed Ethan on the cheek and turned to go. He hooked his thumbs onto the belt loop at the back of her jeans and tugged her to him.

"Thanks for the help with the letter," she said.

Ethan wrapped his arms around her torso and pulled her against his chest. "Happy Birthday, star girl," he whispered against her ear.

WHEN SHE MADE it home after dark, Stella felt like a tea kettle just about to boil, all pent-up energy. Nothing had gone as she wanted, and now she was waiting for this mystery school's reply. She wiped her phone's browser history and plugged it in on the counter when Oliver rounded on her.

"How was the visit?" he asked, depositing his AR glasses in their charging case.

"Um, great. How was the tournament?"

"We won, thanks to you. How'd you get Mom to change our visit?"

"Just a well-timed question, that's all. Congrats on the win."

They hadn't grown close in the last three years. Oliver spent most of his time absorbed in gaming while she was busy staying out of the way or doing chores.

Oliver grasped her arm as she passed. "Listen, if you need help with Mom, just let me know."

"Sure, thanks," she replied, a bit stunned. She didn't think he looked beyond the screen long enough to register what happened in the house. "Do you want some lasagna?" she asked, sliding the rectangle dish into the *nanowave*.

A grin played on his lips. "Nah, but I'd take a plate into your room if I were you. The power went out during her live sell-a-thon, and she's been in a rage all night. It wouldn't be good for her to find you out here."

Stella nodded, and he released his grip. "Thanks for the heads-up." She watched him grab a bag of chips and retreat into the family room. What was he up to? Normally, Ollie said two words to her a week. Stella shrugged and started the nanowave, eager to get back to the solitude of her bedroom.

FOUR DAYS LATER, Stella awoke to Margaux standing over her bed, something clutched in her hand.

"What's this?" Margaux asked, waving the phone in the air.

Stella looked up bleary-eyed, reaching for the phone. The screen came into focus slowly. "Looks like a text alert."

"Go on. Open it."

Typically, Margaux wasn't interested in Stella's communications, but this unfamiliar area code must have piqued her curiosity.

"It's probably spam," Stella said, swiping the screen.

"Read it," Margaux demanded.

"Greetings, Miss Dallas. You are indeed on our roster, and your tuition has been paid in full. We look forward to your arrival at the end of the month to begin classes on September 3rd. Do not reply to this message."

Stella grinned at the screen in disbelief. It was real. If her father wasn't going to tell her the truth, she bet the people at this school knew about her family's past, and she intended to find out.

"Well…" Margaux said.

"I wasn't going to mention anything," Stella began, grappling with the situation, trying to quickly come up with a way to mold the truth into something plausible for Margaux without actually telling her the truth. "I…uh…applied for a culinary training school scholarship. You said yourself I'm gifted in the kitchen. If I got in, I'd tell you … and Dad. But if I didn't, no one would need to know, and I'd just finish my last two years at Bailey High."

Margaux narrowed her eyes at Stella. "Is it close?"

"No, but the scholarship covers room and board, everything," she replied, blood pounding in her ears. *Please let this interrogation be over soon.*

"How are you getting there?"

"I…uh, I hadn't gotten that far yet. I only found out about it when you handed me the phone just now."

"Excuses are not productive. Make your plans. It's nice to see you showing some initiative. Finally." Margaux made a quick turn and left the room. "I'm going to hot yoga. Make sure breakfast is ready in seventy minutes exactly," she called before slamming the door to the garage behind her.

Stella leaped out of bed. Ms. Oscura, the headmistress, was undoubtedly clever. She had given just enough information without revealing too many details. Stella couldn't be more grateful. Although she'd hinted as much in her letter, sometimes people didn't notice those things. When Stella heard the garage door *thud* into place, she tiptoed upstairs. Oliver should still be sleeping, but she didn't want to chance it. This was the first moment she'd had to retrieve the birthday present from her father. She could have asked Margaux for it, but knowing her stepmother's mercurial nature, it was a coin toss between actually receiving the ring and Margaux taking it for Oliver.

The bedroom curtains were still drawn, and a sour odor permeated the room. Stella tiptoed around piles of clothing and discarded shoes strewn across the plush carpet. Her foot caught on something, and she stumbled forward, catching herself on the edge of the bed. Stella reached back and untangled the item from around her ankle. She held it up, then dropped it in disgust. It was Mr. Phan's tie. Clearly, he had been back to 'go over blazer designs' when Stella was out today. She rolled her eyes. Yep, Dad was certainly clueless about what went on while he was away. Mr. Phan was not the first.

Dad's valet was on the end of his dresser in the corner. She raised her hand, ready to wipe the layer of dust off the top with a quick swipe of her sleeve, but stopped. *"Don't leave any trace,"* she heard Nonnu warn from her memory. Instead, she flicked open the lid with her thumbnail and stared at the contents. There were bits of paper, some crumpled bills, and loose change from his pocket; his holy medal and ID bracelet were also there. Where had he said the ring was? In a compartment? She pushed the contents aside with her finger and located a small flap at the bottom of the valet.

Grasping the tab with her thumb and forefinger, Stella gave a tug. It opened to reveal a sizable gold ring. Seriously, it was big. If Margaux had known this was here, she would have pawned it years ago. A solid gold ring would be worth a hefty sum today. Which must mean he didn't wear it anymore, hence being in the secret compartment. It was a signet ring, the kind men used to wear decades ago. She slipped it on her ring finger, curious why Dad wanted her to have it. It was too large, even for her thumb, so massive, she'd never be able to wear it. How had he worn it? Dad didn't seem like the type to don flashy jewelry.

Then again, he had said it was a gift from her mother. Stella wondered what the occasion had been and thoughtfully regarded the ring. It was slightly cockeyed on her finger since it was so top-heavy. Was it maybe a Christmas gift? Or a family heirloom? Perhaps she found it in a thrift store or had it made especially for him. Did it have a deeper meaning, like a private couple code? Or was it just something pretty that had reminded her of him? By the worn shoulders and scratch marks along the side, whatever its story, this ring definitely had a past.

Stella was honored Dad wanted her to have it.

When she shook her finger, the ring slid off and dropped solidly into her palm with the signet side down. She held it up to the hazy light filtering in through the curtains and studied the details of the design. A braided band of gold encircled the profile of a man. He wore a laurel crown set with four diamonds that glimmered in the dim light, which made her assume it was a Greek or Roman man. A champion of some kind, she thought, turning it over to inspect the inner band, but it was smooth. Any markings or engravings had been worn away by years of use. More mysteries she didn't have time to solve.

"What are you doing?" Oliver asked from the doorway.

Shoot, she'd stayed too long. Stella palmed the ring and turned slowly. "Hey, Ollie. I was missing Dad, so I wanted to reconnect. You know, smell his stuff and feel like he's around."

He looked at her quizzically.

"Don't you ever do that?" she squeaked.

"No," he replied. To her surprise, he crossed the room to where she was standing. For only being thirteen, he towered over her. "How do you do it?"

"Uh, I just look at his stuff or smell his cologne. You know, things that bring back unconscious memories."

"Huh," Oliver said, bending low to sniff the valet. He

shrugged, then flipped the box closed. "It's been kind of cool having you around," he admitted, bumping her with his left hip. "I'm not sure I would have enjoyed sharing Christmas and stuff when I was little, but now it's like…a…um…shared experience. Like I'm not in this alone."

"What do you mean?"

He shuffled his weight before looking up. "Mom won't let me tell anyone where Dad is, so it's not like I can share it with my friends. But you know what it's like having him gone and all."

Stella nodded; she did know. In that instant, she realized she wasn't in this alone either. Not like when Mom and her grandparents had died. She was the only person, besides her father, who remembered their little quirks. She couldn't text anyone when she saw a woman shuffling down her driveway in slippers and a house robe to reminisce about Granny's muumuu collection. She alone carried those memories, but with Oliver it was different.

"I'm glad you're here too," she said. "Now, let's get down to the kitchen. Your mom is gonna be pissed if breakfast isn't ready when she walks back in the door from yoga."

"Yeah, you'll undo all her relaxation work," Oliver said, chuckling.

Stella glanced at the dresser. Nothing was out of place. Of course, now she had an alibi. There was something to be said for little brothers. She slipped the ring into her pocket and closed the door behind them. For a moment, she considered pawning it for the fare up to Monterey, but she had a feeling that this ring was more than an ornamental bauble. Maybe it even held the mystery of her family's past. There was only one way to find out.

# Chapter Five

After a couple of weeks, Stella managed to scrounge up enough money for the bus fare to Monterey. The train was faster but also three times as expensive. Usually, she received a voucher that allowed her to ride for free when she visited her father. Margaux kept those locked away, like most things of value in this house, and she would know if one went missing. It was easier this way. Besides, doing odd jobs around the neighborhood had been a good chance to say her goodbyes. There was one goodbye she had been dreading.

Two days before she was set to leave, Stella steadied her nerves and walked into the library.

"Hey, didn't think I'd be seeing you today."

"Almost finished?" Stella asked. Ethan peered around a row of books and shook his head. "Want some help?"

"Always," he replied. "But you may change your mind when you see the mess." She followed Ethan to the receiving room. Instead of being crammed with donations, there were a few half-full boxes. Stella punched Ethan in the arm. "Hey," he replied, rubbing his bicep.

"Is this it?" she asked.

"Sadly, yes," he said. "But I'd still love the help."

Stella robotically pulled open the closest box and began removing books. After years of volunteering together, she and Ethan had developed a system and got to work quickly sorting the piles.

"You're being unusually quiet," Ethan said, plopping a book beside her.

It was now or never, she told herself, wiping her clammy hands down her pants before turning to face him. "I got accepted to a culinary school." Ethan's eyes widened in surprise.

"The letter," he said. Stella nodded. "That's incredible." Before she knew it, Ethan had grabbed her around the waist and pulled her upright.

"There's just one thing, it's not close." Ethan dropped his arms and stepped back, joy falling from his face.

"How far?"

"Far enough. I won't be coming home on weekends or anything like that. We won't see each other for a long time."

"Do you have to go?" he asked, tucking his hands into his pockets.

"How can you ask me that when this is my chance to get away from Margaux."

"But you don't even want to be a cook. Why would you go so far away?"

"For the chance at a better life."

"But you can have a good life here," he said.

"That is so selfish. We aren't even at the same school. You have no idea what it's like to have no options. Next year, you'll attend whatever University your father has made the biggest donation to."

"You think I can't get in on my own merits?" he spat.

"Of course you can, but you won't have to. It's different for you. You have options. I don't."

"I know you like to cook, but I didn't think you wanted to make a career out of it. Why culinary school?" he asked quietly.

"Because it's what Margaux would agree to," she said, her voice thick with emotion.

"I just wish you weren't leaving."

"A year from now, would you have given up going to college just to stay here with me?" she asked.

"That's different."

"It's not," she replied. "No one is looking out for my future but me."

"How can you say that?" he asked. "When I've looked out for you this whole time." He raised his hand and attempted to brush her cheek, but Stella stepped out of reach. The look of hurt that passed over his face sent a stab of pain through her heart. Stella had to get out of there.

"I really just came by to say goodbye. I'm leaving the day after tomorrow." Stella turned for the door but paused before crossing over the threshold. "Thank you for everything, Ethan." When he didn't reply, Stella turned and walked out.

THE NEXT MORNING, an envelope was wedged under the doormat containing a note wrapped around a couple of bucks. Ethan thanked her for helping process the donations and wished her luck at school. He also apologized for being self-centered and asked her to stay in touch. Stella hugged the note to her chest.

Stella didn't have time to dwell on sentiment; there was still one final thing to do. And she had been dreading it. Telling her father. However, she wasn't sure how much to reveal. Instead of being one hundred percent honest, she went with the fib she'd already told Margaux. It was easier, and it saved her from not having to explain why she'd lied to her stepmother. Sometimes, Dad could be so clueless.

He was ecstatic at the news. Of course, he thought she'd been accepted to a culinary school. He explained that secondary school now was vastly different from when he'd been a kid in the *Before*

*Times*. You went through four years of high school with everybody else, then some went to college, some to trade school, and some right into work. Only a select few with the means and aptitude transitioned into university programs after four years at an elite high school. The world still needed doctors and lawyers, but it had become clear that post-secondary education had become bloated and less necessary for the needs of society. Now, if you were lucky enough, you combined the last two years of traditional high school with another year of an apprenticeship program. If you didn't have the funds or any interests or aptitude, you finished four years of general-ed high school and got a job when you graduated.

That had been Stella's plan before the letter. She still had no idea what this finishing school entailed. It had to be better than Bailey High School, with its mismatched desks, sagging acoustic ceiling tiles, and inedible school lunches. Anything would be a step up from that, even a finishing school where they would train her to be a good wife. Stella shook her head. It had to have changed. No institution that antiquated could still be in operation now. Could it? She'd soon find out.

The school did not contact her again. All pertinent details, sparse as they were, had been contained in that single text. On August 31st, she walked down to the bus station, ready to see what Nonnu had gotten her into. A dry, hot breath of wind pressed in on her face, and Stella wondered if they had Santa Ana winds in Monterey. She'd never been that far north. Since the text hadn't mentioned a school uniform, she'd packed the warmest clothes she had into her backpack, along with her atlas, new cookbook, Scruffy, her plush bunny (tucked all the way at the bottom), a pair of boots, and all her socks and underpants. It wasn't much, but hopefully it would be enough. She didn't dare wear the signet ring yet and instead had it tucked in the lining of her bra. The bulky ring pressed uncomfortably against the soft tissue there.

She wished Dad could have been here to send her off. She'd seen old movies where parents drove their kids to college in cars packed to the roof with "essentials." Then they'd help them decorate their dorm, embarrass their kid in front of the new roommate, and shed a tear as they said their goodbyes, professing their love. Margaux just looked at her indifferently and said, "Is that today?" when she retrieved her morning smoothie and went back upstairs.

Stella hadn't expected anything different. Still, it had stung. At least Oliver had given her a hug and wished her luck. Then, without a backward glance, Stella had slipped on her backpack and walked out the front door, but not without first making herself several sandwiches for the road. It was going to be a long trip.

The bus pulled up at half past six in the morning. Stella climbed aboard, flashing her ticket at the driver from her phone. She'd splurged and bought the more expensive fare. It was as close to non-stop as she could get without taking the train or ride-sharing. She'd change buses at Union Station in Los Angeles, then catch a commuter bus to Paso Robles, and then another bus to Salinas, where she'd get a local bus to take her to the coast. When another of California's bullet trains had gone bankrupt decades ago, the state put its money into clean energy buses and set up transit-only lanes on the freeways. The state was already well traveled by highway, so it was an easy move that allowed people to leave their cars at home and arrive just as quickly. Buses only made drop-offs and pick-ups at one or two depots, so some days, they were faster than the commuter trains. The last open row was directly behind the driver. Stella slid in, taking the window seat. She placed her pack on the floor and propped her feet on it, settling in for the long ride.

Their cookie-cutter suburban scenery flashed past on the way to the freeway. Unlike the train, which was confined to a track and much more isolated, she enjoyed staring at the neighborhoods they passed; it was like looking at microcosms. You got just a glimpse of their life. The person repairing their gutters or watering their grass. Or the houses with a pristine lawn next to one with a rusted-out car in the driveway. Stella made up stories about the people who lived there, always wondering how close she came to the truth. She certainly knew that appearances did not often reflect reality.

"Hey, kid," the driver barked. "Salinas."

Stella stuffed her phone, the sweater she'd been using as a pillow, and the half-eaten sandwich into her pack and hurried up the aisle of the bus.

"Thanks," she said, hopping down from the last step.

The bus had dropped her at the transit center. It was oppressively hot like it had been at home. Ugh, they do have Autumn Santa Ana winds here, she thought, readjusting her pack. She regretted the sweaters and pants she'd brought with her. Stella checked the bus schedule posted on the kiosk. The next bus to Monterey didn't depart for forty-five minutes. It figures she'd have just missed the last one.

"You look lost," a man said as he passed.

"Nope, just waiting for the next bus to Monterey," she said.

"I'm going that way. I could give you a lift," he said, eyeing her appreciatively.

"No thanks," she replied, quickly crossing the street. The other bus patrons had walked this way. Although Stella didn't know where she was going, it was better than standing alone with that creeper hanging around.

It was after five, and her stomach was gnawing at itself as she cut through a parking lot and continued up the tree-lined street. She fished the half-eaten sandwich out of her bag.

In her three and a half years down south, Stella hadn't seen a building over forty years old. After "The Big One," which was far before she had been born, many older buildings had been destroyed or torn down. Even then, they were still decrepit mini-malls or government buildings, like her former high school—nothing as elegant and stately as these buildings existed there. While seeing the Art Deco Union Station in Los Angeles had been a feast for her eyes this morning, it couldn't compare to an entire street filled with history. These two-story turn-of-the-century buildings, with their Greek columns, sweeping arches, and dramatic entrances, reminded her of LoDo in Denver. Immediately, Stella felt at home as she followed several people along Gabilan Street. They made a left onto Main Street, and Stella did the same. She figured if she made two more lefts, she'd have walked a big square and be right back where she started in time to catch the next bus to Monterey.

The sidewalks were crowded for the late afternoon. That was when she realized the office workers were departing their second-story cubicles for home or making a tight U-turn and heading to early dinners at the ground-level restaurant. Stella strolled past them, eating her peanut butter sandwich and enjoying the scenery.

Her earlier plan to make a left, left, and right back to the depot where she started had gone very wrong. The last left she made appeared to be a street but must have been an alley or something because she was alone, facing the backs of warehouses and dumpsters.

*No biggie. I'll just turn around and retrace my steps.*

But when she turned, the guy who had offered her a ride was striding toward her down the alley. Stella turned back and picked up her pace, the gravel sliding under her feet. Up ahead, there appeared to be another passage, although the man didn't seem to be in any hurry. Stella hoped that didn't mean this was a dead end —especially for her.

# Chapter Six

"Up here," someone called. Stella looked up to see a girl leaning over the edge of the building. Her dark curly hair fell forward, obscuring her face. "The fire escape, hurry."

Stella jumped, grasping the first rung of the fire escape, and pulled herself up until she could get her footing and climb the rest of the way. The girl grasped Stella by her backpack and heaved her onto the roof just as the man entered the backstreet.

The girl made a shushing motion with her finger, and Stella tried to calm her panting. A moment later, they heard the man grunting as he tried to climb the ladder. He was so out of shape he couldn't manage one pull-up. Eventually, he gave up and stormed off. They watched him retreat down the alley from the opposite side of the roof.

"That was close, girl. Whatever possessed you to come this way?"

"I was trying to get back to the transit center, but I guess my sense of direction isn't that great."

"I saw him following you from the depot, but you were too engrossed in your sandwich and sightseeing to notice."

Stella winced at the warning. It was careless of her. "Thanks for noticing I was in trouble."

"Of course, us Valentina girls have to stick together. I'm Noemi."

"Stella," she replied, extending her hand. "Wait, how did you know?"

"Who else is going to be trekking all the way up here from the OC?"

"You were on all the buses today?"

"Yep, got on in San Diego. My butt is anxious to get this trip over with. It's still *assleep* from the last bus ride. Come on."

Stella giggled and followed Noemi down the fire escape on the opposite side of the building. They dropped into a parking lot just opposite the transit center. Noemi's springy curls bounced when she walked. Stella liked that she wasn't wearing AR glasses. Of course, that didn't mean she didn't have contacts, but somehow, she doubted it.

"Where's your stuff?" Stella asked, noticing for the first time that Noemi didn't have a backpack. She just winked and kept walking.

"Why didn't you say anything to me on the bus?" Stella asked.

"I like keeping a low profile."

"Except when you're thwarting overweight creepers."

Noemi winked again. "Gotta keep up the skills if I'm gonna make it in Valentina's. It's pretty cutthroat. I mean, that rigorous pre-admission evaluation was no joke." Lightning-fast, she darted behind a row of hedges and retrieved a rolling bag and backpack.

Stella nodded and wondered, not for the first time, just what Nonnu had gotten her into.

THE BUS ARRIVED as they were walking up to the depot. Along with a few locals heading home, they shuffled aboard for the hour's drive to the coast. Unlike the interstate buses they'd been riding all day, this one was updated and flashier, with flat panel screens built into the seat back of each chair, plush seats that weren't upholstered by that sticky faux leather, and scratch-free windows that allowed them an unobstructed view of the passing scenery. The bus lumbered back to life and breezed through town the way she'd originally come. It seemed silly to backtrack like this, but Stella wasn't in charge of the bus routes. They made several stops in town before reaching the flat open farmlands, which were slowly replaced by rolling, green hills and then mountains thick with towering trees. She and Noemi were silent as they marveled at the changing scenery. It was unlike anything they'd seen during the entire trip north.

Stella must have nodded off because Noemi elbowed her in the ribs hard as they crested one last hill and descended into Monterey.

"Ow," she yelped.

"Look," Noemi said. From this vantage point, they had a clear view of Monterey Bay through the front of the bus window. Stella couldn't help but think back to the circle drawn in the atlas.

"I made it, Nonnu," she whispered, face turned away so Noemi wouldn't hear. Her breath had left a foggy patch on the window. She touched the glass with the back of her hand and smiled at the cool sensation. Phew, those sweaters would come in handy after all.

Their view vanished as they descended into the valley, and she closed her eyes, lulled by the hum from the bus engine and the quiet chatter of the commuters around her. They both must have fallen asleep because the next thing she knew, the driver was calling loudly to them.

"Girls. Wake up, girls, your stop is next," the driver informed them.

"How does he know that?" Stella whispered to Noemi, who shrugged as she wiped her eyes.

"Prep school row," he announced a few moments later when the bus stopped at a fork in the road.

The girls gathered their things and waited—behind the yellow line for their stop.

"This time of year, we make a special exception for you guys," he said, pulling up to the curb. "First year?"

They nodded,

"Don't worry. I've seen lots of new students over the years. Everyone is scared at the beginning," he said. "Have a good term."

The door opened with a hiss, and a rush of cool air blew inside. The scent of dry pine and salty ocean filled her nose. Stella couldn't help but smile. This was a long way away from Orange County. For the first time in three and a half years, she felt truly free as she stepped onto the street.

As the bus drove away, Stella looked around and realized they had not been dropped off at the school's driveway.

She turned to Noemi. "Any idea where we go now?"

Noemi pulled out her phone and showed their location. "It looks like we have a couple of miles to walk down this road," she said, grimacing.

"Makes me rethink that jerk's offer for a ride," Stella said. Both girls laughed.

If there was one thing Stella didn't want to do, it was walk the rest of the way, but since that seemed to be their only option, they set off down the oceanfront road.

Stella paused to marvel at the turbulent ocean and rocky coastline, so different from the broad, flat, sandy Southern California beaches. Having only ever been to the beach once, when she'd first arrived before Dad went back to prison, she remembered the glittering ocean and the gentle waves she'd bodysurfed. They had stayed all day, just her and Dad, and as the sun was hanging low in the sky, she had turned to see the perfect outlines of two fish silhouetted inside a cresting wave.

The girls walked on as the road curved away from the cliff. The ocean was soon hidden behind an outcropping of trees. The vibrant sunset peeked through the branches, creating a kaleidoscope effect that Stella found mesmerizing. It was magical.

"Hey, while we're young," Noemi shouted from up the road.

"Sorry. I haven't had much opportunity to see the ocean," Stella said, catching up.

"Not like, even in the OC," Noemi replied, imitating a surfer drawl.

"Not exactly. I lived inland. Way inland," Stella replied.

"Ah, suburbia. Tough luck. I don't know about the OC, but the surfer dudes at Pacific Beach are fire." She winked and gave her the okay sign.

Just then, a massive black SUV careened around the corner. Stella pushed Noemi out of the way. Both girls fell into the soft pine overgrowth along the shoulder. The SUV skidded to a stop a few yards away, hazard lights blinking.

"Are you all right?" Stella asked, dusting herself off.

Noemi grabbed a rock instead and raised it in her fist. The SUV's passenger door flew open, and a flurry of fuchsia fabric popped out.

"OH MY GAWD! Vito, you killed them," the girl exclaimed, running over, her skirt flouncing around her like an undulating jellyfish.

"We're very much alive, no thanks to you," Noemi said, pushing herself up.

"Thank gawd. Vito, I told you to be more careful," she yelled. "You're going to Val's, yeah?" Noemi and Stella nodded. "Word. We'll give you a lift. I'm Theresa, but everyone calls me Tess." She extended her hands and helped both girls up at once.

Vito lumbered out of the car. He must have been seven feet tall, and even in the dim light, Stella could see his muscles straining against his suit jacket. "No room in the trunk. I'll put them in the cab when you alls have buckled in," he said, lifting their bags in his meaty paws as he waited for them to climb into the vehicle.

"You have no class, Vito," Tess teased. "I'm gonna sit in the back with my new friends. Put the bags up front."

Stella thought Tess was being overly optimistic with the new friend comment. She generally wasn't in the habit of making friends with people who could have killed her, but after that fall, her body was not in any shape to walk another mile.

The luxurious SUV was incredibly roomy, with four leather bucket seats facing each other. Stella stepped in and selected one of the seats facing forward. Getting car sick after almost getting run over, after traveling for eight hours by bus, and after getting stalked by a creeper was not how she wanted to start her time at school. Besides, these were her only pair of jeans.

Tess' multi-layered fuchsia and aqua skirt overflowed the bucket seat. It didn't seem like an outfit anyone would wear on purpose, outside of Halloween, or maybe a child's ballet recital, but certainly not to a finishing school.

"I can tell by the accent. You're from the old country," Noemi said, pushing the gauzy fabric out of the way before sitting down. Tess cocked her head to the side. "New York." Noemi clarified.

"Yeah. Long Island."

Vito tucked their bags in the front seat and closed their door, even though Tess was close enough to shut it herself.

"How did you find out about this place?" Stella asked, eager to learn more about Valentina's before they arrived.

"Legacy. What about you girls?"

Noemi shrugged. "You hear things."

"Stella, are you a legacy, too?" Tess asked, ignoring Noemi's cryptic answer.

"Uh, no. My mother didn't go here. Something about being born at the wrong time or something."

"My sister didn't make it either. She is so jealous." Tess cackled manically, tossing her straight, jet-black hair over her shoulder. "But she's not complaining. Daddy sent her away for her finishing. I mean, she is the oldest, so it makes sense. I don't know. I think I'd rather be here. Besides, my Italian is gawd awful. Any sisters?" Tess asked.

"Only girl," Noemi said.

"Same," Stella added.

"Are either of your brothers at Don's?"

"What?" Stella asked.

"The boys' school. Are your brothers there?"

"I'm the oldest," Noemi said.

"Same," Stella replied.

"Lucky. My sister is the worst. Stealing my makeup and clothes all the time. It was the happiest day of my life when she got on that plane for Sici—"

"Ahem," Vito coughed.

"Anyway, I hope the Don Academy is close," she said, staring out the window. "Their location is secret, just like Valentina's, but I think it's actually on the same grounds. You know they have to keep things private."

Stella wondered what Tess had been about to say but forgot as Vito turned into a driveway and paused at a set of massive gates. His window rolled down, and he raised his glasses. Shockingly, a state-of-the-art retinal scanner popped out of the dented and rusted intercom. A robotic voice identified him, and the gates squeaked open as the scanner retreated into the box. The narrow lane curved down to the right; Stella's pulse quickened at the thought of an oceanfront school. But instead, they turned up the hill away from the bluff. An ocean view would be too much good fortune. Granny always said, "Perfection is an illusion created by dissatisfaction."

Then, as if by magic, the school appeared as they rounded a bend in the road. The girls fell silent and gaped at their new home. It sat at the top of the bluff, shielded from the wind by Italian cypress trees and arborvitaes. A stream of smoke trailed out of two chimneys on either side of the building.

"Those liars," Stella said.

"Who?" Tess said.

"Miss Valentina or whoever. This looks nothing like the image on their website," she said, feeling cheated.

"Of course not. They have to keep a low profile," Noemi said, her eyes glazed over as if she'd discovered a vast treasure.

The school did not resemble the pristine institution she had studied from the homepage, but a dilapidated mansion that had clearly seen better days. Even from this distance, the deterioration of splendor had continued for some time. Still, the swanky elegance of a bygone era permeated the property. Stella wondered what it had been before... At least the fireplaces worked, she mused.

It was two stories, possibly with a basement. There appeared to be smaller windows closer to the ground floor, but she couldn't be sure from this distance. A tower, slightly off-center, stood sentry on the roof. The color was the most striking difference between the reality and the website image. The entire building was seashell-pink. Had that been someone's idea of a joke? Paint the girls' school pink? The sarcastic thought struck her: Was the Don Academy blue?

As they drove closer, details began to emerge. The second-floor windows were arched and had decorative wrought iron balconies, rusted from decades of salt air. Orange stains ran like mascara from under the windows. There were two identical wings on either side of the entrance. Situated in the center of the building was a tower. Stella could make out small round porticos in the facade, and she wondered—more like fervently hoped—it was the library. Wait, was that a person up there patrolling? She pressed her cheek against the glass, straining to get a better look, but Vito turned sharply and drove up the semi-circular driveway to the entrance. A wide stone staircase led to the covered patio with sleek stone column supports and an intricately carved stone railing. The last rays of the setting sun flashed and illuminated the facade in a golden-pink hue before disappearing and leaving them in the semi-darkness of twilight.

The girls piled out of the car, Noemi first. She seemed quite eager to get inside. Before Stella had even set foot on the brick pavers, Noemi had pulled her rolling luggage, *thud-thud-thud*, up the first steps to the landing.

"Leave your bags. Vito doesn't mind bringing them in, do you?" Tess said, batting her eyelashes at the stoic driver.

"Whatever you say, Miss Theresa," Vito dutifully replied.

"Thank you. Have a good drive back," she said, bounding up the steps. "Ready?" she asked when Stella joined them.

"I guess," she replied.

Tess looped her arm through Stella and Noemi's before steering them across the veranda.

"Wait, you drove out here?" Noemi asked. "Just you and Mr. Hulk back there?"

"Daddy wanted to be extra safe. And you wouldn't know it, but Vito is a great conversationalist."

Stella almost laughed but suppressed her guffaw to spare Tess' feelings. Now that they were out of the car, she realized how strangely quiet it was here. Stella hadn't expected a parade but thought there would be more of a welcome. Where was everyone else? Were they the first to arrive, or maybe the last? Were they walking into a trap?

# Chapter Seven

The three girls paused at the top of the stairs before the massive, intricately carved wooden double doors. A story seemed to unfold within the six panels on each door, but Stella didn't have a chance to study the images.

"Ready?" Tess asked.

No, Stella thought, as Noemi pulled the braided rope. A clang tolled from somewhere above, the tower perhaps. Nothing happened. As Noemi reached for the cord again, the door opened.

"*Signorinas, benvenute,*" a tidy man in a nondescript dark suit said. "*Entra, per favore.*"

Stella's Italian was rusty, but she understood a polite invitation to enter.

"*Grazie,*" Tess replied, sweeping ahead of the others.

The entry was not what Stella had expected, given the exterior of the building. It was dim; the only light was from a trio of uncovered windows in the opposite room, which appeared to be a dining hall. Since the sun had just set, it wasn't providing much illumination. The ornate chandelier overhead was off, as were the wall sconces to the right of the front door. Stella squinted to discern the details of the room. The dark wood paneling didn't help. What this place needed was some white paint, she thought. *I hope the rest of the building doesn't look like this.*

The man showed them down the hall and gestured to the tufted, worn leather bench. She sat, unsure what to expect. Stella turned to ask the man, but he had soundlessly disappeared the way they'd come.

The pop opera popular long before her time was booming from the closed door directly across the hall. Nonnu had played the Three Tenors occasionally. It wasn't a style of music Stella generally appreciated, but hearing the soaring vocals relaxed her nerves. Maybe she would fit in here. The girls looked at each other and muffled giggles.

"What is that?" Noemi whispered.

"The Three Tenors?" Stella guessed.

"It's Il Volo," Tess replied. "They performed at my parent's wedding; my mom loooooves them," she whispered back, not that they'd be heard over the crescendo of the harmonizing Il Volo trio.

"It's very dramatic," Noemi said.

As the song reached its emotional conclusion, Tess stood and began gesturing wildly, pretending to sing along. Stella clutched her stomach as fits of silent laughter coursed through her. Then the door swung open. The light from inside the room silhouetted the woman, obscuring her features. But her slim figure was accentuated by a halo of curly hair that reached her shoulders. The woman's arms were crossed; she was clearly not amused. Noemi made a motion, and Tess turned slowly, still in mid-gesture.

"Just wait till I break out the Old Blue Eyes records," the woman said. The girls looked at each other in confusion. The woman shook her head. "Since you're already standing, why don't you come right in," she said, stepping aside.

Wide-eyed, Tess gave her friends a nervous backward glance and closed the door behind her.

"Tough break," Noemi whispered.

They settled against the dark wood-paneled wall and waited, straining to hear what was happening inside. The other walls and doors must be soundproof because Stella didn't hear movement or voices from anywhere else in the building. Just the muffled conversation of Tess and the headmistress. Which left her wondering, once again, if they were the first students to arrive. If that was the case, maybe they could explore the house and choose their own room, she thought, hopefully.

They waited silently for what seemed like hours, neither daring to check the time on their phones in case the woman returned and caught them. There were no posted rules saying phones were not allowed. Somehow, Stella understood that the woman who took Tess inside would be displeased to find them bent over their devices instead of appropriately dreading her return.

Stella craned her neck and peered down the hall. It was as dark as the rest of the house. No lights had been turned on during the time they had been waiting. Did this place not have electricity? Blackouts were a common occurrence in some areas, usually less affluent neighborhoods. In the *After Times*, when all cars were mandated to be electric, blackouts became common, mainly due to droughts that rendered hydroelectric plants useless and power grids that hadn't ever been updated to handle the new surge of demand. At least that's what Granny said during the occasional times their electricity faltered. Maybe that was the case here, she wondered, peering down the hallway that went on for what seemed like forever before disappearing into a dark abyss.

The door opened, but Tess didn't step out. Instead, the woman motioned for Noemi to enter. She gave Stella a wink before setting her shoulders and marching inside.

That left Stella to wait alone. After a long day sitting, her glutes hit the snooze. She stood and paced in front of the bench to get her blood flowing. She didn't want to wander too far away. Where had Tess gone? Were they going to have their welcome interview together? Remembering her necklace for the first time since she'd secured it in her bra, Stella checked to make sure no one was around, then slipped her hand down her shirt and retrieved the necklace bearing the two keepsakes. The gold was hot from being pressed against her skin all day. She slipped the chain over her neck and tucked the trinkets under her sweater in the hollow space of cleavage.

Stella wished she had kept her pack and not allowed Vito to carry it inside. She could use a snack; more than that, she wanted the comfort of Nonnu's note in her hand. Then the door opened. With a nod of encouragement from the same woman, Stella crossed the hallway into the office.

The room was empty. Where had Tess and Noemi gone? Sweat began to slick her palms, as it always did when she was nervous. The office was as dimly lit as the entry, but it was more inviting thanks to several desk lamps spilling golden honey light onto the floor. The walls were lined with bookshelves that were filled with leather-bound volumes. Across from the desk was a fireplace. The portrait of a woman hung above the mantel. She was painted to look like a Hellenic goddess, with laurel decorating her flowing wavy hair. As Stella turned and took a seat before the imposing desk, she realized that this woman and the one in the portrait bore a striking resemblance. They had the same almond-shaped eyes, Roman nose, and untamable mane of curls.

This was not the headmistress she had been expecting. Stella had pictured Sophia Loren, older, not in her youth, but still vibrant, an ageless beauty. Instead, this woman was a few years older than herself, maybe ten or twelve years at the most. She looked like a suburban mom, not a headmistress, dressed in tight-fitting slacks, flats, and a striped boat neck top. The woman gathered a file and brought it close to her face, then lowered a pair of glasses hidden in her wild mane onto her nose.

"Stella," she said, finally lowering the file. I'm headmistress Oscura. Welcome to Valentina's Academy."

"Where are Noemi and Tess?"

"With the others," she replied.

"Academy? Isn't this some fancy finishing school?"

"We've decided to update our school's name. Now, can you tell me what the most important rule is?"

"Um…uh," Stella stuttered, not expecting a test this early in her arrival, "take the cannoli?" She smiled lamely.

"From a legacy, I expected more." She scribbled something in her file.

"Maybe if I knew what rule you meant. Like the golden rule?"

"Nothing comes before the family," Ms. Oscura stated. "This institution and your fellow students are your family now." The headmistress held Stella's gaze. "Never betray the family."

Stella nodded in agreement, then wiped her slick palms on her thighs. "Could you tell me, uh…more about *my* family?" Stella asked.

"Pardon?"

"It's just that my being here is sort of a mystery to me. I had no idea until a few weeks ago that my grandfather had planned for me to attend. Since he's passed, I can't ask him why, and my dad had no idea—except I think he was lying. Anyway, from the acceptance letter, it seemed like you knew him—my grandfather."

Ms. Oscura consulted the file and then looked up. "That would have been my great-aunt Velia. Two headmistresses ago. Yours will be my first class." She pursed her lips as if she hadn't meant to reveal that bit of information. "Anyway, I'm still getting everything sorted.

Look, you know as much as I do, but maybe that's a good thing. I get you are trying to figure out where you come from, and I'm sorry I don't have answers, but maybe your grandfather knew best, and you'll thrive at our little school."

Stella chewed her bottom lip, unsure if she should continue. Actual tears were threatening to slide down her cheeks. She'd come so far only to reach a dead end. She lowered her gaze and quickly pressed her palms against her eyes.

"Ms. Oscura, can I have … a refund?" The woman's eyebrows ascended into sharp points. When she didn't respond, Stella swallowed the lump in her throat and continued. "I was hoping to get some answers here, but since you don't know anything more than I do. I think a different sort of school would be better for my future."

"What sort would that be?" Ms. Oscura asked.

"Uh…culinary." She shrugged. "My stepmother thinks I should be a cook."

"And she's known to want what's best for you?" she asked, almost as if she knew Margaux.

"Not exactly, but a finishing school, sorry, an academy like this really isn't me."

"Is that so," she replied. "What is it you think we do here?"

"Prepare us for…marriage?"

"Life, Miss D'Angelo. We prepare you for life in a cutthroat world."

Hearing her real last name aloud was jarring.

The headmistress continued. "If marriage enters into the equation, so be it. We like our students to have good matches, but it is paramount that when our ladies graduate, they are prepared for their future. Is that something you can handle?"

Stella nodded, still wanting to ask more questions, but she was too intimidated. Ms. Oscura slid her glasses down the bridge of her nose and peered at Stella. "All of our students are from prominent families. I'm not acquainted with your people, but I am sure they are a fine family."

"Like I said, I don't know anything about my family. I didn't even know our real name until I opened that letter."

"Most extraordinary. I'm sorry I don't have any other information for you. As I mentioned, my predecessor did not leave a tidy office, and I'm still organizing. Perhaps you can do some research on your own now that you know your familial surname."

"Yeah, I guess that would be a place to start."

"There is one final item: if you will be staying?" Stella nodded. "Very good. You and your new friends broke a fundamental rule."

Stella was about to protest but didn't get a word out.

"Not about betraying the family. That's the cardinal rule. This one is about your identity, which we keep concealed here. From now on, you will not be known as Stella D'Angelo."

"Dallas," she corrected, still holding on to the identity she'd always known.

"Irrelevant. We give our charges code names in order to protect them. No one is to discuss their true identity while enrolled here. As I said before, this school is now your family. Any biological family allegiance or bad blood ended when you stepped across that threshold. Hence the new name. You start fresh."

"I don't understand," Stella said.

"You don't have to. Just remember, from now on, you'll be Pepper."

Stella gave a start. She hadn't been expecting that. Ella, maybe, or Star, Estella, Estelle... but certainly not Pepper. She wondered what names Noemi and Tess got stuck with.

"You are dismissed."

Stella stood, pausing momentarily, unsure if she should say something, but ultimately deciding to wait for a more opportune occasion—like when the headmistress was not in her office. She began to cross to the door.

"Not that way," Ms. Oscura said, gesturing in the opposite direction. "Join your classmates through that door for your welcome reception."

Stella crossed the office and stood before what appeared to be just another bookshelf. It swung inward, revealing a narrow hallway.

"Whoa," Stella exclaimed. "This place is awesome."

"Yes, my great, great, great uncle took exceptional pride in designing this house. It was his hideaway before he was taken in for tax evasion."

"How sad," Stella replied.

"For him perhaps, but a great turn of fortune for us, don't you agree?" Ms. Oscura said, glancing up. "Welcome to the family, Pepper."

# Chapter Eight

Still in a haze from her encounter with Ms. Oscura, Pepper stumbled into the hallway. The hidden door swung closed behind her, leaving the narrow space in almost pitch darkness. What kind of a school was this? She decided to ask Noemi—or whatever her new name was—at the reception. Pepper took a moment to collect herself. That was a lot of information to receive at once. Disappointment clung to the edges of her consciousness. At least she would have a chance to figure out who her family was while she was here, Pepper thought. But right now, it was time to get out of this creepy, deserted hallway.

She felt along the wall for a light switch; there was none. This place had a serious issue with lighting. She pressed her back to the wall and took several measured breaths. Valentina's would be better than being around Margaux. It had to be. She hoped. Then she pulled the necklace from her shirt and grasped the signet ring tightly in her fist.

"Nonnu, help me fit in here. I don't know why you wanted me at this school, but I trust your judgment."

A moment later, the panel behind her slid open, and Pepper fell backward. She shoved the ring under her sweater and jumped up.

Around forty other girls were inside, most dressed in some

variation of casual party attire, and all turned at her commotion. So that's why Tess had been dressed up, she thought.

"Bless your heart, are you okay?" a strawberry blonde with long ringlets asked, rushing forward.

"Yeah," Pepper replied, feeling everyone's eyes on her. What else did she not know about this school?

"You're so clever. It took me a lot longer to find the trigger."

Pepper stared at the girl blankly. "Trigger?"

"Yeah, for the secret door. Come on, let me introduce you around. I'm...uh..." the girl wrinkled the bridge of her nose in concentration, "Ginger, phew! I'm never gonna remember that." She laughed nervously.

"Y'all, this is..." Ginger turned and looked at her expectantly.

"Pepper!" she shouted. What an awful first impression she was making. Where were Noemi and Tess? She glanced around the room again, but there was no sign of them.

"Hey, how ya doing'? I'm Chili. Yeah, ridiculous name, right? Ya think she's messing with us?"

"I hope so," the platinum blonde beside her said. "Going through the next four years as Chutney is going to blow."

Ginger giggled. Chili instantly shot her a look that could kill, which silenced the ringleted blonde.

"Do you think she was hungry when she picked our code names, or do they have a deeper meaning?" Chutney asked.

"Does everyone have a condiment name?" Pepper asked, relieved to have been given such a normal-sounding nickname.

Chili shook her head. "Nah, that girl over there, the one with the too-tight dress, she's Peach, and that tall one who looks like she owns the world is Cherry."

It wasn't hard to see how Ms. Oscura selected that name. The girl had bright red hair and matching lips. Cherry caught Pepper's eye and raised one eyebrow as she looked her over, wearing a superior smirk on her perfectly painted pout. Pepper surmised that behind that vivacious facade was a calculating disposition.

Pepper fidgeted with her sweater's ragged sleeves, then tucked them under so the dark stain on the rim of the cuff wouldn't be visible. Why did this school not give instructions? She would have liked the chance to be a tad more presentable. Clearly, everyone else had gotten the memo.

"Are you guys legacies?" Pepper asked, turning back to the group.

"Not exactly. My mom said none of her Italian had made it to me." Chutney indicated her blonde bob and ice-blue eyes. "She sent me here to be toughened up."

"Yep," Chili said, "fourth generation, legacy."

"Noe—" Pepper gasped, clutching her hand over her mouth. "No, uh, no wonder you fit in so well. Excuse me." She sprinted to the opposite side of the room where Noemi had emerged through a different secret panel set into the wall. "Where were you?" Pepper demanded.

"Whoa, how did you get here first?" Noemi asked.

Pepper shrugged. "Different passageway, I guess."

"Wait, you mean there are more?"

"Must be, Tess hasn't shown up yet."

"This place certainly doesn't disappoint."

"Hey, what name did you get?"

"Looks like the scholarship gang's here," Cherry said as they passed.

Pepper steered her friend past The Fruit Bunch.

"Who are they?"

"Fruits," Pepper said. "I'll tell you later."

"Looks like you two already know each other," Ginger said, stepping forward to greet them and introduce the other girls.

"Pepper, huh? Yeah, I like it. I'm Azucar," formerly Noemi replied.

"Is that a fruit or a condiment?" Chutney asked.

"It's sugar in Spanish. When Ms. Oscura anointed me, I was a bit disappointed. I could not foresee going through life here as

Sugar. I told her I'd only answer if it were in Spanish. Gotta keep it real, you know. I mean, white sugar, for me?" She raised her hands, snapped, and did a turn, showing off her curvy figure. "I do not think so." The girls laughed at her antics.

"What if she refused?" Ginger asked.

"One of us would have given in, and it would not have been me. What are we doing, just hanging out or something?"

"Getting to know each other, I guess," Chili said.

It was clear cliques were already forming, but Pepper wasn't about to let that stop her. She took Azucar by the crook of her arm and marched over to Cherry's ever-widening flock of followers when the ceiling opened, and Tess tumbled onto the sofa.

The girls gasped.

"WOW! What an entrance!" Ginger exclaimed.

"What a *sfigata*," Cherry said, laughing.

Pepper and Azucar rushed forward to help their friend up.

"Are you hurt?"

"Salty," Tess said. My name is Salty." She waved her arms, trying in vain to extract herself from the tentacles of her skirt. The multi-colored tulle had flipped up, tangling itself in a mess around Salty's face. Pepper pulled the fabric back, revealing Salty's tear-stained face. She whimpered, seeing it was Pepper and Azucar helping her up. "How am I ever gonna live with this Gawd awful name?"

"I think it's an adjustment for everyone." Pepper gave her friend a sympathetic smile and helped her up. "Just be happy she didn't name you Chutney," she whispered.

"At least you finally made it," Azucar said.

"Am I the last one? How embarrassing." Salty smoothed down her skirt, composing herself.

"Come on, I'll introduce you around, and we can get something to eat. I'm starving," Pepper said, noticing, for the first time, platters of appetizers on tables evenly spaced around the perimeter of the stately room. *Had those been there earlier?*

• • •

"Ladies, welcome," Ms. Oscura said, her voice emanating from an unseen location. She was definitely not in the room. "Your evening is not yet complete. Hopefully, you have noticed this room has no discernible exit. There are packets with your name on the banquet table. Inside, you will find instructions and a list of your teammates. The first team to find a way out will be given first pick of the dormitories. Good luck."

The energy in the room surged as girls flocked to the table to retrieve their folders.

"Piece of cake," Cherry announced. "Out of my way, girls. I've got this handled."

Pepper watched as the crowd of students parted for Cherry. She selected her folder and sauntered back to the couch with that same self-satisfied smile on her overdrawn lips.

Pepper hung back, waiting for less of a frenzy, but she didn't need to wait long. Azucar bounded over, announcing they were in the same group, along with Salty and Ginger.

"That must mean we're roommates, too, right?" Ginger exclaimed, joining them.

"Guess so," Pepper replied, looking at the instructions over Azucar's shoulder.

Salty joined them in perusing the clue from her folder.

"Hey, do you see that," Pepper whispered, "they're different."

Ginger removed her clue and compared it to Salty and Azucar's.

"Wait, let me get mine," Pepper said. Hers was the only one left on the credenza. As she approached, she glanced at yet another portrait of a former headmistress on the wall. She got the distinct impression she was being watched but shook it off. On the off chance that the tower had a dorm room, Pepper was not throwing away her shot at claiming it.

The four huddled together away from the other groups and

compared clues. Pepper had been right. All the clues were different, but they would have been misinformed without consulting the other folders. Which clues came first? They played with the various combinations until two seemed to be the best fit.

"All right, so we have a clock, dog portrait, bookcase, and this weird rhyme," Ginger said, reviewing their clues.

Pepper held up the riddle. "Spin me around. I'm the same from every angle. Quarter turn to the right, half a turn to the left. Spin me around."

Cherry dramatically announced to the whole room that she had solved the challenge, and everyone could give up because her team would get the best room. Thanks to her. She dragged a chair across the room and fluffed her hair before grabbing a canister atop the bookshelf. Still standing on the chair, she inspected the can and opened the top. Something jumped out. Cherry screamed, threw the canister, and fell to the floor.

All the girls laughed, then returned their attention to their clues.

"They're just those dumb plastic snakes," Chili said, tossing one to Cherry's group. "Maybe there's a clue on it."

"Beware of hubris." Ms. Oscura's voice intoned otherworldly from the ether.

*She is watching*, Pepper thought.

"The riddle must've been the only clue they uncovered. Which is why she went for the canister on top of the bookshelf," Salty said.

"It figures she wouldn't consider the other team members clues and just focus on hers," Azucar noted.

"We're smarter than that, but not if we don't work together," Pepper said.

"What spins around?" Ginger asked.

"No. That's where she wants us to start, to throw us off, like Cherry. How can the other clues fit together? These four clues need to be combined. Then, they become the first clue. Without using all the pieces together, they lead to misinformation."

"As Cherry just found out," Azucar said gleefully.

"Right, but they all make sense in different orders," Salty reminded them.

"From what we know about Ms. Oscura, what combination works the best?" Pepper asked.

They looked around. The other teams seemed to be having as much trouble as they were, which was a relief. Pepper spread the four clues out on the floor: bookcase, clock, portrait, and the riddle.

"Hmm, maybe we're looking at this wrong. Maybe it's not just about the clue, but who got which clue. Take yours and hold it up," she said.

Everyone reached for their clue and held it for Pepper to see. She shook her head, unable to find a link. Maybe there was none.

"Could they be alphabetical?" Salty wondered.

"Say that again," Pepper replied.

"Well, if you put our new names in alpha order, the clues are in alpha order, too," she explained.

"But mine is first," Azucar said, flashing the riddle.

"If Ms. Oscura counted on your name being Sugar, it's last."

"That's brilliant," Pepper said.

"Yeah, but what does it mean?" Azucar asked, pointing at each item around the room as she named it.

"Each of those is in a corner, or close to a corner, and when you go in alpha order, there is one object in the last corner left unnamed, the vase," Ginger said.

"Which is the same on all sides. Come on," Pepper said, jumping up.

Once on the far side of the room, Pepper turned the vase on the platform a quarter turn to the right and then a half turn to the left. A drawer on the base of the vase's pedestal slid silently open. Pepper retrieved a matchbook and flipped open the cover. The matches had been torn out, but numbers were written inside the flap, clearly a code or combination.

The instructions had stressed that clues be returned to their rightful place so the next team could decipher it themselves. Salty wrote down the numbers, and Pepper took a picture of the front and back of the matchbook before returning it to the hiding place. The drawer slid closed. Cherry noticed them huddled around the vase and stormed over. She looked inside the vase, tried to pick it up—to no avail—then yanked on the drawer handle. It didn't budge.

"What was the clue?" she demanded.

"Cheaters never prosper," Ginger replied.

"Oh Ginger, that nickname is working its spicy magic on you already," Azucar said, then turned to Cherry. "Adios." The redhead turned on her heel and returned to her frazzled-looking teammates.

"Can't say the same for you, sugar." Ginger winked.

Witnessing Cherry's tantrum motivated Pepper to decipher the code that much quicker. She couldn't let that brat have the pick of the best room. Besides, now that they'd found the first clue, she wanted to figure this puzzle out.

"Numbers..." Pepper said, tapping the pen on her bottom lip. "They probably need to stay in this order. 978-1-7328534-1-6."

"A phone number?" Ginger said.

"Too many numbers," Pepper replied.

"A geo-location number?" Azucar suggested.

"Nah, those are separated differently," Ginger replied.

"What else could these numbers mean?" Salty asked.

Shortly after their matchbook discovery another team was turning the vase and retrieving the first clue. Pepper noticed they only wrote down the numbers. Of course, one of them could be using their AR contacts to record the image on the front and back of the match cover, but she hoped not. In her gut, she knew that was the cipher.

Pepper studied the image from the matchbook. It was a lone cypress pine on a bluff overlooking the ocean. That type of simple line drawing was only reserved for easily identifiable icons, but she didn't know it.

"Anyone recognize this?" she asked, holding up her phone.

The girls shook their heads, but Salty gasped.

"Yes, that's Lone Pine right down the road in Pebble Beach."

"What does that have to do with these numbers and this room?" Azucar said.

"How about a serial number?" Pepper suggested. "You know the numbers on the backs of cereal boxes and canned foods."

"Right, but do you see any of those things here?" Azucar countered.

"No," Pepper agreed, "but I see a ton of books, and those have barcodes too." The girls moved to stand, but Pepper held out her hand to stop them. "Wait, there has to be a hundred books in that case. We don't know what we're looking for just yet. Let's not show our hand." Pepper squeezed her eyes shut and tried to block out the noise from the room. What did that picture on the front cover mean?

Another group had figured out the vase clue and rushed past them to retrieve the matchbook.

"Maybe it's a book about that pine tree?" Salty suggested.

Pepper's eyes sprang open. "Of course! Come on, let's look."

"You go. It'll look suspicious if we all go up there. Let's spread out and search different parts of the room to throw everyone off. If you find something cough twice in a row, then we'll all meet back here," Azucar suggested.

"Great plan. Let's go," Pepper said, crossing to the bookcase.

Cherry's team finally figured out the first clue and was squabbling over what the numbers meant when Pepper passed them on the couch. Thankfully, they were too busy fighting to pay much attention to her. She reached the bookshelf and began to scan titles, starting with the top row. She honestly didn't know what she was looking for. A title with pine in it, or Pebble Beach; maybe there was a picture of the pine tree on the cover. As she reached the bottom shelf, something caught her eye. The same line drawing of the tree on the spine of a large volume. She slid the book from the shelf. *17 Mile Drive* was the title. She turned the book over and held her breath. The numbers matched. She had expected a card or note to be attached to the book. She flipped through the pages and stopped at a flash of copper. There it was, the next clue! She coughed twice and discreetly slid the key into her palm. The girls were already gathered when she returned.

Pepper held out her hand, revealing a small key—not the kind that opened the locks on doors, but something smaller. It had a heart-shaped embellished top and a jagged, uneven bottom. What would a key this small, no bigger than an end-of-the-year pencil, unlock, she wondered?

"Did you look at the page?" Ginger whispered. "Maybe there was a clue there."

"Shoot, I didn't," Pepper said, chastising herself for the error. "I don't even know which page it was on. I just slid it out of the book."

"Well, the one good thing about that is, no one else will either," Salty said. "What in this room has a lock?"

"Could it be for something made of that kind of wood? You know, from the tree on the match cover," Ginger suggested.

"It's a thought," Azucar said, turning the key over in her hand.

"The only trouble is, most of this place is made of wood," Pepper said, surveying the paneled room.

"Do you think we were supposed to put the key back like the instructions said?" Ginger asked.

"Not a chance. I think at this point it's finders keepers," Azucar replied.

"She's right. One key means one winner, and I'm betting this is the last, or close to the last round," Pepper said.

No one noticed any distinct markings, but as Azucar tossed the key to Salty, Pepper noticed something and grabbed it out of the air.

"Did you see that?" she hissed, turning the key over. Sure enough, a slip of paper protruded from the hollow end of the key. "Ugh, my fingers can't grasp it."

"Allow me,' Salty said, pinching the corner of paper with her pointed nails. She slid the curled note from the key and dropped it into Pepper's open hand. "And my mother said these were a waste of money." She blew on her nails and pretended to shine them on her sleeve.

Pepper unrolled the slip and stared at it for a moment. "It's… not in English…or Italian"

"Shoot…" Ginger said, peering down at the phrase.

"Not Spanish either," Azucar added.

"It looks like Latin. We have a ton of books. Do you think one might be able to help?" Pepper suggested.

"Wait, let me see that," Salty said. "Yes, I've seen that phrase before." She thought for a minute before her eyes rounded in realization. Salty reached for the Valentina folder they'd just received and turned it to face her team. She tapped the crest in the center of the folder with one long pink talon.

"The school logo," Salty said.

"*Nunquam minoris aestimo domina,*" Pepper read.

"Never underestimate a lady," Salty translated.

"I like that," Ginger said. "But how does it help with our clue?"

"What about the lady hanging above the credenza?" Azucar said, gesturing to the painting Pepper had noticed when she arrived.

"It's worth a shot. Let's get a closer look."

The four girls casually made their way across the room, trying not to attract the attention of the other groups, one of whom was perusing the bookshelf. This painting was of another headmistress.

She was in more modern clothing, probably circa the 1960s, by the cat eye style glasses and bouffant hair. In the background, very small, was the lone pine on the bluff. Around her neck was a locket, and at the bottom of the frame was a small heart encircling a keyhole. Pepper looked at the three girls and inserted the key. Then nothing. No secret drawer popped out of the frame, as Pepper had expected.

She turned back to her team. Instead of seeing disappointment register on their faces, they stared in awe above her head. The painting was moving; actually, the woman was clapping politely, her mint green gloves muffling the sound. Was the volume turned down? Then, the woman pointed to the exact location of the key still inside the frame. Pepper turned the key to the right, and the woman's voice emanated from unseen speakers around the room.

"Excellent job, ladies," she began. The other students stopped their clue-hunting and searched the room for the voice's origin. "Being a Valentina graduate requires all the skills you just exhibited in deciphering the various clues. I am rewarding you with top honors for your cleverness and ingenuity in discovering myself, Headmistress Castellano. Pass through this door and to the adjoining stairwell. You will have fifteen minutes to select your dormitory for the year. Just remember, looks can be deceiving." The screen went still, and Ms. Castellano returned to her neutral pose, staring off into the distance.

The bookcase to the left of the portrait swung open, revealing a narrow staircase. Pepper's team yelped in jubilation and rushed for the exit.

"I knew that's where it was," Cherry exclaimed, folding her arms across her ample chest.

"What about the rest of us?" Chutney asked the portrait, which remained impassive.

Their current headmistress's voice echoed through the room. "Congratulations to the champions. The remaining room assignments will be announced once the winners have made their selection. Continue enjoying the reception. You'll be allowed to settle in for the night shortly. Hurry up, girls, you only have fourteen minutes remaining.

# Chapter Nine

Pepper, Salty, Ginger, and Azucar rushed for the bookcase exit. Unlike the earlier passageway Pepper had walked down with its dark wood-paneled walls that matched the headmistress' office and the formal living room, this area was completely utilitarian, with no embellishments whatsoever. It had rough stone walls and an unadorned spiral stairwell so steep they had to ascend one at a time.

"At this rate, we won't even make it to the second floor to pick our room in time," Azucar said.

"Do we even know what we're looking for?" Ginger asked. "I mean, it's not like there was a map in our welcome packet. How are we supposed to know where the bedrooms are?"

"She didn't say we could only select a bedroom," Pepper said.

"What's that supposed to mean?" Azucar replied.

"Did you guys notice the tower when you arrived?"

"Sure, how can you miss it?"

"I think we should pick that for our room," Pepper exclaimed, pausing at the second-floor landing. She turned around. The faces of her four roommates held various expressions of apprehension.

"What if it's small?" Azucar said.

"What if there's no bathroom?" Ginger added.

"What if we have to climb down this awful staircase instead of the regular one we saw in the entryway every morning," Salty said.

"What if it's amazing?" Pepper countered.

No one seemed willing to budge.

Azucar checked the time. "Ten minutes left," she said. "If we stay here debating, we won't get any choice."

"Let's split up and meet back here in three minutes, then we'll switch again and decide."

"Cutting it close, but if you think it's for the best," Salty said. "I'm exploring down here first. Come on, Ginger."

The two girls threw open the door and ran out as Pepper and Azucar charged up the stairs to the third floor. Pepper was hoping this stairwell led right to the tower. Instead, the door at the top of the circular staircase led to a large open room. Pepper's heart sank. This was not the cozy space she had been imagining. It was empty except for a couple of folding chairs. It was brighter than the rest of the property due to the windows on all sides letting in a flood of moonlight. The tower, or what she had assumed was a tower, was merely set into the ceiling. The walls and floor had been painted white. It was a refreshing change from the dark decor downstairs. There was a single light fixture hanging from the apex of the turret roof.

"This is awesome," Azucar exclaimed, startling Pepper.

"Really?"

"It's huge, for one thing," Azucar exclaimed. "With killer three-sixty views and, best of all, privacy."

Pepper spun around. She had a point. The room was spacious, and they'd probably have a view of the ocean during the day.

"Pep, look!" Azucar said, motioning her over. "There's an exit onto the roof." She twisted the purple glass doorknob. The knob turned, but the door was warped and wouldn't budge; just as Azucar was getting ready to give it a big tug, there was commotion from the stairwell. Salty and Ginger burst through the doorway.

"Whoa," Ginger exclaimed.

"What happened to meeting up?" Pepper asked, checking the time.

"We decided that whatever was up here had to be better than what was down there. It's all dreary and sad, like the dorm of a…"

"Run down prep school," Pepper said.

"Kinda, yeah," Salty agreed.

"And none of the rooms are as big as this," Ginger added. "What an amazing view. Do y'all want to check out the rooms downstairs to be sure of your decision?"

Pepper shook her head no.

"Not a chance," Azucar said.

"Who do we tell our room selection to?" Ginger asked.

"That would be me," Ms. Oscura said, emerging from the stairwell and flicking on the light. "Don't worry, I wasn't spying on you. I noticed your ascent up the servants' stairs and thought I'd see what you were up to. This cupola, unfortunately, is not a dormitory." She held her hand up, silencing the girls' protest. "However, you are proving to be both clever and cunning pupils. It's my fault we did not stipulate what rooms you could or could not choose. Well done exploiting my loophole," she said, glancing at Pepper. "I will agree to this selection on one condition: you will not use the secret staircase to access the ground floor. You'll exit on the second-story landing and continue to the main floor with the rest of the ladies using the main staircase."

"Agreed," the girls replied in unison.

"Can we start bringing our stuff up?" Salty asked.

"Marco and the others will do that when you are at dinner. However, I will not allow you to select the room from which your furniture will come. The last remaining room will provide your furnishings."

"What?" Ginger said, "Some of those rooms are—"

"That's fine, thank you, Ms. Oscura," Pepper said.

"If you'll excuse me, I need to assign the rest of the dormitories.

See you in the dining room in exactly half an hour. Don't be careless with your things, ladies." She handed their welcome packets to Ginger and departed.

"Pepper, you are a genius!" Azucar exclaimed. "Wait till Cherry finds out we have the best room!"

"Now, now, I think you got that nickname because you need a little sweetness in your life, sugar," Pepper teased.

"What about you?" Azucar shot back.

Pepper paused. "Maybe I need a bit of a kick?"

"Come on, let's start deciding where we want to have our beds," Salty suggested.

Pepper stood back, marveling at everything that had transpired today. From her cramped and tiny bedroom off the kitchen back home to this place, sharing a room with three other awesome girls in the tower of this old mansion, about to start a new life.

"Thanks, Nonnu," she whispered, before joining the girls on the floor.

SINCE THEY WERE REQUIRED to be at dinner in half an hour and had to wait for Marco to bring up their furniture and luggage, Salty had a great idea to mark out where they wanted the beds, desks, and dressers using the items from their welcome packet. They spent the next half hour fussing with the details until it was time to go to dinner.

Their radical choice was all anyone could talk about that evening. Cherry hadn't been the least bit bothered by their decision, having gotten the room she deemed the best. Someone whispered that Cherry had commandeered the soon-to-be-empty room as her personal closet. Her suite-mates were less than pleased. Pepper imagined that Cherry was great at faking her enthusiasm for many things to appear superior.

When they returned to the cupola tower, their beds were placed against the four walls under the windows, and all the desks were grouped in the middle of the room.

"Seems a lot smaller with the furniture in place," Azucar said.

"Yeah," Ginger agreed, walking around the desks. "But we did sort of miscalculate the size of the beds," she said, examining the layout they'd set with the pages from their welcome pack, which were now strewn around the room.

"What we need is a big rug," Salty said, making notes on her tablet.

It was clear who the decorator was going to be. Salty had already made a list of things they needed: blinds, reading lamps, and simple cloth bed canopies for privacy. The rest of the girls agreed to keep all the beds, draperies, etc., the same style and color in order to make their space feel larger and more cohesive. But since they had to agree, their pallet was neutral, which wasn't making Salty happy.

Pepper had a look at the dormitories when they went down to dinner and was relieved that Salty and Ginger had loved the cupola, too. The other rooms looked so uninviting, mainly because all the furniture was mismatched. It was like this institution updated things one decade at a time, making each room look like an outdated thrift shop display. Pepper was grateful that their room was totally white. The suites downstairs had the same odd, outdated furniture but also the original floral wallpaper, walls painted different colors, and blinds that had matched decor long since gone. She wondered if Ms. Oscura was planning on redecorating now that she was the new headmistress. From their earlier escape room challenge, she had a feeling Ms. Oscura was here to shake things up.

The desks Marco had brought up were all vastly different. If she hadn't seen the other rooms herself, Pepper would have thought they reorganized and selected the worst desks for them, but this had no doubt come from one empty dorm downstairs. One was that white plastic prefab material, another was solid wood painted green but desperately needed an update, the other was unfinished wood with peeling wallpaper from some former student beautification attempt, and the fourth was chrome and glass.

"They all look so…sad," Ginger said, running her thumbnail along a deep scratch in the glass.

"Don't forget what Ms. Oscura said at dinner. We can customize our furniture however we like," Salty reminded them.

"You're right, and with the one light fixture overhead, this is the best place for the desks," Pepper replied, stifling a yawn. "I'm exhausted. How about we continue decorating later?" she suggested, grasping her backpack.

"I'm too excited," Ginger said, unzipping her suitcases. "I want to unpack now."

"Well, enjoy, I'm going to bed," Pepper said, retreating to her corner single bed. She'd selected the spot that would, she hoped, overlook the ocean. As she sat on the bed, it creaked loudly. Hopefully, the rest of the frames wouldn't be as noisy, or no one would get any sleep. As she snuggled into the lumpy mattress, she wondered if anyone else had ever used this room as a dormitory or if they were the first. She smiled, knowing Ms. Oscura had been completely surprised by their decision. She was proud of herself and the others for working together and besting Cherry and her fruit bunch. She wasn't sure what their first day of classes would hold tomorrow, but if tonight was any indication, she was up to the challenge. For the first time in years, she was excited for tomorrow.

# Chapter Ten

Without window coverings of any kind, the morning sun illuminated their room at first light. The girls groggily sat up in bed, bleary-eyed and disoriented. Their uniforms, which they had picked up along with their sheets and duvet covers after dinner last night, were waiting to be worn. It had been hard to make out the clothing details in the dim light last night. Pepper reached for her uniform and unfolded it on her bed. There was a selection of white crew-neck T-shirts, a navy-blue crew-neck sweater with the school's emblem just under the collar, slim gray and navy plaid pants, and a matching plaid skirt. Some things never changed, like school uniforms. The others had been less than thrilled about the uniform, but Pepper was relieved. From what she'd seen last night, her roommates had brought tons of clothes. That's one of the reasons she opted to go right to bed; she didn't have much to unpack. Heck, she didn't even own that many clothes—at least this way, she'd fit in most of the time.

"First day, get up, ladies," Salty sang, hopping out of bed.

Ginger turned toward the wall, pulling the pillow over her head.

"Are you gonna be this cheery every morning?" Azucar asked, scowling.

Pepper just chuckled and gathered her bathroom items. That was one downside of this room selection; their closest bathroom was down one flight of stairs and two hallways away. She looked outside. The ocean view peeked through the trees, revealing a gem-blue sea. Some things were worth a little inconvenience.

Pepper padded downstairs, still half asleep, and stumbled into the bathroom.

"Does anyone smell greasy pepperoni pizza?" Cherry said, stooping over the sink to spit out her toothpaste foam as Pepper stepped inside the oblong bathroom.

"Good morning to you, too. Enjoying your walk-in closet?"

Cherry wiped her lips, now noticeably less full than yesterday, and grinned. "I am. It'll give me some space away from everyone else. My private sanctuary."

"Ah, so you're going to make it into a single room," Pepper said.

"That's the idea. Thanks for taking the attic. I mean, you girls should be up there. After all, that's where unwanted things belong."

Pepper ignored the jab and breezed past Cherry toward the row of showers. Let her think their room was a stuffy, horrid attic. Pepper wasn't going to tell her the advantages of having the cupola room. Besides, with Cherry, Pepper imagined, it was probably best if she thought she'd won.

When Pepper returned to the cupola, Ginger was still in bed, but Azucar was at least sitting up, and Salty was dressed.

"Better get a move on if you want a shower," Pepper said. "I think Cherry and her crew are gonna be tough to share a bathroom with."

"No fooling?" Ginger exclaimed, jumping out of bed. "How much time do I have?"

"That depends. Do you want breakfast or not?"

"I need at least an hour to straighten this curly mess of hair," she said, rushing around collecting bottles and makeup bags.

"Without breakfast, for sure," Azucar said.

"Sixty-five minutes until first period starts," Pepper replied.

Ginger yelped and dashed out of the room. Azucar flopped back in bed.

SALTY AND PEPPER decided to get down to breakfast and maybe do some exploring before class. Pepper didn't want to appear too ignorant in front of the others, but not knowing the full details about Valentina's Academy kept her at a disadvantage, no matter what Ms. Oscura thought about fresh starts.

"Salty, you seem to know a lot about this place," Pepper said, stopping her on the landing.

"Fifth-generation legacy," she replied, tossing her glossy black hair over her shoulder.

"Right, and…well, you've got to promise not to tell anyone, but I didn't even know this place existed until about three weeks ago. It was my grandpa's dying wish that I attend."

"That's so exciting," Salty said.

"Yeah, but Ms. Oscura said we'd be prepared for anything in the future."

Salty nodded as if this were the most normal thing in the world. "Right, so if it's not all posture and table settings, what do we learn here?"

"Don't know." Salty shrugged. "When you finish, you are sworn to secrecy. Isn't that the best! Come on, I'm starving." She took Pepper's arm and pulled her onto the second floor.

"Do you know who everyone is?" Pepper whispered as they joined the group of girls descending to the first floor.

Salty just waggled her eyebrows and made a shushing motion with her finger.

"Hey girls, how was the first night in the tower?" Chutney asked as she passed them on the stairs.

"So quiet," Salty replied. "I love it up there. How's your room?"

Chutney shrugged. "Chili snores."

"I do not," Chili said, brushing past as they entered the dining room.

About half the students had opted to get dressed after breakfast, while the other half were already prepped and ready for their day. Ms. Oscura was at a long table at the front of the room, along with several other adults Pepper did not know, teachers presumably. She wondered if they all lived on the premises, perhaps in some other wing of the building. The delicious smells quickly diverted her attention. Pepper's mouth watered as she approached the buffet. Pepper could enjoy a breakfast that wasn't scraps for the first time in years.

"Bacon!" she exclaimed, taking a sizable serving. "And it's crispy!"

Four long tables were set up two by two in the dining room. Salty and Pepper selected a couple of seats at the center of the last table near the wall of windows overlooking the wild garden. Actually, wild probably wasn't a fitting description; untamed was more like it.

"All right, spill. Who's who?" Pepper whispered, crunching on some bacon. It was delicious.

Salty sipped her smoothie and stirred her yogurt and granola in a small bowl. "Well, I don't know everyone, and I'm not supposed to say, am I...? But that girl over there, the one with the braids? Her father is the head of the Chicago Mitchell crime family. Very powerful. And Cherry's real name is Brittany Bianchi. One of the East Coast Bianchis. They run, like half of Brooklyn, and, if you believe the rumor, Washington DC, too."

"Fascinating," Pepper said, making a bacon sandwich with her toast.

"Are you gonna eat that every day?" Salty asked.

Pepper shrugged. "Maybe. Why?"

"Cholesterol, duh."

"Dude, I have been living on scraps for years. I am going to enjoy some greasy bacon." She took a crunchy bite and smiled. "What about you?" Pepper asked. "Who are your people?"

Salty smirked. "That's a secret."

Just then, Cherry burst through the double doors, looking like she was prepped for a fashion shoot. Her sweater was at least two sizes too small, and her skirt had been rolled to graze her upper thigh.

"Who is she trying to impress?" Chutney said, sitting opposite Pepper.

"My stepmom is like that. It's like they have this consuming need to present one image to the world, or everything will come crashing down."

"Such a princess," Salty commented.

Pepper hid a smile. Coming from Salty, who'd had a virtual melt-down when she got dressed this morning because she hated navy and there wasn't enough glitter on the emblem, that comment was a little on the nose.

"What class do you have first? Mine is history, snore," Chutney said.

"Hey, us too," Salty replied. "At least it's not gym."

"Ew, do we have to take that?" Chutney said.

"Only Wednesdays, but it's two hours long. I hope we aren't running that whole time," Pepper said. "Hey, we were going to check things out before class, wanna come?"

"Nah, I think I'm gonna read. I stayed up late to finish this great romance novel but fell asleep. I wanna find out what happens."

They finished eating quickly and said goodbye to Chutney in the entryway just as Azucar was plodding down the stairs, looking still half asleep.

"Is there still food?" she asked.

The girls nodded.

"Is Ginger coming down?" Salty asked.

"Last I saw, she was mid-blow-out. She might make it."

"The bacon is so good," Pepper gushed.

"Vegetarian," Azucar said. "I want to live in a kinder world." She shuffled into the dining room.

THEIR EXPLORATION YIELDED LESS than exciting results. There was the dining room, front entrance, and a handful of classrooms. There had been a few locked doors that were intriguing, but when it came down to it, the school seemed quite ordinary but sorely needed updating. This morning, what had been invisible in the dim lighting last night was painfully obvious. The threadbare rugs, the tarnished metal fixtures, the peeling corners of wallpaper. What happened to this place, Pepper thought, following Salty down the hallway.

THEIR HISTORY CLASS overlooked the courtyard—or it would have if the ivy hadn't been allowed to grow over the windows. A candle was burning on the teacher's desk, contributing to the stuffy, oppressive feeling. However, a pleasant wet moss smell was intermixed with the scent of old books and dust. A wall of bookshelves filled with books and, in some cases, double-stacked lined the wall opposite the windows. Pepper took a seat near the back, between Azucar and Salty.

Ten minutes after class was supposed to begin, but there was still no teacher. All the girls looked at each other and consulted their schedules to ensure they hadn't shown up on the wrong day or time. Then, a petite woman, presumably Mrs. Sabatini, their history teacher, stepped inside and closed the door behind her. Pepper inwardly groaned. With twenty bodies in here, it was going to get even warmer. She debated taking off her sweater.

"Chutney?" the woman said, looking at the sheet she was holding as she walked to the front of the room.

"Present," Chutney replied, her cheeks flaming as several girls stifled laughter.

"Honey," Mrs. Sabatini continued, calling role.

"Here," replied the girl Salty had pointed out in the dining room. She had long, toffee-colored braids and skin that definitely resembled honey. Pepper wondered if Ms. Oscura named her ironically, as she had with her friends, or aptly.

"Sugar"

"I prefer Azucar."

"Whateva curls your hair," Mrs. Sabatini said, scribbling on her role sheet. She smirked. "You think the headmistress was hangry when she assigned names this year or what?"

"What are the code names usually?" Pepper asked, noticing the teacher had a subtler version of Salty's Long Island accent.

"Next time, raise your hand. Usually, it's flowers. We did have an Oakley one year."

The entire class groaned.

"Great, we get the eccentric headmistress," Salty whispered to Pepper.

The woman completed taking role and looked up. She was older than Pepper had first thought. Her face was lightly lined, and there were streaks of gray throughout her shoulder-length black bob.

"I'm Mrs. Sabatini. This is my twentieth year at Valentina's. I'm happy to welcome you to Her-story 101. Just so you know, we'll be together for the next three years. Although the subject matter will remain rooted in history, we will explore different aspects relevant to your specialized Valentina education. This semester, we are focusing on female rulers, their ascent to power, their accomplishments, and, in some cases, their demise. No woman, least of all a Valentina woman, should be without the complete knowledge of powerful women throughout history."

"This is gonna be *firme*," Azucar said, preparing to take notes.

Pepper just stared at Mrs. Sabatini. This was undoubtedly going to be a different education than she'd anticipated.

Ginger burst into class. Half her hair was straight, and the rest was curly, but not in half the way one might imagine. The underside was straight, and the top was curly. It didn't look half bad, but from Ginger's flaming red cheeks, she was clearly upset.

"I'm so sorry," she said, sliding into the last seat in their back row.

"Ginger?" Mrs. Sabatini said, making a notation in her chart. "Next time, detention. Take a seat."

"What happened to you?" Azucar asked, turning around in her chair.

"I realized I was going to be late, so I abandoned my hair but forgot to change staircases on the second floor. I actually went all the way down to the first floor, but then I couldn't figure out how to get out. Ms. Oscura heard me crying and let me in through her office. I'm mortified." She dropped her head to the desk.

"It could happen to anyone," Salty said.

"But it didn't. It happened to dumb 'ole me."

No matter how exciting the course material was, this was still history class, and they spent the next fifty-five minutes taking notes and then writing a synopsis of the life of Grand Princess Olga of Kyiv. A fascinating woman, Pepper decided, twisting in her seat to crack her spine in several places. Once Mrs. Sabatini had looked over their notes, they were dismissed.

"Anyone know where our next class is?" Pepper asked, consulting her schedule.

"I'm off to algebra down the hall," Chutney said.

"Ew, we still have to learn that?" Salty said, pulling a face.

"I have math, too," Ginger replied, checking her schedule. "Let's walk together."

Pepper perused the schedule, noting FL 0 alongside their

cooking class. The rest of their classes had FL 1 and a number; clearly, they were on the main floor.

"What does FL zero stand for," she asked.

"Hmm," Salty replied, biting her bottom lip in concentration, "basement?"

"Let's find out," Azucar said, leading the girls down the hallway to another set of stairs.

The temperature significantly decreased as they descended. The damp, musty odor of wet earth permeated the air, which was not appetizing.

"I thought we'd be in the school's kitchen," Pepper whispered. "Not a dungeon."

"Maybe this is Cooking Poison 101," Azucar replied.

"What happened to wanting to live in a kinder world?" Pepper asked.

"For animals," Azucar replied. "People are the worst."

They reached a set of double doors and pushed them open. Pepper groaned. Cherry and her cohorts were in this class, too. Well, they couldn't avoid them all day. That would have been too much to hope for, she thought.

The cavernous room had eight kitchen stations, each with an oven, sink, and prep station. Like the rest of the building, these appliances were mismatched with older models that had been replaced in various decades. If all the fixtures and appliances were to be upgraded to stainless steel or even white, the room would look refreshed and modern, thanks to the aesthetic of the white subway tile serving as a backsplash. Pepper guessed it had been the economical choice when this room was being retrofitted as a kitchen classroom. Still, it held up remarkably well over time. The floors, on the other hand, could use work. As she lifted her foot, the sole of her sneaker made that sticky sucking sound as if it were suctioned to the grime on the floor. She shuddered.

Hopefully, they wouldn't be in charge of scrubbing the floor clean before they started cooking, but she certainly hoped someone would.

The door banged open, and to Pepper's surprise, a youngish man sauntered into the kitchen. He was slightly taller than Pepper, with close-cropped, sandy brown hair and a trim figure with just the hint of a soft belly rounding his olive-green sweater.

"He's cute," someone whispered, loud enough to be heard by everyone, including their teacher.

"Good morning, I'm Mr. Tonelli, your cooking instructor. We will be exploring the cuisine of Italy." He perused the roster, brow knitted in confusion. "Is this correct? Cherry, Pepper, Salty, Apple, Peach, Coconut, Honey? These are your names?"

"Yes, sir," Coconut said. "But I'd prefer to go by Coco."

"Is the headmistress mocking me?" he wondered aloud, scratching his cheek with the end of his pen.

"Apparently, she was hungry when she selected our code names," Cherry said, fluttering her eyelashes.

"This is highly unusual. How are you supposed to know if I'm talking to you or referencing an ingredient?" He blew a frustrated breath noisily between his lips, then set down the roster. "I guess that's her prerogative. Split up into groups of three and convene at a station."

Pepper, Azucar, and Salty stuck together. Each workstation's prep table was covered with kitchen tools.

"What is this stuff?" Salty whispered, regarding the table full of doodads and gleaming silver objects.

"This stuff," Mr. Tonelli said, "Miss...?"

"Salty," she replied.

"So strange," he murmured to himself. "Very well, Miss Salty. These things are the tools you will be using to create culinary masterpieces. There will be no machine to chop your veggies or wash your dirty pots. There are no robots to open and slop sauce in a pot. Not in my kitchen. Here you will learn how to prepare meals from start to finish, with your own hands, and you will like it. Let's begin."

Salty stared at her perfectly manicured nails in horror.

"Italian American cuisine is entirely its own category, separate from the old country. Authentic Italian food has been melted away in the big cultural pot of America. Not in this kitchen! No deep-dish pizza. No fried anything. No garlic bread baguettes. We are making everything from scratch. Yes, pasta, too. Get ready—"

"Are we going to learn to cook anything besides Italian food?" Cherry interrupted.

"Right now, you are going to learn the names of these tools. Cooking won't even enter into the curriculum until next quarter after you learn and understand authentic Italian cuisine."

Salty looked a bit more relieved at that news, but Pepper's heart sank. She had been looking forward to getting into the kitchen again. This hadn't exactly been what she had in mind, but it was familiar territory that put her at ease. They spent the rest of class cataloging their tools and watching Mr. Tonelli demonstrate how to use them. It had been boring. Did they really need that ten-minute lecture on the differences between the chef, boning, pairing, and bread knives?

"Is he, like the cook for the school, or does he just teach cooking?" Salty asked as they marched up the stairs for lunch.

"I guess if we only get pasta, that'll be a big clue," Azucar replied.

The girls' laughter echoed down the empty hallway.

"And the way he went on about my name. It's not like I picked it," Salty exclaimed.

"I think he just found it strange. I mean, every time a recipe calls for pepper, I'm going to be looking up, wondering what he wants," Pepper replied.

"Looks like we know who his favorites are," Salty said as Cherry shoved them aside to ascend the stairs without a backward glance.

"I'd rather be interesting than obvious," Azucar said, but it was too late. Cherry was through the door.

"It was a nice try," Salty said.

"I always think of insults too late," Azucar said.

"What do you think she was doing in class, just her and the teacher?" Pepper wondered aloud.

"Nothing I want to know about," Azucar said, "especially not before lunch. Come on, let's find Ginger and see what horrors await us in algebra this afternoon."

STRETCHED out in a warm patch of sunlight on the cupola floor, Pepper started her homework. English had been a colossal disappointment this afternoon. Where was the fun in just reading a novel? Weren't they here to be preparing for life? That was what Ms. Oscura told her just one day ago. How was reading Shakespeare preparation for life? The rest of the girls were working on their algebra homework in the study room downstairs. Pepper sighed and rolled onto her back, thinking about the lazy summer afternoons she and Ethan had spent in the corner of the library reading vintage magazines together. She felt terrible about the way she'd left. Before she'd thought it through, Pepper had sent a chat request.

"Hey," Ethan said as the screen filled with his smiling face. "How's it going?"

"It's crazy here." Pepper paused, wanting to tell him all the unbelievable details, but she didn't dare.

"Are you showing all the other students how it's done?" he asked.

"Hardly." She laughed. "Our teacher isn't letting us cook until at least next quarter. Today, he went on for twenty minutes about the cheese grater!"

"Ouch, that's rough. What's interesting about a grater? I mean, it does one thing, right?"

"Not according to Signore Tonelli."

"Well, when you do get to cook, you'll blow them all away. I know it."

"I hope it's soon. Margaux expects me to know how to cook when I get home."

"Eh, just tell her you're saving your talent, and she can cook dinner for once."

Pepper looked into Ethan's deep brown eyes. She'd missed sharing her day with him. She wished she could tell him about the escape room challenge. He'd be so proud of her. But instead, she just asked how everything was going at the library.

"Same as always," he replied, turning the screen to scan the empty room. "My dad's threatening to cut funding. I'm not sure how much longer it's going to survive."

Pepper gasped. "That's awful."

"Yeah, but after I graduate, there won't be anyone around to run it, so…" He shrugged.

This wasn't like Ethan. He was always a fighter, a champion of causes he believed in, like the library. Something was wrong.

"Is there something I could do," she said.

"Nah. Not unless you have a spare million. Hey, are you coming back, like on holidays?"

Pepper hadn't been expecting that. Her gaze darted to the door as Azucar bound inside. "Uh, no. We aren't allowed."

"Allowed what?" Azucar said. Then, realizing Pepper was on a chat, she grabbed for the phone. "Who's this? Boyfriend back home?"

"No, we're just friends," Pepper said, wrestling the phone away from Azucar.

"Sorry, my bad," Azucar replied, retreating to her bed.

"Roommate," Pepper said, grinning sheepishly. She could see her guilty face in the small square at the top right of the screen. She couldn't stand the hurt look that passed across Ethan's face. Ugh, why had she reached out? It was better to leave it a clean break.

But she had been homesick for something, someone familiar. This wasn't fair to him.

"Gotta get busy closing up. Nice to see your face, St—"

"Yeah, you too," she shouted, cutting him off before he could utter her real name. Not that Azucar didn't already know it, but it felt wrong suddenly. Like the person she had been had already faded away in the short time she'd been here.

The screen went black. Ethan had disconnected while she was lost in thought.

"Don't tell me, it's complicated, right?" Azucar said. "Girl, end it now. I hear we are consorting with the Dons for PE on Wednesdays. Y-U-M."

Pepper gave her friend a hollow smile, still preoccupied by the realization that who she'd been just a few days ago was not who she was becoming. Could Stella and Pepper coexist, or was Stella disappearing for good?

# Chapter Eleven

The grating drone of a leaf blower echoed through the room. Pepper lifted her head. Hazy morning light filtered through the clouds. Their curtains hadn't arrived yet, and they were still subject to the fickle fog for their a.m. wake-up. It's too bad this morning was nice and overcast. The light in the cupola was still dim enough to sleep without shoving a pillow in your face. The noise, however, persisted.

"Sounds like they're tackling that mess of a garden this morning," Pepper said, sitting up.

"Ugh, did they have to do it on our late start day?" Ginger moaned, pulling her comforter over her head.

Wednesday was their delayed start morning, giving them time to finish assignments or catch up on sleep. Pepper wanted to explore the grounds a bit. Having been in class the past two days, she hadn't gotten a feel for her surroundings. She asked if anyone wanted to join her but was met with a series of groans. She slipped on some joggers and shrugged into her school hoodie before heading downstairs.

Salty had managed to get a set of lockers in the bathroom for their things, which made getting ready a lot easier. This morning, Pepper had the bathroom to herself, which was a relief. Most mornings, she had endured snide comments from Cherry and The Fruit Bunch, not unlike the jabs from Margaux. Pepper was used to ignoring such barbs, but it wasn't the most pleasant way to begin her day.

There were a handful of girls in the dining room. Pepper had pledged to herself to be more social. When confronted with the opportunity to sit down and talk to people, she shied away. Instead of sitting at the table with her fellow students, Pepper grabbed an apple and headed out the front door.

The morning air was biting. She regretted not putting on another layer under the sweater as she ventured down the stone steps and across the mostly green lawn to the bluff. Pepper loved how the tall cypress pines shielded the view like a screen. The rambunctious sea thrashed against the jagged rocks below. The wind whipped her hair into a tangled mess around her face. Pepper parted the untamed mass of hair and attempted to tuck it into a low bun with little success. When it was clear the wind was winning, she dragged the hood over her head and cinched the ties tight so only her face was peeking out of the dark blue fabric.

Low clouds blocked the sun and created a hazy, dreamlike landscape. Pepper peered over the side of the bluff. The ocean was a swirl of white foam and a vibrant cerulean blue. A path along the bluff's edge led away from the school toward the beach below. Pepper glanced back and took off down the path at a brisk pace. The rules stated that they were allowed to wander the grounds, but they never specified how far. Since there were no fences, Pepper figured this was safe; at least, that's what she'd argue if she got caught.

Within a few moments, she was breathing heavily, the cold air stinging as she pulled it in through her nose before making vapor clouds as she exhaled. The salt-laden breeze was exhilarating. Unlike down south, where it was sweltering before noon, and you were dripping with sweat the moment you left the house, here, the fierce wind off the ocean made her want to outrun the cold and build heat from inside her core. She took off along the path, marveling at the expansive ocean vista.

Pepper darted down the gently curving path when the trail dipped between two boulders. She could no longer see the ocean, but the sound of the crashing waves was amplified in this alcove. She pulled back her hood to feel the wind through her hair, closed her eyes, and spun around. WHAM! She hit something solid and tumbled down the rest of the embankment before landing in a heap on the sand.

Disoriented, Pepper reached out, her fingers brushing fabric. She tried dusting off her face, but her hands were also covered with sand, so it didn't do any good.

"Don't you watch where you're going?" Pepper said, squinting at the person who'd tripped her.

"Sorry, guess I was looking down, concentrating on maintaining my form," he said, panting.

Her pulse quickened, and she scooted back. What was a guy doing here? Unless…

"Are you hurt?" He reached out and brushed the sand from her eyes with the cuff of his sleeve. "Is that better?"

Pepper nodded. He was clearly one of the Don Academy students. He was almost too good-looking, even with sand sticking to his sweat-slicked forehead. The kind of guy who might be a fitness influencer. His deep brown eyes were rimmed with long lashes that matched his dark brown, almost black hair. Which was pulled away from his face at the nape of his neck, but tendrils had escaped and were framing his face like a halo. He jumped up, shaking his head, sending sand everywhere. His hair tie slipped free, and his curls cascaded to his shoulders into the kind of loose waves Pepper had always envied.

She grasped the hair tie and handed it back. "Are you at the boy's school?" Even as the words were leaving her mouth, Pepper couldn't believe she was saying them. He looked down and gave her a lopsided grin before taking the tie and pulling his hair back. "I guess that's obvious, duh."

"Yeah, I am. You must be at Valentina's," he said, holding out his hand; it was hot against her palm. She hoped he couldn't feel her pulse pounding against her skin.

He wasn't wearing a school uniform but a plain white undershirt that clung to his well-defined chest and folded-down joggers, revealing a slim line of tanned waist.

"It's nice to meet you...." He paused and raised one eyebrow.

Pepper looked up, paralyzed. What name should she give him? Did they have secret names there, too? Her code name was for Valentina's, but this was kind of school-related. Weren't they going to have their gym class at The Don Academy later today? Then again, maybe since he wasn't part of her school, she should give him her real name.

"Is it a secret?" he asked. "No worries. I like a challenge, but it's after nine-thirty, and I've got to get back for my first class at ten. See you around...Sandy."

She shook her head, trying to look annoyed, but a fresh wave of sand avalanched down her shoulders, making them both smile. "Yeah, see ya," she said in reply.

He turned and ran back down the beach. Pepper was mesmerized and couldn't look away until he was just a tiny figure bouncing in the distance.

Wait, did he say it was after nine-thirty? Pepper bolted back up the bluff to school. They had etiquette class at ten, and even though it was their first class, Pepper knew she could not show up with sand in her hair.

AT TEN ON THE DOT, Pepper was racing down the stairs, hair still wet, and slid into the main hallway just as the entry clock stopped chiming. She was surprised to see her classmates lined up alongside the wall, silent. Pepper joined the end of the line and tapped Chili on the shoulder.

"Hey, what's going on?" she whispered.

Chili shushed her without turning around.

Pepper's stomach gurgled just as someone opened the classroom door and stepped into the hall. The woman zeroed in on Pepper and made her way down the line. A cloud of fragrance preceded her trim frame. Her clothes were timeless in the way a pair of classic jeans would always be in style. She sported a crisp white blouse with sleeves rolled to the mid-forearm, revealing a two-inch section of gold bangles, slim black slacks, and red loafers. Her hair was short and an ashy blonde, which accented her round red-framed glasses and red lipstick. Pepper sensed a color preference, but she had to admit that even for her age, she was stylish and imposing.

"You're late," the woman said, reaching Pepper at the end of the line.

"I was in line at ten exactly," Pepper replied defiantly.

"Don't answer back. On-time is late. Early is on time, and late is unacceptable. Understand." Pepper nodded. "Secondly, a lady always makes a good appearance unless she is incognito for some surveillance. You will not come to class with wet hair again, understood?"

Pepper tucked the dripping strand behind her ear, knowing this teacher would have had more to say about a head full of sand, but she decided it was best not to answer back again. She didn't have high hopes for this class to begin with, but after encountering their teacher, her heart sank. The woman gave a slight nod, and the class filed inside. This was going to be one tea party, place setting, snooze fest, she thought, stepping inside.

The classroom, if you could call it that, was not what Pepper had been expecting. Unlike the other standard but tidy classrooms, this room looked like it hadn't been touched, let alone updated in decades. Instead of desks, there were bistro tables and tufted olive-green chaise lounges. Crystals hung from the windows, sending prisms across every surface. Books were piled on almost all tabletops, including some student workstations. Inside, Pepper realized what she had mistaken in the dim light of the hallway for Ms. Powell's ash blonde hair was, in fact, a silvery gray.

"Good morning, my little *farfalle*. For our first task, we will begin creating your astrological natal chart."

Pepper searched the faces of her classmates; everyone wore the same puzzled expression.

"Sorry. Ms. Powell, what does this have to do with etiquette?" Chutney asked.

"Firstly, don't talk out of turn." She waggled one gnarled finger at Chutney. "Were you under the impression that we would be doing posture drills and elocution lessons in my etiquette class? Is that it?"

The girls nodded.

She chuckled. "Hardly. Before we begin espionage, surveillance, counterintelligence, and all the other goodies we'll be studying together over the next three years, I need, and more importantly, you need, to know your strengths and weaknesses. In my many years of experience, these have been best revealed in the alignment of the planets at the moment of your birth, which is what natal means: birth. There, bonus vocabulary lesson." She smirked.

Pepper had expected a long syllabus explanation or at least a rundown of their curriculum as Seignior Tonelli had. Ms. Powell just prattled on about the importance of knowing one's exact birth time and location. Pepper's breath began to quicken. She didn't know the time of her birth, and no one was alive to tell her. Her hand automatically went for the necklace. She pulled the ring up from her shirt and grasped the signet ring between her thumb and forefinger.

"The tablets have all been queued up to the correct website. Enter your birth date to reveal your astrological sign."

At least she knew this. Pepper entered her birth date and selected enter. A lion appeared on the screen.

"This is your sun sign—the driving force of your personality. Save these results in your natal chart folder—again, already created for you. I'm a Capricorn. We are very organized and goal-oriented. Share your results with your table partner, and you'll begin to understand the zodiac's ability to highlight your natural abilities."

"She seems awfully rigid for being so...spiritual," Salty whispered.

"Another Capricorn trait," Ms. Powell said.

Salty jumped. "Sorry, I didn't mean..."

"Of course you meant it. First impressions are often incorrect, but if we know their power, we use them to our advantage. What is your sign, dear?"

"I'm a, uh...Pisces."

Ms. Powell narrowed her eyes and pursed her lips. "Yes, I see it. Very sensitive. And you?"

"Leo," Pepper replied.

"Ah, that makes sense. Queen of the Jungle must have attention at all times."

Pepper shook her head. That didn't seem like her at all. In fact, she was quite the opposite. Before she could contradict Ms. Powell's assessment, the woman stepped away to check on Chili and Chutney's progress.

AS THEY LEFT THE CLASSROOM, still a bit dazed from their unusual lesson, Salty informed them that her mother had given her a heads-up about Ms. Powell.

"She's been here that long?" Azucar whispered.

"Apparently, and still just as weird, but Ma said it gets better. As we advance, we'll learn espionage techniques."

"What else?" Ginger pressed.

Salty shrugged, "Ma said she shouldn't have even told me that, but she knew I'd freak out after the first class. I guess we'll have to wait and see."

"It certainly is a strange hybrid," Pepper commented.

"I liked her," Azucar said. "I think she has something up her sleeve. This is gonna be our best class. Wait and see."

"You only liked her because she said your natal chart progress was perfection," Salty said.

"It's not my fault my Abuela was into astrology, and I know my moon sign. Don't get all jelly on me—Pisces."

Salty rolled her eyes and kept walking.

So far, their education at Valentina's had been a bit unconventional. Pepper had no idea how etiquette translated into surveillance and birth charts. It was only the first week, but this certainly wasn't the education Pepper had imagined. Still, it was a vast improvement on the general education she would have received back home. Being here was better, Pepper decided, joining the lunch line.

# Chapter Twelve

alf an hour after lunch, half the school, the same group in etiquette class, met on the lawn for their first physical education class. One benefit of living at Valentina's was changing into the PE uniform in privacy in her room and not in front of twenty other girls in the middle of a drafty locker.

"Do you think we're getting picked up and taken to a fancy gym?" Azucar asked.

Pepper shrugged. At this point, nothing would surprise her.

"Hey, so tell us all about that cute guy you ran into this morning," Ginger said while they were waiting.

"Literally ran into," Pepper reminded them as she recounted the incident.

"I wonder who he is," Salty said dreamily. "If you see him this afternoon in PE, you have to point him out."

Pepper agreed, but sort of hoped they wouldn't be having PE together as the other girls did. He was very fit, and this morning's run made her realize just how out of condition she had become since moving to California. In Denver, Nonnu had encouraged her to exercise by jumping rope and doing the obstacle course he'd made in their backyard. Of course, she had been younger, but she loved running and ducking in and out of the tires, rope swing, and other obstacles. It was so much fun. She smiled at the memory.

Ms. Oscura bounded down the steps wearing the same uniform as the girls: navy leggings with the school logo printed on the right hip in silver and a gray T-shirt. The girls gawked at her.

"Good afternoon, ladies. Since this is Valentina's first-ever physical education class, I will be escorting you today. This is not going to be a habit. I'm just showing you the way this first time. Coach O'Loughlin will be waiting for us. In the future, you will meet on the soccer field of the Don Academy for class."

"If their coach is our PE teacher, are the boys joining us for class?" Cherry asked.

"They are not," Ms. Oscura replied.

"What are we going to be doing?" Salty asked.

"Whatever the coach deems appropriate. Let's get going." She took off at a brisk jog. "Keep up, girls. This is your warmup."

"Ugh, I hope it's not miles away," Ginger moaned. "I didn't pack my sports bra, and doubling up on the support is not cutting it."

"It just figures that our new headmistress would add exercise to the curriculum," Salty whined.

They labored across the lawn, past the trail down to the beach where Pepper had run into that guy this morning, and beside an ivy-covered wall that seemed to go on forever. Then, the Don Academy rose from the rolling landscape like an imposing mountain. The edifice of the school was brick and, unlike Valentina's, looked every inch like an impressive prep school. They had to have at least quadruple the students as Valentina's. Coach O'Loughlin was waiting at the soccer field gate when the girls approached the school's perimeter. It seemed like this fence surrounded the entire property, which left Pepper wondering how that guy got out this morning.

"Here they are, Coach. Send them on back when you're through," Ms. Oscura said, not even slightly out of breath. "Girls, we will be taking roll upon your return, so don't get any cute ideas."

Coach stepped forward. "I was wondering if you and I could demonstrate what we'll be doing this year in physical education."

A ripple of laughter passed through the class, followed by a low whistle. Ms. Oscura gave the girls a death glare.

"My pleasure. Shall we demonstrate a catch-release combination?" Coach nodded.

Ms. Oscura turned, and to Pepper's surprise, Coach lunged forward, grasping her around the waist from behind. In an instant, her feet were above her head, and then Coach was flying through the air, landing in a heap on the grass. It all happened so fast that Pepper barely had time to register Ms. Oscura's precise movements.

Coach stood, and to her surprise, he was smiling. "Thank you, Headmistress. I'm not sure I could have found the words."

"My pleasure. Whip 'em into shape, Coach," Ms. Oscura said before jogging away.

"You got it. Now that you are warmed up let's get in some stretches before tackling the circuit course."

"Circuits? What about all that Kung Fu stuff?" Azucar asked.

"Self-defense will be our focus this year, but you must be strong first. Judging by the number of red, panting faces I see, we need to do some basic training first."

Ginger collapsed inside the gate. "Y'all, I think I'm gonna die."

Pepper helped her up. "Can we get some water first, Coach?"

"Sure, that's a good idea. Stay hydrated. There's a hose on the way."

"A hose?" Cherry balked. "That's disgusting."

"You aren't obliged to use it," he replied, not bothered.

The girls listlessly followed.

"Hustle up, girl . . . lady . . . uh, students, let's get going with some stretches. Follow my lead."

"Coach seems a little out of his element teaching us," Pepper whispered.

Salty raised the hose to her lips but handed it off to Azucar without drinking. "It's just my luck to get the eccentric headmistress who chooses food code names and adds exercise to the curriculum."

THE STRETCHING routine allowed Pepper and her classmates a moment to catch their breath and prepare for circuits. Not dissimilar to her grandfather's course, Pepper was excited to give it a try and was the first to volunteer, along with Cherry, who seemed to just want to be competitive. Two could play that game, Pepper decided. Coach demonstrated each station. While it wasn't exactly an obstacle course, Pepper liked the variation rather than the monotony of running.

There were six stations, and they were supposed to do ten reps at each and then move on to the next until they finished the circuit. Coach clearly hadn't thought this through because, with twenty-four students, it would take quite a while for them all to cycle through the whole circuit. Then again, it was a two-hour class.

"Ready, Peppercorn," Cherry said.

"Clever. Did you come up with that on your own, or did you need a thesaurus?" Pepper asked, stretching her calf.

Coach selected four more girls to join them and then gave the signal. Pepper and Cherry raced in opposite directions. Cherry went for the battle ropes. Pepper smirked. She'd tire out her arms quickly and be unable to do the rest of the arm exercises. Pepper started with the push-ups. She planted her hands on the dewy grass and lowered herself to the ground. After eight, her arms were shaking, and she was grateful they only had to do ten reps. She finished the last two to the shouts of encouragement from Salty, Azucar, and Ginger. Then she began the lunges, which were a piece of cake. She always had strong legs. Cherry was struggling with her push-ups as Pepper moved on to the burpees. Ugh, I should have done these first, she thought, struggling to complete the push-ups.

"It's not a race, girls, don't overdo it," Coach said, clearly noticing Pepper and Cherry's private competition.

Pepper ignored him and began her bicycle crunches. Her abs burned with the effort, but she pushed through. Next up was the jump rope, which, after the lunges, burpees, and bicycle Vs, left her legs a bit tired and uncoordinated. Pepper's feet got caught in the rope numerous times. She cursed and started again. When she successfully completed her ten jump ropes, which was more like twenty-five because she kept starting over, she reached the final circuit. Pepper grasped the heavy, coarse ropes in her hands, took a deep breath, and let it out as she heaved the first rope in the air, sending it rippling like a wave. Who used these, their football team? She lifted her left hand.

"Coach, is it ten on each side or all together?" she panted.

"Each side," Coach called back. "Or as many as you can do."

Basically, the rest of the girls were sitting until it was their turn. After that run, no one was complaining about the inactivity. But Coach noticed and sent them off to walk the track to keep their heart rate up while waiting. They groaned but obliged.

Pepper finished and collapsed beside the ropes.

"Good job," Coach said.

She lay there as the rest of her team finished their circuit. Cherry completed the course a couple of minutes later. Pepper smiled inwardly at her victory.

"All right, get some water and join your classmates walking on the track," Coach said, motioning the next group over. She lay there for another few moments, not wanting to be subjected to Cherry's insults.

Once Cherry and her fruit bunch were a safe distance away, Pepper hobbled over to the hose. Her face was burning with heat, which meant it was probably beet red. She took a drink, then doused her head. The cool water trailed down her neck, sending cool shivers along her limbs. Pepper lifted the corner of her shirt and wiped the drips from her face.

"You're a beast, Sandy," a male voice said.

Pepper quickly pulled her shirt down and looked up. It was the boy from the beach. He stepped onto the field with a group of guys.

"Uh … thanks, I guess," she replied. "Do you have PE after us?"

He grinned. Pepper did not appreciate the nervous summersault flips her stomach did when he smiled.

"Soccer practice," he replied, stopping beside her.

"Right. Do you guys have a team?" She smacked her forehead. All this exercise was siphoning blood from her brain. "Duh, of course you do. I meant, who do you play against?"

"Other private schools in the area. We're ranked number one."

His teammate kicked a ball in his direction. *Beach Guy* casually caught it with the tip of his cleat, then bounced it on the top of his foot before he headed the ball back across the field.

"You should come to our first game in two weeks," he said, turning back to her. "It's at Loyola."

"Dude, come on," one of the guys yelled, motioning him over.

"Have a good practice," she said, thoroughly annoyed with how lame she sounded.

"Thanks. I hope I'll see you at the game," he replied.

"Sure, maybe," she said, watching him jog across the grass, his tanned legs pumping with minimal effort. She wouldn't mind watching those legs run up and down a field for ninety minutes.

Salty ran up, startling her. She grasped Pepper's arm and steered her down the track. "Was *that* the beach guy?"

"Shh, yes," Pepper replied, watching him casually bouncing a soccer ball on his knee, pretending he wasn't showing off for her.

"Why didn't you tell me you met *Il Principe!*" Salty squealed.

"What?" Pepper said, turning to face her friend. "Probably because I had no idea. He's a prince?"

"Don't you know anything?" Salty replied, looking around. "That's Nico Rossetti, son of the biggest family on the East Coast. He's basically going to inherit Manhattan and a whole bunch of other places. What did he say?"

"Uh…wait, how do you inherit a city?" Pepper asked.

Salty stopped short and eyed Pepper suspiciously. "What are you playing at?"

"Nothing. I just…"

"Are you a mole?" Salty asked, narrowing her eyes.

Salty gave Pepper a sharp look and coldly walked past her. For her unicorn sparkle personality, this departure was alarming. Who knew sweet Salty had a tough side. No, no, no, Pepper thought, hanging back. What could she even reveal to Salty without harming herself? Her cover was blown. She had to come clean.

# Chapter Thirteen

They limped up the stairs, sore from their circuits and the run. Ginger plopped down at her desk and retrieved a journal from the top drawer.

"Ooohhhh, is that your diary?" Azucar asked, trying to peer over Ginger's shoulder.

"More like a journal. I do brain dumps here."

"Pardon? You dump what?" Azucar asked, stepping back.

"I get everything that's in my head down on the page so I can concentrate on other stuff without my mind wandering."

"Hmm…everything that's in your head. Well, that shouldn't take long," Azucar teased.

"Does that really help?" Pepper asked, wondering if she should try it.

"Sure does."

"I can't keep a journal or diary," Salty said. "My mom trained me never to write anything down."

"Why?" Pepper asked.

"Evidence," Salty replied simply, with a pointed look in Pepper's direction.

Things had turned cold between them quickly. She needed to fix it. When Azucar announced that there was one other shower

109

free, Ginger jumped up and raced downstairs. Pepper crossed the room and tried the door leading onto the roof. The handle turned smoothly, but the frame had been painted shut. She gave it a couple of forceful tugs, and finally, the sealed paint split with a crack, and the door popped open. Salty looked up at the noise.

"Hey, can we talk?" Pepper asked. "Out there."

"You gonna try to push me off the roof, mole?"

Pepper gave an exasperated sigh. "I'm not a mole, but I need to explain some things, and I'd rather not do it where we can be overheard."

Salty eyed her suspiciously but agreed. Pepper stepped onto the flat, gravelly roof. The air was cool, but the setting sun had burned away the earlier mist and warmed her face. She took in the surroundings. There was a walkway that stretched along the length of this wing. Pepper assumed it was the same on the other side of the building. She noticed a cigarette butt discarded in the corner.

"What is it?" Salty asked, leaning against the waist-high wall surrounding the rectangular parapet.

"This afternoon, I wasn't pretending. I really don't know exactly what you're talking about. And it's not because I'm a mole. If I were a mole, I would understand what you were saying, wouldn't I?"

Salty's frown dissolved, and her usual bright expression returned. "Yeah, that's right."

"But I'm not exactly who you think I am either." Pepper twisted her hair into a bun, then let it fall down her back. "I need you to keep this dry," Pepper said. Salty nodded and leaned forward, tantalized by the promise of a secret. "My grandparents raised me."

"That's not so weird. I bet a lot of girls here were," Salty interrupted.

"The thing is, they never talked about our family. They died several years ago, and I've been living with my dad and stepmom ever since. A few weeks ago, I opened a letter left to me from my Nonnu that said I had full tuition here, but it contained no other information." Pepper hesitated, unsure if she should reveal more. "And as you already know, this school is pretty secretive, but it's not normal. He said I belonged here, and this school would help me find my place, but I feel like such an outsider. It's like everyone is in on the secret but me. Can you help?" To her surprise, Salty had tears in her eyes.

"That is so tragic. I'm sorry I accused you of being a mole."

"Forgiven, if you'll help."

"Of course." Salty rushed forward and grasped Pepper's hands. "What do you want to know?"

"What kind of a school is this? It's not just a private school. That much is very obvious."

Salty laughed. "This is a prep school for mob wives."

Pepper gave a start. "For what?"

"Mafia brides," Salty replied. "All the women in my family, well at least one a generation, have attended Valentina's. That's why my sister was so upset. She wanted to better her odds of finding a high-powered Don."

"A Don? You mean… a Godfather."

"Exactly."

"And Nico, I mean, *Il Principe*, he's going to be…"

"Head of the Rossetti crime family, one day. Probably after a long career as a professional soccer player."

Pepper felt the blood drain from her face as she sank to her knees, lightheaded. It all made sense. The stories Nonnu told, the trips to Little Italy, her father's time in prison. They were all involved in organized crime. But why the secrecy?

"Are you okay?" Salty said, kneeling beside her.

"Yes, I'm just…it all makes sense now."

"*Perfetto*," Salty said. "To tell you the truth, this is not exactly the experience I had anticipated either. This new headmistress is shaking things up. To hear my grandma tell it, what she learned was how to cook, keep house, and eavesdrop."

Pepper smirked. "During my orientation, Ms. Oscura said she was preparing us for life with or without a betrothal."

"I think she's progressive," Salty replied. "So why do you think your family never talked about their involvement?"

"I don't know. The last time I visited him, my dad told me not to ask questions."

"Typical man. They never tell the women anything. Why did you have to visit him if you live with him and your stepmom?"

"Uh…he's in prison."

"Such a drag, right? I hate those visitation rooms. Awful lighting."

"Is your dad in prison too?"

"He was a long time ago. It's no biggie. I bet most of the girls here have family that's been in jail at one time or another. TCN"

"What's TCN?"

"That's Cosa Nostra. TCN."

"That doesn't make sense."

"Gosh, you really are a zip. Cosa Nostra means it's our thing. It's like a slang way to

say mafia."

Pepper didn't want to seem clueless once again, so she refrained from asking for the

definition of zip. Maybe it meant clueless? She thought, still reeling from the reveal.

"Your Nonnu was right. You belong here."

Pepper had her doubts, but it was nice to hear. "Thanks, I've never really fit in anywhere,"

"I'll make sure you fit in here. I'll be like your mafia godmother!"

"Thank you, I guess. Hey, Nico said there's a soccer game in a couple of weeks. Want to go?"

"Get out! He invited you to watch him play?"

"I guess, yeah," Pepper replied.

"Girl, you do not seem to understand. He is the most eligible guy out of all the guys at Don's. Everyone at Valentina's would kill to be in your shoes."

"Huh, well, maybe we should sneak over instead of announcing it to everyone."

"Now you're thinking like a Mafiosi."

A prickly, hot blush crept up Pepper's neck. "Thanks. Hey…do you think you could help me with something else?"

"Anything, shoot."

"I don't know much about my family. We had a different name than the one I had my whole life. And, like I said, my dad won't tell me anything."

"Do you know your real last name?" Salty asked.

"Yes, but before I tell you, promise you won't ever repeat it to anyone, ever."

"You have my solemn oath. I won't tell another soul," Salty said.

"D'Angelo. That's what it said in my letter. Stella D'Angelo." It felt odd to say her real name aloud, especially after getting used to being called Pepper.

Salty puffed her cheeks, then blew out the air quickly. "Nope, doesn't ring a bell. Not for a crime family, anyway. I mean, it's Italian, but I don't remember a family headed by a D'Angelo. Are they from New York?"

"I don't know for sure, but I think so."

"There are a lot of moving parts in a family organization. Maybe your grandfather was a made guy," Salty offered.

Deflated, Pepper leaned against the latticed parapet wall and looked down to the garden. The landscapers had done a great job pruning the overgrowth away today.

"And your mom didn't go here, right?" Salty asked.

"Nope," Pepper said, fiddling with a loose piece of concrete.

"What about your grandma?"

Pepper looked up suddenly. "Yeah, there was this weird sentence in my acceptance letter. Something about how my grandfather would know Valentina's produced ladies of quality. Do you think that means my grandmother went here?"

"It's worth a shot," Salty said. "Want to go down and ask Ms. Oscura now?"

Pepper shook her head.

The wind whipped up, sending debris and leaves into the air. Pepper squeezed her eyes shut too late. Grit scraped against her eyeball, causing her eyes to water. Pepper wiped away the tears with the back of her hand.

"Don't cry," Salty said. "We'll figure something out. What about an archive? A school this old and prestigious has to have one, right."

Pepper stopped rubbing her eyes and stared at her friend. "You are brilliant. Of course. There will be a record of my grandma if she went here."

"We make a pretty good team," she replied

"Salty and Pepper, who would've guessed."

They laughed and helped each other up. The next moment, Azucar stuck her toweled head out the open door.

"Whoa, secret exit. Way to go, ladies."

"Um, I'm not sure we can get to the ground from up here," Salty said.

"Besides, we don't want Ms. Oscura to banish us back to the dorm rooms," Pepper added. "If you think Cherry is a witch now, imagine how much she'd hate us for stealing her closet space."

Azucar eyed them skeptically. "Well, it's at least a good place to get some alone time, right?"

Pepper and Salty looked at each other and then nodded.

"Showers are free," Azucar said, ducking back inside.

"You go ahead," Pepper said. "I want to think for a bit."

Salty hugged her, then disappeared inside. Pepper pressed her back against the wall and slid to the floor. Mafia. The word sat in her stomach, heavy and solid. It was all so clear. That's what Nonnu meant about Valentina's preparing her to take her rightful place in their world. Although being a mafia wife wasn't exactly how she pictured her life, she had a feeling Ms. Oscura was preparing them for a more varied future. It all made sense, except for the secrecy. Why did she grow up with the last name Dallas instead of D'Angelo? And why wouldn't Dad talk about their past?

She pulled the necklace off and slipped the signet ring on her thumb. The gold warmed to her touch. Now that she knew, Pepper didn't feel quite so alone anymore. She had the overwhelming urge to call Ethan. What would he think? As far as she knew, his family were big supporters of law and order. His father made a lot of speeches about "taking back our cities from lawlessness," which she could only assume, now, that he meant people like her family. Their little enclave in Orange County had seemed relatively free from organized crime, but what did she know. All this time, she thought she came from a regular family, not a "family." Pepper decided it would be her mission to learn the truth about who she came from. If Salty were right, Valentina's Academy would have kept archives of past students. If her grandma had gone here, and it seemed promising that she had, there would be records. Finally, she'd find out who she was.

# Chapter Fourteen

To their surprise, after two weeks of constant schoolwork, Ms. Oscura announced during breakfast on Friday that the school van would be going into Monterey that evening if anyone wanted to visit the town for a few hours. The dining room erupted in shrieks of excitement. Once the squeals quieted, Ms. Oscura informed them that this would be a regular occurrence if the girls didn't abuse it.

Salty kicked Pepper under the table.

"Ow, what was that for?"

"Foot slipped, sorry," she replied, winking.

Pepper realized what she was trying to communicate. The soccer game was tonight, and this was their opportunity to go. Heeding Salty's advice, Pepper hadn't said a thing to anyone else, but they agreed to include Azucar and Ginger. Leaving their other two roommates out of a prime boy meeting opportunity would be unforgivable. Salty and Pepper agreed not to tell them until they were in town. That way, they'd up the odds of not being overheard —or followed.

. . .

THE REST of the day was a snooze fest. Mrs. Sabatini continued their lessons on strong female leaders, and now Pepper understood why. Learning about the women who shaped history but were mostly forgotten was fascinating. None of that mattered right now, though, as Pepper and her roommates sprinted up the stairs. Their caravan was leaving for town at four-thirty, and they had to get ready. Plus, everyone was tired of being cooped up in the school for two weeks.

"WHOSE BRIGHT IDEA was it to only have four showers for eight girls?" Ginger said, grabbing her towel and shower caddy before dashing back downstairs.

"Wow, that girl's fast," Azucar said.

"If Ms. Oscura had given us some warning, I could have showered this morning instead of hitting the snooze for thirty minutes," Salty said.

"Yeah, thanks for that," Azucar said, heading downstairs.

Pepper had managed to snag a shower this morning. Instead of trying to rush through washing her hair while praying the hot water held out, she stared at her armoire. She couldn't wear the school uniform into town; that would be pathetic. But all she had was a pair of jeans, some shirts, boots, sneakers, a sweater, and her jacket.

"Whatcha doing?" Salty asked.

"Trying to find an outfit," Pepper replied.

"Too bad we aren't the same size. You could borrow some of my things," Salty said, disappearing down the stairs.

It was true; Salty was about five inches shorter than Pepper. Salty's pants wouldn't make it halfway up Pepper's long legs. She sighed. Jeans and the school hoodie were probably her best bet. She changed quickly and looked at herself in the mirror on the back of the door. It was a strange image. Her bottom half looked like normal Stella, while the top was definitely Pepper. She sighed and took a brush to her hair.

An hour later, they were all ready. Pepper rubbed her lips together, getting used to the feel of the slick pink lip gloss Ginger had swiped on her before they headed downstairs.

"Salty, why are you so dressed up? It's not like we're going to Prom or anything."

"Ohhh, do you think they have one here? With the Dons, I mean," Salty replied, fussing with the tulle of her skirt.

Azucar shrugged.

"What are we gonna do in town, y'all?" Ginger asked. "I have a mountain of math homework that I do not get at all. Maybe I should stay here."

"You'll regret it," Salty sang, pushing open the front door.

Half the school was milling around on the patio.

"Phew. You guys are going, too," Chutney said, rushing over. No one from my suite wanted to come."

Salty and Pepper eyed each other.

"See? Not everyone is going," Ginger whined.

"Trust me, you'll want to," Pepper said.

Before Ginger or anyone had a chance to question her, Mr. Oscura stepped onto the patio through the French doors of her office. Immediately, the talking ceased, and the students turned their attention to the headmistress.

"The van will be here momentarily. They will be back for one more drop-off if you do not get a seat right now. Pick-ups will be at six, seven, eight, and eight-forty-five. Have an enjoyable time. Remember who you are, and do not tarnish the name of our school with the community."

"Ms. Oscura," Chutney said, raising her hand. "What if we miss the last van?"

"Don't," she replied. "Doors will be locked promptly at nine p.m." She turned, her gray and navy plaid cape flaring behind her as she went inside.

The girls managed to make it onto the van first, but over half didn't.

"Guess we need a bigger bus," Mario said, setting off down the curved driveway.

After a ten-minute drive, the bus pulled onto Cannery Row. The door swung open. "Right back here at six, seven, eight, and last call at eight forty-five. Everybody out," the driver said.

The girls filed off the bus. Some went straight for the aquarium, others down the street to the shops. Salty and Pepper grabbed Azucar, Ginger, and Chutney, steering them up the hill toward the main street.

"What's the big idea? I want to go see the otters," Chutney whined.

When they reached the street corner, Salty explained their plan to catch a ride share to Loyola to watch the soccer game. To their surprise, Chutney and Ginger opted to stay in town and visit the aquarium. But before they left, the girls promised to keep the soccer game a secret.

"You two are so sneaky. Why didn't you say anything? I would have worn a cuter outfit," Azucar said as they walked up David Ave to Hawthorne Street.

"There's a burger place," Salty said. "Do we have time to get fries or something? I'm starved."

Pepper checked the time. The game started at five. "I guess we don't have to be exactly on time."

"By your tone, I'm thinking we do," Salty replied.

"Let's get takeout," Azucar said. "We'll eat on the way."

"Good compromise," Pepper said, typing in their location and destination in the ride app as they walked up to the burger joint. "They'll be here in ten minutes."

"Perfect," Salty said, swinging the door open.

With seconds to spare, the girls ran to the corner and waited for their WI-Ride. A sleek silver sedan pulled up. The window rolled down, and a voice emanated from the empty, self-driving vehicle.

"Ride to Loyola for Pepper?"

Pepper walked to the driver's seat and entered the code on the door panel. Before they even had a chance to sit down, the doors slammed in their faces, and the locks clicked into place.

"No food inside," the automated voice blared.

"We won't eat it inside," Salty said, shaking the closed bag in front of the video monitor.

"No food allowed," it said again before speeding off.

"Great. What are we going to do now?" Pepper asked.

"What else," Azucar replied, waving her thumb at the passing cars.

"I don't know. Daddy forbids me from hitching," Salty said.

"Then go to the aquarium," Azucar said as a beat-up EV with a surfboard balanced on the roof pulled up. "Hey, can we get a ride to Loyola?"

"Yeah, sure thing," the man replied. "Hop in."

Pepper shook the bag of fries. "We won't eat in your car."

"No worries. Ono Grill has the best grinds! Eat it before it gets cold."

Azucar and Pepper got in the backseat. Salty was still on the curb, looking conflicted. "Do you want to meet cute boys or not?" Azucar snapped.

"Fine," Salty said, sliding into the back seat.

THE TWENTY-MINUTE RIDE was fun as Gavin, their surfer driver, regaled them with stories about his epic waves. They pulled up out front of Loyola to find a mass of students walking to the field.

"Thanks for the ride," Pepper said.

"No probs. Glad I could help. Have a good time. Go Knights!"

Pepper didn't have the heart to tell him they were supporting the other team. When she turned around, Azucar and Salty were already walking up to the gate with the crowd. She ran to catch up.

Pepper realized that the rest of the students were flashing an ID on their phone, or a physical card to enter.

She tugged Azucar's sleeve. "Hey, how are we gonna get in there?"

"Leave it to me," she replied.

The ticket scanner held up the device, flashing red against their empty hands. He looked up. "ID card or code."

"The thing is, we don't have them yet," Azucar said, smiling sweetly. "Our school just started, and they haven't handed them out."

"No ID, no entry. Next," he barked.

"Are you going to punish us because our school didn't get its act together?" Azucar asked.

"How many are you?"

"Just three of us," she said, motioning to the others. Pepper and Salty smiled sweetly.

"Go in, but no re-entry. If you leave, you can't get back."

"Thank you, honey," Azucar said, kissing his cheek.

When they were firmly inside the gates, Pepper turned to Azucar. "I thought Ms. Oscura miss-named you, but I was wrong. You can be sweet as sugar."

"When the occasion calls for it. Come on, let's get seats."

As they rounded the corner of the bleachers, a vibrant green field came into view. A restaurant-quality snack stand stood off to the right, with a line that practically reached the width of the field. Salty rubbed her belly and smiled. At least she wasn't pouting and hangry.

"Kinda makes you think our parents are wasting money at Val's if the parochial school is this nice," Salty said, gawking at the pristine bleachers.

Instead of having two sets of bleachers facing each other across the field, theirs were side by side, which was okay with her. It gave them more students to interact with. Pepper scanned the crowd. She hadn't realized how starved she was to meet different people.

Not usually an extrovert, she'd felt a bit bored at Val's seeing the same handful of girls each day. This was a feast for her eyes and ears. The constant stream of voices coming together was a symphony of sound. Pepper closed her eyes and got lost in the cacophony for a moment.

"Hey, Sandy."

Pepper's eyes sprung open. Only one person called her that, and he was walking right toward her. She turned to discover that the girls had walked ahead without her. She waved at Nico as he wove through the crowd.

"I made it," she said.

"I can see that," he replied, giving her that stomach-flipping smile. "Nice to see you here. My sister's around here somewhere, too."

"I'd love to meet her," Pepper said, scanning the crowd as if she could tell automatically who his sibling was.

"You know her, or you probably do. She's at your school."

Pepper froze. Don't be Cherry, don't be Cherry, she chanted over and over.

"There she is," he said, waving at a girl Pepper vaguely recognized.

"OMG, Coco," Pepper said, smiling.

Nico guffawed. Coco slapped his arm.

"I can't get over your dumb nicknames."

"Hey, leave my school traditions alone," Coco shot back. She pushed her wavy black hair out of her eyes and grinned. "Hey Pepper, I didn't know you were going to the game. You could have come over with us."

Nico stopped laughing and looked at her, eyebrows raised. Pepper's cheeks flamed. "Yeah, we decided at the last minute when we got off the bus in town."

"We can give you a ride back," Coco offered.

"Will you have enough room?"

Coco scrunched up her face, then shrugged. "We'll make it work."

"Don't worry. We'll just grab a WI ride. No biggie," Pepper replied.

Nico stepped forward. "You should go with Coco-nuts. Those ride apps are really dangerous. Their computers can be hacked easily."

Pepper laughed.

"He's right. Daddy doesn't like me using rideshares for that reason." She stepped closer and dropped her voice to almost a whisper. "Last year, Don Vito's daughter was abducted from one of those self-driving car apps."

"What did they want?" Pepper asked.

"Money. But he couldn't raise it in time." Coco swallowed hard. "They found her body in a dumpster behind a club in Manhattan."

"Did they ever find out who it was?"

Nico shook his head.

Pepper was positive no one cared enough about her to plan a kidnapping, but she wouldn't want to put her friends in danger.

"Hey, thanks for the heads-up," Pepper said. "The other girls are around here somewhere. Come sit with us."

"Let me round up my crew," she said, melting back into the crowd.

"Coco's your sister," Pepper said thoughtfully.

"Twin, to be exact," he said.

"Interesting." Pepper thought back to what Salty had told her about Nico inheriting the Rossetti position as Don someday, but why couldn't his sister inherit that same position?

"Hello…did I lose connection?" he joked.

"Sorry. What?"

"I just said we were thinking of having a celebratory bonfire on the beach after we win."

"That sounds fun. Wait, are we allowed to do that?"

"Such a rule follower. I get why she named you Pepper." He winked.

"I am not, but you know fire is dangerous and stuff." She hated that she sounded so dumb when she talked to him.

"The ocean will be right there. I promise to bring a bucket. Anyhow, connect with me after the game, and we'll figure it out... if you want."

"Nico, stop flirting. We have a game," Coach yelled.

Now, it was his turn to blush. "I gotta..."

"Go, yeah. Good luck," she said. He smiled and darted through the crowd onto the field.

Pepper turned and scanned the bleachers, quickly locating her friends in the top middle section. Then, she raced up the stairs.

"Why didn't you tell me Coco was Nico's sister?" Pepper hissed when she sat down between Salty and Azucar.

"Sorry. I forget you don't automatically know who everyone is."

"She's coming to sit with us," Pepper said.

"Shoot, she is?" Salty looked genuinely scared.

"What's wrong?" Pepper asked.

Salty leaned back, partially shielding herself from view. "She's held a grudge against me since we were in the same catechism class." Salty paused for effect. "Sister Mary Teresa of the Holy Cross sort of thought Bell—AH, I mean Coco—was the one responsible for writing the curse words on the back of the Sacred Heart of Jesus statue...but it was me, and I never confessed."

"You get saltier by the minute," Azucar said, clearly delighted.

"And she didn't tell them?" Pepper asked.

"First thing we learn is not to snitch," Salty replied. "Technically, she dared me to do it, but she got in a lot of trouble and never forgave me."

Just then, Coco and her crew mounted the steps of the bleachers. Pepper waved them over. Shoot! Cherry was with them.

Pepper had been afraid of this. It seemed like those high-ranking families stuck together, code names be damned.

"It's pepper spray and her benefactor," Cherry said, glancing at Salty.

Her overly sweet perfume filled Pepper's nose. Did she pour the bottle over her head, Pepper thought, as a sharp stab of a headache bloomed between her eyes. Pepper felt sorry for Cherry's roommates. Then she remembered the extra room and Cherry's plans to use it as her own. Figured. These girls always got what they wanted.

"Be nice," Coco said. "At Val's, there are no sides. Only one family, remember. How have you been, Salty?"

"Good. It's been so crazy getting settled that I haven't had time to come and say hi."

"How did *you* find out about the game?" Cherry said, sneering at them.

"Nico invited Pepper," Salty said. Pepper shot her a warning look.

"I've known Nico for years," Cherry replied. "We are very, very close."

"How nice for the two of you. Did he invite you tonight?" Azucar shot back.

Cherry coolly ignored the comment.

The game began, and the girls focused their attention on the twenty-two guys running up and down the field. How they kept up the stamina to run the length of the field again and again was impressive. Now, Pepper knew why Nico had been doing such extensive training that day she literally ran into him on the beach. His earlier invitation to the bonfire replayed in her mind, as did Cherry's comment about the two being very, very close. She wondered how much truth there was in her comment. To Pepper's knowledge, Cherry wasn't a liar, but she was prone to exaggeration.

The Dons missed a goal, and the stands erupted. It was clear who had come to cheer them on. Instantly, she felt bad for not telling the rest of the girls about the game. Of course, they might have opted to stay in Monterey like Chutney and Ginger. She glanced down the row at the Val students. Cherry had a dazed look on her face and was clearly watching something on her AR contacts. The rest were zoned out or talking.

"Hey, are we here to support the Dons or what?" Pepper asked, surprised by her sudden burst of spirit. "They're our brother school, right? Let's support them!"

Coco, Salty, Azucar, and Apple were alert. Cherry did not shift her gaze one millimeter. Coco elbowed her friend in the ribs.

"Ow! What was that for?"

"We are here to support my brother and his team. Turn that dumb thing off, and let's think of a cheer."

Yikes! That wasn't exactly what Pepper had meant. She was thinking more like just paying attention and clapping. But Coco had already started putting together a plan. Pepper couldn't back out now, not since it was sort of her idea. Filled with dread, she scooted closer to listen to Coco's rhyme.

It was clear Salty and Coco had been friends. They collaborated well, and soon, they had created a simple cheer, complete with hand motions. Pepper resigned herself to go along with it and climbed through the crowded bleachers to the sidelines to join her classmates. They lined up and waited for Coco to start them off. Pepper hung back a bit, but soon, she was clapping in time with the others, urging on the crowd.

A rush of euphoria enveloped her as everyone got to their feet and cheered with them. Even the Loyola cheer squad got in on their dance. It was awe-inspiring to see two groups, supposed rivals, joining forces to support one another. That was until Cherry decided to turn her back on the crowd and flash the field. Two players ran into one another and were knocked out. Then, the Loyola team got the ball and scored. That was it for the game. Plus, because technically, they were on the Don Academy's side, they got a penalty card for Cherry's shenanigans, which meant another point for Loyola when their penalty kick made a goal.

After that, the girls sat separately and kept to themselves. Salty and Azucar debated leaving early, but Pepper begged them to stay. She wanted to see Nico again and didn't want to ride back with The Fruit Bunch alone.

Cherry's antics cost the Dons their win. The guys shuffled off the field after the game, their heads down, deflated of all energy.

"Good game," Pepper said, as Nico was shuffling past.

He looked up, almost in a daze, and caught her eye. "We should've won. We had them."

"Yeah, until Look-At-Me Bimbo ruined it," Azucar said.

"Still on for the bonfire tonight?" Pepper asked.

"Nah, don't feel like it," he replied.

"Maybe another time, before it starts getting too cold," she said.

Nico nodded and walked away. Pepper's heart sank. She hadn't realized how much she had been looking forward to that bonfire.

"Looks like that guy back home is getting a Dear John letter," Azucar said.

"Shut up," Pepper replied, aware that her feelings for Ethan were precarious. "I don't even know Nico. I'm just sad they lost. Come on, let's catch up with everyone and get back. It's almost curfew."


As THEY FILED out of the SUV, Pepper grabbed Salty's sleeve and pulled her back from the group so they were alone. "How did they get a family car here so fast?"

"Rossetti's have connections everywhere."

"Even in Monterey? It doesn't seem like it. I mean, no one acts like they know about our school or Don's," Pepper said.

Salty shook her head. "Nope. They have no clue that most of Monterey is now run by...well, us." She shrugged.

"So, the Rossetti family has people here?"

"Now that their kids go here. Yeah, probably," Salty replied.

"What about your family?" Pepper asked.

"We don't have that kind of power. But if I was in trouble, we have sympathetic families in the area that Daddy could call on for a favor."

It was all so intertwined and fascinating. It made Pepper even more anxious to figure out how her family fit in. If the answers were anywhere, they would be here.

# Chapter Fifteen

**P**epper had been looking forward to Wednesday since last week. Not only because she might catch a glimpse of *Il Principe* on the field later, but she loved her morning routine of getting down to the beach, feeling the spray on her face, and getting her toes in the sand. True, she also hoped to run into him, but this morning, she had the foggy shoreline all to herself. She had slipped out of bed before the others were awake and tiptoed down the stairs. This time, she stopped for a quick breakfast of buttered toast before heading out. Knowing what was in store, or more like fearing what awaited her at PE later, Pepper took her time crossing the lawn to the bluff trail.

Mornings were shrouded in a cool gray mist that carried the salty brine of low tide. Pepper inhaled deeply. The crash of the ocean was interrupted by the cry of the seagulls overhead. It was a lonely sound that tugged at her heart. Most days, she didn't have time to notice because she was in a mad dash to make it down to breakfast and get to class on time. Somehow, living at school made it trickier to be on time. Maybe because class was just downstairs, so she didn't build time into her morning for setbacks—like no free showers.

Pepper carefully side-stepped her way down the embankment.

It was steeper than she remembered. No wonder she'd lost her balance and fallen onto *Il Principe*. She looked hopefully down the beach, but there was no sign of him. Actually, she did want to be alone for a few minutes. She longed for a few moments of solitude to think.

Every moment of free time, she and Salty spent exploring the school. However, they hadn't made any progress in discovering the school's archives. Thanks to Salty's special lock-picking skills, they found out what was behind the locked doors on the main floor—empty classrooms. It made Pepper curious how reduced their staff and enrollment was currently. The building and grounds were extensive, yet they only had forty-eight students. What had this place been like in its prime, she wondered, looking out at the fog-shrouded ocean.

A barking sound that clearly wasn't a dog echoed off the bluff and collided with the sound of the surf pounding the shore. Pepper searched the beach but saw only rocks scattered on the sand. Funny, she hadn't remembered this area being so rocky. Must be low tide, she mused, returning to her thoughts. Again, the same barking noise echoed down the beach. Then the massive boulders began to move, and that's when she realized they weren't rocks at all but half a dozen blubbery harbor seals that were bouncing up the beach toward her. They did not look happy. Of course, it was hard to tell when a seal was in a good mood, but the way they were charging up the beach probably wasn't because they wanted a hug.

She stood slowly and backed toward the trail, and that was when she saw the cluster of small adolescent seals. They had probably just swam up, and she hadn't noticed them because of the heavy fog.

"Don't blame me because your kids wandered off," she said, making a wide circle around the pups. The adults were still charging down the beach, making quite a racket.

When her path was finally clear, Pepper darted back up the

embankment. Once she was in the curve of the trail and no longer visible, the barking stopped so much for a peaceful morning. She rubbed her temples. It was probably time to get back up to the cupola and get ready for etiquette class anyway. They had class once a week for ninety minutes. It was all still a little weird, and Pepper had no idea what their astrological chart meant about their futures, but she was intrigued.

Last week, Pepper had stayed behind to voice her concern over the natal chart assignment. When Ms. Powell originally mentioned it, Pepper figured she could just fudge the details. As the weeks progressed and their natal charts got more and more detailed, she realized that her plan was no good. Finally, last week, when the assignment had been due, she confessed to Ms. Powell that she didn't know many of the details necessary to complete the assignment. Ms. Powell assured her that she would speak with Ms. Oscura and see if there was anything she could do. Pepper was confused about how that would help. Didn't teachers at this school determine their own lessons and grades? But when she turned around to ask what she meant, the woman had disappeared. Pepper entered class five minutes early, hoping to have a word with Ms. Powell, but she was not inside so much for being early.

"Good morning, my little *farfalle*," Ms. Powell said, gliding into the room. She had on her same uniform of a crisp white shirt and black slacks. Today, she wore turquoise mules with matching glasses and lipstick., Pepper wondered if she owned anything else. "I have surveyed your natal charts and am placing you in groups based on the findings. As you are aware, your chart revealed certain traits indicative of leaders, supporters, and followers, commonly referred to as Alphas, Betas, and Pack. Your teams for the remainder of the year will be divided as such."

"Wait. Ms. Powell. You're telling us that you've determined which of us are leaders and followers and are going to pigeonhole us in groups?" Honey asked.

"Raise your hand, dear. And yes, that is exactly what I am

saying. In this world, the sooner you accept your natural abilities, the sooner you can find your place and thrive."

"No. No, ma'am," Azucar said, hand raised. "That's not how it works. We all have equal abilities and should get the opportunity to lead."

"Next time, wait to be called on." Ms. Powell looked over the room. Many of the girls were nodding in agreement with Honey and Azucar. "Very well. We will do it your way. Give me a moment to rearrange the groups in order to satisfy your demands." She took a seat at her desk. No one spoke as she scribbled on her tablet.

Pepper caught Azucar's eye and mouthed, "What did you do?"

Azucar shrugged, but a self-satisfied smile played on her lips.

"Attention girls, here are your groups." Ms. Powell projected a list of teams on the touch screen at the front of the class. "You will have assignments throughout the year to work on with these groups. I will not designate an Alpha, Beta, or Pack. You can make those decisions among yourselves. Is that acceptable?"

The girls nodded.

"Very well. I've put your assignment on the board. Break out into your groups." Ms. Powell stared at the list and let out a snort. "Pardon me, just seeing all your code names together, this looks like a shopping list rather than a class roster."

"Dude, I thought we were gonna get to choose our groups," Azucar whispered.

Pepper searched the list for her name. She was in a group with Salty, Chutney, and Olive. At least she hadn't ended up on Cherry's team. That would have been unbearable.

Squabbling began right away in Cherry's group. She and Honey were in a power struggle while Chili and Pear looked uncomfortable. Pepper noticed that Azucar's group was casting ballots. She turned back to her group members.

"How do you want to do this?"

Chutney shrugged. "Whatever."

"Let's just decide who wants to do what." Pepper glanced at

the board. "We'll need a tech specialist, a presenter, a researcher, and a project coordinator. Who wants what?"

"Can I be the presenter?" Salty asked. No one objected, and Pepper wrote her name down next to that position.

"Who's good at tech stuff?" Pepper asked.

"I always do videos and coding and stuff," Chutney said.

"Perfect, that's your job. What about project coordinator?"

"Seems like you're already doing that," Olive said. "Besides, I'm pretty competent when it comes to research."

"Uh…sure," Pepper said. She wasn't sure she wanted to be the coordinator, but since everyone else was happy with their jobs, she figured it worked out for the best.

"Ms. Powell," Honey yelled, jumping up. "I need to switch groups. I can't work with her," she said, glaring at Cherry.

"What's that dear? Having a bit of difficulty, are we?" Ms. Powell looked up from her screen. "I'm sorry, but the class decided to do things your way. Figure it out."

Honey crossed her arms and returned to her seat, still clearly fuming. Cherry looked smug and began giving orders. Pepper returned her attention to her group, grateful they weren't having those issues.

Pepper waited as everyone filed out after class, then approached Ms. Powell.

"Yes, dear?"

"Last week, you said you'd talk to Ms. Oscura about my natal chart assignment. Did she agree to let me take an incomplete, get partial credit, or maybe do a different assignment?"

Ms. Powell slid her turquoise spectacles off her nose and studied her momentarily. "No, my dear, she did not. However, she did show me a copy of your birth certificate."

"What? How?"

"Applications require birth certificates to prove date of birth.

You wouldn't believe how many people fake their daughters' ages to get them admitted to Valentina's."

Pepper patiently waited for her to produce the document, but Ms. Powell switched off the tablet she was cradling. "Did you need something else?"

"Yes, my birth certificate."

Ms. Powell seemed taken aback. "I don't have it, dear; Ms. Oscura does."

"Can you tell me where I was born, at least?" Pepper pleaded, close to tears.

The teacher smiled and nodded. "Of course, dear. Let me see," she said, rummaging through her leather portfolio. "Ah ha, here is your chart. I filled it in myself. You'll still get a chance to complete it on your own for full credit; don't worry. But I needed to know so I could create your groups for class today." She ran her finger through the list. "Let's see...ah yes, I remember, you're a Leo, born in Brooklyn, New York. This puts your moon in Capricorn, which is very advantageous. A naturally magnanimous leader, an empire builder, if you will. I really am quite looking forward to seeing your progression here." She wrote Pepper's birth time and location on a sticky note and handed it to her. "Have all the planets and their meanings completed by the next class. We need the time and place to account for the time change. It aids in accuracy. If we hadn't known that, I could have confused you for an Aquarian ascending, and that would have changed everything. Fortunately, we found what we needed. I mean, I would have been placing you in a beta role when you are clearly an alpha."

Pepper was half listening. She was born in Brooklyn? The pieces still didn't fit. If she was born in New York, and Dad was in New Jersey, why hadn't he known about her? They must have moved to Denver when she was a newborn. The postmark on her original letter from Nonnu was from Colorado, a month after her birth. But why go in such a hurry and with so much secrecy?

"Did you hear me, dear?" Ms. Powell asked, gently shaking Pepper's shoulder.

"Due Friday...right. Thanks for the info." Pepper was so involved in her own thoughts that she walked right past the dining room, completely forgetting about lunch, and headed straight up the main staircase. *I wonder what else was on the birth certificate. Was her father's name listed? How about her last name? Was it D'Angelo or Dallas?* Ms. Oscura had lied to her, Pepper thought, reaching the cupola. She flopped onto her bed and reached for the signet ring. She slipped it on her thumb. Then, she began to fill in her natal chart. Not that she believed in all this star stuff, but it was a graded assignment.

As she entered the information and read the traits for each house, Pepper began to get a weird feeling in the pit of her stomach. Sure, some of the descriptions were not totally correct, but the more she read, the more all of this added up to her. How was that possible? Although Ms. Powell definitely had the Alpha part wrong, Pepper did not lead. She hung back and tried to remain invisible. That was how she'd survived until now, and it had worked just fine.

THE CUPOLA DOOR SWUNG OPEN, and Salty walked in, carrying a to-go container.

"Brought you a sandwich when you didn't show up for lunch. You can't go to PE on an empty stomach," she said, placing the food on Pepper's bed.

"Thanks," Pepper's stomach gurgled. "I guess I didn't realize how hungry I was."

"Yeah, I saw you walk past the dining room in a bit of a daze. Anything wrong?"

"No. I just have to finish this assignment by Friday. Thanks for this," she said, taking a bite of the turkey club.

Salty smiled but didn't press her further, and Pepper was

grateful for that. She pulled the privacy curtain around her bed and finished her lunch in quiet solitude. By the time they had to leave for PE, she'd completed her natal chart assignment. She had also decided to break into Ms. Oscura's office to retrieve her birth certificate. It was hers; why shouldn't she be allowed to see it?

AFTER A GRUELING PE SESSION, Pepper pulled Salty aside as everyone left the field. They pretended to tie their shoes to avoid being overheard.

"What is all this secrecy about?" Salty said, tapping her foot.

"I needed to talk to you when no one could eavesdrop."

"Are you planning on robbing a bank or something?" Salty inquired.

"No, the school," she said, pulling the bow of her laces taut.

Salty gasped. "You are not serious."

"I certainly am. Oscura is hiding my birth certificate. I have a right to see it. But since it's obvious she isn't going to show it to me voluntarily, I need to go get it."

"How do you know she has it?" Salty asked as they began to walk back to school.

Pepper explained her earlier natal chart assignment talk with Ms. Powell and how it had been jarring to learn details about her life from a teacher.

"How are you gonna do it?" Salty asked, clearly intrigued.

"That is what we are going to figure out," Pepper said, slinging her arm over Salty's shoulder.

"I don't know…" Salty drifted off.

"We are in a mafia school. Don't they expect us to do things like this?"

"It's not a spy school," Salty replied.

"Still, they have to realize they are training us to skirt the law or the rules anyway. Come on, help me…please," Pepper said, batting her eyelashes.

"Ugh, fine," Salty replied. "What's your plan?"

# Chapter Sixteen

"You aren't ready yet?" Salty said, returning from the bathroom. Her long black hair was twisted up in intricate tendrils. Ginger must have helped. Why did girls always want to style their hair in the exact opposite way from what they were born with?

Salty sat on the end of Pepper's bed, toppling the stack of books Pepper had lugged up from the library.

Ginger and a few others declined the bonfire invite and decided to have a movie night in the dining room. Ms. Oscura had been accommodating in providing snacks, a projector, and speakers for the event. She also didn't make a fuss about the bonfire. A dusk bonfire was well within the bounds of their weekend curfew. The headmistress said it would be good for them to get to know their neighbors, but she would be checking in on them from the bluff.

Pepper talked Salty out of an outfit that rivaled Cherry's shoes at the soccer game in inappropriateness. Instead, she helped style her in boyfriend jeans and a cute and casual sweater combo. For her own outfit, she surveyed her meager closet with resignation. Jeans and a hoodie were her best options, yet again. Better casual and aloof than trying too hard, she reasoned, slipping the sweater over her head.

They met Azucar at the entrance and set off together. The sun had almost set, casting a rosy glow over their faces as it illuminated the sky in vibrant pink rays. Pepper stared out at the ocean. She would never get tired of that view.

"Do we even know where we're going," Azucar asked.

"I do. This path will take us down to the beach," Pepper said, leading them along the bluff to the trail.

She was grateful for the sweater as they rounded the curved path. The wind off the ocean stung her cheeks. Pepper wondered if maybe a bonfire wasn't the best idea tonight. She pulled her hood up, and they continued down to the beach, joining the group of students.

"Hey, you're here," Nico said, a genuine smile brightening his face. "Look, I brought the bucket, as promised."

Pepper leaned over. "There's nothing inside it."

"I didn't say I'd fill it," he replied.

She grasped the handle. "I will. Can't have us setting the coastline on fire."

Pepper swung the bucket at her side as she walked down to the shoreline. Hmm…this was going to be trickier than she imagined without getting wet. The waves pushed onto the shore but not forcefully enough to send water into the bucket when she laid it on its side. If she waded out into the surf, she'd be able to get the water in the bucket, but then she'd be wet. That's when she noticed the boulders and had an idea. If she could hop on them out about halfway to the breakers, she'd be able to easily lean over and fill the bucket.

Pepper studied the black shapes, making sure they were not, in fact, sea lions; then, when the tide went out, she dashed for the first rock. She hopped up and almost lost her balance. Maybe this wasn't the best idea. Still, she was already here, and the waves were rushing back, filling the once squishy sand she had run across with a shallow amount of water. Now that she was here, Pepper realized that she could easily hop across to the next few stones; it was the last one she'd need to worry about. She walked easily from rock to rock. By this time, several waves had rolled by, and she was in trouble if she fell. Not because of getting wet but because she couldn't swim. Why was she being so reckless. A noise caught her attention, and she glanced back at shore. Nico, his friends, and her classmates were cheering her on from the beach. Right, that's why.

The rock farthest away wasn't too far to jump; it was the coating of green algae making her pause. *All right, you got yourself into this mess. Go all the way.* Pepper gauged the distance and leaped forward, landing easily on the lopsided rock, but her foot slipped off, and she fell forward just as an incoming wave slammed into her. Saltwater stung her nostrils as she fought for breath. Her head collided against the jagged edge of the rock she'd just fallen from. Pepper thrashed her arms and legs to no avail. Her water-logged clothes and shoes impeded her movement. She couldn't find up, even when she opened her eyes. The cold, dark sea had her.

Then something was around her waist, tight and insistent. Pepper's head broke through the water's surface, and she gulped a ragged breath of air. Seconds later, she coughed up the sea water trapped in her throat.

"Let's get you standing," Nico said, righting her.

That was when she realized the water was only waist deep. Despite the cold shock of the wind, Pepper's face burned like an inferno.

"So much for the bonfire," she said as they slogged through the knee-high waves, "and your bucket."

"It made it back to shore already," he said, nodding toward the bobbing red object ahead.

Pepper rolled her eyes. "I knew I should have stayed in and researched…uh, that paper. Sorry, I ruined your bonfire."

"You didn't."

"Right, you were planning on going for a swim."

He shrugged. "You never know. But I probably wouldn't have with all my clothes on."

She smirked.

"Don't go. We have lots of blankets and brew, and we can dry your clothes off on sticks over the flames or uh … beside them."

"If you think I'm getting nake—"

"No, no! I just meant you could take off your sweater and shoes and stuff. You'd be more comfortable. Nothing is worse than wet socks." He smiled. Pepper realized that he still had his shoes on but had managed to pull off his jacket before diving in to save her. Nico was in just a short-sleeved T-shirt. His teeth were chattering slightly.

"Maybe I'll stay," she said. It was slow going in sopping wet clothes and shoes. Every step felt like she was being sucked into the sand. Like the sea wanted to claim her for its own.

"You know we could always have thrown wet sand on any fire that got out of control," he said.

"And you let me go out there to get a stupid bucket of water," she replied, aghast.

"As I recall, you insisted. Besides, I think telling a Valentina girl to do anything is dangerous."

"Thanks for the rescue," she said, "but I think it's best if I go back."

"Please stay…just for a little," he said, tugging on the sodden hem of her hoodie.

People were rushing toward them as they reached the dry sand.

"Give her mouth to mouth," one of the guys said, laughing.

"That's when people are unconscious, *stupido*," Nico replied.

Soon, Pepper was being bundled off by her friends.

Salty leaned over and whispered in her ear. "Nice move being rescued by *Il Principe*. Cherry stormed off the minute he jumped in the water."

"I totally did that on purpose," she replied wryly. "Strategic, that's my style."

"Next time, Ms. Strategy, could you tell your friends? I almost died when you were knocked off that rock by that monster wave," Azucar said.

"Is that what it looked like?" Pepper asked.

"Yeah, why?" Salty replied.

"Because that's what happened," she said, grateful no one noticed she slipped.

When more Valentina students arrived, the girls fussed over her and helped her peel off her soggy sweater. She was infamous by the time the first spark began consuming the dry logs. Luckily, the flames were hungry, and soon, the pallet or whatever the guys had dragged down to the beach was fueling a massive bonfire. It was so wide that Pepper couldn't see people on the other side. The heat it threw was intense, but Pepper hovered close to the flames, grateful for the alcove they'd selected. It blocked the worst of the windy gusts. The Valentina girls mainly were grouped together, while the Dons kept to themselves. It resembled a middle school dance. Boys on one side, girls on the other. At least she was finally drying off.

It was dark now, but coastal clouds meant the star visibility was nonexistent. The orange glow from the fire cast an amber bubble around them, like a protective shield against the darkness. When Pepper's hair was finally dry, she pulled it into a messy top-knot, hoping to salvage some shred of cuteness. Although, after being rescued and dragged from the beach by *Il Principe* himself, she was sure he wouldn't be giving her the time of day. The nubby blanket the girls bundled her in smelled of pine and gasoline. Was it from the depths of someone's car trunk or maybe a garage? Still, it reminded her of Nonnu and helped shield her from the biting wind. Most of her was warm, but each time she tried to warm her toes by stretching her legs out in front of her, they'd pinch and burn. She couldn't find a happy medium, so she tucked her feet underneath her legs and tried to be content.

As THE EVENING wore on and the alcohol flowed, the two groups began to mingle. The once towering inferno had dwindled, and their entire group was visible around the bonfire. Salty and Azucar were talking with guys she didn't recognize from the soccer team. Pepper wished there was food instead of just beer. But this was organized by boys, so what had she expected? Next time, if there was one, they would bring snacks. She rotated her shoes so the tongues were pulled through the laces at the bottom, allowing the toe box to receive some heat. They were still squishy with seawater. Truthfully, she was getting sort of bored, and the headache she'd had intensified, but Pepper didn't want to make anyone leave early. Salty and Azucar looked like they were having fun, and she knew they'd never let her walk back alone, not after her earlier fall.

Pepper's heart jackhammered in her chest when Nico stood and circled the group. He plopped down beside her on the large piece of driftwood they were conveniently using for seating and handed her a flask.

"It'll help you get warm," he said.

"I think the fire is already doing that," she replied.

"No, in here," he pointed to his chest. "It takes the chill off from being in the water."

Pepper nodded and grasped the offering. She'd hadn't much experience with hard liquor before and hesitated to take a sip, but he was watching. The liquid ran to the back of her throat and burned with a fiery warmth as it went down her esophagus. She coughed once and handed the flask back.

"Mmmm, burning," she said.

Nico smirked and took a swig. "I'm not sure if I should call you Sandy or Soggy."

Pepper swatted his arm. "How about Pepper?"

"How about your real name?" he countered, looking up at her through long dark lashes.

She shook her head. "Not a chance." She rubbed her temples.

"You okay?"

"Just a bad headache. I think I may go back. I'm really tired." The longer she sat there, the more the heat from the fire made her drowsy. As her eyes drifted shut, she felt the delicious pull of sleep. Then, something cold was next to her cheek. Pepper opened her eyes, startled. "What was that?"

Nico held up a bottle of cold beer.

"I guess it was rude of me to drift off while you were talking, but did you need to shock me?"

He grasped her chin between his thumb and forefinger and gently turned her face toward him. Pepper had never wanted to be kissed more than right at that moment. She and Ethan had kissed a few times, but their relationship generally teetered on the edge of the friend zone. Then Nico reached up, using his index finger, and pulled down the delicate skin under her eye.

"What are you doing?"

"Checking for a concussion," he replied.

"Are you a doctor now?"

"We get all kinds of training at Don's," he replied.

"Sounds like Valentina's in a way," she replied, pulling away, "But I'd hardly call you an expert just yet."

"I'm kidding, but the soccer team has had its share of concussions, myself included, so I know the signs. You probably have a slight one." He stood. "Come on. Let's go for a walk." Nico offered her his hand. Pepper could feel everyone's eyes on her. Instead of sitting there worrying about her possible concussion, Pepper agreed to the walk.

Her shoes were still soggy, so she left them by the fire and continued barefoot. Maybe freezing feet would help keep her alert. Although, after Nico touched her face, Pepper was wide awake. She wasn't going to mention that to him.

They walked in the opposite direction of Valentina's bluff. The beach was wider here as the land gently sloped away and eventually became a rolling hill that flattened into the landscape. The soft glow of lights in the distance drew her attention.

"What's down there?" she asked.

"Carmel," he replied. "You haven't been?"

"It's not exactly easy getting away from Valentina's. I mean, with the exception of your soccer game, I haven't left the school grounds since I arrived."

"Seriously? I've heard Carmel described as "cute." You'd probably really like it. We should go sometime."

Pepper stopped in her tracks. Was he asking her out, like on a date?

"That would be...nice." She turned to avoid looking at him, afraid he'd be able to see the nervousness that was bubbling over in her stomach and causing her to sweat. She pulled the blanket tighter.

"That's a great view of Don's. It's so...imposing all lit up," Pepper said. It was a far cry from her school's meager dwelling. Maybe being unassuming was an advantage. She wondered why the country's most prestigious mafia girls' school appeared to be so underfunded.

"Best prep school in the world," he said.

"Ever wonder why boys get prep schools and girls get finishing schools? Technically, we're all being prepared for the future, but it's like a girl is finished when she completes her education. While your education has prepared you for the future."

"I guess." He shrugged. "Maybe it's just a holdover from another era, and it doesn't mean anything?"

*Maybe that's why Ms. Oscura changed the school name,* she wondered.

"If you say so," Pepper replied. "What do you guys study up there?"

"Probably the same stuff you study."

Hmmm…was he being cagey on purpose? "Like, do you have a study emphasis for when you get out?"

He cocked his head and looked at her, puzzled. *Real smooth, Pepper.* Of course, he knew what he was doing when he finished school, taking over 'the family business.'

"I just mean, are you interested in anything outside of…uh… you know, the obvious."

"I want to play professional soccer," he replied. "Not that my father will let me, but while I'm here, I get to pretend as if I'm headed for that path. What about you?"

Pepper shook her head and shrugged.

"No outside interests?" he asked.

"I never had the option of outside interests. Until recently, I was on track to attend a public high school and get a job when I graduated. My interest didn't factor into my future one bit."

She spread out her blanket and sat, motioning for Nico to join her.

"That's so strange. I mean, we come from pretty different backgrounds, but we had the same outcome. It doesn't matter what I want to do—I have something I'm destined to do."

"Yeah, but running an organization versus sitting in an office are two very different paths."

"A prison is still a prison no matter how you dress it up," he said, looking away toward Carmel.

"So you really don't want to take over…"

"It's not that. All my teachers say I have the natural talent of a Don, but it's the lack of choice. You know … what's that thing some early Christians believed."

Pepper wrinkled her brow.

"You know, how it's already decided if you're going to hell or heaven when you are born, and there's nothing you can do about it."

"Uh…predestination?" she replied.

"Yeah, it's like that. My life is predestined!" he exclaimed, gesturing wildly with his hands. "I can't screw it up. But now that you aren't on your original cubical farm track, you get to choose. Why did you come here?"

"When you put it like that, my reasons for coming seem pretty shallow. My main reason was to get away from my awful stepmother. It's that simple."

"Step-monster, huh?"

Pepper chuckled. "Something like that."

"Well, that was the first reason. But now that you're here, what do you want to accomplish? I mean, it is a prestigious school. Valentina's could open doors for you."

"Now you sound like my Nonnu." Pepper grasped her knees and leaned back. This was a question she hadn't considered. "I haven't thought about it. Although I do like cooking. Not sure if we will ever be allowed to do any," she said, then regaled him with stories of Signore Tonelli's no-cooking, cooking class. He laughed at her impression of the stern chef. Which made a warmth that had nothing to do with the earlier whiskey bloom in her chest.

"Looks like you have an interesting road ahead of you," he commented.

"Yeah, it's been a whirlwind so far, but maybe I have some options I hadn't considered."

She stared out at the pitch-black ocean. The sky was almost undetectable from the sea, except for the foamy white patches of waves as they pushed toward the shore.

"Do you have a brother at Don's?" he asked.

"I don't have a full-blood sibling. My half-brother is younger, and we just met three years ago."

"You just met?"

"Uh, yeah…" Pepper chewed her bottom lip. Always with the

secrets, she thought, considering how much to reveal. "My parents weren't exactly married, so I didn't know my dad or his new family until recently."

"Whoa, that's intense."

"That's one way to put it. Lonely, terrifying, scary, and joyful are other words I'd use to describe the experience." Without thinking, she reached for her necklace and pulled the signet ring from inside her shirt.

"What's that?" he asked, leaning closer.

She held her breath. It was such a habit she'd barely registered doing it. *Shoot.* "Uh, it's ...."

"It's okay if you don't want to tell me. It was rude of me to ask."

Pepper was grateful for the out, but she searched her feelings and wanted to share this piece of her history with Nico. "Remember how I said my parents weren't married?"

He nodded.

"This was my father's." She held up the signet ring. He reached out to hold the ring between his fingers. It was dark, but the light from the Don Academy illuminated the shiny gold face of the Roman soldier.

"That's legit," he said, turning the ring so the small diamonds in the laurel crown caught the light.

"My mother gave it to him, but I don't know anything else beyond that."

"Why don't you ask your dad?"

"He's...not big on sharing stuff. He just said he wanted me to have it. It's the one thing I have from their relationship," Pepper replied. "Think we should head back?" she asked, noticing the moon peeking through the parting clouds. "It's probably close to curfew, and my toes are going to fall off in a minute." Pepper slipped the ring back down her shirt. It felt good to share something real with someone. People that live with mountains of secrets must be so lonely. She thought back to Granny and Nonnu.

Maybe that's why they hadn't had friends. It was easier to keep secrets if no one was around to ask questions.

Nico didn't make a move to get up. Instead, he leaned back. "I got trapped in a car on a mountain road one winter with Bell...uh, Coco. Sorry, I keep forgetting her super-secret code name. Why do you have those, by the way?"

"To foster togetherness. Our past identities are forgotten, and we all got clean slates when we walked through Valentina's door."

He snorted like that was the most ridiculous thing he'd ever heard.

"You were saying?"

"Right, we were trapped in a car during a blizzard. We didn't know how long it would take for help to reach us. The extremities are the first thing to get frostbite." He scooted around to face her. Pepper nodded, curious about where he was going with this random story. Then he grabbed for her right foot. "We had to keep our feet warm like this." He tugged her leg so it was elongated, tucked her foot under his armpit, and repeated the same action on the left foot.

"This is weird," she finally admitted after a moment of silence.

"Are your feet warmer?"

"In your sweaty armpits? Yes, they are."

He chuckled. "Mission accomplished then."

She couldn't help but grin. "Can I ask something kinda personal?"

"In this position, I think that's only fair."

She was grateful he couldn't see the raging blush spreading across her face, most likely in red blotches of embarrassment. "If you and Coco are twins, why are you automatically going to take over?"

"Technically, I am the eldest, born two minutes and seventeen seconds before Coco. But it's a man's job—always has been. I guess that's why."

Pepper yanked her feet from his grasp. "That's it then? Men

have always done it, so that's what's happening?" She jumped up. "Thanks for…whatever that was." And she stormed down the beach.

"Yo, wait up," he said, chasing after her. "That's not what I meant. It's just that when there has been a male in line to take over, that's what typically happens, but each family is different. Besides, Coco doesn't want the job."

Pepper swung around to face him, and they collided. He caught her by the arm and pulled her close. Nico didn't step back. His breath was warm on her face, and his chest brushed her lightly each time he inhaled.

"I'm sorry," she said. "It's your family business. It seemed strange for you to be honored with that position if you don't want it when you have a twin who could easily take over."

"I don't know about honored. Do you know what a Don has to do? The kind of responsibility he shoulders?"

Pepper shook her head.

"It's not easy. Coco and I have talked about it—a lot. She's willing to take over if…anything happens to me, but she doesn't want it. Ask her yourself if you don't believe me."

"But it's not unheard of for a woman to be the…?"

*"Comare?"* he said, supplying the word for godmother she was searching for. "Not unheard of, just unusual."

Her hair had come down from her earlier bun, and the wind blew it across her face.

Nico reached up and smoothed a strand behind her ear. Then he removed his hair tie and offered it to her. "You're a strange girl," he said. "Unlike anyone I've ever met."

"Thanks, I guess," she replied, wishing she fit in this world better. Pepper pulled her knotted, damp hair into a low ponytail. "Maybe we should head back. My feet are starting to get cold."

Nico nodded and then abruptly turned around. "Hop on, I'll carry you."

She hesitated, but her feet were aching. She climbed onto his back, and he grasped her thighs, sending her temperature skyrocketing once again. They were still far from the bonfire party, and Pepper couldn't resist temptation a moment longer. She reached up and ran her fingers through Nico's wavy locks.

"I've wanted to do that forever," she said.

"Is that so?" he replied, his voice thick with amusement.

"Your hair is usually so tame, but it's tantalizingly wild right now," she said, unable to resist one more pass of her fingers through his curls. Did she imagine it, or did a sigh of pleasure escape his lips?

"Yeah, gets like that when…it's wet," he replied, clearing his throat.

"How'd you get all wet," she teased.

"This beautiful girl fell into the ocean, and I rescued her," he said.

"How heroic. Well, I guess that's worth messing up your do."

Pepper wiggled to be released as they approached the bonfire. Nico stopped as she slid down.

"She's one hundred percent worth it," he said, reaching forward to grasp her hand.

To Pepper's utter shock, they walked back to the party hand in hand. The fire had long since turned to ash, and the crowd had dwindled considerably. Only a few small groups were huddled together. Pepper noticed Azucar and Salty sitting back-to-back, their heads lolling to one side.

"Thanks for the rescue," she said, releasing his hand. "Let's not make near-death experiences a thing with us," she joked.

"It's a deal," he said. "Are you gonna do some more beach runs this week?"

"Maybe Wednesday morning if the weather holds out," she replied.

"Hopefully, I'll see you."

"That would be nice."

He grinned and then began gathering up the blankets. She

folded the one she had been wrapped in and handed it to him. Then she undid her hair and held out the hair tie. "Keep it. So you can remember tonight," he said.

"I don't think I'm going to forget almost drowning," she said. Or you rescuing me, she finished silently.

"Keep it anyway. Come on, goombahs, let's get back up the hill," he said to his friends, who were pounding beers and having a burping contest.

Pepper started to gather bits of clothing that had somehow ended up all around the bonfire. She needed those socks, as she only had a few good pairs.

"Hey, Nico," one of the Don's students shouted. "Did you she repay you for saving her life?"

"*Basta*," Nico said, with such authority, the drunk jock went mute instantly. "Throw wet sand on the fire and carry these up to the supply room." He dropped the blankets he'd collected and strode down the beach.

Pepper marveled at the way he commanded authority. She slipped her sandy feet into the shoes, which were cold but mostly dry. Then she woke up her friends with a gentle nudge. The other Valentina girls were already trudging up the trail back to the school.

"Where were you?" Azucar asked.

"Walked down the beach," Pepper replied.

"This whole time? Did you…" Azucar said, waggling her eyebrows.

"You are as bad as the dudes," Pepper said, pushing her to stand.

"I think he likes you," Salty said as they hiked to the embankment.

"Maybe," Pepper said, not willing to admit that their walk had nothing to do with his feelings but was entirely about her possible concussion. However, they'd had a moment after she ran off that made her doubt her doubts about his feelings.

"But next time, be a bit...I don't know, flirtier," Azucar said, yawning.

"Like how?"

"Girl, if you don't know..." Azucar said.

"What she means is, like you talk...a lot. Just don't ask so many questions."

"Should I just flash him, like Cherry?" Pepper shot back, increasing her pace.

"That's not what we're saying. Be more Audrey, less Katherine," Salty replied.

"Who are you talking about?" Pepper said.

"She just means flirt more and rely on your intellect a bit less. He has to know you're interested."

"Like you two?" she said over her shoulder.

"Yeah, the guy I talked to definitely knows I'm interested," Azucar said.

"They're guys, Pepper. They're uncomplicated creatures," Salty said.

Pepper crossed her arms and continued along the trail. Her sweater and shoes hadn't dried thoroughly, and she was beginning to feel the dampness against her skin. What were they talking about? Why was it wrong to be inquisitive and have conversations? She enjoyed talking to Nico and learning his views on current events. Wasn't her constant attention the whole night proof that she enjoyed spending time with him? What did those two know? She bounded up the steps to the school two at a time. She wasn't about to tell them Nico was concerned that she had a concussion and that was why they had wandered off...or about the private things they'd shared.

THE FOLLOWING DAY, when Ms. Oscura heard about Pepper's near-drowning, she forbade bonfire meet-ups on the beach. By Cherry's smug expression at brunch Saturday morning, Pepper was sure she had something to do with it. So much for learning how to flirt, she thought. The glares she got from the other girls made her want to crawl under the table. It wasn't her fault...well, it sort of was, but she didn't snitch. Actually, Ms. Oscura could have been watching from the bluff, but why wouldn't she have come down to help? The girls tried to puzzle out the clues but came up empty-handed. They'd have to find another way to meet up with the Dons. Besides, she had other things to worry about now, mainly uncovering the truth about her past.

# Chapter Seventeen

As they neared midterms, assignments began piling up. Some classes, like algebra, would have a test before they left for winter break, but as Pepper noticed by the essay Ms. Samson just assigned for English, projects would probably be assigned in the rest of their classes. However, Pepper's mind was not on her classwork. Instead, she was preoccupied with plans to procure her birth certificate.

Pepper crafted plan after plan but scratched each out as she realized how impossible they would be. She just couldn't come up with the right approach for this mission. Finally, she put down her pen and refocused on the lesson. Mrs. Sabatini was in the midst of a lecture about the wives of Henry the Eighth, and, to the rapt expressions of her fellow students, she was the only one who found this lecture less than thrilling. Pepper put aside her preoccupation with liberating her birth certificate and tried to refocus. Try as she might, her mind was not in class but diligently working on how to find that important document. Ugh, if only Ms. Powell had brought it to show her. Pepper crossed out an idea she'd been concocting on the edge of her paper when she realized that forging the art teacher's signature on a note and asking for the document again would look suspicious.

"Each of these women sparked change in some significant way or another. From the annulment of legitimate marriage and the changing of England's religion to the beheading of queen consorts. Their lives—"

"Were at the mercy of a maniacal misogynist," Azucar interrupted. The class laughed but was quickly silenced by the sharp look Mrs. Sabatini swept over her students.

"Sounds like an opinion," the history teacher replied.

"It's not," Azucar fired back. The class gasped and turned as one to see how Mrs. Sabatini would reply.

"You will have ample opportunity to back up that *opinion* with facts if it is defensible since your assignment is to write a six-page term paper on one of Henry the Eighth's wives—your choice which—describing how her marriage to the King changed culture, policy, and the perception of women in positions of power. Now, if Ms. Azucar has no more interruptions, I'll continue." She clicked her slideshow forward to an image of the Tower of London. "The Bloody Tower, where the nobility went to die, was the spot where King Henry had his wives beheaded. It is rumored that after Anne Boleyn was beheaded, her eyes blinked, and her lips parted as if she were trying to speak."

"Now that sounds factual," Azucar whispered to Pepper. These bouts of head butting were becoming increasingly frequent, and Pepper was learning to tune them out. Azucar had become more argumentative and acerbic than before.

The slideshow presentation continued, but Pepper stared out the window, lost in a daydream.

"Which wife are you going to research?" Salty asked.

Pepper shrugged.

"Anne Boleyn," Azucar replied. "I'm going to prove that she was more than a slutty replacement for the first queen."

"Don't forget the catalyst for an entire country's religious switcheroo because of a lascivious king," Salty added.

"Touché," Azucar said, scribbling notes on her tablet. "Which wife are you going to write about?"

"Catherine Parr. I like her best because she had her own opinions, worked behind the scenes to manipulate policy, and brought stability to court. At least, that's what my argument will be. Hey, what's up with you?" Salty said, hip-checking Pepper.

"Huh?"

"You are a space cadet. What's going on?"

"Just preoccupied," Pepper replied.

"With the heist?"

Pepper chuckled. "You are quite perceptive."

"Is it worth possibly getting expelled over?"

She paused and looked up. "To me, it is," she said. "Look, if you don't feel comfortable…"

"Just tell me what you need, and I'll be there," Salty replied.

Pepper hugged her friend.

"Come on, you two, we're going to be late for cooking class," Azucar yelled from down the hall.

Ms. Powell stuck her head out of her doorway and tsked. "Ladies, do not yell," she said and abruptly shut the door.

The girls rolled their eyes and shook their heads as they passed by her room on the way to the basement.

PEPPER HAD SKIPPED her last few Wednesday morning workouts to finish projects or snoop around the school while everyone was still in bed. After failing to devise a cohesive plan to retrieve her birth certificate this morning, she got up early and headed to the beach. It had nothing to do with the fact that the boys' soccer team hadn't been practicing during their PE class, and she hadn't so much as caught a glimpse of Nico since the bonfire—not that she'd been hoping to.

The mornings had turned quite chilly, and she layered up in the PE leggings and her old joggers. She slipped a breakfast bar into her hoodie pouch and tiptoed out of the cupola.

Pepper slipped the school-issued navy fleece headband over her ears and trotted down the stairwell. The later it got into the semester, the more the other girls took advantage of the late start day and stayed in their rooms. Before, a handful of students had been in the dining room or the halls, but the house was deserted this morning. She carefully closed the front door behind her and began to run. Cardio really builds body heat, and by the time Pepper had reached the beach, she was an inferno. She decided to slip off the joggers before she continued.

A low whistle came from behind her. Pepper spun around, catching her foot on the waistband of her joggers, and toppled to the damp sand.

Nico rushed over. "When I started on my workout, I didn't expect to see a girl stripping on the beach," he said, grasping her under the arms and hauling her to her feet.

"Don't get too excited, Romeo," she replied, "I'm just removing one layer because I got too hot."

"You can say that again, but removing that one layer only adds to your hotness."

She was already warm from the run, but her face flamed at his compliment.

"Are you too distracted by my hotness to get in a good workout?" she teased, throwing her joggers at him.

He waggled his eyebrows, which made her laugh. "Never." Nico rolled up her joggers and placed them on the closest rock. "Race you down to the end of the bluff."

Pepper didn't wait for him to say go but took off down the beach. She looked back and laughed at his stunned expression. Within moments, he had caught up. She pumped her legs as fast as she could on the uneven sandy terrain, but he zipped ahead and did a victory dance until she caught up.

"How are you not even winded?" she asked, panting.

"I run for almost ninety minutes at a time during games. This"—he made a general gesture around them—"is nothing."

"For you, maybe."

"How come I haven't seen you around for a while?" he asked.

"Got busy," she replied, twisting a strand of hair that had come loose from her braid.

"I thought maybe it was because of the bonfire or something."

"Where I made a complete fool of myself? Why would you think that?" she said, playfully pushing him.

"Fool? Nah, I'd say you displayed bravery by trying to uphold fire safety standards."

Pepper rolled her eyes.

Nico ran his hand through his damp hair. "Maybe we could think about that Carmel trip in a little."

Pepper was taken aback. She wasn't going to mention it, thinking he'd forgotten or hadn't actually intended on taking her to see the quaint hamlet next door.

"That would be nice, but things are getting so busy."

"Yeah, mid-terms. We're starting them too...."

Pepper felt the opportunity slipping away. She didn't want him to think that she didn't want to go, but how could she manage it with her birth certificate heist, two term papers, an algebra test, and who knew what Signore Tonelli had in store for them?—organizing the kitchen tools by date of invention? She smirked at the thought.

"What about before we go home for break?" he asked.

Pepper exhaled and could feel the tension in her jaw relax. "That's a great idea. Then neither of us will be preoccupied with assignments."

His crooked smile made her stomach flip.

"Are you on the school chat?"

Pepper nodded. It seemed antiquated, but after so many email and phone security hacks, people started using private chatrooms about ten years ago. Both Valentina's Academy and the Don Academy shared a network. She wondered why he hadn't asked if she was on the virtual AR chat that was more popular with students. There, you could interact with anyone and do...pretty much anything.

"My handle is *FutbolRossetti17*. We can chat if we don't see each other on Wednesday."

"I'd like that," she replied. Just then, her alarm went off. "Shoot, I've gotta get back for etiquette class."

One eyebrow shot up. "For what class?"

"Uh...it's not exactly what you think, but she'll kill me if I'm late."

"Sure. See you around," he said, turning up the hill for Don's.

"Or online," she said before racing back down the beach to retrieve her joggers and return to Valentina's. This was cutting it close. She couldn't show up all sweaty, and she couldn't show up with wet hair again. Still, she thought it had been worth it, reflecting on Nico's invitation to chat. So much for her friend's advice to be more eye-flutteringly flirty. Nico seemed to enjoy her inquisitive brain just fine.

She ran down the hallway and was in her seat long before the bell. When Ms. Powell walked in, she looked over the assembled class and nodded, clearly pleased by their punctuality.

Honey raised her hand. "Are we getting new groups now?"

"New groups?" Ms. Powell echoed. "No, my dear, these are your groups for the year. You are going to have to learn how to make it work." The class groaned in unison. Mrs. Powell smiled at them.

"Espionage," she began, "is an art form with different dedications and applications. Covert surveillance, for example, may suit one of you and not another. Be assured each of you has a special gift to bring to this subject. Surveillance, cloak and dagger, undercover work, and eavesdropping are all areas in which you can utilize your innate talents, which you have not yet uncovered. That is why you will learn them all. But, as you might have guessed, we will start with something simple. This afternoon, we will be beginning our lip-reading segment."

"That's it? Lip reading," Azucar blurted out.

"You have to learn to crawl before you run, my precious *farfalle*," Ms. Powell said. "First lip reading, then eavesdropping while holding a conversation, and on and on, until you are so good at espionage that you will not even realize you are doing it."

Pepper leaned forward. Unlike Azucar, she did not think this was a waste of time. In fact, she was anxious to learn.

"Ah, how I love this day. It's blessedly so silent," Ms. Powell said. "Pencils ready. We will begin with a short video. Write down what you believe the person is saying, and then I will play the clip with sound."

"Why do we need to learn this when we can just text?" Cherry asked.

Azucar turned and caught Pepper's attention. She mouthed something. Pepper smiled and decided to have some fun with her.

"Do I want to play a game?" she whispered back.

"No. This is lame," Azucar whispered, clearly annoyed. Pepper just laughed silently.

"My dear, this is precisely for those moments when you cannot utilize technology. Remember, girls, your greatest asset is *you*, not a device. Let's get started."


IT SEEMED THAT MOST of her fellow students hadn't felt that their education up until that point had been living up to the hype heard from their female relations. With the introduction of the espionage coursework, a new energy pulsated through the halls. Pepper was excited that they were starting to utilize their new talents.

"It finally feels like we're starting to learn the real stuff," Ginger said, helping herself to a generous scoop of ice cream. "Do not give me that look, Salty. With the sprints we ran today, I could eat two gallons of this stuff and still be calorie-deficient."

"Have you guys thought about what you are doing after school?" Pepper asked.

"Like this summer?" Ginger asked.

"No, I mean after we graduate," Pepper said.

"Getting married to the richest Don I can trap," Salty said.

"Is that it?" Pepper asked.

"It? Do you realize what it takes to be a Mob Wife? It's no joke. But you'll learn, we all will. I mean, that's why we're here, isn't it."

"Yeah, I guess," Pepper said.

"Remember the school motto," Azucar said. "*Nunquam minoris aestimo domina.*"

"Never underestimate a lady," they replied in unison.

"This school is nothing like I imagined. When I get home at the break, they're going to expect me to know something—at least how to cook," Ginger whined.

"Don't be so disheartened. I'm sure Signore Tonelli will let us start cooking soon," Azucar said.

"I hope so. It's getting super boring in there," Pepper added. "I am not sure how many more ways I can learn from a picture how to chop a carrot."

The girls laughed. That was when Pepper got a brilliant idea.

In a school full of lip readers, one couldn't take a chance on being overheard or seen. Salty and Pepper hung back at the end of the PE class to discuss their heist plan uninterrupted. This way, they wouldn't need to talk in code, which made things infinitely less complicated.

"Meals are the only time Ms. Oscura is for sure not in her office, right?" Pepper said to Salty on their walk back to school. The wind off the ocean was ice cold today, biting her cheeks and lips. Pepper pulled her school hoodie over her ears and cinched the ties so only her eyes, nose, and mouth were visible.

"Won't she think something's up?" Salty asked, chewing her bottom lip.

"I've missed meals before. Just make a plate for me like you did for Ginger when she was sick a few weeks ago."

"What if she asks?"

"Tell her I have cramps."

"That's a good unverifiable symptom," Salty said, nodding.

"Exactly."

"But how are you getting into her office?" Salty asked. "I'm not okay picking the lock."

"Hmmm…it would be suspicious if both of us were missing." Pepper searched the horizon for inspiration. "What about our secret passageway?"

"But we promised never to use it to get to the first floor again!" Salty exclaimed.

"I know, but this is an emergency. Besides, I'll be in and out so fast she'll never know."

"I guess," Salty said, not sounding entirely convinced. "How are you getting into the computer without a password?"

Pepper stopped in her tracks. Shoot. She hadn't thought that far ahead. Of course, the computer would be password-protected. "I might not need it," she conceded.

Chutney ran up behind them. "Hi, guys. Wow, Coach was really tough today. I can't believe he made me stay behind to put all the equipment away just because I came in last on the sprints."

"He's a tyrant," Salty agreed.

"I'm sorry we didn't stay behind to help," Pepper replied. "I lost track of you and didn't realize you weren't finished."

Chutney shrugged. "No biggie."

"Hey, thanks for handling all the tech stuff for our etiquette project. I swear your crazy skills helped us ace that project," Salty said.

Pepper gasped but then covered by clearing her throat. "Yeah, did you have any trouble getting things set up?"

"Nah, it's simple coding. I've been doing this stuff forever."

"I'm glad the three of us ended up walking together. You know I stayed behind to talk with Ms. Powell a while back." The two girls nodded. "She let it slip how bad the school's cyber security was, but Ms. Oscura isn't concerned about it."

"What? That's shocking," Chutney said.

"Yeah, she asked if I knew anything about computers, but I don't," Pepper said.

"My parents got me into it when I was a kid," Chutney said. "Not many girls are into coding and stuff."

"She was curious how easily someone could get the password for the headmistress's login to show Ms. Oscura how vulnerable our information really is."

Chutney furrowed her brow. Pepper's heart raced, fearing she'd said too much.

"A password…that's it?"

"Yeah. Well, you know Ms. Powell, she doesn't seem that tech-savvy herself."

"For reals." Chutney chuckled. "But I could probably do it."

"Seriously?" Salty said.

"Can you show us…now?" Pepper asked. "I mean before dinner. I'm so curious, being a tech dummy and all."

"Sure, come to my room and see how the peasants live."

Salty gave Pepper a knowing look as they followed Chutney inside.

# Chapter Eighteen

A week later, Pepper made a big show of curling up in a ball on her bed and moaning dramatically. The other girls sympathized. Cramps were never fun. They promised to bring her back snacks and goodies from dinner. Ginger even offered to see if she could find a hot water bottle. Pepper thanked her before doubling over in pain and groaning again.

Once she heard the second-floor landing door close, Pepper jumped up. She and Salty decided it would be best to wait ten minutes before she actually tried to break in to be sure Ms. Oscura was in the dining room. But Pepper wanted to be in position well before then. She slipped off her shoes and stuffed her phone into the waistband of her leggings, then padded down the stairs. Pepper paused at the second-floor landing and pressed her ear to the door. She heard talking and the clomp, clomp of footsteps as students headed to dinner. Pepper continued down the tightly twisting circular stone stairwell. When she reached the bottom, Pepper turned on her phone's flashlight. She recognized the escape room exit and wondered if there was an entrance to the headmistress' office along this hallway without her having to get back into the escape room. She deduced that there must be surveillance in the Reception room, remembering the way Ms.

Oscura could track their progress during the competition. Staying out of there would mean she could stay completely covert if there were an entrance to the office.

Chill bumps rose along her arms as she progressed down the dusty hallway. Pepper flashed her phone light along the wall, searching for an indentation or button, any sign that a hidden door existed. So far, though, there was only the smooth stone and the seam of grout between them. Maybe this had been a bad idea. If she were caught, would Ms. Oscura make them move downstairs? Was she risking her friends' cupola oasis for a document that probably didn't have any new information on it? Or worse, would she be sent back to Margaux's house?

As she snuck down the corridor, her toes cold on the frigid stone floor, Pepper wondered if perhaps she was mistaken. Maybe this secret passageway did not lead to any other room. But who would build an elaborate, secret hallway that only went one place? Surely, if the builder had wanted secret escapes, he would have designed multiple exits. She flashed her light along all the walls. They were perfectly uniform gray stone rectangles. Pepper lowered her phone and noticed a strange gap between the wall and the floor. She knelt and touched that portion of the wall. It had the look of stone but was flat. It had been painted to look exactly like the stone.

Pepper pushed on the section. Nothing moved. She ran her hands along the wall on either side of the panel, but there was no variance that she could feel. Maybe it only worked one way, she thought, disheartened. No, Bugsy or whoever it was that built this house wouldn't leave himself trapped in a corridor. What if the light is deceiving me, she thought. Playing tricks with my eyes, the way the faux stone did to make it appear to be a part of the wall. Pepper switched off the light and waited a few moments for her eyes to adjust. That's when she saw it. A dim, glowing disk in the ceiling the size and shape of a doorbell. Lucky me, the ceiling is low, she thought, reaching up.

She said a quick prayer that it was not, in fact, a doorbell and pushed. The panel before her slid into the wall. The same sweet citrus scent she recalled from her first meeting with Ms. Oscura flooded her senses. This was definitely the right place. It was eerie as if the headmistress was still present somehow. As she stepped inside, the door silently slid closed behind her.

There was a single lamp in the shape of a water lily glowing on the corner of the desk. Since her eyes were already adjusted to the darkness, the single decorative light fixture provided enough brightness for her to see. She tiptoed behind the desk and gently touched the top to activate the tablet inset on the desk surface. It came to life with an ocean image, which Pepper recognized as the view from the bluff. So, the headmistress was an amateur photographer as well. Pepper retrieved her phone and brought up the note with the password Chutney had been able to hack in two minutes. Seriously, they needed to think about upgrading their security. When she entered the password, the ocean screen dissolved into what looked like the actual wooden desktop, complete with piles of papers, an old-fashioned inkwell, a clock, and a notepad. Pepper chose the default search tab in the bottom left screen and typed: student records. Zero results. She tried again: student files. Zero results. Could their files be under a code word or hidden? Ugh, this was impossible. Why did she ever think she'd be able to find her paperwork. Then it dawned on her. Paper. Maybe they weren't electronic, she thought, looking around.

The last time she was here, Pepper hadn't paid much attention to the furniture. There were only forty-eight students. Their files could all easily be kept here, she reasoned. There didn't appear to be a filing system in sight. Where would Ms. Oscura keep current student files, she thought. After what seemed like hours of looking in drawers, pulling out books, and feeling behind paintings for a safe, she returned to the desk and plopped down in the headmistress' worn leather chair. She slid open the top drawers, but they were too shallow to be a reasonable place to keep files;

mostly, there were just pens, stationery, device chargers, an extra pair of glasses, and a selection of chocolate that Pepper was tempted to sample. She tugged at the largest drawer in the desk, but it didn't budge. She slid open the last drawer in the center of the desk, only to be disappointed by a neat arrangement of well-organized pens in trays. She leaned forward, pushing the drawer back in place with her mid-section.

The hall clock chimed on the hour, and Pepper knew her time was up. They'd be close to finishing dinner. She needed to get back upstairs. Before she got up, Pepper tried the large drawer one last time. Miraculously, it slid open, revealing rows of paper files. Realizing she had left the pen drawer ajar, she pushed it, but it wouldn't close all the way. That was when she understood that the file drawer was locked when the pen drawer was closed. Seriously low-tech but clever. She hurriedly flipped through the files. They were not in alphabetical order. Pepper squinted to read the unfamiliar names on the tabs: Evangeline, Jade, Lilith, Ellery, Annabelle, Juliet… She wondered which name belonged to which of her peers, but she didn't have time to check now. Finally, she found her file at the very back and slid it free.

Ms. Oscura's voice echoed down the hall. She opened the folder and shuffled through the pages until she found the document she needed. Pepper took a quick picture with her phone, wishing she had more time to review the other pages. She stuffed the file into the drawer and quickly pushed it closed, then ducked out of sight just as the door opened. This is it, I'm caught, Pepper thought, crouched alongside the massive desk.

"Headmistress," Salty said from the hallway. "Can I ask you a question?"

"Of course, come in,"

"Oh, it'll only take a second, but I have to show you," Salty said.

Their voices trailed down the hall. Pepper peered over the desk. The door was open. Shoot, she couldn't get back across the room because someone could easily see her as they left the dining room, blowing her cover. There were other exits. But where were they? Pepper felt under the desk for a button or lever.

Maybe she should have slipped out the open office door and pretended to be coming downstairs. But it was too late for that. Ms. Oscura's heeled step was edging closer. Finally, she located a release on the underside of the pen drawer. She sprinted for the opening between two bookcases at the opposite end of the room. Rather obvious, she mused, darting inside the dark space. She immediately tripped and fell hard against something solid directly in front of her. Stifling a cry of pain, Pepper clamped her hands over her mouth. She'd fallen onto a set of metal stairs. The secret door hadn't yet closed, and she looked up in horror as the office door swung open.

# *Chapter Nineteen*

Ms. Oscura stepped inside and turned toward Pepper's hiding spot when something on her desk caught her attention. Shoot, I didn't log out of the computer, Pepper thought. Ms. Oscura looked up just as the secret door clicked into place.

Pepper let out the breath she was holding and massaged her right knee, which had landed hard on the sharp corner of the narrow stairs. If the headmistress had noticed anything, she surely would have opened the passageway door and discovered the intruder. Pepper waited a few moments, and when she was sure Ms. Oscura wasn't looking for her, she felt her way up the steep staircase. She didn't dare turn on her flashlight for fear of the light seeping out through the seam of the secret door. But this staircase, which felt more like a ladder, seemed to go on forever.

She hoped this wasn't the way Salty had gone that first day. She didn't want to drop out of the ceiling into that escape room, or any other room for that matter. Then again, there were probably more exits than Salty had realized.

Soon, she reached a plateau and figured it was safe to use her flashlight. As she coughed from the dust swirling into her nostrils, Pepper saw she was in a small crawl space. More than likely between the first and second floors. She proceeded forward on hands and knees, stopping every so often to shine her flashlight in search of an exit. Pepper chuckled to herself. Salty had probably been having a fit up here in her party tutu with all the dust.

By now, the others would be wondering where she was, especially since she was supposed to be laid up with crippling cramps. She needed to get back to her room. Pepper crawled on, reaching hand over hand into the pitch-black darkness. As she reached forward, her hand landed on something furry. Pepper gasped and recoiled, shrinking away from the creature. In her haste, Pepper dropped the phone and fumbled for it in the dark. But by the time she finally found it and shone the light down the tunnel, whatever had been up here with her was long gone. If small, furry things were living here, she wanted out. Now.

The passage twisted and turned so many times Pepper wasn't sure what part of the building she was even in anymore. Thankfully, though, she had not encountered her fluffy friend again. But she didn't want to tempt fate. Perhaps this was just an air duct and not a secret passage, she thought, her sore knee throbbing as she shuffled forward. Pepper was starting to lose hope that there was a way out when she heard the sound of running water. She followed the noise until she saw a metal grate above her. She paused, listening.

"Did you finish that algebra assignment for me, or what?" It was Cherry!

Pepper had managed to crawl all the way to their wing of the building.

Her phone buzzed in her hand, echoing through the tunnel.

"What was that?" Peach asked.

"It's you wishing you were never born, that's what," Cherry said. "Finish my assignment already."

"No, wait. There it is again."

Shoot, Pepper glanced at their phone. It was Salty.

The girls are getting worried. Where ARE you?

On my way. STALL. And stop texting!

Pepper shrank back as Peach stepped toward the floor grate. If they only knew what was under here. She made a mental note to sidestep this part of the floor when she was clad only in a towel.

"Stop messing around and finish my homework," Cherry said, "Or I'm telling my father, and that means your father will be in a world of hurt."

"I'll get it finished," Peach said.

The sound of retreating footsteps echoed through the tiled bathroom until there was silence. Pepper positioned herself under the grate and gave it a push. It moved aside easily. She climbed out and replaced the grate. In order to cover her disappearance, Pepper doused her hair under the faucet, wrapped it in a towel, and proceeded upstairs. The door to the cupola stairwell opened just as she reached for the octagonal, purple glass handle. Ms. Oscura stepped out.

"Headmistress," Pepper squeaked.

"I was just coming to check on you. Funny, your roommates didn't know where you'd gone."

"Shower," she replied. "Sometimes the hot water helps relax the muscles. Actually, a bath really helps, but since we don't have one, I decided to try this."

"And were you successful?"

"Uh...yes, ma'am," Pepper replied.

"I'm pleased you are feeling better," Ms. Oscura said, moving aside.

"Thank you."

Ms. Oscura stopped and regarded Pepper from head to toe. She realized too late that her clothes were covered in dust from the tunnel. Ugh, why hadn't she stripped and left her clothes in her bathroom cubby!

"I think we'll have to ask Marco to clean that stairwell thoroughly," Ms. Oscura said, walking away.

"Yeah, it's pretty dusty," Pepper replied before darting through the door and up the stairs.

She burst into the cupola and headed straight for her bed. The girls looked up at her entrance.

"That's where I thought you were," Azucar said. "I mean, there aren't a lot of places to get to in this school. I don't know why Salty was so worried." She turned back to the assignment she was finishing.

Pepper collapsed onto her bed, still covered in dust. She couldn't debrief Salty out loud, but they could still communicate.

"It's obvious you two are texting each other. What's going on?" Ginger asked.

"Nothing," Pepper replied. "I...well, I heard Cherry threatening Peach in the bathroom. She's forcing her to do her algebra homework."

Ginger snorted. "Figures. She also gets the rest of us to do all her work in Etiquette. I wish Ms. Powell would let us change groups."

Pepper and Salty nodded at each other across the room and put their phones down.

"Did you get it?" Salty mouthed silently.

Pepper nodded and smiled. Their debriefing would have to wait. But that didn't mean Pepper couldn't look at what she'd found.

"We brought you some dinner if you're feeling up to eating," Ginger said, indicating the plate on Pepper's nightstand.

"Thanks, yeah, I'm feeling better and famished."

Ginger smiled and returned to reading. Pepper realized that she needed to continue the ruse for a while longer. She brought the plate to her lap and ate. The document was too important to glance at one-handed while trying to cut chicken Parmesan with her fork. She'd have to delay gratification a bit longer.

· · ·

ONCE THE GIRLS had settled in for the night and were either watching shows on their devices, reading, finishing homework for tomorrow, or getting a head start on future assignments, Pepper retrieved her phone and opened the photo app. The single image she'd captured was off-center and washed out because of the camera flash. Darn that dim room, she thought, zooming in. But she'd managed to capture the vital part. Certificate of Live Birth, State of New York, Kings County, was written at the top of the form. A smudged purple seal was in the bottom right corner. Pepper's heartbeat sped up, and she recognized the dampness under her arms as fear sweat. But what did she have to fear? Ms. Powell had told her several surprising facts. She just wanted to confirm what she knew or thought she knew about herself and her family.

The other section headings were challenging to read. Still, Nonnu's familiar firm handwriting was easily legible: Stella Valentina D'Angelo, birth date, time of birth, she scanned lower. Mother: Giada Florentine D'Angelo. Pepper traced the letters of her mother's name. Mother's Birthplace: Brooklyn, New York. Father: Unknown. She gawked at the blank spaces that followed. Did her mother never reveal who her father was? It was undeniable that Santiago Candella was her father. Their matching emerald eyes were enough to prove parentage, but why wasn't he listed on her birth certificate? Since Nonnu had filled out the form, he was either unsure of paternity or had left it off for a reason.

Nonnu, why were you so secretive? Pepper continued searching the rest of the document. She kept returning to her middle name, which she'd never known. Was it a coincidence that it was also the name of this school? The school Nonnu insisted she attend. Pepper put down the phone and rubbed her eyes. Instead of answers, all she'd found were more questions.

Growing up in Denver, she recalled a stark contrast between her grandparents. Nonnu had been vibrantly Italian, cooking authentic food, teaching her the language, and telling her all those mafia stories. Which she now realized were *not* just stories. Granny, on the other hand, was a typical American grandma. She had made grilled cheese sandwiches, cut the crust off, watched afternoon soaps, and never joined in with Nonnu's stories. In fact, she often interrupted and had him do some chore or another. Pepper thought back. What was her name, the name the neighbor ladies had used when they came by to borrow sugar or deliver a misdirected piece of mail?

Tina…Tina Dallas. That was the name they'd used. Nonnu never did call her that. He used pet names, but maybe there was something more. In Pepper's acceptance letter, the headmistress had alluded to the fact that Granny did attend this school, so she must have been part of the "family." Before now, she'd always taken Granny's identity at face value. Now, she understood that there was more to this mystery. She could feel it in the knot that had formed in her stomach. Pepper switched off her bedside lamp and pulled the curtain around her bed, knowing she'd be awake for hours. What secrets was Granny hiding?

# *Chapter Twenty*

Pepper had been selected to go last for their wives of Henry the Eighth presentation. She was half listening to Chutney while putting the finishing touches on her essay. She'd meant to do it sooner; it was only that her mind was consumed with the information she'd found last week. The class clapped politely as Chutney concluded and took her seat. Cherry was next, and Pepper fully intended to zone out. To Pepper's surprise, a chat bubble popped up on her screen. It was Nico, under his chat name, *FutbolRossetti17*. They'd started communicating more and more frequently, but usually in the late evenings.

Hey-whatcha doing?

I'm in history class.

Whoops. Sorry. Real quick. Do you want to meet up tomorrow morning for a different kind of workout?

What did you have in mind?

It's a surprise.

I don't like surprises.

I think you'll like this one. Besides, I didn't want to wait until after finals to see you.

Me either.

A charge of excitement shot through her limbs.

I'll agree to your secret workout on one condition. No swimming.

It's a deal. Meet me at your entrance gate at six sharp.

PEPPER REACHED FORWARD to tap out a reply when her tablet was yanked off the desk. Mrs. Sabatini peered down at her, lips drawn in a thin, disapproving line.

"I'm really sorry. I was finishing my paper."

"No one grins at their lap while writing a term paper," Mrs. Sabatini replied.

"I was admiring a brilliant sentence I had just written," Pepper replied.

Mrs. Sabatini began to turn the table toward her. "Should I read this brilliant sentence to the class?"

"No," Pepper yelped. "Fine, I was on the school chat."

"You've earned yourself afternoon detention, and you are presenting next. Continue, Cherry."

Pepper slid down in her seat, unbothered by the detention. A glow of happiness blossomed in her chest. Nico wanted to see her and was planning something for tomorrow morning. However, she wondered what the nature of an alternate workout would be. She hoped nothing too strenuous.

. . .

Mrs. Sabatini pulled her aside after class. "You will serve detention tomorrow morning with Marco."

"Tomorrow morning?" she exclaimed. "But you said afternoon detention. I can't in the morning."

"Tough cookies," she continued. "Report to Marco in the courtyard at eight a.m. on the dot."

"Mrs. Sabatini, I am very sorry for not paying strict attention to my classmates' presentations. I apologize and take full responsibility for my actions, but could I please have detention another day?"

"I know you girls love sleeping in on your late start day, but why not just get it over with?" she replied.

Pepper debated outright lying or telling the truth. "Since one of the reasons we are here at Valentina's is to make a good match, it seems counterproductive to keep me from spending time with one of the most eligible bachelors in organized crime." That should do it, she thought.

Mrs. Sabatini regarded her student for a moment. "Yes, Ms. Powell was right about you. A definite alpha. Okay. You can write a paper about why it is rude to not pay attention during my class instead of serving detention with Marco."

"Thank you—"

"*And,*" she continued, "you will bring back intel from your date."

"I wouldn't call it a…wait, did you say intel? You want me to spy on Nico?" Pepper asked.

"Life's full of tough choices. You will use the skills you've acquired to find out which bakery the Rossetti's purchase their cannoli from."

"Can't you just ask Coco?" Pepper asked.

"I am asking *you* unless you'd like to weed the lawn instead of doing whatever you had planned with *Il Principe.*"

"You know we call him that?"

"Honey, everyone calls him that. He's the prince of the mafia.

Kudos for momentarily capturing his attention. But if you want to keep that date, you will agree to these conditions. After all, we are preparing you to be mafia wives, and good wives know how to get information."

This seemed unfair, but Pepper couldn't see a way out of it. The fire that had been burning in her chest turned to ice. Pepper agreed to Mrs. Sabatini's terms and took a seat to write her one-page essay about paying attention in class. But she couldn't concentrate. How would she find out about cannoli, of all things, without simply asking him? It wasn't like they casually discussed baked goods.

After a few moments of clacking away on her keyboard, Mrs. Sabatini's chair screeched across the floor as she pushed back and stood. "I need to speak with Ms. Oscura. You may remain as long as necessary to finish your assignment. Just leave it on my desk when you have finished. And find me tomorrow to report on what information you recover."

Pepper agreed and returned her attention to the page. Mrs. Sabatini was old-fashioned, insisting she handwrite the essay. Pepper stretched out her hand, unused to this much writing. She couldn't bring herself to write about why she couldn't pay attention to Cherry's ridiculous speech about Anne Boleyn's sex appeal, making her the best queen, so she kept her comments generalized instead. Getting to a full page was challenging, but Pepper looked over her work, pleased with her progress, and then placed it on Mrs. Sabatini's desk. That was when she noticed the computer screen. On it was a chart of Valentina students and what appeared to be Don students. She didn't find her name, but at the top was Cherry with a dotted line to…Nico? The computer screen dissolved into an image of a sun-drenched tropical beach. Had she seen that correctly? Pepper touched the screen. The image disappeared, but the locked screen log-in prompt was in its place. She wanted to run downstairs and tell Salty but decided to keep this information on ice for the moment.

Now, she wished she'd asked Nico to reschedule their workout, but it was too late. She was duty-bound to find out about cannoli, of all things. With no idea how she was going to accomplish that, plus the glimpse of that chart still swirling in her mind, she made her way down to cooking class with the tardy slip Mrs. Sabatini had written clutched in her hand. To her amazement, the delicious smell of sautéing onions and garlic filled the stairwell. She took the stairs two at a time and burst into the kitchen.

Each team was clustered around their stove. Pepper headed straight for her group, but Signore Tonelli intercepted her. She explained how Mrs. Sabatini had held her back and handed over the tardy slip. Instead of allowing her to join the others, he made her copy the recipe by hand before watching the video on preparing a vegetable broth. It was tedious, and Pepper envied her classmates for their first cooking experience. She loved to be in front of the stove and cursed Mrs. Sabatini under her breath for the unfair and extreme punishment. Even when she'd finished her assignment, Signore made her sit up front and wait until the rest of the class completed the assignment.

As Salty ladled the broth into bowls, Signore Tonelli nodded and allowed her to join her group.

"What happened to you? One minute, you were behind us, and then, poof! You were gone," Salty said, handing her a warm bowl.

Pepper dipped her spoon into the clear broth, bringing the steaming spoonful to her lips. She sipped the liquid. It could use a dash more salt and certainly more garlic, but it was decent. After a few more slurps, she explained the encounter with their history teacher—leaving out the cannoli intel mission. Some things were best kept to yourself, she decided. The girls sympathized with her plight but informed Pepper she would be the kitchen clean-up crew for this assignment.

"Sorry," Salty said.

"You weren't here, and no one else wanted to be in charge of washing the dishes," Azucar explained.

Pepper looked over the mess. There were piles of vegetable

peelings, stacks of dishes, and quite a few dirty knives. "Did you guys need to use everything in the kitchen to make this?" she asked.

"We were all in charge of chopping a different vegetable," Azucar said.

"Here, have some more broth," Salty said, pouring another spoonful into Pepper's bowl.

"Do you guys know anything about cannoli?"

"That's a subject change," Azucar replied. "Why?"

"No reason just thought they'd go with this dish," Pepper said.

"My Nonni makes them for us. Says it isn't right to go to a bakery, but to be honest, Buddy's in Long Island has better ones. But if you ever tell her I said that I will fit you for concrete stilettos," Salty said.

"Buddy's, huh," Pepper said aloud, even though she was mostly talking to herself.

"Yeah, my parents get all our birthday and holiday cakes there, too," Salty continued.

Pepper slurped the rest of the broth from her bowl, then lugged the heavy soup pot to the sink and began filling it with water.

"Do you want some help?" Salty asked.

"No, fair is fair, but next time I'm cooking," she said, wiping down the counters with the wet dish rag.

By the time Pepper finished clean-up, lunch was over, and it was time for English class. For a day infused with such a hopeful moment, it was proving to be quite dismal. At this point, she was so consumed with her assignment that she wanted to cancel the meet-up altogether and help Marco pull weeds. She didn't want to deceive Nico but couldn't reveal the truth. Why was she always in a paradox of lies? Salty was leaving the dining room as Pepper made her way to class.

"Here, I swiped this for you," Salty said, handing her a chocolate chip cookie. "How are you doing?"

"My arm is about dead from scrubbing that pot. You forgot to put in the olive oil first, didn't you?"

"Guilty," Salty said. "But it's not that. Something is bothering you. I could see it on your face when you walked into cooking class."

Pepper shrugged.

"Is it something about your family? Did you discover something?"

"No, nothing."

"Oh. Maybe that's it. Don't worry. Your family isn't from outer space. There have to be records about them somewhere. You'll find them." Salty gave her a bright smile and walked into her algebra class as Pepper continued down the hall to her English classroom. If there was such a thing as natural alphas and betas, not that she believed there was, Salty was the quintessential and perfect beta. She was supportive and encouraging, anticipated others' needs, and was fiercely loyal. In fact, she was also the perfect friend.

THE NEXT MORNING, Pepper got up early, as usual. No one made a fuss or even turned over to inquire about where she was going. Since Nico had promised not to make her go swimming, she pulled on her school leggings and her hoodie and headed downstairs. Too nervous to eat anything, she placed a protein bar into her pouch and slipped out the front door. The mist was low and heavy this morning. She loved how it amplified the sound of the waves crashing just beyond the bluff. It felt like she was in the midst of the turbulent sea. Pepper cut across the lawn to the entrance gate. She had no idea what the code was to open the gate, but thankfully, a tree was growing along the fence. Pepper shimmied up and dropped down onto the other side of the wall in minutes. Getting back inside would be another issue, but she didn't have time to worry. A black SUV appeared, silently parting the mist, startling her. She had expected Nico to arrive on foot. Instead, he jumped down from the vehicle's passenger side.

"So, this *is* an adventure we're going on," she said.

"I told you it would be different," he replied.

"By different, I thought you meant seeing the other side of the bluff." She gestured down the street.

"Not a chance. Come on. It's a bit of a drive, and I want to spend as long as possible there.

Intrigued, Pepper climbed into the car.

"A driver and everything, huh?" she said, fastening her seatbelt.

"Yeah, I'm getting my license over break. Then I can pick you up in my vintage roadster."

A shiver of delight passed through her. They drove south for under an hour, turning along the highway adjacent to the ocean. It was so unlike her view of Monterey and Carmel from the bluff. This area still seemed wild and untamed. Then, the highway curved into the mountains, enveloping them in soft green light and towering trees.

"I thought we were going running on the beach, back there," she said.

"I told you this was going to be different."

Pepper nodded and returned her attention to the passing scenery. She'd sort of figured a new beach was a different sort of workout. Clearly, Nico had other plans. The driver stopped to let them out at the state park and informed Nico he'd be having a cup of coffee at the inn when they were ready to leave. And to call him if they weren't going to make it back in time.

Nico thanked the driver, and they set off through the parking lot to the trailhead.

"What did he mean if we don't make it back?" Pepper asked. "You planning on kidnapping me in the wilderness?"

Nico stopped and turned.

She met his unwavering gaze. After she had said it, Pepper realized its horrible mafia connotations.

"I'd never do anything to hurt you," he said. The way he said it, softly and with such intensity, she believed him. "The truth is, it's a long trail. I don't want you to miss class, but I hoped we'd have enough time to grab breakfast at the inn beside the river. I guess we could have saved this trip for a weekend, but…never mind," he said, grasping his right foot to stretch his quads.

"I'm glad you didn't wait," she said, giving him an encouraging smile.

He straightened up, regaining his usual swagger. "Ready to run?"

"You did promise me a workout. Lead the way."

The mist had mostly lifted here but still lingered at the tiptop of the trees. They set off together down the trail into the forest. It was incredible how the insulation of the forest muffled sound, the way the mist had done back at school. Their footsteps were almost silent as they ran over the layers of cushiony pine needles. The trail was narrow, and it seemed like Nico knew the way; she followed behind at a close pace. Since their first meeting, she had regained some cardio stamina and was proud of herself for keeping up with him.

Although the setting was tranquil, her earlier comment rubbed between them, chafing as they ran. When Nico stopped and turned to look out over the river, she knew it was time to speak up.

"I didn't mean anything earlier," she said. "I realize it might have been a bit insensitive. Because…"

"Of who my family is and what they do," he finished.

"I wasn't going to say that, but yeah."

"TCN. Violence is part of who we are, I guess, but I don't hurt people I care about."

"I understand."

"What about your family? I mean, no one in our world is squeaky clean."

"That's the thing," she said as a tight sensation gripped her chest. Was she really going to divulge her greatest secret? "They are uh…not involved."

"Come on, let's walk a bit farther up the trail. We have time," he said. "By not involved, do you mean regular people, like dentists or librarians?"

The word librarian caught her off guard, and she automatically thought of Ethan at home, getting ready to start his day. Her heart constricted. How could she be here with Nico, with these new and powerful feelings emerging, and still chat with Ethan on the regular? He knew her better than anyone, but she couldn't deny that she was falling for Nico. She and Ethan were just friends, well, maybe a smidge more than friends. At least that's what he wanted. Pepper sighed; she didn't know what they were. It was complicated, too complicated for this early in the morning.

"Sorry," Nico said, breaking in on her thoughts. "Forget about it. It's none of my business."

"No, it's fine," she said. "My father is in jail, and my mother and grandparents are dead. Pretty straightforward." Then Pepper picked up her pace and brushed past him. Salty knew the truth, of course, but no one else. It was still a gaping wound she never discussed. She was not in the mood to start now, not even with him. Thankfully, Nico took the hint, and they continued in silence.

Pepper kept her lead. She pushed herself to outrun the pain pressing against her chest like a boulder. The trail was well-defined; there was no way to get lost. He hadn't been kidding about a different sort of workout, though. On the beach, they had one elevation. Sure, the sliding sand made traction tougher. Here, the constant elevation changes made her muscles scream with fatigue. Still, Pepper didn't stop.

"How are we on time?" she called back.

"We should turn back soon, but I want you to see what's ahead. Do you mind if we walk?" he asked.

Pepper readily agreed. Her legs were so fatigued she wasn't sure how she was going to make it back.

"Easy there," he said, catching her when she tripped over a tree root that had decided to arch a few inches above the ground across the path. "I didn't think you'd faint into my arms until we reached the surprise."

"Don't count on that, Romeo," she said, smirking. Although now she wondered what was up ahead.

Pepper heard it before it was visible. When they turned the bend, she caught a glimpse of the waterfall steadily cascading over the rocks and closed her eyes. The sound was soothing in a way the forest's silence wasn't. Despite her aching muscles, she opened her eyes and rushed up the path to get closer. The craggy cliff was covered in mossy green lichen. There wasn't a large pool waiting for them to swim in. It was too chilly anyway, and she was not stripping down in front of Nico, not yet. There was a shallow body of water sprinkled with a smattering of boulders. She ached to use the protruding rocks as stepping stones so she could put her hands under the falling water. The thought sent a prickly sensation of fear coursing over her skin as she remembered her last attempt at rock hopping at the bonfire. She decided admiring the water was just as lovely.

"This is spectacular," she said.

"I'm glad you think so. You know, in February, this pool is high enough to go swimming."

"Except I can't swim," she replied, "remember?"

"I could never forget that night. But…I could teach you."

"Here? In the middle of winter? Pass. But you find a heated pool, and I'd be willing to give swimming another try."

"Heated pool…hmmm, that gives me an idea. Remind me to look up something when we return to the inn."

"Are we gonna have time to eat?"

"Yep, you outpaced my estimate. We'll be good on time."

"That's if I can motivate my legs to get us back."

"Hop on," he said, turning his back to her.

"I can't. You're tired, too."

"Not for the whole way, just to give you a chance to rest. Besides, this will count as my weight training."

She hesitated but decided to agree. Her legs felt like overcooked spaghetti, perhaps due to Nico rather than muscle fatigue. She wrapped her legs around his waist as he held her upper thighs, keeping her steady.

"So what's it like at Don's?" she asked, propping her head against his so her breath washed over his reddening ear.

"You're gonna make me hold a conversation while I'm doing all the work, huh?"

"Absolutely," she laughed.

"It's like your school, except we have all the grade levels. So it's not just my class, but upper and lower grades."

"You're not a first-year?"

"No, second. That's how I know about all these places already."

She had wondered about his intricate knowledge of the area. "You were probably upset when the last class graduated," she said.

"At Valentina's? Nah, they were stuck up. They didn't want anything to do with the first years. There were bigger fish to catch, if you know what I mean."

"So you know the whole point of Valentina's?"

"My sister goes there, so yeah. Why?"

"No reason. Do you get to take electives?"

He paused and straightened up. Pepper slid down. "Sorry, needed a break."

"It's all right. I can walk from here," she said.

"Electives?" he replied. "Sports mainly, some guys take a language, but *lo parlo italiano.*"

"*È cosi?*" she replied.

"*Anche tu?*"

"*Parlo un po d'italiano.*"

"That's good to know," he said, grinning. "Now we can speak in code."

"Assuming no one else around knows Italian either. Odds are high the people in our circles do."

He shrugged. *"Conosco i miei polli."*

Pepper burst out laughing. It was a phrase Nonnu used often. She had taken it literally as a child and thought he knew chickens. Now, of course, she realized it meant he knew his people. She hadn't heard it in years. The fact that Nico used it so conversationally made her want to throw her arms around him. She refrained and, instead, playfully slapped his arm. "Yeah, I bet you do."

"Smell that?" he asked.

Pepper took a deep breath. "Woodsmoke?"

"Breakfast," he replied.

"I hope they have cannoli," she blurted out.

"After that great workout, you want to eat dessert?"

"Why not? I earned it," she said.

Nico shook his head. Shoot, he wasn't taking the bait.

"Is that a dessert your family likes?" she continued, hating herself for asking.

"Sure, I guess," he said, stopping to retie his shoe.

"Any bakery in particular you go to get them?"

He looked up through his dark lashes. "Nope. Well, there's a place down the street, Contino's Bakery, but I think Mom goes anywhere. Dessert's not really my thing."

Relief flooded her like being doused with cool water on a hot afternoon. That should be good enough for Mrs. Sabatini. Now she could enjoy the rest of their date—uh, workout.

"Don't have a sweet tooth?" she teased.

"Not that type of sweet," he replied, pinching her waist. Pepper yelped, then swatted his hand away when he reached out to grab her again. They sprinted down the path, their earlier fatigue forgotten in a rush of flirtation.

. . .

WHEN SHE GOT drowsy on the ride back, with her head on Nico's shoulder, she replayed their perfect breakfast overlooking the meandering river. They feasted on towering stacks of pancakes topped with mountains of whipped cream and omelets stuffed with gooey cheese and crispy bacon. It had been a perfect morning. Nico draped his arm around her shoulder, and she snuggled in close to his chest before promptly falling asleep.

# Chapter Twenty-One

After mid-terms, their teachers did not ease up as Pepper had hoped. Workloads were doubled with no regard for their students' personal lives. Pepper lamented that there had been no time to further her research of the grounds and reluctantly conceded it would have to wait if she wanted to keep her grades up. Even seeing Nico had dwindled to an occasional glimpse on the soccer field during PE. She felt bogged down with schoolwork, a first for her. Public school had always been a breeze. It was rare she had assignments she didn't finish in class. In some ways, it was good to be preoccupied with homework.

Every so often, when walking down the hall, Pepper would try a door handle to see if it would open. Salty always shook her head at Pepper's attempts. It was worth a try, she'd remark. There had to be records here somewhere, and she was still determined to find them even if she had been coming up empty.

FRIDAY AFTERNOON, Pepper sat up in the cupola staring out the window, desperately trying to figure out a way to discover some new shred of evidence about Granny's identity. Of course, she'd done internet searches. Unless you had access to the paid info databases, which only affluent schools, rich people, or institutions did, anything she turned up online was unreliable, at best. When she asked Ms. Oscura why they couldn't access the databases, the headmistress marched her into the library and pointed out the encyclopedias, which annoyed Pepper. It was true that most everyone else stopped relying on the internet for legitimate information decades ago and now used it as a sort of…what had Nonnu called it? A productivity vortex, nothing more. The way he described it, the birth of the internet held so much promise, but unregulated artificial intelligence polluted the whole system.

There were tons of Tina D'Angelos and even more Valentina D'Angelos online, but zero vital records for Tina Dallas in Colorado. At that point, she knew she was on to something important. Her father's words echoed back to her about letting the past stay in the past, but Pepper needed to know, and since he wouldn't tell her, she'd find out for herself if she could.

A pillow hit her face, knocking her head against the windowpane.

"Hey!" Pepper yelled.

"Oops, sorry," Salty said. "Are you gonna continue moping when we finally have a Friday to ourselves without an assignment hanging overhead?"

"Yes. Leave me alone," Pepper teased, chuckling as she hurled the pillow back at her friend.

"Get ready. The van is coming in an hour. It's First Friday at the aquarium. Students are half-price. There's gonna be a DJ, and they're doing otters encounters. It's going to be amazing. Get up."

"I just feel like I'm so close to a breakthrough," Pepper said. "Since Nico has an away game, and everyone is taking the van to town, I thought I could snoop around some more."

"Maybe you should wait a bit before you start breaking into other off-limit sections of the school. Ms. Oscura is already suspicious. She'll probably be expecting you to try something. I'm certain she knows a student broke into her office."

"But she doesn't know it was me," Pepper said.

"Are you positive?"

"No, but it's a chance I'm willing to take. Salty, you don't know what it's like not to have any idea who your family is."

"Believe me, sometimes I wish I did," Salty replied.

Pepper cocked her head to the side. "Why?"

"The people in my family have done some terrible things. My own father even. I'm not saying it wasn't necessary, but think about reconciling your Nonnu with someone who chopped some guy's fingers off with wire cutters."

Pepper recoiled in horror. "That's awful."

"TCN. Yep, that's what I mean. You never see them the same again." Salty stood and crossed to her bed on the opposite side of the room. Pepper turned back to the window. The soft golden rays of the setting sun lit up the room.

Maybe Salty was right. What if she learned something horrible about her parents or Nonnu? It would tarnish their memory forever. These thoughts circled in her mind over and over in an infinite loop. But if Nonnu hadn't wanted her to know, he never would have told her about Valentina's. It was his wish for her to understand her origin. He knew her well enough to know that she couldn't find her place without learning where she came from. No, it wasn't time to give up. She had to find the truth. No matter what. Looking at her best friend's sad expression, Pepper decided that maybe searching for the truth could wait for one night.

PEPPER NEVER IMAGINED when Salty said students were half price that the aquarium would be swarming with other high schoolers. It really shouldn't have been quite such a shock. Monterey was a sleepy town, and there wasn't much for people their age to do. Of course, students from all the surrounding schools were here as well. Pepper glanced around the group, moving toward the entrance, but she didn't recognize anyone. Salty pulled her along the queue and passed her phone under the checkout scanner to pay for both their tickets. When Pepper protested, Salty waved her off.

The atrium of the aquarium, usually a dull, industrial, cavernous concrete space with bare ductwork looming overhead, had been transformed by vibrant, jewel-toned spotlights. To the right, a huge gray whale had splashes of sapphire blue light around the massive mammal, making the already strange site of a flying whale seem otherworldly. She'd been here on a handful of free days they hosted each month but never for a special event.

"So why are we allowed in for half price?" Pepper asked.

"Well, we can only stay until five, then it's for the twenty-one and up crowd, but it's still fun to look around for a couple of hours, right?"

"Absolutely, what do you want to see first?" Pepper asked, consulting her map.

"The otters, duh," Salty said, yanking Pepper to the crowded viewing area.

They squeezed onto the platform, but the exhibit was so popular Pepper couldn't see anything above the heads of the other patrons except rippling turquoise water. Salty was so tiny that she squeezed through the crowd to the viewing window. Finally, when the group oohed and aahed for the tenth time, she'd had enough of wondering what cute activities the otters were up to and left to explore the rest of the aquarium on her own. She wandered upstairs, but even the second-floor otter experience viewing loft was packed. Pepper made a sharp left and headed for the open ocean exhibit.

She passed a few of her fellow Valentina peers on her exploration, but not nearly as many as had driven over with them from the school. It seemed like most of the girls in the van with them had opted to explore Cannery Row instead of the aquarium. Pepper trailed behind a tour group, the guide barely audible over the constant chatter from the students ahead. A part of her wished she had stayed at school and done some more exploring until they turned the corner, and a bright blue window appeared. The tour group rushed forward, pressing in on itself to get close to the exhibit.

She waited for them to depart and then took in the magnificent sight of vibrant orange jellyfish undulating through a neon blue sea. It was like a moving portrait. She stood back to appreciate the tableau. It was mesmerizing. Pepper felt her mind drift away as she followed the movement of the invertebrates' dance, their tentacles trailing behind them like sashes on a woman's evening gown. Pepper stayed transfixed until the next group showed up and crowded the window, interrupting her private experience.

Pepper continued through the aquarium, pausing at different exhibits and wondering where Salty had gotten to. Most likely, she was still at the otter exhibit. She was definitely a cute and fuzzy creature lover. It was doubtful that fish held much appeal for her friend. Pepper wove through the dim maze, past illuminated windows full of vibrant fish until the path opened to a two-story underwater fantasy world.

Pepper gasped. She'd never seen anything so beautiful in her entire life. She chastised herself for bypassing this exhibit during her other visits. Shafts of light sliced through the deep blue water. A school of silvery fish moved as one, flashing as they darted in and out of the beams of light. Pepper stepped forward as if she were in a trance. The room was deserted. The groups passed through some time ago. She plopped down at the edge of the viewing window and lost herself in the magical undersea world. More so than the jellyfish, this mesmerizing display of turtles, sharks, and hundreds of fish swimming by took her thoughts away from the search for Granny and Nonnu's past. A break she dearly needed. She slid down in front of a rectangular block that served as a bench. A turtle glided up the glass just in front of her, and for the first time in weeks, Pepper's mind released its hold on her obsession. It felt like she was floating in the tank now that she wasn't fixated on a single task running in the background like an open browser window trying to load.

Time passed slowly or not at all while she watched the lazy laps the various sea creatures made. She lay on the ground, hypnotized into an altered state by her surroundings, believing she, too, was a part of the vast blueness. Pepper couldn't be sure, but on the edge of her consciousness, she was positive she heard voices. She tried to focus as she drifted in and out of sleep, as she did when waking from a nap. Was that Cherry she heard talking with…she couldn't place the second voice, but it was familiar. They were arguing. Pepper willed herself to wake up, but the drowsy pull of sleep kept dragging her back. Then, the sharp smack of flesh hitting flesh jolted her awake. She sat up. A brief glimpse of red hair flashed as the exit doors opened. Pepper looked around for the second person, but the room was empty. They must've gone back through the exhibit, she thought, jumping up.

Pushing open the doors, Pepper stumbled into the bright light. Someone hip-checked her. Pepper tried to take a defensive position but wobbled unsteadily. The person reached forward, wrapped their arms around Pepper's torso, and jostled her up and down.

"Did you see the puffins!" an excited voice asked.

"Dang it, Salty," Pepper said, detaching her best friend's arms from around her body. She rubbed at her eyes, trying to regain visibility after being in the almost completely dark open ocean room. There was no sign of Cherry anywhere. That didn't mean much since she had been unable to see for a few moments, which would have given Cherry plenty of time to slip away.

"Why so grumpy?" Salty asked, steering Pepper to the puffin enclosure.

"I thought I saw something," she replied vaguely, still scanning the crowd.

"What?" Salty said, gazing at the birds.

"Tell you later," Pepper said, returning her attention to the display. Cartoon-like birds hopped around their enclosure. Of course, Salty had ended up here.

An announcement blasted through the sound system. There were only twenty minutes remaining of the high school portion of the aquarium's First Friday. Salty gasped and insisted that they hit the gift shop. Pepper followed along, still wondering what exactly she had heard or didn't hear back in the open ocean exhibit.

# Chapter Twenty-Two

The weather was a gloomy gray, which Pepper observed from the cupola window above her bed. She had found some risers, and with the bed curtain, it now felt like a window seat, which she'd always wanted. It had been over three months since she'd arrived, and Pepper didn't have more answers, only more questions about her past. She and Salty had been exploring their labyrinth of a school whenever they didn't have class. So far, they'd found two new secret staircases and a handful of passageways, none of which led to a room full of archives. It also didn't appear that this building had a level lower than the ground floor kitchens, which, if she was being honest with herself, was sort of a basement. They discovered a dusty storage closet crammed with cast-off furniture pieces and desks in need of repair but no archives. They had managed to drag an antique bureau up to the cupola to hold Salty's ever-expanding wardrobe, so it hadn't been a complete waste of time.

Still, Pepper was anxious to discover her roots. Over breakfast the week before winter break, Salty and Pepper puzzled out their dilemma.

"If this school was so prestigious, wouldn't they have kept

track of their students? That way, they could put in a brochure that Miss Fontina Fontana married Carmine Carmichael."

"That's the kind of stuff people usually remember," Salty said.

"Right, but not for hundreds of students over decades. The records have to be somewhere."

"Maybe they burned down in a fire," Salty offered.

"Thanks for that," Pepper said.

"Sorry. Hey, maybe I can ask around when I go home," Salty offered.

"Do you really think your relatives are going to remember my relatives, especially when I don't even have a maiden name for my Granny?"

Salty shrugged. "It's worth a try. My Aunt Angela is a super gossip. Maybe my Gran remembers your Granny. They could have been here together." Salty gasped. "They could have been best friends, too!"

Pepper smiled. "You, Salty, are anything but salty."

They ate in silence for a few moments. Pepper wondered if Salty's relatives really could give her the clues she'd been searching for.

"What if they're off-site?" Salty said suddenly.

Pepper looked up. "You are a genius."

"What did I say?" Salty asked, dipping her toast into the runny yolk of her fried egg.

"It's off-site."

"Why would that make you happy? Those records could be anywhere."

"They might," Pepper said, "but I'm betting they're just over the hill." She pointed her spoon west.

Salty gasped. "At Don's," she mouthed.

Pepper nodded. "They're partner schools, right? Why not keep the records secure over there? Keep all their students together. I mean, we're supposed to be marrying them, right?"

"It sounds reasonable, but how will you get over there to check?"

Now, that was a challenge she hadn't been anticipating. Pepper shrugged and shoved a spoonful of cereal into her mouth.

"Don't be sad. You can keep checking the school during Winter break. It'll be so much easier without the teachers hanging around and fewer students," Salty offered.

"Maybe we can loop Chutney in to find some info," Pepper said.

"Like what?" Salty replied, narrowing her eyes.

"Floor plans for Don's."

"Do you think there's gonna be a room marked Valentina's archives?"

"No, but at least we can eliminate sections of the building we aren't familiar with, and maybe we could check with people who are more knowledgeable."

"Are you referring to *Il Principe* by any chance?" Salty asked. Pepper winked. "How are you going to trick Chutney this time?"

Pepper didn't like the word trick. She preferred to think of it as persuasion, but Salty was right. Chutney didn't deserve to be deceived. She'd have to come up with a way to entice her to find the plans.

"It's too late now with exams this week, and then it's winter break…but I'll think of something," Pepper replied.

"Of course you will, evil genius."

Pepper snatched a curvy piece of bacon from Salty's plate and wiggled it under her nose. "*Grazie, signorina,*" she replied, then laughed maniacally.

PEPPER WATCHED as her roommates packed to go home for vacation. Honestly, she didn't mind not going back to Orange

County, not that Margaux had even suggested it. Dad hadn't gotten early parole, so there was little point in returning. Besides, being at school alone or almost alone would be a nice break. She assured Salty that this would probably be her best Christmas since Nonnu had died. Pepper didn't bother mentioning that Margaux made a big show of decorating the outside of their house with Christmas lights and animated figurines that synced up to traditional carols. Inside, it was an undecorated melancholy. The first year Pepper had been living with them, she had been so excited to spend the holiday with her family. On Christmas morning, Margaux had just shoved a shopping bag with underpants and socks at her. Oliver had received mountains of gifts. Margaux covered by saying she didn't know Stella well enough to shop for her yet, and they'd go shopping during the after-Christmas sales. Dad had been satisfied with the reply, but Stella doubted her sincerity. It turned out she'd been correct. The underpants and socks had been her only gift. Practical, sure, but not what she had been anticipating. Of course, now that he was older, Margaux just handed Oliver her credit card and told him to order something he wanted. With Dad still away, Pepper doubted Margaux would even bother with the pretense of gifting her anything this year. And she was completely fine with that. She was tired of faking enjoyment from the so-called gifts she'd received over the last three years. Sometimes nothing was better than complete crap.

Now that classes were over, she had one thing to be excited about. Her Carmel date with Nico. He'd been busy with soccer tournaments, and she had mid-terms. But he was flying home tomorrow morning, so he'd asked if she wanted to visit Carmel tonight. She'd accepted and couldn't wait. Thank goodness Salty hadn't left yet because she needed serious help figuring out an outfit. Meeting up for morning jogs was one thing; dinner in Carmel was completely different.

"Well, I hate to say it, but you have nothing to wear," Salty said, standing before Pepper's open wardrobe.

"That's the same conclusion I came to. Which is why you are supposed to be helping me fix this predicament."

Salty flitted back to her wardrobe and extracted several entirely unsuitable gauzy tutus. Pepper gave her "the look."

"I'm not a magician. I can't just make something out of nothing. Why won't you ask the other girls if anyone has a dress you can borrow?"

"Because they'd want to know why, and if what you said about Nico being the most eligible mafia bachelor is true, then I do not want that kind of mean girl attention."

A knock at their door interrupted them. Coco poked her head in.

"Hi, what's up?" Pepper greeted her.

"You got a delivery," she said, holding out a package the size of a cake box.

"That's weird," Pepper said, crossing the room. "Thanks for bringing it up."

"No problem. Have a Merry Christmas if I don't see you later."

"Thanks, you too," Pepper said. "Huh, it's from Irvine."

"See! They did send you presents," Salty exclaimed, rehanging her skits before plopping beside Pepper on her bed.

Pepper eyed her skeptically. It was true that her family didn't know where she was. She had set up a mail forwarding service to a P.O. Box down south once she realized that it would look very strange for letters to be returned marked Person Unknown if they did try to send her something at the culinary school she was supposedly attending. Not that she ever, in a million years, expected to receive anything, but now she was glad she'd set up the ruse. She tucked the package under her bed.

"You aren't gonna open it?" Salty asked.

"If it's for Christmas, don't you think I should wait?"

"No," Salty replied.

"Fine to humor you." Pepper retrieved some scissors from the flower pot they used as a communal supply holder in the center of their desks. With trepidation, Pepper slit the shiny tape and pulled the flaps of the box open. She removed the first item, unfolding the apron she'd used at home. It wasn't unique or even clean. There was a sticky note attached saying Margaux thought it would come in handy at school.

"That's thoughtful, I guess," Salty said, opening the stained white apron.

"Did you get presents?" Azucar asked, stepping inside the cupola.

"Define presents," Pepper said, peering into the box. Nothing was wrapped, and it looked like Margaux had simply tossed items into the box without a care for their wellbeing. Pepper picked up half of an aubergine pie bird she'd saved up to purchase a year ago. She pushed a few items around and found the other half.

"We can glue it," Salty said, patting her friend's arm.

Pepper put it aside and reached back into the box. There was a stack of sticky notes, some pens, and a pair of girl's underpants that were not hers or new.

"Looks like your little bro is having friends over and stashing their *chones* in your laundry hamper," Azucar said, joining them.

Pepper chuckled. Leave it to Azucar to find the dirty humor in the moment. Her hand brushed something, and Pepper jumped when she realized it was a dead cockroach. She wished she hadn't opened the box. This was embarrassing. She'd seen some of the gifts other girls had received: luxurious cashmere sweaters, perfume, and even AR glasses. Now, there was no place for her shame to hide. Her friends knew the horrid truth of her family situation.

Ginger pulled back the curtains around her bed and shuffled over, covering a yawn with the back of her hand.

"Y'all woke me up," she said, sitting on the floor beside

Pepper's bed. She picked up the broken pie bird and apron. "Is this a white elephant gift exchange?"

"I wish," Pepper replied, unsure she had the stomach to continue.

She removed a slim old cookbook to find a wallet underneath. Pepper held it up. The girls made strangled noises of approval. She knew they were trying their best to be supportive, but who could fake liking these obvious attempts at destroying her holiday joy? She opened the black wallet, but the price tag fell out, so she stuffed it inside the credit card slot. It wasn't as horrid as the other gifts, but it wasn't really something needed, not at school anyway. However, it *was* newish. Next, she pulled out a wad of cloth that turned out to be a wrinkled chartreuse blouse with a second-hand store price tag of five dollars.

"Does she know what you look like?" Ginger said. "I mean, why?" She took the article of clothing and held it up. "This is simply…awful."

"I guess it's better you opened it now," Salty said. "Now it can't…"

"Ruin Christmas," Pepper replied, lying across her bed. "Yeah." A tear slipped down her cheek.

"Screw her," Azucar said, tossing the package onto the floor. Several pennies and broken pencils rattled around the empty box. "That wallet still has the price tag on it, right? Return it for cash, and toss the rest of this junk."

"It's probably seasons old. It looks like something from the back of Margaux's closet or leftover from Oliver's fundraising auction," Pepper said.

"Stores take old crap back all the time. You'll just get less money," Salty said.

"You think so?"

"Dude, it's high-end. They'll take it back. Trust," Azucar said.

"I bet there's a store in Carmel. Return it tonight," Salty suggested.

"Right. Just hold on a minute, *Il Principe*. I need to exchange this horrid holiday gift," Pepper replied sarcastically.

"He's got a sister. I'm sure he's used to it. I make my brothers go shopping with me all the time," Azucar said, inspecting the wallet.

"Seriously, don't let her win," Salty said.

"Thanks," Pepper said, wiping her face dry. "I'm not sure how I would have survived this if you all weren't here."

The girls gave her a group hug that felt like pure sunshine.

"Let's get all this crap out of here and find you something amazing to wear tonight," Salty said.

"Wait, we don't love this?" Azucar said, holding up the blouse. They erupted in a fit of giggles. Pepper realized that the true gift she'd received was their friendship.

INSTEAD OF DEALING with the awkwardness of Nico picking her up, he sent a car, which, to be honest, was also pretty embarrassing. Since they were on the cusp of winter break, it seemed like no one had anything better to do than gather in the entry as she descended the stairs.

"You look so pretty," Chutney gushed.

"Thanks," Pepper said, looking down. Salty managed to talk her into her pale pink tutu skirt that flared over her hips and ended below her knees. Pepper had felt slightly ridiculous when she'd put it on. Azucar insisted they pair the ultra-feminine skirt with her vintage Guns 'N Roses band T-shirt and a jean jacket. Thankfully, she and Ginger wore the same shoe size, and Pepper didn't have to wear her boots—which were the fanciest shoes she owned. Instead, she borrowed a cute but not ridiculous pair of shimmering pink heels that weren't too high to walk in.

Then, there was the fight over her hair and makeup. Pepper insisted her hair be kept as close to its natural texture as possible. Salty acquiesced a little begrudgingly and gave her a sleek blowout while Ginger did her makeup. It really did take a village, or in this case, three best friends, to get her ready. While she wasn't convinced this date was a big deal, the girls assured her that all signs pointed to yes.

"Where's lunch meat going?" Cherry asked, walking up from the basement.

"Date with *Il Principe* in Carmel," Ginger answered smugly.

Pepper wished she hadn't. All the girls at school enjoyed taking sides in their feud, but Pepper found it all tiresome. The fact that she and Cherry hadn't been on good terms since the bonfire only added fuel to the inferno. Still, Pepper didn't want to give Cherry more reasons to hate her. Besides, she had better things to think about than Cherry. Surprisingly, instead of saying something nasty, Cherry turned an alarming shade of red and marched upstairs.

The driver honked, and Pepper rushed outside. The same black SUV that had brought them home from the soccer game weeks ago was waiting on the stone driveway. The driver stepped out of the vehicle. This one was much scarier than Salty's driver, Vito. He looked the part of a mafia hitman. She walked unsteadily toward the car as he opened the rear passenger door.

"Thank you," she said and climbed inside.

Pepper stepped on the hem of the skirt and pitched forward, landing in a heap on the closest bucket seat. She twisted around and fastened the seatbelt over the pink poof in her lap. *How did I ever let Salty convince me to wear this?* Pepper gathered a section of her hair and ran her fingers over it, repeatedly smoothing the strands. A few moments later, they pulled up in front of Don's, where Nico was waiting. Pepper stopped fidgeting, unsure if she should get out and greet him, open the door, or just sit there. While she was debating, the driver exited the vehicle and opened the opposite rear passenger door. Nico climbed in. He was wearing dark jeans and a suit jacket over a T-shirt. A wave of intoxicating aftershave followed.

"Hey," he said.

"Hey…" She shifted uncomfortably, feeling overdressed and a bit silly in her tutu. The silence ballooned between them, filling the space. "Thanks for sending the car to get me. I don't think Ms. Oscura would have been okay with my asking to use the van since so many girls are going to the airport tonight."

His shoulder twitched, and his head tilted slightly. "It's nothing."

She wondered if that was true. Using their family's resources probably was nothing to him and Coco.

"What's that?" he asked, pointing at the bag she held between her knees. "A Christmas present for me?"

Her eyes opened wide. Shoot, should she have gotten him something? "Uh, not unless you like ladies' wallets. I got the wrong one, and I need to return it. There's a shop in Carmel. If that doesn't screw up your plans too much."

"Of course not," he said. "What's the store?"

Pepper opened the wallet to read the brand. "Winfield."

Nico tapped the driver on the shoulder and told him to stop at Winfield's before dinner.

"You look nice," he said. "Very…fluffy."

She ran her hand over her sleek hair and realized he was talking about the skirt puffed up around the seatbelt's constraints. "Thanks. Salty, let me borrow it. Actually, she practically pulled it on over my head and insisted."

They sat in silence as the scenery whooshed past. Why was it so hard to talk to him? Their conversations on the beach were effortless. "You smell good."

"Aqua de Nico." He winked.

"You're sassing me, aren't you?"

"Sassing?"

"It's something my Granny used to say. Sass is like a way to tease someone or to be really disrespectful, but if you knew my Granny, you wouldn't even attempt disrespecting her."

He chuckled. "I'm not sassing you. That's really what it's called."

"It's cool you found a cologne with your name on it," she replied. "I've never seen my name on anything."

"What? It's on every dinner table, restaurant, and every grocery store."

"Ha-ha. Not that name. My real name."

"Which is…?" he asked, leaning as close as his seatbelt would allow.

"Not telling," she replied, giving him a sweet smile.

The car rolled to a stop in front of a shop Pepper realized must be Winfield's.

"I'll be right back," she said, hopping out.

If affluence had a smell, it would smell like this place. The moment she stepped inside, heels echoing against the glossy tile floor, it was obvious she did not belong. But Azucar was right. Why not try to get something good from what Margaux sent in the holiday horror box? Pepper strode up to the cash register and waited. Three sales associates were a few feet away, chatting. She knew they saw her. Heck, she was the only person in the store. But she waited for what felt like forever before they acknowledged her presence. She could feel the eyes of the sales associates on her as she removed the wallet from the bag and set it on the counter. A moment later, a man walked up.

"Is there something I can do for you?" he asked.

"Yeah, I'm returning this."

He looked down at the black snakeskin item and sneered. "I would need your receipt."

"It was a gift," Pepper replied.

The man harrumphed and pushed the wallet across the counter.

"It still has the tag from your store," Pepper said, opening the front flap and pulling it free. "See?"

The man made no move to take it from her. "Yes, but it is quite a few seasons old, and without a gift receipt, we can't guarantee that you did not…" he drifted off.

Pepper played with the zipper tab as heat flooded her face. This guy was clearly not going to offer to return the wallet. She hung her head, resigned to keeping the awful gift.

"That she didn't what?" Nico said from behind her.

Pepper spun around.

"Winfield's return policy states that all returns shall cheerfully be accepted with or without a receipt," he read from his phone.

"Yes, that is…corr…correct, Mr. Rossetti," the man stammered.

"Then what is the issue?" Pepper asked, her resolve returning as she turned to face the sales associate.

"Uh…not a thing," the man replied, glancing occasionally at the door. Their intimidating driver had just stepped inside and was waiting by the door. "I'm afraid all I can offer you is store credit," he said.

"Is that acceptable?" Nico asked her.

"Sure. Whatever," she agreed, secretly disappointed not to receive a wad of cash. What was she going to do with store credit here? After this experience, she never wanted to step foot inside this place again.

"Very good, Miss," the salesman said, reaching for the wallet. A few beeps and keystrokes later, he presented her with a gift card for eighty-seven dollars and sixteen cents. Thank you for shopping at Winfield's, Mr. Rossetti, Miss." The sales associate nodded at them.

"Thank you," Pepper said, tucking the card into her jacket pocket.

"Would you like to shop or head to dinner?" Nico asked.

"Are you for real? What dude wants to shop?" Pepper said.

"I have a twin sister. I've done this a lot," he gestured to the store. "Besides, I enjoy spending time with you."

A lightness filled her chest, dissipating the earlier embarrassment. Pepper didn't know what she wanted in a store like this. It was the kind of place where Margaux shopped. She'd never allowed herself to fantasize about owning things that were this beautiful. There were racks of luxurious throws, pillows, and tables overflowing with soft sweaters. She flicked the price tag on a camisole and almost gasped. It was a hundred dollars. What would her eighty-seven dollars buy in a place like this? Likely nothing. Too embarrassed to paw through the clearance rack with Nico standing by, she sighed and turned to him.

"I guess I'm not in the mood to shop," she said, stopping to run her hand over a faux fur throw draped along the back of a low sofa. "Let's go to dinner. I'm hungry anyway."

"Whatever you want," he replied, holding the door open for her.

As they stepped outside, Pepper realized that the smell of money from the store was clinging to her hair. She couldn't stand another moment and asked if dinner was close enough to walk. Nico nodded, told the driver to meet them at the restaurant, and held his arm out to her. It was such an old-fashioned gesture, like something he might have seen in an old movie, that she couldn't help but smile. Pepper slipped her arm through his, and they began to stroll down the street. It was awkward initially, as they were out of step, and her hip kept bumping against him. A gust of frigid wind sent chill bumps up her arm, and rather than remove her hold on Nico, she pulled him in, tucking his arm against her side. Suddenly, they were walking in unison, pressed together in a cozy bubble.

"Thanks for coming to my rescue back there, but I did have it under control."

"Of course you did," he replied.

She couldn't tell if he was being sincere or patronizing. "And I did not steal that wallet. It was a crappy gift from my stepmother."

"I believe you. Don't let that salesjerk make you feel bad. They can't even afford the stuff they sell, but they love making others feel inferior."

As they strolled down the street, Pepper noticed the spotless sidewalks and beautifully decorated window displays. Lights were strung from the eaves of several buildings, giving the town an otherworldly quality, like it existed out of time.

"Carmel is a pretty ritzy place, huh?" Pepper said, glancing in the windows of the art galleries and jewelry shops they passed.

"You don't like it," Nico said, notes of disappointment in his voice.

"I love it. It's adorable and quaint, like a village from a fairy tale. It's just not what I expected after seeing Monterey."

Nico nodded. "Yeah, they're like distant family members. One is sophisticated, the other is…more laid back."

"That's a diplomatic way of saying poor," Pepper replied.

He chuckled. "I wouldn't call Monterey poor."

"I guess not," she replied. "They're similar but also very different. I'm glad we live right between them. It's the best of both worlds."

Nico stopped in front of a fancy French restaurant. Pepper stepped forward, reaching for the door, but Nico turned down a dark adjacent ally.

"This way." He grinned, beckoning her onward.

"We aren't going in there?" she asked, following him down the brick-lined passageway.

"Nope. Someplace better."

When they were halfway through the alley, twinkle lights blinked on overhead. Pepper gasped. Nico turned and held his hand out to her. It was warm and comforting. Her imagination was concocting wild scenarios, from a waiting helicopter to an intimate candlelit dinner for two, ala *Lady and the Tramp*. They stepped through an archway into a charming courtyard open to the twilight sky. Strings of bistro lights crisscrossed over a small, deserted ice rink.

"Is this where we are going?"

"Were you expecting something…different?" he asked, running his hand through his hair.

"Yes, but not something so perfect," she replied. "Can we go skating?"

"Of course. I rented it for us for an hour unless you're too hungry?"

"I'm too excited to be hungry," she said, grasping his hand and pulling him to the rink entrance.

The attendant handed them ice skates and directed them to low benches. Pepper was grateful she had taken Ginger's advice and put on tights. At least she didn't have to worry about putting her bare feet into community skates. She pulled the laces tight, then tucked Ginger's heels under the bench.

"I have a confession," Nico said, looking up at her. "I've never done this before."

Pepper tried to keep the surprise from registering on her face. "You're an athlete. It'll be easy," she said.

"I'm an athlete on grass or dirt, not ice."

"Then why did you organize all this?" she asked, grasping his hands to pull him up.

"I thought you'd enjoy it," he replied. "And I sort of thought maybe I'd just watch you skate."

"Nice try." She pulled him up. He wobbled on the blades but stayed standing. "That's a good first step." She led him to the opening. Nico gripped the railing tightly, knuckles white.

"Watch me," she said, stepping onto the ice. It was true that she hadn't been skating since she'd been a kid in Denver, but some skills never left. The surface was slick, and it took her a few moments to find her rhythm. Pepper glided across the ice, crisscrossing her feet as she went.

"Yep, watching you is much more fun," Nico said, attempting to turn around and sit down.

"Not a chance," Pepper said, grasping his arm.

"What if I eat it?"

"There's no one around to see," she said gently. "Trust me."

Pepper held out her hands. A moment later, Nico grasped them and took one step onto the ice. His skate teetered, and he looked at her skeptically.

"You can't skate with one foot on the platform. It also works best when you keep moving."

He placed his other foot onto the ice and grew wide-eyed as he wobbled. Pepper pushed off, slowly pulling Nico forward, encouraging him to move his feet from side to side. She watched as he tested the new movements, a look of determination on his face. In a few moments, they were doing unsteady laps around the rink, and Pepper had taken her place beside him, no longer needing to pull him across the ice. For the first time, she noticed the holiday music swirling around them like snowfall.

"I think I've got it," he said.

"You are doing so great."

"This is kind of fun." He looked at her, grinning with pride. They held hands and circled the tiny rink. Nico tugged on her. Thinking he was about to fall, Pepper turned sharply to catch him, but instead, they ran into one another.

"Whoops, sorry," she said, grasping his arms to steady herself.

"It looks like we stopped in an interesting spot," he said.

Above them hung a twig of mistletoe. Pepper's breath grew shallow. The world slowed, or maybe the music just changed tempo. Nothing was in focus but the two of them. His cologne mingled intoxicatingly with the chocolate aroma from the nearby hot cocoa stand.

"Dance with me?" he asked.

"Um...do you think that's a good idea?"

"I think I can handle it."

Pepper wasn't so sure, but his version of ice dancing really just consisted of wrapping their arms around one another and swaying to the music, which was fine by her. As the song finished, Nico pulled her in closer and attempted to lean her into a dip, but his skate slipped, and he fell back, taking her down on top of him. They landed with a loud crack that echoed around the rink.

"Are you hurt?" she asked. "Did you hit your head?"

"Ugh, my phone," he said. "It's in my back pocket."

Pepper exhaled, relieved. "Phew, I thought I broke the soccer star. Coach would have killed me."

"Well, the season's over," he said, tightening his grip around her waist.

"I told you stopping was worse than skating. You always fall when standing still on the ice," she said. With her panic dissipated, Pepper realized their compromising position and attempted to roll off him, but Nico kept her in a tight embrace. She placed her hands on his chest and lifted herself slightly. "Aren't you uncomfortable?" she said.

"Not even a little," he replied.

"Cold?" she asked, thinking of the ice he was lying against. Nico shook his head. Truthfully, Pepper wasn't either. His eyes were pools of dark chocolate with little dots of white reflecting the lights overhead, like marshmallows bobbing in a cup of hot cocoa.

"Time's up, guys," the rink attendant said. "I need to get the mini-Zamboni out here to clean up the ice before tonight's sessions."

With measured movements, Pepper stood, then reached down to help Nico, who was on all fours and looking like he might crawl to the exit. Eventually, he took her hand and was upright in moments. She was about to push off when he called her name. She turned back, realizing they were still holding hands.

"Tradition," he said, gesturing to the white berries overhead.

She hoped he meant a mistletoe kiss, not some obscure tradition she didn't know. Pepper skated forward, anticipating what it would feel like to be in his arms and feel his lips against hers. She'd imagined this moment a thousand times but never allowed herself to hope it might come true.

As the twinkle lights shimmered above, like stars, their eyes locked. Then Nico's warm hands cupped her chilled face. It felt like they were moving in slow motion, probably because he was trying not to lose his balance, but she loved every measured movement. She wanted this to last forever. They were almost the same height, but Pepper closed her eyes and tipped her face to meet his. Then she waited, but instead of feeling his warmth pressed against her, Nico stopped just a breath away. He was so close...and yet felt so far. Pepper closed the distance between them, unable to endure the temptation a moment longer.

Nico's lips were cold as they brushed against hers, but they were also soft and inviting. He was restrained and respectful. She adored each of his sweet, playful kisses but wondered if the heat building inside of her was reciprocated. When they broke apart for an instant to pull in a quick breath, he slid one hand behind her neck, the other around her waist, and pressed her against his solid frame. They slid back at his quick motion but stayed upright. Pepper tangled her fingers in his curls, keeping him close, then nipped a little bite on his bottom lip. She felt him smile. That was all the encouragement he needed. Nico's earlier restraint melted into a flurry of fiery kisses, each more intense than the last. As things heated, Pepper felt her knees give out, and her skates slip. She clutched Nico's coat, but he had a firm grasp around her waist.

"I've got you," he whispered before teasing her with another kiss that left her wishing their skating session could go on forever. Just then, the rink attendant eased the mini-Zamboni onto the ice and was bearing down on them. Nico placed one more sweet kiss on her lips before they stepped off the ice together.

THE LIGHT from under the cupola door spilled into the dark stairwell. Pepper knew the girls were waiting up to get the details, but she wanted to keep tonight all to herself. Instead of going inside, she quietly backed down the stairs to use the bathroom. By the time she returned, their curtains were drawn. Pepper switched off the light and crawled into bed.

"How was it?" Salty whispered in the dark.

"Really fun," Pepper admitted.

Salty squealed with delight. "You guys are so cute together! I'm so happy."

"It was one date. Keep it in perspective," Pepper replied, maintaining her detached facade.

"Every love story starts with a first date," Salty whispered.

A warm glow of hope Pepper was unaccustomed to feeling blossomed in the pit of her stomach. Maybe she thought…maybe.

# Chapter Twenty-Three

The winter sun blazed overhead, not nearly as intense as it had in the previous months, but strong enough to heat the top of Pepper's uncovered head. She ran her fingers through the long strands, noting the still damp sections, then she reclined in the patio chair and drew her knees up to her chest. Being so far out on the bluff meant sunny days had been few and far between, which she didn't mind. The gray mist created an atmosphere that matched her melancholy mood. However, since they'd been blessed with a rare blue-sky day on Christmas Eve, she decided to soak up what brightness she could and sat in the courtyard with the novel Ginger had let her borrow. Well, more like insisted she read. It wasn't exactly her style, but her mind had been so preoccupied with secret passageways and hidden clues that a straightforward love story was a nice departure from her racing thoughts.

Pepper pulled the bonfire beach blanket over her legs. It still held the faint aroma of motor oil. She smiled at the memory it sparked. The wind was still sharp and biting, an ever-present reminder that it was winter. Pepper wrinkled her nose as the earthy scent of manure wafted toward her on the breeze. *Ugh, hadn't that dissipated yet?* They'd been keeping their windows closed for months. During the second week of school, workers arrived and began transforming the courtyard by pruning out the dead and overgrown plants. After a while, she could appreciate the size and scope of the entire space and had begun to imagine lunches outside on the rusty patio furniture or on blankets on the chipped tiled patio once spring arrived.

The last step had been dumping what smelled like tons of manure over the dry, dusty earth and seeding it with grass. Strange time of year to be gardening, she'd thought, but as Pepper looked out onto the lawn, long, delicate shoots of bright green danced in the breeze. Perhaps they would be able to utilize this space in a few months. She returned her attention to the novel. It had been a wonderfully lazy day, and there hadn't been many of them recently. A trip to experience midnight mass at the Carmel Mission was set for this evening. Pepper decided a nap in the sunshine would be the perfect antidote to stay awake later and snuggled into the sun-warmed blanket, quickly drifting off to sleep.

THAT EVENING, they pulled into a full gravel parking lot in front of a low, walled property. Mario asked Ms. Oscura to save him a seat while he found a place to park the van. Pepper followed Ms. Oscura and the other girls staying at the school over the holidays through an arched gate into the open courtyard of the mission. The lights went out as they arrived, and it was difficult to decipher how many people were there in the darkness. Then, almost as if by magic, a spark appeared, hovering at the far end of the courtyard. Olive bumped Pepper's arm and pressed a candle into her hand. Soon, light after light began appearing out of the darkness, creating a sea of dancing flames. One strong voice began singing *It Came Upon A Midnight Clear*. After a moment, they all joined in. The voices of everyone in the courtyard, combined in harmony, made Pepper feel a deep sense of belonging as she looked at the illuminated faces of Ms. Oscura and her fellow students.

As the song finished, the bells chimed, resonating through the frigid air. Silently, everyone assembled and filed into the church. The courtyard dimmed as the processional moved inside. They were at the back of the group, and Pepper loved how the light followed them, constant and comforting. The church was illuminated only by candlelight, not just by the parishioners, but by a display surrounding the altar and creche. They stepped into an empty pew as the organ sounded. The church patrons were silent as metal scraping against metal echoed from behind. Pepper turned around. Mario rushed up the aisle just ahead of a young man waving a canister suspended by a long chain. Smoke was billowing from the container as he slowly walked along the center aisle toward the front of the church. She was alarmed at first, but no one else seemed concerned. Then, as the altar server passed, a sweet, earthy scent followed, and she realized that the metal device contained incense. Ms. Oscura passed her a hymnal as the music started up again. Pepper was transfixed as the smoke swirled high into the air, seeming to dance with the notes from the organ.

SOMETIME IN THE EARLY MORNING, the van lumbered along the twisting seafront road back to Valentina's. There was a palpable Christmas magic in the air. Being with her classmates, experiencing the processional tonight, and singing carols had been unexpectedly uplifting. There were no expectations, at least not for her. It had all been an enchanting surprise.

"I'm hungry," Olive whined from the back row of the van.

"Me too," Chutney added.

"Why didn't we stop for a snack?" Pepper asked.

"Because you've been asleep for most of the ride," Ms. Oscura replied.

"I'm wide awake now and hungry, too," Apple said.

"Can I make everyone a midnight snack of…cookies, maybe?" Pepper asked.

The headmistress sighed and turned around in the passenger seat to look at the girls.

"Since it is Christmas, you have my permission, but be sure to clean everything, or Signore Tonelli will have a fit at the start of the next term."

"Then he'll never let us cook anything again," Olive said.

The girls promised to keep the kitchen spotless and thanked Ms. Oscura for her permission. Pepper knew they would have snuck down without it, and she had a feeling Ms. Oscura knew that, too.

THE GIRLS CHANGED into pajamas instead of staying in their fancy church clothes. Pepper, who had not realized they were supposed to dress up for church, nor did she have fancy clothes, went to the kitchen, still dressed in the school uniform, leaving her jacket on the hook in the entryway. She plodded downstairs, feeling along the wall for the light switch. She missed her friends already. A midnight cookie-baking party was just their style. Pepper let herself into the classroom kitchen. The surfaces were spotless, of course. It was eerie being in the cavernous room alone. She wished the others would hurry.

Pepper opened the refrigerator and found an assortment of eggs, butter, and a carton of milk close to its expiration date. She realized she didn't know where the pantry was and opened the nearest cupboard. There were only mixing bowls and other tools inside. Hmm…where would Signore Tonelli keep essentials? She surveyed the room. She'd always wondered what lay behind the doors on either side of the demo kitchen. Pepper tried the handle of the first door. It was locked. Must be his office, she thought. The door to the left, though, was open. It was pitch black. She held up her phone and shone her flashlight inside, discovering a hallway with three more doors leading off it—one directly opposite her and two on either side of the hall.

Pepper flicked on the light switch and stepped inside. She tried the first door; it swung open easily. Inside were floor-to-ceiling open shelves filled with staples. She flipped the door stop down and took a closer look. Industrial tubs of flour and sugar were stacked on the floor while shelves of canned goods, four rows deep, rose to the ceiling. There were shelves filled with cake forms, cooking sheets, baking mats, and state-of-the-art mixers stacked in the corner. She shook her head. They better be able to use this stuff next term.

The other two doors in the hallway intrigued her. Pepper left the pantry door ajar and stepped into the hall. Behind the door opposite the panty was a windowless room with a dusty desk and metal chair pushed into the corner. It appeared to be a long-forgotten office or maybe a detention area. Pepper quickly shut that door, as chill bumps rose on her arms, and headed to the opposite end of the hallway. The handle was stiff, but she managed to twist it. However, when she pushed the door, it stayed closed. Pepper leaned against it with her shoulder and shoved. Slowly, it creaked open, scraping against the floor and eventually stopping halfway. Pepper felt alongside the inner wall, but there wasn't a light switch. She held up her phone, switched on the flashlight, and gasped.

# Chapter Twenty-Four

Pepper couldn't take her eyes off what she had just discovered: a room full of filing cabinets. This had to be the school's archives!

"Hey, you in here, Pepper?" someone called from the kitchen.

She quickly pulled the door closed and raced back to the pantry. "In here," she yelled. "Help me get some of this stuff."

Olive appeared a moment later. "Look what you found!"

"Maybe someday Signore Tonelli will let us use some of it."

"Well, we are tonight," Chili said from the doorway. "Are there cookie cutters in there?"

"Probably. Take a look," Pepper said, heaving the tub of flour off the shelf and scooting it across the floor.

"What are we gonna make?"

"How about the always enjoyable gingerbread cookie?"

"Hmm...I didn't see any molasses in there," Pepper said. "What about sugar cookies with frosting?"

"How about snowflake cookies with powdered sugar on top?" Olive said.

"No icing?" Chili replied.

"We get to eat them sooner if we dust sugar on top," Olive said.

"Deal! I am starved," Chili answered.

"Wait. Before we start, we need the proper holiday atmosphere," Chutney said, switching on the monitor behind the demo station.

"Uh, can you work that thing?" Chili asked, gathering mixing bowls from the cupboard.

"She's got it covered," Pepper replied, walking past. She and Chili scoured the pantry until they found a container of cookie cutters. Luckily, an assignment in the past must have been winter cookies because there were a ton of snowflake-shaped cookie cutters. Pepper instructed the girls on what ingredients they needed. By the time they had everything set up, Chutney had managed to get the monitor working and stream a classic holiday movie from her device.

"Ah, I love this movie," Olive shouted.

"I knew all the words when I was a kid," Chutney said.

"The best way to spread Christmas cheer is singing loud for all to hear," they recited in unison.

"Did you guys ever notice that Buddy's list of things he's gonna do with his dad is like the perfect winter date?" Apple said.

"Yeah," Chutney replied. "Ice skating, eating cookie dough, uh...."

"Making snow angels," Olive added.

"Do you ever miss snow?" Pepper asked as she measured the flour. "It's beautiful here, and I wouldn't trade tonight for anything, but it doesn't feel like Christmas without snow."

"I thought you were from Orange County," Apple said.

"Yeah, but I grew up in Denver. Each December, my Nonnu would put lights on the house, and Granny would bake cookies. Then we'd drink cocoa and watch the snow fall while listening to Christmas carols. I guess I miss them," Pepper said.

"I hear that," Chili said. It's not the holidays without snow." Then, with a mischievous gleam in her eye, she took a handful of flour and threw it at Pepper. It hit her right in the face. Pepper sputtered and coughed, sending clouds of white into the air. Then she grabbed a fist of confectioner's sugar and threw it across the island. But being lighter than flour, the sugar separated and drifted over everything.

"There, it's snowing, now cut it out, you two," Olive said. "I don't want to be cleaning this up till dawn."

It did look like snow. Laughing, Pepper and Chili agreed to a truce and continued the cookie-making process. Soon, they had a neat assembly line going, and in minutes, their snowflake cookies were in the oven. They wiped up the remains of their earlier flour and sugar fight, then settled in to watch the film while their cookies were baking.

As the minutes passed, the scent of vanilla filled the kitchen, making Pepper's mouth water. She yawned and checked the time —one more minute to go. The other girls seemed to be wilting as well.

*Ding.* The timer sounded, and they jumped up, ready to inspect their confections. They were golden brown perfection. Olive slid the cookies out of the oven and placed them on the stovetop, where Chutney scooped them onto cooling racks.

"These look so good I want to eat one right now," Chili said.

"We sure made a lot," Chutney exclaimed, looking over the dozens of cookies. "I don't know about you, but I'm so sleepy that I can probably only eat one tonight."

"What if we wrapped up what we don't want and gift them to the other girls tomorrow morning."

"You mean this morning?" Olive said.

"Right, in a couple of hours," Pepper replied.

"It's a great idea. Besides, Christmas is about sharing." Chutney said.

When the cookies were cooled, they dusted them with confectioner's sugar. They looked perfect and tasted delicious, but Olive had been right. It was far too late to indulge in sweets. They all sampled their creations and then decided to head to bed. Pepper volunteered to finish cleaning up. She could tell the others were getting drowsier by the minute, plus she needed them out of the way to get back into that file room.

"No, really, go on ahead. I don't mind one bit," Pepper said. "Think of it as my Christmas present to you."

"You are the sweetest. Thanks, Pepper," Chili said.

"Merry Christmas," Olive said as she left the kitchen.

"Same to you guys," she called after them.

What the girls didn't realize was that behind what looked like a cabinet was a dishwasher. Signore Tonelli was sure sneaky. When the door swung closed, Pepper swiftly loaded the machine and switched it on, eager to get into the archives. As the dishwasher hummed to life, Pepper ran a wet cloth along the counter, grabbed a plate of snowflake cookies, and headed for the back room.

The contrast in temperature from the warm kitchen to the damp inner archive room was jarring. Pepper shivered as she stepped inside, wishing she hadn't left her jacket upstairs. Using the phone flashlight, which was almost out of battery, she located a light switch. It flickered on, and then one of the two bulbs flashed and went dark. Of course, she thought, considering it might be wise to come back tomorrow when that slim window would at least give some light. But Pepper was anxious to find any shred of family connection. After all, she'd spent weeks searching for this place. She wanted to start at least exploring. Pepper slid open the first drawer, wincing when it made an ear-splitting screech. She stopped, hoping the sound wouldn't carry, then pulled out the first file to check the drawer's contents.

"Please let everything be in alphabetical order," she whispered, opening the folder.

There was just a bunch of yellowed bits of paper. Old newspaper clippings, she realized. Pepper searched for dates, but only the articles had been cut out of the paper. Discouraged, she flipped through the clippings. They were all about someone named Carmina Sangiovese. Apparently, she was a famous nightclub singer when she left Valentina's. From the hazy black and white picture alongside the articles, Pepper guessed these were from the nineteen-thirties, but it was tough to be sure. She put the file back and reached for the next one. It also contained newspaper clippings with no dates attached. Was that on purpose?

Pepper surveyed the room. A dozen filing cabinets and even more boxes piled on top of them. Maybe she should come back later when she wasn't so tired. But she knew she'd never be able to sleep if she didn't at least check a few more. Since this drawer seemed to contain nothing but old newspaper articles, she moved on to the next filing cabinet. If this school had been in use since the mid-nineteen thirties, maybe each cabinet was for a separate decade. She moved down to the sixth cabinet. If she were correct, then this one would contain the records from the nineteen nineties. She didn't know her grandmother's exact age, but she counted back by twenties from her birthdate and figured it was as good a place as any to start looking. Thankfully, this drawer slid open noiselessly. Unlike the first drawer, this contained files with neatly typed tags affixed to the tab. They were alphabetized by last name, followed by an initial—presumably, the student's first name.

Pepper popped a cookie into her mouth, pulled a file from the drawer, and combed through the pages. These records were more of what she had expected to find in school archives. It contained the entrance exam scores, transcripts, and other noteworthy school-related paraphernalia. It was also from nineteen ninety-two.

Pepper slid the file back where she found it and began reading the tabs, hoping they led to a clue. Not knowing her grandmother's last name, she searched for a T or V following the surname. The first drawer had no promising name combinations, so she dropped down to the next drawer. Again, there was nothing. Pepper pulled a box over and sat down, sliding the third drawer open. The alphabetical order began again. She pulled the first file free. It contained a class photo. All the girls were lined up in front of the school on the stone steps. The building looked about the same, maybe in slightly better condition. That was a new class,

Pepper realized. She scanned the faces. One girl in the back row caught her eye, but she couldn't be sure if that was Granny. Plus, the image was old and cracked, so it was tough to see the details.

She returned her attention to the files. As her fingers touched each tab, Pepper whispered the surnames.

"Angelo, Avinari, Battaglia, Bianchi, Carbone, Candella." She paused.

Had her father's family gone here too? Pepper folded back the yellowed page, revealing an acceptance letter for Carlotta Candella. Was this her paternal grandmother? Pepper flipped through the file, looking for a photo, before she realized that Candella would have been her grandmother's married name. Disappointed, she slipped the file back in place and continued her search: Caputo, Castellano. Wait, was that a V? Yes, Castellano, V. She extracted the bulging folder and brought it to her lap. Then she shoved another cookie into her mouth and opened the file.

# Chapter Twenty-Five

There was a snapshot paper clipped to the front of the manilla folder. A yearly school photo, perhaps. Pepper gasped, sending a piece of cookie to the back of her throat, which caused a coughing fit. Although not a carbon copy of herself or images she'd seen of her mother, there were undeniable family traits. The arched eyebrows, the almond-shaped eyes, even the same long straight caramel-colored hair. This was, without a doubt, her grandmother. Transfixed by the image of this young and vibrant woman, Pepper marveled at the stark contrast between it and the grandmother she knew.

With her unlined face, bright, carefree smile, and mischievous sparkle in her eyes, this young woman was ready for the world. Compared to the careful and often worried grandmother she had known, this person was a stranger. Pepper reluctantly tore her eyes from the photo and began searching the documents for answers.

Transcripts from her time at school showed Valentina Castellano was a diligent student. Pepper marveled at the variety of courses they had offered back then: pottery, painting, music, and more, alongside the core classes Pepper was currently taking. This, of course, was not the information Pepper truly cared about. She flipped the page. A handwritten note from Ms. Powell had been tucked in with a detention slip. Wow, the etiquette teacher really had been here forever. Pepper tried to make out the curvy, looping letters in her handwriting. Since she typed almost all her communications, reading cursive was especially difficult. It's almost like it was in code. From what she could decipher, Granny had talked back in class. Pepper smiled, thinking about her detention weeks ago. Behind that was an immunization card. Pretty boring stuff. Was this all that was in the often-threatened permanent record?

The box she was perched on suddenly split open, sending herself, the file, and countless documents spilling across the hard concrete floor. It was like the school didn't want her to know her family's secrets. Pepper picked herself up and began sorting through the loose pages. There were typed pages, handwritten notes, newspaper clippings, and photographs, all mixed together. Ugh. It would take her until sunrise to finish reorganizing all of this. She considered leaving the mess for another day. She reasoned that it wasn't like anyone ever came down here when something caught her eye.

It was a photograph of a wedding party. She crawled over the files across the floor to pick it up. Not only was it a wedding portrait, but it was also her grandparents' wedding portrait. She quickly scooped up the rest of her grandmother's file and headed to the kitchen. She needed to spread everything out on a table and go through it piece by piece. Plus, she was exhausted, and a chair to sit in and maybe a mug of hot cocoa would help keep her alert.

WITH A FULL PLATE of cookies and a steaming mug of chocolate, Pepper settled in to make sense of the photograph. Nonnu looked so young and handsome. And Granny, she was a sophisticated beauty. There were six bridesmaids and seven groomsmen on either side of the happy couple, along with people she assumed were the bride and groom's parents. It was strange to see images of people she did not know, but she wouldn't exist without them. She stared at the smiling faces of the bridesmaids in their matching, floor-length sage green satin dresses. Granny wore a cascading, beaded princess dress. It was another era entirely. She'd never daydreamed about her own fairytale wedding. Maybe it was because there weren't pictures like this to pour over with her mother. Pepper turned the image over. Someone had taped a newspaper notice to the back. It read: Miss Castellano, daughter of the famed Castellano clan and recent Valentina graduate, marries Don graduate and up-and-comer Vincenzo D'Angelo of the Red Hook D'Angelo's. Red Hook? Pepper scribbled the words on the inside of the file. She'd have to look it up. It sounded ominous.

The article went on to describe the ceremony and the attendants. She didn't recognize any names until she reached the wedding party. Wait, did she read that correctly? The Maid of Honor was the bride's cousin, Ms. Fiorella Oscura. Wait. Valentina and Oscura? Was this all a curious coincidence, or did these names have significance? Oscura is the last name of the current headmistress. Valentina was my grandmother's name and the middle name of the past headmistress. It's also my middle name. Pepper dropped the photograph.

"Am I related to the school? I mean the founders," she thought aloud, flipping the photograph over and staring hard at the young woman beside Granny. There was an undeniable family resemblance. Pepper wondered if the woman was still alive and if Granny had any more living relatives. She set aside the photo and combed through the rest of the folder.

BRIGHT MORNING LIGHT streamed in through the high windows. Pepper blinked; her tired eyes were crusted with sleep. She was face down on the stainless steel work table, having fallen asleep at some point that morning. By the crick in her neck, Pepper surmised she'd been in this position for a few hours. There was a polite cough, and Pepper sat up too quickly and grasped her neck, massaging the stiffness away.

"You are a liar," Pepper said, looking up.

Ms. Oscura regarded her with a serene expression still on her face. "May I join you?"

Pepper nodded.

"My middle name is Valentina, like the past headmistress. I thought it might be a coincidence until I remembered that my grandma was called Tina. So I decided to go looking and found my grandmother's file," she said, pushing the open folder across the table. "Not only am I a legacy, but I'm part of the Valentina dynasty."

"And how did you discover this?" Ms. Oscura asked, her right eyebrow arched.

"Clues from my birth certificate led me to my grandmother's school records."

Pepper knew she'd shown her hand too soon from the cool nod she received. Now, the headmistress knew she had broken into her office. Still, that betrayal, which could get her expelled, paled in comparison to keeping a secret of this magnitude from a blood relative.

The headmistress looked down at the newspaper clippings and the wedding photograph, then back at Pepper. "Yes. It would appear you are indeed part of the Valentina dynasty," Ms. Oscura said.

"Why didn't you tell me?"

"I was as unaware as yourself."

"Right, cut the act," Pepper demanded.

"Truly, I had no idea who your grandmother was. At one time, it was customary to go through a student's familial history before their admittance. You, of course, have been on our roster practically since birth. Presumably, my aunt verified your pedigree. As I mentioned earlier, she did not leave a tidy office. I've been sorting through her documents since last May, when she passed. Once term began, I had to decide to focus on my duties and responsibilities to the incoming class. After all, it's not where you come from that will determine your success here, but what you can do with your natural talents."

"But why has all this been kept from me?" she yelled, eyes brimming with tears. "It's like no one wants me to know where I come from, and I can't figure out why."

Ms. Oscura reached across the table and patted Pepper's hand. It was the most human show of affection she'd seen the headmistress express. "I can't begin to understand what you must be feeling. But if those who care about you think it is best to shield—"

"No!" roared Pepper. "No more protecting me from the unseen forces. Nonnu sent me here to find out who I am. Maybe he meant for me to simply find a husband in the world of organized crime, but that's not good enough for me. Not knowing makes me feel untethered. Each clue I discover is like grasping at a blade of grass to keep me from floating away. I want roots. And I'm going to find them."

"Very well. As I said, I don't have any information to give you, but you may continue searching the archives for your relations. After you clean up the mess in there, of course."

"Thank you, headmistress, or should I call you cousin?"

Ms. Oscura gave her a sharp look that caused Pepper to shrink back. "As for your punishment for breaking into my office," She paused. Pepper's heart hammered in her chest. "You will serve a month of detentions with Marco cleaning the grounds every Saturday and Sunday morning."

Pepper almost groaned but stopped herself. It could have been much worse.

"Never admit to anything outright without proof. I suspected it was you, but there was no way to say for sure. You did a good job hiding your tracks. Let this be a lesson. Never admit to wrongdoing unless, of course, it is dire."

"Thank you."

"Pepper, never break into my office again, understood?"

"Yes, ma'am."

"Now, why don't you leave all this for today and enjoy your Christmas. Cook has prepared a sumptuous holiday feast. You must be tired from sitting up all night."

Pepper stood but hesitated, looking between the headmistress and the folder.

"You may take the file to review, but do not mention it to anyone. It is strictly against protocol to allow students to review other students' files, even archived files."

For a family reunion of sorts, it was underwhelming. Pepper hoped to be regaled with stories of their relations, but she had to be satisfied with not getting expelled. Truthfully, she didn't know what she'd have done. This place felt like home now.

Ms. Oscura waited for her to collect all the papers into the folder, then switched off the light before the two exited the kitchen.

"Do you know anything about my grandmother?" Pepper asked. "Valentina Castellano?"

"Castellano…hmmm, come to think of it, I do. If she's who I'm thinking of, your grandmother was slated to take over as headmistress of our school but didn't for some reason. I believe that's when the line shifted from Castellanos to Oscuras. My great-aunt Sophia took over instead. I'm not sure why your grandmother didn't join us. Usually, the Valentines are groomed to take over the role of headmistress, but it's like she just disappeared."

"Am I…being prepared?" Pepper asked as they reached the top of the stairs.

Ms. Oscura swung the door open and paused. "Would you like to be?"

"I'm not sure," Pepper replied.

"Nothing is set in stone. The outgoing headmistress either appoints a replacement before retiring or names one in her will. It was quite a shock for me, but my career as a sculptor hadn't gone where I'd imagined, so I accepted." Pepper stared at Ms. Oscura, feeling like she was seeing her with fresh eyes. "You have a lot of living left to do before making any decisions regarding lifelong commitments. Come on, before all the hash brown casserole is gone."

Pepper realized she was still dressed in last night's clothes and excused herself to go up to the cupola for a shower and to change. She ran up to the second floor, her mind swimming with information. There was so much to absorb, not in the least was the possible opportunity of being headmistress of this school. True, Ms. Oscura wasn't offering it to her, but it was an opportunity where none had existed before. Where there was opportunity, there was hope.

CHRISTMAS DAY PASSED IN A BLUR. Mainly because Pepper was preoccupied with the contents of her grandmother's file, she knew there was more critical information there. At least, she hoped there was. After breakfast, the six girls used Olive's Christmas gift from her father. He had sent the school a supply of new rackets. They trekked across the lawn to the Don Academy's tennis courts, singing Christmas carols there and back. After dinner, Ms. Oscura let them watch movies in the kitchen since everything was still set up from the night before. The girls dragged pillows and blankets from their rooms downstairs and created a cozy pile to lounge on, eventually falling asleep under the flickering light of the film.

This was the second night Pepper hadn't slept in her bed. When she dragged her things upstairs in the morning, she was astonished to see a massive leather-bound book the size of a dictionary propped up on her pillow. A note slipped out as she dropped the bedding to pick up the book.

PEPPER OPENED THE COVER AND, with a shock, realized it wasn't a bible but a detailed book of Castellano/Oscura family history. The first two pages contained a detailed family tree. She immediately found Granny's name with a line extending to the right connecting to Nonnu and one single line from the two of them to her mother, Giada. Neither Pepper nor her father were listed. She grabbed a pen off her desk, drew a line under her mother, and then added her given name: Stella Valentina D'Angelo. With a satisfied smile, she turned the page, eager to discover her roots.

# Chapter Twenty-Six

P epper spent the rest of winter break in the cupola, a mug of something sweet and hot on the windowsill and the book in her lap. She poured over each page, taking notes as she read. Their family had a fascinating history. Perhaps all families did, but their stories got forgotten and boiled down to banal details of so and so married, lived eighty-four years, and then died. This book was more than a list of dates; it was a treasure trove of stories with exquisite details about their life in Sicily, immigration to America, and the eventual rise and fall of their mafia empire.

There didn't seem to be any rhyme or reason for it to be dubbed "Maria's book," except for the fact that the wives of the mafia Dons had transcribed each story and bit of family lore and history. Pepper couldn't wait to share these stories with Salty. The fact that she'd promised not to hardly registered in her mind. After all, Salty was as much a part of this discovery as she was. Pepper couldn't keep it a secret.

She was especially drawn to the dramatic life story of the "big cheese," Fortunato "Lucky" Castellano, the founder of The Don Academy. She wondered if any rhyme or reason would be revealed for the curious way this house had been designed. Lucky's legacy had been recorded by his wife, Violetta Oscura, or Letti, as she fashionably referred to herself. Lucky's father had been a prohibition-era Don. Dealing in illegal liquor took the family from meager community guardians and transformed them into multimillion-dollar businessmen. Letti, a neighbor of Lucky's, had watched the family's rise to affluence. She mentioned that the best thing about Don Gio, Lucky's father, was his compassion. He didn't cut his ties and leave or neglect his duties as Don when he began pulling in money literally by the barrel but helped the young sons of the community by securing them work, sometimes within his organization. He also gave money to the widows and even donated a large sum to establish St. Joseph's Orphanage, which was where she was about to go when Mama Castellano, Don Gio's wife, took Letti and her younger sister Lorenza in after their mother died of typhoid. She was only fifteen, but it was then that she and Lucky became close and eventually married a year later.

Lucky was the second son, nicknamed Lucky, for overcoming a sickly childhood. His elder brother Giovanni the Second had been groomed to be Don Gio's successor, but he was gunned down in a territory dispute before his twenty-fifth birthday. Lucky was suddenly slated to become Don Gio's successor. There was one problem. Lucky had already begun his chosen career by investing in local restaurants and stores. This, of course, was the key to his ultimate success. When the depression hit America in nineteen twenty-nine, Lucky and his father were well positioned to do what the banks could or would not — lend money. When some borrowers couldn't pay, the Castellano crime family took over their business, which left the family poised to make substantial financial gains once the economy roared back to life, and it did. Lucky wasn't the typical Don or Don-in-training; he wasn't as concerned with running the family and often struggled to fill his father's shoes. In many people's opinions, Gio the Second had been the perfect man to take over, not Lucky. He had never really felt comfortable as the head of the family.

Lucky and Letti preferred to live a glamorous life among Hollywood royalty, regularly traveling between the two coasts to attend parties and invest in the burgeoning film industry. If there was one thing Lucky was adept at finding, it was opportunity. He'd say, "Opportunity doesn't knock. You have to find it and invite it in." Lucky wanted to change his family from wealthy outlaws to the level of elite philanthropists he rubbed elbows with. As far as he could tell, the philanthropes were just as corrupt as the mafia but simply appeared more respectable.

There was just one hiccough during this period of financial prosperity. Lucky, now Don Gio's official understudy, was lured to the docks to settle a dispute between two of their rivals. But it was a setup to frame him for the murder of several city council members blocking the path to clandestine gambling halls the Gambian family was running. It didn't matter that he was innocent. Lucky was immediately whisked away to Monterey to live with a Sicilian family of fishermen as their "son" from the old country for the next several years. During that time, Letti was inconsolable without her husband by her side. While he was away, she gave birth to their second child, a daughter. In fact, he didn't meet his daughter, Valentina Luciana Castellano, until she was four years old.

By that time, the clever Lucky had quietly purchased the bluff where Valentina's and Don's now stood under a dummy corporation. He pitied any young man who had not been fully prepared to meet the demands of being a Don the way he had, and the Don Academy was born. The building that was now Valentina's Academy was their family home, completed just before Lucky's luck ran out, and he was arrested for the murder he had been framed for many years ago. He had been sentenced to life on Alcatraz, which was close enough for regular visits from Letti and his children. As the years progressed, their funds diminished, and Letti decided that the future Dons were not the only ones needing training.

She wrote about her early days as a young mafia bride. When Mama Castellano and Don Gio were alive, she didn't have a care in the world. But once Lucky was sent away, she began to realize that life could change in an instant. From that moment on, she stuck close to her mother-in-law, learning what it took to run a household and much more. Being a mafia wife wasn't simply stirring spaghetti and popping out babies. It was an art, a delicate dance between the Don, the head of the crime family, and his wife, the head of the house. She was also the closest confidant of the Don—at least, that was how it worked in the Castellano family.

Pepper took more notes while reading Letti's pages than almost any other place in the book. There was one other woman who was as fiery and determined as her four times great-grandmother, and that was Fiammetta Castellano, the woman who'd traveled across the Atlantic Ocean on a cattle ship with her two young sons. But her handwriting was cramped and hard to read. So Pepper skipped some of her sections in favor of others since she had a deadline to return the book by January 2nd. But she'd definitely wanted to borrow Maria's book from Ms. Oscura again; that was if she'd let her, or even if she wouldn't. Pepper thought back to her confession about breaking into the headmistress' office and prided herself on not revealing how she had done it. Even though Ms. Oscura scolded her for admitting to the theft, she still had no idea how she'd accomplished such a feat.

THE PASSAGES about her grandmother were sparse and not incredibly satisfying. During that era, Maria's book seemed to have been kept by an aunt who was not too familiar with Valentina Castellano. As Ms. Oscura had mentioned, Valentina Castellano was slated to become the next headmistress of Valentina's finishing and prep school. At that time, there was just one short paragraph noting the change. It stated that Sophia Oscura would be taking the position of headmistress. Then, there were a lot of details about her niece. There had to be other records somewhere. Now that she had her great grandparents' names and the names of her grandmother's siblings, Pepper was in a place to make real progress.

At least within the pages of Maria's book, Pepper had been able to form a connection with her past. It hadn't revealed the motives she had been looking for, but she at least had more information and some great stories. There was one passage Pepper found especially poignant. A saying Lucky Castellano often used:

"When the law is corrupt, there's nothing wrong with being corrupt with the law."

Pepper considered this and found it to be sound logic before inscribing it on the inside cover of her journal.

# Chapter Twenty-Seven

To usher in the new year, Ms. Oscura gave her permission for the girls to light sparklers on the bluff at midnight. They cheered and made resolutions under the inky sky. For the first time in as long as she could remember, Pepper felt hopeful. Maybe Nonnu had known what he was about when he'd signed her up. She began to think that this school really would help her discover her rightful place in the world.

Soon, her quiet cupola sanctuary was filled with boisterous activity once again. Pepper didn't mind. Two weeks of solitude had been enough. She was grateful for the time alone to review Maria's book but was ready to have her roommates back. They returned with luggage bursting with new clothes, shoes, and trinkets. Pepper didn't envy their gifts. She had returned to Winfield's in Carmel and bought a luxurious, sea-green silk pillowcase that she couldn't believe was on clearance. It had been from several seasons back and overlooked in the stock room—thus the super discounted price. At least this experience had been better than the first. The salesperson treated her like a prized customer and even gave her a student discount. Pepper hugged the soft, green pillow to her chest as Salty proudly showed off her holiday haul.

"How are you going to fit all of that in your wardrobe?" Pepper asked, staring at the growing mound of clothing on Salty's bed.

"Good question," she replied, glancing at Pepper's mostly empty storage space. "Can we share? I promise you can borrow anything—except my cashmere sweater dress."

Pepper couldn't help but smile. They were not exactly the same size. "What are friends for?" she replied, sliding her few pieces of clothing to the end of the wardrobe. She had to admit it was a simple solution. She barely had any clothes. Not that she minded. Other than an occasional trip to town, she hung around in the school uniform. Simplicity was best, she decided, watching how hard both Ginger and Salty were working to unpack and organize their new belongings.

"What happened to my bed?" Ginger asked as she pulled back her bed curtain.

"Oh, that," Pepper said, excited. "I totally forgot. I washed all your bedding and the curtains, then ironed and re-hung them."

"That must have taken forever," Salty exclaimed.

"Took me an entire day. Not that I had any other pressing plans," Pepper replied.

"That was too thoughtful. Thank you," Ginger said.

"Hey, remind me to give you your Christmas gift. I'm not sure which bag it's in at the moment," Salty said, staring at the mound of luggage beside her bureau.

"You didn't have to get me a thing, but I'm touched just the same," Pepper replied. "You really are sweet."

"Not according to my code name, but thanks."

"Speaking of inappropriate code names, wasn't Azu coming back today?" Ginger asked.

"I thought so, but maybe the bus is late. I may venture down to the gate in a bit to catch her," Pepper said.

"We should have coordinated," Salty said. "I could have given her a ride in from the depot."

"Did you drive again?" Pepper asked.

"No, it would have cut into winter vacation. Daddy let me fly, first class, of course."

"That goes without saying," Pepper said.

"I wish I got to fly first class. I was stuck in a cramped seat between a squirmy toddler and a talker. She chatted at me the entire flight. I'm not sure I said more than two words. How was your break?" Ginger asked.

Salty was trying to shove the last of her new sparkly tutu skirts into the wardrobe when she paused and turned to look at Pepper. Since her back was to Ginger, Salty mouthed, "Did you find it?"

Pepper nodded slightly before replying with a shrug. "Not much. It was pretty quiet, with everyone gone. But I got a lot of reading done." Pepper tossed the novel Ginger had lent her across the room. "Thanks. It was cute." Then she slipped onto the roof via the door they'd pried open months ago. The sky had turned an ominous shade of gray, and the wind blew in from the ocean in gusts that almost toppled her over. She peered out across the lawn. The van was lumbering up the driveway, dropping off more returning students. Pepper smiled. It would be good to have a full house again.

After a few moments had passed, Salty joined her along the roof's railing. "I've been dying to find out what you discovered," she said.

"What's Ginger doing?" Pepper asked.

"Went downstairs for a shower. What did you find out?"

Pepper recounted the entire ordeal, from cookie making to this morning, when she reluctantly returned Maria's book to Ms. Oscura. Salty was appropriately gob-smacked. This was the longest Pepper had seen her be silent, and it was slightly alarming.

Salty turned and stared into the distance.

"Hey, snap out of it," Pepper said, shaking her friend. "I know it wasn't the news we had been hoping for, but it's a big piece of the puzzle."

Salty returned her focus to Pepper and grinned. "It's incredible! I can't believe you're related to Ms. Oscura."

"Shh. Keep it on ice for now," Pepper said. "Besides, I'm not getting special treatment. If anything, I think she will be tougher on me now since I'm a double legacy."

"Legacy squared," Salty said, giggling.

"Now I just need to find out more about Nonnu. There has to be a reason Granny didn't take over as headmistress. Which would have been a few years after I was born, but they were already in Denver by that point."

"Isn't this enough?" Salty asked, "I mean, look at all the cool things you learned. We don't even know which of our family members came from Italy. Sometimes, it's better to stop while you're ahead."

"Meaning?"

"Nothing," Salty replied, chewing her bottom lip.

"Not nothing. What is it?"

"What if you spend the rest of the year searching for something you never find? And what if you do something crazy and get expelled for it?"

This didn't seem like Salty, but she had a point. Some people knew even less about their ancestors. Still, something nagged at Pepper. She needed to know more, but instead of arguing, she simply nodded.

"We'll see. Maybe I'll get lucky," she said. "Hey, it's close to dark. I'm gonna go down and wait for Azu. Wanna come?" Pepper asked.

"Nah. I have a suitcase full of shoes I need to put away before dinner."

"See you later," Pepper said, crossing the flat part of the roof that adjoined their tower.

"Pepper," Salty called out before she stepped back inside, "I really am very happy for you." She smiled and ducked back into the cupola.

• • •

THROUGHOUT WINTER BREAK, Pepper discovered all kinds of secret passageways and exits from the school, like this one. Down the left wing corridor and past the library was a small door leading to a tiny room, which led to this exit on the south corner of the building. These newfound spots would definitely come in handy in the future, she thought proudly. Winter break hadn't been singly focused. She silently thanked her fourth great-grandfather, Lucky Castellano, for the shortcut. Then she ducked through the bushes toward the main road to wait for Azucar. It wouldn't be any fun to walk that entire way back alone, especially not with a storm threatening to unleash its bounty at any moment. She paused and thought about returning for an umbrella but decided against it.

The wind whipped up in a tornado-like frenzy, tossing her hair into a tangled mess. Pepper tried to smooth it out, but her two hands were no match for the ferocious wind. She gave up and let the few strands she'd managed to secure escape. It was almost as if they were trying to take wing and fly away on the breeze. Oh well, it's just Azucar. She won't care if my hair looks like a rat's nest, Pepper thought, approaching the main entrance.

An engine revving caught her attention as she approached the gate. Pepper peered down the road but saw nothing. A honk startled her, and she turned to see a red Lamborghini rolling toward her. The car stopped just before the gates. As Pepper approached, her heart hammered in her chest. She held her breath as the passenger window descended.

"What are you doing here?" Pepper asked as she peered inside the dark car.

"Just dropped off Coco-nuts," Nico said. "I messaged you, but someone hasn't been on the chat."

"Sorry, yeah, I've been a little preoccupied."

"Have you ever heard of vacation?"

"Well, it wasn't schoolwork," she replied, grinning.

"That's good to hear...or is it?" he replied, furrowing his eyebrows comically.

"It's not bad news for you. If that's what you're worried about."

"I'm not worried." He held her gaze until Pepper felt the blush creeping up her neck and looked away.

"Is this yours?" she asked, gesturing to the car.

"Yeah, Christmas present from my old man. I was hoping you had time for a drive."

A drive. It was such an old-fashioned notion she couldn't help but smile. With gasoline prices beyond the financial reach of most consumers and electricity heavily regulated, people did not idly drive anywhere. Manufacturers rarely bothered making internal combustion models once all cars had been mandated electric in the *After Times*. Fancy cars like this were practically non-existent and more often indoor showpieces rather than functional vehicles. She had even heard of a woman who had one in her living room just so she could sit in it and read the newspaper. Nico reached over and popped open the passenger door. Pepper slid into the seat, giddy with excitement. She'd never been in a car this fancy in her life.

"Ready?" he asked as the gate creaked open. She nodded, and he peeled out of the driveway, fishtailing on some gravel before regaining traction and speeding down the road.

They roared through the streets by the bluff until they reached a turnoff. Nico slowed down to a respectful speed and approached a guard gate. A sensor lowered and scanned a barcode on the front of his windshield. The lever raised, allowing them entrance into what appeared to be a regular neighborhood. Nico didn't resume his earlier street racing tactics but kept the car at a leisurely pace.

"Where are we going?" Pepper asked, a bit nervously. No one knew where she was other than going to walk Azucar back to school. *Stupid, Pepper,* she chastised herself. *"The first rule of personal safety was always to tell someone where you are going,"* she heard Ms.

Powell say in her head. But this was Nico. She should feel completely safe with him.

"You'll see," he said, a hint of a smile on his lips.

They continued in silence. The light had started to dim as they passed an open golf course green. Then, just beyond was the ocean. The street suddenly left the neighborhood behind and flowed alongside the ocean through small clusters of trees and outcroppings of rocks that jutted out to the ocean below. It was so beautiful—more so than anything she'd seen.

"How is this so close to school and yet so different?"

"You really don't know where we are?" he asked.

Pepper shook her head, feeling foolish.

"Seventeen Mile Drive. It's famous."

She shrugged. "It is stunning. Look! It's that tree we can see from our bluff—the one from our, uh, never mind."

"Lone Cypress," he corrected, "not that tree." Nico pulled into the empty parking lot. "I missed you when I was home," he said.

Was he waiting for her to say she missed him? Honestly, she didn't have a chance. Pepper didn't want to lie, but she didn't want to hurt his feelings. "It wasn't the same without my workout buddy," she replied. There, that was truthful without being nakedly honest.

"Yeah, having Coco as my running partner was not the same."

"I don't see her as the running type," Pepper replied.

"Exactly. Come on. Let's get out and watch the sunset."

Pepper glanced up at the dark sky, doubtful any sunset would be visible, but she joined him at the wooden railing. The violent sea crashed against the rocks just below, and the wind picked up again. Pepper decided that from now on, she'd always be one of those girls with a hair thing on her wrist. She leaned against the fence and gazed out at the solitary tree.

"It's pretty famous, huh?"

"Very," Nico replied, resting on his elbows.

"Must've been here for a long time," she said.

"There's a plaque around here somewhere."

"I don't need to know years, but how does something grow and remain for decades—"

"Centuries even," Nico added.

"Right, centuries, probably. How is it possible to survive such inhospitable conditions?" she wondered as the wind whipped up again, the cypress trees around them creaking as they swayed.

"Grit and determination, I guess," he said.

Pepper had to agree. "The will to survive is a powerful force."

Nico turned to her. "You seem different than you were before Christmas. Is there anything on your mind?"

"Me? I'm the same as I was before."

He shook his head. "It's not bad or anything. You just seem more…I don't know, in focus."

"Did you get contacts over break?" She teased.

"No, it's you. There's just something more present in your behavior."

"Maybe I'm finally feeling like I belong here," she replied.

"You definitely belong here," he said.

Pepper allowed herself to be wrapped up in his warmth. It was a welcome respite from the coming storm. She leaned back against his chest, watching the clouds build around them. On the horizon, a piercing ray of ruby sunlight shone brightly against the darkness. She gasped. The clouds parted for one moment of pure, brilliant sunset perfection. Nico loosened his grasp just enough for her to turn around. His lips caught hers in a moment she'd been dreaming about since their ice skating date. His lips were chilled by the wind but soon warmed up against her own. He paused and lifted her onto the wooden railing. They were eye to eye now. She wrapped her leg around his waist as he leaned in closer. Nico rested his hands on her thighs, where her jeans creased just below the pockets.

Unlike the first date, when he'd overloaded on aftershave, today, the aroma of soap, spearmint gum, and something natural like freshly dug earth radiated off his warm skin. It mingled with the crisp freshness of the ocean. It was delicious. She much preferred him this way. Here, where it was just the two of them, Nico was bolder, or perhaps in the two weeks they'd been apart, he had imagined this moment as many times as she had. As his kisses intensified, Nico slid his hands from her thighs to her hips. Pepper's heart raced as his fingers began playing with the edges of her sweater. Teasing. Her hands explored his solid and well-muscled chest. Then she reached up and lightly brushed the top of his slightly pointed elf-like ears with the tips of her fingers before grasping the back of his neck and threading her fingers in the hair at the base of his head. Thunder sounded in the distance, but neither reacted, too focused on the heat building between them.

"May I?" he asked, pulling back slightly. His eyes were dark pools of desire.

Pepper nodded. "Yes," she answered, delighting in the electric trail of sensation of his fingers against her bare skin as they lightly traced the top of her waistband.

Then, he stepped back abruptly and turned toward the car. Pepper hopped down, pulling her shirt in place before placing her hand on his shoulder. Nico jumped at her touch and practically ran back to the car.

"I should get you back," he called over his shoulder.

She was confused. Why the sudden change in demeanor? Had she done something wrong? Too embarrassed to ask, she simply agreed.

"Yeah, I guess it's close to dinner time. And you probably need to be getting back to school yourself."

This time, he didn't open the car door for her. She slid into the passenger seat, still confused by his behavior. He started the car and peeled out of the parking lot. Their ride was quiet. Nico responded to anything she asked in one- or two-word replies. Eventually, she just gave up and stared at the passing houses out the window.

When he pulled up to the gate, Pepper unfastened her seat belt.

"Where are you going?" he asked.

"Home," she replied, gesturing to the glowing lights of Valentina's in the distance.

"Don't be silly. I'm taking you the whole way," he said, lowering the window before turning to the retinal scanner.

This time, he didn't perform any car acrobatics but respectfully drove along the curved driveway and stopped in front of the stone steps.

"Well, that was...unique. Thanks for the drive and for showing me your new car," she said before hopping out. After his behavior, she wasn't going to linger in that car another moment. Pepper bounded up the steps two at a time, anxious to get inside, when something caught her left arm as she reached the front door.

"Wait, what's the rush?" Nico asked, his eyes full of concern.

"Are you kidding? You ran hot then frigid with me tonight. I thought you...I don't know what I thought. I just want to go inside."

A pained expression crossed his face. "It's not you, it was... uh...a guy thing." She narrowed her eyes at him and tried to utilize the fierce look Ms. Powell had been working with them on before winter break. "Look, I'm not running cold at all. I'm very much hot over here for you."

"Is that so?" she said, crossing her arms.

"Yes. And you are adorable when you pout."

Darn it. Her look clearly needed improvement. He seemed quite earnest, so she let him tug her closer, closing the space between them.

"Can I prove it to you?" he asked.

Pepper barely nodded yes when he planted a very hot kiss on her lips that lasted longer than a goodnight kiss probably should have.

"Think you'll be on chat tonight around ten?" he asked, hands in his pants pockets as he backed away.

"I think I can arrange that," she replied.

"All right then, have a good night."

"You too. Thanks for the drive," she said, reaching for the door handle. Pepper realized he was actually going to wait until she got inside. She waved and stepped into the entry.

"Got a hot date there, Pepper?" someone said from the top of the stairwell.

"Didn't you learn it's not polite to spy on people," Pepper shot back as her face grew hot with embarrassment at being seen. She raced up the stairs, but the interloper had already retreated to her room.

Pepper was flushed from the cold...and Nico's kisses. She wanted to run some water over her face before dinner but hadn't replenished her shower cubby with fresh towels, so she hiked up to the cupola. As much as she loved their room, it was a hassle when you forgot something. To her surprise, Azucar was crouched in front of her bed unpacking when she walked in.

"Hey, you're back!" Pepper exclaimed.

"Yep," Azucar replied shortly.

"How was break?"

"Fine," she answered, not turning to look at Pepper.

They were alone in the cupola, so Azucar couldn't be pissed with anyone but her. Pepper wondered why. "Is something the matter?"

"Nope," she said.

Pepper knew that was a lie, but if Azucar didn't want to talk about it, she wouldn't force her. After all, what could she have done? Pepper wasn't even here when Azucar arrived. Her friend's cool demeanor dampened her earlier joy at seeing Nico. Pepper grabbed her new set of towels off her bed and headed downstairs.

EVERYONE WAS upstairs in the cupola, putting the finishing touches on their new decorations or still trying to get their things put away before the term started tomorrow morning. Azucar had closed her curtains. Pepper checked with Salty, but she didn't know why Azu was so taciturn, and they let her be.

"So this unexpected date…" Salty said. "Tell us everything."

Pepper thought she heard a disgruntled noise coming from Azucar's side of the room but ignored it. She did not do well with passive-aggressive behavior.

"He drove me along Seventeen Mile Drive to look at the Lone Cypress," Pepper said.

"So romantic," Salty gushed. "I can't believe you got so lucky. I'd kill to be dating *Il Principe*."

"We're not dating…okay, maybe we are," Pepper admitted at her friends' unconvinced looks. "But something bizarre happened at the lookout."

"Did he want to go too far?" Ginger asked.

"No, nothing like that," Pepper said. We were kissing, and all of a sudden, he stopped and wanted to take me home."

"That is weird," Ginger said.

"Were there cops around," Salty asked.

"No, we were alone," Pepper replied. "When we got back here, he walked me to the door and said it was a guy thing, then he kissed me—like *really* kissed me."

"Strange," Ginger echoed.

"I do not get guys running hot and cold like that," Pepper said.

"Ugh," came the exasperated reply from Azucar's bed. "You are so naive." She flung the curtains open.

"Ah, look who's talking to me again," Pepper said.

"Serves you right. I thought you were walking down to meet me when you jumped in this Guido's sports car and kicked up a dust storm on your merry way down the road. I had to use my inhaler," she said.

"Azu, I didn't even know you were there," Pepper said.

"Yeah, no kidding," she replied.

"I'm so sorry. Forgive me?"

"I guess," Azucar agreed. "And he was having an erection."

Salty gasped. "That is so blunt of you."

Pepper's eyes widened in shock. She thought back to his behavior. "Are you sure?"

"Yeah," Azucar said. "I have five brothers who aren't exactly shy about discussing their dating life. Trust me. It was his little friend waking up."

"Oh…" Pepper said, realizing she was right. "I'm so embarrassed."

"Why?" Azucar said. "He reacted to you. That's a good thing. It means he likes you—really likes you. Wait. You mean to tell me, Mr. Librarian Boyfriend, and you never…"

"No, and we were never together. Like, we're on the step before together when you're still friends, mostly," Pepper said.

"Wait, you are two-timing *Il Principe*?" Salty asked, aghast.

"No!" Pepper replied. "Ethan and I are friends. That's it. He probably wants more, but we are not a couple. Period. And for that matter, I'm not even sure what Nico and I are."

"You two are something, that's for sure," Ginger said.

"Can we just drop it, please? This is complicated enough," Pepper pleaded. "And this doesn't leave the cupola, understood?" They agreed to give Pepper a break about Nico and Ethan.

"Well, congratulations on letting him know you definitely like him," Salty said.

"And vice versa," Ginger replied.

They burst into giggles that barely subsided long enough for the welcome-back banquet that evening. It was a good thing they were able to keep their composure. Ms. Oscura had a special announcement.

"Welcome back and happy New Year and new term, ladies," she began after dessert. "At the end of each school year, we have a co-ed dance with The Don Academy." The dining room was filled with excited chatter. "This, however, is not an ordinary dance. It will be your year-end combined final for all classes." The room grew silent. "You will utilize everything you have learned over this year to complete an assignment at the dance. Each teacher will explain further details specific to their class in due course. Now, upstairs to get a good night's sleep."

The girls filed out of the dining room and up the stairs, conspiring on what these mysterious assignments could entail. There were a lot of rumors, but one thing was clear to Pepper: the second half of the year just got interesting.

# Chapter Twenty-Eight

Mrs. Sabatini was tight-lipped about the history component of the end-of-year assignment. However, she promised it would dovetail with their etiquette portion. Wednesday couldn't come soon enough, but Pepper was excited to find out what they were finally going to be doing in cooking class. If they had to use their skills for the dance, they certainly wouldn't be taking notes about the proper sauces for different pasta shapes; at least, she hoped not. She and Azucar walked down the dungeon steps, as they'd taken to calling them, when Cherry and The Fruit Bunch pushed past them. Cherry, seemingly deliberately, shoved Pepper aside, almost causing her to tumble down the stone steps.

"Is it just me, or does she seem nastier than before break?" Pepper whispered, regaining her balance.

"It might just be you," Azucar replied.

"Wait, didn't you see that?"

"I did. But she was sweet to me this morning at breakfast. Let me take the last jelly donut."

"Lucky you."

"I'm not saying we're besties, but it seems like her nastiness is only being directed at you."

Pepper didn't want to admit it, but she had been thinking the same thing.

They walked into class, and the room went silent. Pepper looked around. Something was off. Pepper could feel it. Thankfully, Signore Tonelli entered and started their lesson.

"*Buongiorno*, welcome back. We will build on your soup course and begin sauces today," he said.

Chili raised her hand. "Wait, *signore*, aren't you going to tell us what our final will be?"

"Ah yes, the end-of-year assignments. Apparently, Ms. Oscura has already told you about the dance. Normally, that announcement is made closer to the end of term, but I suppose a new headmistress means new traditions." There was a buzz of excitement in the room. "You will be preparing all the appetizers and desserts for the dance. Grading will be based on presentation, flavor, and ability to execute the dishes."

The bubble of excitement burst. This was going to be a lot of work, especially since they were just now starting on sauces. Pepper cringed at how much they needed to learn in four months. Hopefully, they'd be ready, or the guests would be enjoying cups of marinara and cream sauces with chasers of broth.

WEDNESDAY MORNING, Pepper was up bright and early. She and Nico had chatted each night since their drive on Sunday. He seemed eager to meet her for their weekly workout. Maybe Azucar's guess was correct. If that were the case, then they'd need to keep things a little more PG—if they got heated up again, that was. Pepper ran over scenarios as she trod down the stairs. She was surprised to see a handful of students already in the dining room when she walked in before seven. Dinner last night was a heavy meal, and she only wanted a protein bar or a banana. It had been so long since the house was full, so she decided instead to have a bowl of yogurt with granola and catch up with her classmates.

Pepper set her bowl at the end of the long table where five other girls were happily chatting. When she pulled out the last chair, Pear turned around.

"That seat is taken," she said, pushing the chair back against the table.

"Okay, sorry," Pepper said. "How about that one?" she asked, pointing her spoon at the empty seat at the other end of the table.

"Taken," Chili replied.

Pepper removed her bowl of granola and turned to join the other table of students, but when she set her food down, they all got up, leaving their breakfasts half-eaten. There was a titter of laughter from the five girls. Pepper considered sitting down to show them their mean-spiritedness didn't bother her, but when the tears pricked behind her eyes, she knew it was pointless to stay. She left her uneaten breakfast on the table and grabbed a protein bar as she left the dining room.

What was wrong with everyone? It was like they all took mean pills over vacation. Even Chili, whom Pepper had counted as a friend, had been especially cruel this morning. She thought back over the last twenty-four hours, trying to pick out a moment where she could have offended everyone. Then it hit her, Nico. There was that person who had seen them saying goodnight Sunday. The interloper had been on the second-floor landing, and Pepper couldn't tell who it was. They had undoubtedly seen her and Nico together. She wracked her brain trying to figure out who it was but came up blank. Still, that was just one person…unless…they told their roommates, and then word spread around the school. That had to be it.

Hadn't Salty said he was the hottest catch in the mafia world? Parents probably sent their daughters to Valentina's with the intention of getting close to the future head of the Rossetti crime family. Still, that shouldn't turn people against her. Would it? Then again, position and money were two of the most powerful motivators. Perhaps that was the reason…

As she walked down the embankment to the beach, Pepper was deep in thought. She didn't see Nico run up until he scooped her into his arms and twirled her around.

"Hey, beautiful," he said, planting a kiss on her neck before setting her back on the sand.

Pepper hurriedly reached up to wipe away the tears she'd been crying when he surprised her.

"What's this?" he asked, taking her face in his hands.

"Rough morning," she replied. "It's nothing."

"The angry red blotches on her cheeks say otherwise. What's up?"

She couldn't deny it. Nico could read her like a book. "Some of the girls were mean to me this morning." A bubble of laughter that sounded like a sob escaped her lips. "God, that sounds so childish when said out loud." She began to walk down the beach.

"What did they do?" Nico asked, sliding his arm across her shoulder. She relaxed against his strong embrace, some tension and anger ebbing away like the tide rolling back into the ocean.

"It's silly, really."

"No, it isn't. Not if it upset you. Tell me."

"Well, they wouldn't let me sit with them this morning at breakfast. And not just one set of girls. Everyone in the dining room either ignored me, told me the seat was taken or got up when I put my tray on their table. It was blatant."

"Damn, girls are brutal. Dudes wouldn't do that. He'd tell you he has a problem with you, and either you fight it out or forget about it."

"Sounds juvenile."

"Better than the psychological games these girls are playing," he said. "Any idea why they suddenly hate you?"

"I didn't say they hate me, but … yeah, maybe." She took a

breath, unsure if Nico was the right person to help with her issue. But he was here, and he was asking. "I think maybe word has gotten around about you, and they're …"

"Jealous?" he guessed.

"Yeah, maybe. I mean, not that I think we're … together or anything official, but they might," she stammered, fiddling with the pull ties on her hoodie.

"Hmmm, you don't think we're official?"

"I wasn't sure," she confessed.

"I don't just let anyone into my Lamborghini."

"So, I'm special?"

"Very," he said, kissing the tip of her nose. "Enough sadness. Those *puttane* are just jealous. Let's get your blood pumping. That always makes me feel better when I want to rip someone's head off. Drills?"

"Lead the way," she said, more grateful than ever that she had bumped into him that first Wednesday of school.

It was well after the time she should have headed back, but Pepper's motivation to return to school was low. She wanted to stay in this alcove with Nico, sheltered from the harsh wind and the sea crashing just beyond. But time pressed on, no matter how she willed it to slow. As she hiked up the embankment, Pepper remembered that today, they'd learn their end-of-year etiquette class assignment. She'd probably have time for a quick shower, but she would have to wait until this afternoon to wash her hair. Not that she figured Ms. Powell would mind. A wet head seemed to be her main pet peeve, not a sweaty one. Pepper bounded up the stairs two at a time and decided to hit the showers before going up to the cupola. Why make two trips? Besides, her quads were still fatigued from Nico's drills.

Pepper strolled into the bathroom where Chutney was bent over, blow-drying her platinum blonde hair. The only shower with decent water pressure was free. Pepper snagged a towel and stepped in. Each shower stall had an entry with a bench and then the shower itself. Like a changing room, plus a shower. Except they had curtains across the entrance and not doors. Pepper stripped and left her sweaty clothes in a pile on the floor. The heat from the shower relaxed her tired muscles, and she stayed under the powerful stream, letting it massage her back for a few moments.

Switching off the water, Pepper reached for the towel she'd hung up on the hook an arm's reach away. Instead of the scratchy, thin school towel, her hand brushed the cold tile. She opened her eyes and looked through the evaporating steam. It was gone. Pepper searched the floor, thinking it had fallen. It wasn't there either. Was she going crazy? She'd grabbed one, hadn't she? Pepper stepped onto the slatted wooden floor mat that was supposed to be antibacterial or something and realized that her clothes were gone, too.

This meant that this morning's mean girls' display at breakfast wasn't a fluke. Fine, she thought, I'll just grab another towel from the rack. Pulling back the curtain to shield herself, Pepper peered down the shower corridor. It was empty. She hugged the wall and tiptoed to the cabinet. It creaked as she swung it open. Empty. Pepper flung the door wide. Shelf after shelf was bare.

The downstairs clock chimed. There were fifteen minutes before class. *What am I going to do? I can't just run through the house naked.* If someone was doing this on purpose, and it seemed very plausible that they were, they could be waiting to record her bolting, buck naked, to the cupola stairs. Pepper desperately looked around. She was trapped. Her options were to wait until everyone was in class or run for it. Pepper paced the shower hallway, and that's when she got an idea. She returned to the shower stall, unfastened the curtain, and wrapped the cold, clammy, white plastic around herself. It clung to her skin and made walking difficult. Still not wanting to be seen, Pepper looked around the corner into the bathroom sink area. It was deserted. She shuffled past the double mirrors, only glancing at herself once. The shower curtain was thin, and she could see the outline of her whole body. It was better than being nude, she reminded herself.

Pepper took a deep breath as she opened the bathroom door, readying herself for what might be waiting for her in the hallway. She had, if she was lucky, probably five minutes to get downstairs. She pushed open the door and calmly walked to the cupola stairwell. If there was one thing she had learned from Nonnu, it was never to let them see you sweat. There was a gasp followed by some grumbling and unenthusiastic laughter. She pulled open the stairwell door, turned, and curtsied as best she could.

"Thanks for the challenge, ladies," Pepper said, then closed the stairwell door behind her.

Getting across the hall had been the easy part. Making it up the stairs in a stiff plastic shower curtain clinging to her wet skin was another thing. Try as she might, Pepper couldn't manage to get onto the first step. Eventually, she just gave up, peeled the curtain off, and bounded up the stairs two at a time. What did she care if her roommates saw her bare? They changed in their room daily. It wasn't as if they all hadn't caught a glimpse of butt cheek every now and then.

Luckily, though, the cupola was empty. Pepper threw herself at the wardrobe, extracted her school uniform, pulled it on, along with a pair of sneakers, and rushed downstairs. She made it into her seat just before ten, to the astonishment of several incredulous-looking classmates, particularly Cherry. It didn't surprise Pepper and confirmed her earlier assumption that these mean girl tactics were about Nico.

"I didn't think you were going to make it," Salty said, leaning over.

"Almost didn't," Pepper replied. "I'll tell you about it later."

The door opened, and Pepper breathed a sigh of relief. At least she had gotten here on time.

"Welcome back, my little *farfalle*," Ms. Powell said, sweeping into the room wearing her usual uniform of a crisp white button-down shirt, black slacks, and coordinating colorful mules, glasses, and lipstick. Pepper wondered how many of those shirts and slacks she owned or if she regularly laundered a few pieces.

"I see by your rapt attention you are eagerly awaiting news of this year's final assignment. I will not reveal it until the end of class. So you can relax." She set down her mug of tea and perched on the edge of her desk, a vibrant coral mule dangling from her foot. "Last class, we wrapped up our lipreading and eavesdropping unit. This week, we will begin surveillance." A groan rose collectively from the students. "Mmm-hmm, I know you think these are rudimentary skills, but a simple task utilized with ease is pure elegance. When you are further along in your coursework, we will build on these skills, and you will thank me for drumming them into your brain until they are second nature. But first, I have a small gift for each of you." She picked up a satchel that was on the desk and held it up. "A small token to help facilitate and aid in your growth, my *farfalle*."

Ms. Powell passed by each desk, and one at a time, the girls put their hands into the depths of the cloth bag and extracted a crystal. Some were brightly colored, others dull and craggy. Pepper watched as Salty pulled out a milky white stone. Ms. Powell took a step to the right and held the bag open before Pepper. She reached in and felt around before finally closing her fingers around a smooth, lopsided stone. It was a stunning bright emerald color with captivating swirls and patterns of varying shades of green.

"Today's lesson will be to research your stone and write about why it chose you and how it can aid your journey."

"I don't understand how any of this crap is going to help us in the future," Cherry said, slamming her stone onto the desk.

"My dear, the first thing a successful mafia wife learns is to take orders from her elders and not ask questions. Get to work." There was a steel edge in Ms. Powell's voice that Pepper hadn't heard before. Cherry also seemed to notice because she acquiesced immediately and began the assignment.

"You're lucky you got Amethyst, dear. It aids in elevating one from the baser emotions and into the light," Ms. Powell said to Cherry.

The class chuckled. The blotchy red patches on Cherry's neck indicated she was not amused. Pepper began researching her stone. It was a malachite, not an emerald as she had hoped from the bright green color. This stone seemed to do everything but cook dinner. She took diligent notes but made sure to transcribe one sentence as she was reading through the lore of the malachite: *while its beauty is unmatched, this stone isn't just around for its looks; it is a spiritual powerhouse capable of assisting in times of great turmoil, and transformation.* Pepper smiled inwardly. She could use a heavy hitter in her corner about now. Not that she truly believed, but it was nice to think this little green stone was on her side, especially after this morning.

Salty leaned over, flashing her tablet at Pepper. "Does this look like regular quartz or smoky quartz?"

Pepper studied the images and then the crystal on the desk. "It's hard to tell. Better ask Ms. Powell."

"Snow quartz, dear," Ms. Powell said before Salty had gotten up.

"Thanks," she replied. "Since she's taught us to read lips, I guess she does it too."

Pepper smirked. That was an astute point. She'd have to remember to watch her conversations when Ms. Powell was in sight. They worked diligently for the next forty minutes before Ms. Powell transitioned into their surveillance introductory lesson. Pepper's mind was half on the current assignment and half on the assignment to come.

"This will be due at the beginning of the next class with an additional paragraph about how your stone has aided you during the week."

Cherry snorted in amusement, garnering another stern look from Ms. Powell.

"Now, about your end-of-year final. You will be assigned a mark, or a gentleman, as it were, to gather specific intel without being discovered. What intel will be an absolute secret until just before—it is your end-of-term final, after all. I will not answer any questions. Put your hands down. You are dismissed."

They rushed to leave the classroom in a flurry of energy and conversation. Pepper had just made it to the door when she went sprawling into the hall, landing hard on her shoulder when she tried to catch herself on the doorjamb and got twisted around. Salty was instantly by her side, fussing over her, as Azucar chased down the malachite that had flown out of Pepper's hand and was tumbling down the hall.

"Looks like that stone isn't good for klutzes," Cherry said, stepping over her.

Pepper could hear Cherry's laughter echoing all the way from the dining room.

Azucar helped her up and handed back the deep green stone. "Did you run over her grandma during winter break?"

Pepper shrugged. "I think she's jealous about Nico. But whatever I did, she's out for blood this semester."

"Forget her," Salty said.

"It's kind of hard when she's actively trying to make my life hell. I mean, it's the first week back, and I've already been snubbed, humiliated, and tripped. What's next? Beheading?"

"Let's just get something to eat."

"You go," Pepper said. "My shoulder is throbbing pretty badly. I'm going to see if I can get some ice in the kitchen."

"Go see the nurse," Salty said.

"We have one?" Azucar replied.

"Didn't you read your welcome packet? Yeah, Ms. Samson."

"The English teacher is also the nurse? What a crappy school," Azucar said.

Pepper chuckled. "See you later. Can you bring me up a plate of something? I don't want to face Cherry right now."

"Sure," Salty said, giving her a sympathetic smile. "See you later."

Pepper turned in the opposite direction and headed down the hall toward the English class. She hoped Ms. Samson would be there since she had no classes today. Wednesdays were like office hours or prep periods for them, but teachers weren't always available. The door was closed. Pepper knocked. There was no answer. She tried the handle, found it unlocked, and peered into the room. The lights were off.

*Guess I'll check the kitchen for some ice.* Before she turned, a seam of light coming from under the bookcase caught her attention. She tiptoed inside. Did Ms. Samson have a hidden office back there? The bookcase was slightly ajar, and Pepper could see someone sitting in a faded, easy chair, but she couldn't make out her features. She was talking to someone opposite her. The voice was familiar. Was it Ms. Samson? Pepper leaned closer.

"Do you think they can be trusted with something of this magnitude?"

"It's part of their final. We're going to have to trust them. Just make sure the right girls get the correct target," the figure in the chair replied.

"Good thinking. We can't rely on chance."

Pepper wished she could hear them better. Was their final some kind of double mission? As she was sure all the girls did, she figured it would be a benign assignment utilized to test their skill set acquired during the year. But what if it wasn't? What if rogue teachers were using them to further some nefarious plot? Pepper backed away and silently closed the classroom door behind her. She was so preoccupied she forgot all about her shoulder and ran up to the cupola to wait for Salty and Azucar, her mind racing with scenarios.

By the time they made it upstairs, Pepper had spun over a

dozen theories about the conversation she had overheard, each more unlikely than the next. Salty listened patiently as Pepper talked while Azucar put on her headphones and closed her bed curtains, completely disinterested in conspiracy ideas.

"They could have been talking about a whole bunch of stuff," Salty said, stealing a chip off Pepper's untouched lunch tray.

"Sure, if it was a normal conversation instead of a secretive one."

"That is a good point."

They hatched theories until it was time to walk down to PE. Salty tried to convince her to stay behind, but Pepper wanted to prove to Cherry that her petty tactics didn't work on her.

When they walked up, Coach was ready and waiting. After their mile warm-up around the track, he paired them off by twos and tossed each a pair of gloves and a punching mitt. They had just started a boxing segment, and Pepper was eager to try some of the techniques they'd learned. The teams spread out across the field, but when Pepper turned around to face her partner, Olive was hightailing it in the other direction, and Cherry was taking her place.

"Ready?" Cherry said, sliding her hands into the boxing gloves.

"Let's go."

Cherry threw a right cross that smacked with a sharp sting into Pepper's mitt.

"If you think he's going to like you more because you're being mean to me, I think you better reexamine your tactics," Pepper said.

"Males have a way of being convinced of what's best for them. He'll come around," Cherry replied before bringing her knee up with lightning speed.

Pepper didn't even have a chance to block the kick before she dropped to the ground, and the pain exploded down her arm. When she looked up, Cherry had already walked off. Clutching her arm, Pepper found Coach and pulled the neck of her sweatshirt down to reveal her injury.

"Whoa, that was quite a kick," he exclaimed. "You better head back right away for some ice."

"Back to Valentina's?" Pepper asked.

"No, use our dispensary." Coach whistled, alerting the soccer crew, and waved Nico over. "Take this girl to the locker room for some ice. You know where all the stuff is."

"Yes, coach," he replied.

Pepper limped off the field, gingerly prodding her shoulder with her finger. It was tender to the touch and looked like she was hiding a softball under her sweatshirt. It was probably not wise to have come to class. They walked side by side toward the school, Pepper's heart rate increasing, not because Nico was with her, but because this would be her first look inside Don's.

"I saw Cherry's roundhouse to your shoulder. Are you sure this is just a bruise?" Nico asked.

"This is part two of her handy work," Pepper said, explaining the earlier incidents.

"She is vicious," he said.

"And besties with your sister," Pepper added. Nico made a face. "What? You don't believe me?"

"About the bestie part," he said, punching in a code at the entrance. He held open the locker room door for her. "They may be friendly, but Coco-nuts is too smart to let a manipulator like that into her inner circle. Give my father credit for teaching us about knowing who to trust."

The door closed behind them, blocking the noise from their PE class and practice. Their sneakers squeaked against the floor as they walked between the rows of lockers. The musty fug of sweaty males assaulted her nose as they went deeper inside. Gross, how did they not smell that? She tried breathing through her mouth. Then she glanced around, memorizing the layout.

"The trainer's room is just in here," he said. Nico switched on the lights to reveal a state-of-the-art facility. It had the lingering scent of the locker room tinged with an antiseptic afternote. They definitely had more money flowing in here than Valentina's, she thought, marveling at the gleaming shelves filled with supplies. Nico retrieved a sizable bag of ice from the freezer and instructed Pepper to sit on the long metal table.

"Yikes," she said, jumping up. "That's frigid."

"Get back up," he said, depositing a roll of plastic wrap next to the ice.

Pepper gingerly eased herself back onto the table. When she pulled down the neck of her sweater, Nico chuckled.

"How do you expect me to get this," he said, holding up the ice, "through that tiny hole? Off with it."

She looked up, stunned. "With what, exactly?"

"Your sweater…and shirt. I need to strap this to your bare shoulder."

"That will be really cold. Can't I have it on the outside?"

"Not if you want to reduce the swelling fast."

Pepper hesitated. She'd never been undressed by a guy before, and while this was not exactly the throes of passion, it was still intimidating.

"Do you need help because of your shoulder?" he asked gently. "Here, let me. Arms up."

Pepper raised both arms, though she gasped when a stab of pain radiated through her shoulder and neck. Nico gently worked the sweater up and over her head. It was an odd sensation to be reeling from an injury but also have the guy you were falling for stripping off your clothes. He did the same with her shirt, but this time, he let his fingers gently brush her bare waist as he lifted the shirt, sending goose bumps up her arms.

Then she was just sitting there in her old threadbare black sports bra on a cold metal table under harsh fluorescent lights. Pepper crossed her arms over her chest, feeling incredibly exposed. But then Nico's lips brushed the back of her neck, and she realized he didn't see the imperfections she noticed in the mirror. He trailed kisses along her back and planted one very light kiss on the injured shoulder.

"Thank you," she said.

"You won't be thanking me in a minute. Take a deep breath, and when I ask, hold the ice to your shoulder—do not take it off."

Pepper nodded, bracing herself. After the shock of cold, a shooting pain coursed down her arm. Cherry certainly had done a number on her today. Nico gave her the signal, and she held the ice in place. He began wrapping the affected area with plastic wrap. Once it was secure, he passed the wrapping under her good arm and back to the injured shoulder before securing it in place.

"You can open your eyes now," he said.

"No, it helps with the pain."

She felt the heat of his skin before his lips met hers. He ran his fingers lightly up and down her mostly bare back. Which quickly took her mind off the throbbing shoulder.

"That certainly made everything less painful," she said when they disentangled themselves.

"It's a trick I learned playing soccer."

"Your teammates kiss you when you have an injury, too?"

He laughed. "No, but I have been kicked in the shins and had my foot stomped on to take my mind off the pain of a dislocated shoulder."

"That's harsh," she said. "Thanks for taking a gentler approach with me."

"My pleasure," he said, kissing the tip of her nose. "You have a solid twenty minutes before you start dripping water everywhere."

"Possibly less now that you've raised my temperature," she said.

"True, maybe ten minutes."

"How am I supposed to get my shirt on?" she asked, pointing to the mound of ice strapped to her shoulder. With the added bulk from the swelling, it was like wearing one of those puffy shoulder pads she'd seen in photos from the nineteen-eighties.

"We just walk around like that," he said.

"I'm not walking around in my bra. Here, maybe I can get the shirt halfway on," she said, attempting to pull it on one-handed.

"What a minute. I have an idea," he said before running out of the training room.

Pepper hopped off the bench, wobbling slightly due to the added weight on her shoulder and the slightly residual giddiness from Nico's kisses.

He returned with a navy T-shirt. Pepper couldn't figure out why. It was the same as her shirt, maybe slightly bigger. Then he retrieved a pair of scissors and cut the sleeves off before she could protest.

"You ruined your shirt," she said as he slipped it over her head. It did not smell especially clean.

"Can't have you running around in your bra," he said, winking. "Let's get you back before they send people looking for us." He grasped her arm.

"What's down there," Pepper asked as they walked back through the locker room.

"Showers. Why, feeling dirty?"

"You wish," she said. "So that must go…?" She trailed off, pointing to the other hallway.

"That's the tunnel that leads into the main school building. It lets out on the basement level. Normally, we just run up the stairs to the dorms, but there's an elevator. Why?"

"Curious. This school is huge compared to tiny Valentina's."

"Yeah, it takes some getting used to. I got lost all the time my first year. Now, I can get around with my eyes closed."

"What else can you do with your eyes closed," she asked, pulling Nico to her as he reached for the door handle. After the last horrible forty-eight hours, she didn't want this magical moment to end. He backed her up against the wall, pressing himself against her while still making sure to avoid her shoulder. Then he slid his hand up her thigh and around to cup the curve of her backside. A moment later, he stepped back, adjusting his shorts.

"We better stop," he said. "Can you find your way back?" Pepper nodded and started to open the door when he grasped her once more for a deeply passionate kiss that left her breathless. Then he disappeared back into the locker room.

Salty was waiting at the edge of the field when Pepper returned. Class had been over for fifteen minutes. The soccer team was in full practice mode, and Salty didn't seem annoyed to have been kept waiting.

"Nice love bite," she said.

Pepper's hand clasped onto her neck. "Help me tie my sweater up there," she said, swinging the sleeve over her shoulders. Salty got up and dutifully and strategically arranged the hoodie to cover the bruise.

"Do you want to stay and watch the guys or come back with me? Nico said I'd start to melt soon, so I probably should get going."

"Yeah, okay," Salty replied, reluctantly turning to follow Pepper off the field. "Nice shirt, by the way. You smell awesome."

"Shut up. I found out something in the locker room."

"Azu was speaking gospel about why *Il Principe* ducked out at the cove?"

"No, well…yes to that, but no, it's about Don's. I found a way inside."

"Are you still trying to get in there?"

"Of course. I want to learn as much about my family as possible. And I think Don's holds the key to my grandfather's past."

Salty shook her head but didn't say another word. Pepper couldn't understand the sudden change. Before winter break, she had been totally on board with Pepper finding out all she could about her relatives.

# Chapter Twenty-Nine

By March, Pepper had enough of the snubbing, supply stealing, and snide comments. She decided to confront Cherry. This had to stop. Getting this worked up over a guy, even someone as great as Nico, was silly. Pepper decided to sneak into Cherry's room after dinner.

She'd catch her off guard and alone. Hopefully, they could have a civil conversation, and Pepper could make her see that this was all silly, juvenile behavior. That or she'd give her a black eye for putting her through hell for these past months. Either way, Pepper expected a resolution by the end of the encounter. She had to be stealthy. All of the mean girls making her life hell were in Cherry's Fruit Bunch. She coordinated with Salty, and just before dinner was finished, Pepper slipped out the door.

Using the new skills she had acquired from etiquette class, Pepper crept along the hallway, listening for movement. When it was clear she was alone, she opened the suite door and stepped in. There were two large bedrooms surrounding a single sitting room. Pepper wished they had a lounging area like this upstairs, but she wouldn't trade the cupola for anything. Maybe they could convince Ms. Oscura to put patio furniture on the roof just beyond their room. That might be really fun. The furniture in this suite was mismatched, but the girls had done a decent job covering the chairs with sheets and piling decorative pillows on the sagging couch.

Now, which one was Cherry's room, she wondered. Pepper started with the room to her right, knowing she didn't have much time. Nope, clearly, three girls were living in here. She couldn't understand why they'd acquiesced to Cherry's demands and let her have an entire room when they could have easily split the rooms two by two. There'd still be plenty of space. Of course, that also meant Cherry wouldn't get her own room. Pepper crossed the living space and opened the opposite door. Yep, this was Cherry's. She'd outfitted it with clothing and shoe racks, installed a vanity, and had two of the twin beds pushed together to make a king. Clever. Pepper closed the door behind her and perched on the edge of the vanity. She looked around the room, marveling at all of the clothes. Most of which she'd never seen Cherry wear. Pepper shook her head. What a waste.

The vanity was covered with bottles, makeup brushes, eyeshadow palettes, and perfume. No wonder it took Cherry so long to get ready in the morning. Pepper picked up a pink bottle shaped like a gemstone and removed the cap. A wave of candy citrus scent washed over her. She heard voices in the suite and jumped, dropping the bottle. It clattered to the floor and rolled under the vanity. Pepper dove down to retrieve it, placing it back on the counter as the door swung open.

Cherry saw Pepper and closed the door behind her. "I wondered when you would show up," she said.

This surprised Pepper, but she didn't reply. In Ms. Powell's class, she had learned to allow the other person to show their hand first, so she waited as Cherry put down her bag and kicked off her shoes. "Are you here to beg me to spare you, precious?"

Pepper shook her head. "No. I'm not sure you have a heart to appeal to. I'm just here to tell you that your efforts are driving

Nico and me closer. He thinks what you are doing is petty and childish."

Cherry laughed.

"Instead of waging a counter-campaign where my friends and I are horrible to you and your friends, I'm here to ask you to stop."

Cherry smirked and crossed the room. Pepper stepped back, but the vanity prevented her from taking more than half a step as the table's edge pressed into her backside.

"If you thought that was unpleasant, wait for round two. You'll wish you were never born."

"All this over a guy? Come on, Cherry. You can't bully him into liking you."

She laughed. "You do not deserve him."

"And you do?" Pepper replied.

"Maybe, but you, Stella D'Angelo, definitely do not deserve him," Cherry said, her voice dropping threateningly.

Pepper was rattled by the use of her given name. Cherry had been calling her variations of pepper all year. It was clear that she meant business. Pepper hadn't even known who she was until a few months ago. How could Cherry? A cold sweat was dampening her shirt, making her chilled. "What is it that you think you know, Brittany Bianchi?" Pepper wasn't a fool. If Cherry knew something, she wanted to know what it was, and she certainly wasn't going to reveal anything just because Cherry knew her real name.

The redhead narrowed her eyes and poked her bright red talon into Pepper's cheek. "Your grandfather was a rat. And everyone knows where rats belong."

Pepper gasped and turned. Cherry's nail scrapped across her cheek. "That's a lie."

"Are you sure about that? Put the pieces together, precious. You'll see I am very much correct." Cherry turned and crossed to the door, flinging it open. "Get out," she yelled. "And if I catch you snooping around my room again, I'll take it up with the headmistress. Your cousin," she whispered as Pepper passed.

Chutney and Chili poked their heads into the lounge area at the commotion. Pepper had been wrong to underestimate Cherry as simply a dumb bimbo. She was much more conniving than she looked. Pepper strode from the room with as much dignity as she had left—which wasn't a great deal. She managed to make it to the cupola before she started shaking.

Thankfully, Azúcar and Ginger were preoccupied with their algebra homework. She motioned to Salty to follow her onto the roof. Once outside, Pepper inhaled the crisp evening air. The tremors that had begun moments ago lessened as she pressed her back against the wall and took measured breaths. Salty appeared a few moments later.

"What's going on?" she asked.

Pepper was about to speak when she realized where they were standing—right above Cherry's room. She facepalmed, then made a shushing motion with her finger. Without speaking, she told Salty the whole thing. They had been practicing reading lips and had improved considerably. When Pepper got to the part about Cherry knowing something about Nonnu, Salty's eyes grew wide, and her lips disappeared into a straight line.

"You know, don't you?" Pepper mouthed.

Salty nodded slowly.

"Why did you keep it from me?"

"I was hoping you wouldn't find out."

"Well, Cherry found out, and she's threatening to use it against me. Probably in a play to get Nico. And now I find out my best friend knew the whole time!"

"I'm sorry," Salty mouthed. "How can I make it up to you?"

"Tell me exactly what you know," Pepper replied.

Salty nodded. "Library in ten minutes."

The library was deserted when they padded inside in their

pajamas and slippers. Pepper closed the door, then checked the alcoves and behind the drapes.

"We're alone. Spill it. What did you find out?" she asked, crossing her arms over her chest.

"Pep, I'm so sorry. I didn't know how to tell you. And I never dreamed Cherry, of all people, would be the one to reveal your family's shame."

"Shame from what?" Pepper asked, exasperated.

"Your grandfather rolled on someone. I don't know the details."

"Rolled?"

"Snitched, ratted…uh tattle tailed—"

"I get it, but about what?"

"That's what I don't know." Pepper gave her a look. "Honestly, I don't. My great-aunt wouldn't tell me. She just said he was a rat and good riddance. I'm really sorry."

Pepper flopped into the nearest chair, suddenly dizzy. This did not fit with her memories of Nonnu. He was an upstanding guy who taught her right from wrong and lived by a code that didn't involve snitching on people.

"How could this be," she said, burying her face in her hands.

"Oh, honey, I know it's hard to believe. Sometimes, family members do horrible things, but you don't have to love them any less. My grandfather…well, let's say he wasn't always so warm and cuddly. TCN, babe."

"Right, but snitching? That's like a cardinal sin, isn't it?"

"He must have had a good reason," Salty offered. "Hey, maybe that's why you don't know anything about your past. Could your family have been in witness relocation?"

Pepper's head was spinning. Everything in her life snapped into clear focus for the first time. That had to be it: their different last name, having no contact with family, no old photos, not even of her mom as a child, and Granny's insistence that Nonnu not tell his stories. It made perfect sense. But then that meant Nonnu had rolled over on someone.

She sighed. "Why would he want me to go here if he was a rat? Wouldn't that defeat the purpose of being in hiding all those years?"

"Maybe he was counting on your family connections to protect you. I mean, the other headmistress would have known your grandparents, right?"

"I guess so." Pepper pulled her necklace from under her shirt and rubbed the signet ring with her thumb. "My life is a web of secrets!" she exclaimed. "If Nonnu wanted me to find my place in our world, this was a complicated way to do it. Why couldn't he have at least told me in the letter?"

"It's like my mother always says: *never write it down*. She doesn't even make shopping lists," Salty added, most unhelpfully.

"This is just…a lot." Pepper sighed again. "I think I just want to be alone."

"Sure, I get it. You know where I am if you need to talk," Salty said, shuffling out of the library.

Pepper sat alone in the dimly lit space for the next hour, replaying her childhood over and over in her mind, trying to find the clues that the conclusion she had just reached was correct. If it was, that meant Nonnu was a rat, and she did not belong here.

# *Chapter Thirty*

It was clear that Cherry had made good on her threat. By the whispers and stares Pepper received walking into breakfast, everyone knew about Nonnu, or at least Cherry's version of who he was and, by association, who she was. No one except her roommates would look her in the eye, speak to her directly, or acknowledge her presence. In an instant, the world she'd come to love had been flipped on its head. Valentina's had begun to feel like home, and now it felt like a prison.

That night, when a chat message dinged on her tablet, Pepper marked her place in Romeo and Juliet and swiped the book app closed. Ms. Samson had begun a new section on gang rivalries in literature. First up was this classic. Their assignments were to read portions independently and then debate the various tactics and missteps of the rivals in class. She'd read the play once before but never studied it from this angle. It was quite a bit more interesting than the love story everyone swooned over. It was quite tragic. Certainly not the type of love story Pepper enjoyed.

Her finger hovered above the chat app, the small red notification button taunting her. The girls at Valentina's used the chat feature sporadically. Of course, no one outside her own roommates was speaking with her at the moment, which meant that she was about to be barged with insulting messages or Nico was writing to her. She said a prayer and touched the screen.

You busy?

Doing homework, why?

I was worried about you.

Ah, then you've heard. News travels fast. I can explain.

It doesn't matter.

Actually, it does.

Not on the chat. Meet me at our spot in twenty minutes.

But it's after curfew.

He sent a selfie of himself looking sad.

Please, I have to see you.

I'll be there.

PEPPER POKED her head out of her bed curtain. The rest of the room was quiet. Azucar's gentle snores emanated from her bed. Salty's light was off, and she seemed to be asleep as well. Through Ginger's closed bed curtains, there were two glowing shapes, probably from her new AR glasses. That or Ginger was radioactive and could see through walls, which was doubtful. Pepper slipped out of bed, pulled on a hoodie and boots, then crept out the door. She thanked "Lucky" Castellano again for his oddly designed house and slid down one of the unused laundry chutes. It let out in a dusty room at the back of the house. From the large metal basins, hooks on the walls, and the drain in the floor, this was probably the washing room decades ago. Luckily, it also had an exit at the side of the building.

Nico was waiting just beyond the embankment trail. When she rounded the corner, he ran up and pulled her into a tight hug. The tears that had been at bay all month poured out of her at once. She couldn't even form words. It didn't matter. Nico held her close and stroked her hair as she cried. A small part of her felt foolish for this show of emotion, and she wondered if Granny would be ashamed of her. Holding it all inside and being brave had been exhausting. It felt good to let her emotions flow in a safe space. Pepper dried her eyes with the cuff of her hoodie. She hadn't realized how much she had kept bottled up.

Nico dried one stray tear as they walked down the beach to the alcove. He guided her onto his lap, and she lay against his shoulder. She told him everything that had transpired over the last few months.

"I'm so sorry. People can be so ridiculous. It's not like you did anything."

"Honestly, something feels off. I can't imagine Nonnu doing anything like this either."

"Sometimes people are faced with impossible choices," he said.

"I want to get to the bottom of it and clear his name…if I can."

"That's honorable, but it might be best to leave it alone. You know, let this blow over and forget about the past."

"That's what Salty thinks I should do, too." Pepper shook her head. "I know you both mean well, but I can't let it rest. I have to know."

"If I can help in any way…" He trailed off as he caressed the tender spot behind her ear with the tip of his finger.

"This is helping," she said, turning to catch his mouth with hers, finding respite and solace in Nico's embrace. To forget the maelstrom that was raging inside her former sanctuary. Pepper wasn't a stranger to upheaval, but this time, it felt different; she was different, and right now, she needed to forget.

PEPPER SLID INTO BED, still reliving the feel of Nico's lips on her neck, when a searing white-hot pain enveloped her foot. She yowled in agony and pulled her legs tight into her chest as a trail of hot blood dripped down her heel.

# Chapter Thirty-One

ights flicked on. Azucar was the first out of bed. She tore back the covers and cursed.

"OMG!" Salty exclaimed.

"Toss me that towel," Azucar commanded.

Ginger ran out the door, yelling for help.

Droplets of blood were splattered over the white sheets. Pepper's mind couldn't focus. Was it her period? No. Something was in her bed. An animal? There wasn't anything moving around unless it ran away. It was getting hard to concentrate on anything but the pain.

"What is it?" she asked between gasps.

"Rat trap," Azucar said. "I'm gonna take it off."

As the lever was released, black spots danced before Pepper's eyes, and a spasm coursed through her toe. Azucar pushed the trap aside, then wrapped Pepper's foot in the towel before elevating it to slow the bleeding.

"Those *puttane*," Salty cursed, holding up the trap to reveal a razor blade attached to the lever. "Hey, something is written on the underside of the trap." She turned it over, reading aloud, *"This is what happens to rats."*

"I think you're gonna need to go to the hospital," Azucar said, indicating the bloody towel.

"Ginger should be back with help soon," Salty said, opening the door.

"Hide it," hissed Pepper.

"What?" Azucar asked.

"The trap. Hide it. I don't want Ms. Oscura to know…please," Pepper pleaded.

The door swung open as Azucar pushed the bloody trap under the bed with her foot.

"*Dio mio*," Ms. Oscura said, her phone pressed to her ear. "Yes, Marco, bring the van around, then get up to the cupola. I need you to carry an injured student. *Subito*," she said, reaching Pepper's bedside.

"I think her toe might be hanging on by a piece of skin," Azucar said quietly.

"We'll get you to the hospital, don't worry," Ms. Oscura said, passing her palm over Pepper's forehead in a rare show of motherly affection. "How did this happen?"

The girls all turned to look at Pepper. Her mind was concentrating on the pain, and she was beginning to feel lightheaded from the loss of blood, but she knew enough to conceal the truth, at least for now. Cherry wanted her scared, injured, and gone. But she wasn't playing Cherry's game.

"I dropped a glass earlier and must've missed a shard…" Pepper took a deep breath to keep from losing consciousness. "I guess I stepped down in the dark when I returned after going to the bathroom."

Ms. Oscura looked down at the bloody scene and opened her mouth to reply when Marco burst into the room.

"*Mama Mia!*" *he exclaimed* before lifting Pepper from the bed effortlessly.

"The elevator, Marco, *subito*," Ms. Oscura said.

"Elevator?" Pepper said. But Marco just crossed the room and pushed a panel in the wall aside. Ms. Oscura punched in a code, and the wall slid open, revealing a vintage iron-gated elevator.

"Once upon a time, this was the crew's lookout," Marco said. Guys would be stationed along the roof. This cupola was their quarters." Ms. Oscura gave him a sharp glare. He looked appropriately chastened and turned to step into the elevator.

"Well, that's certainly a surprise," Azucar said, stepping forward with Ginger and Salty.

"No, girls. You'll have to wait here," Ms. Oscura said, sliding the iron gate closed on their concerned faces.

The elevator bumped and shimmied down the three flights to the main floor. Even in her current agony, Pepper was delighted to have found yet another secret exit. She repeated the code to herself until she was sure she wouldn't forget it. The doors slid open, revealing the entrance hall. Huh, that's what's behind that ugly tapestry, she thought as Ms. Oscura held the dusty cloth aside, allowing Marco to step out. They bundled her into the van and took off. As they pulled away, her roommates ran onto the driveway.

IT WAS ALMOST dawn once she was stitched up and released from the hospital. Pepper had been treated immediately, but reattaching a toe took a minute. She thought she'd need to spend the night, but she'd been back in the ICU only a short while when a nurse announced she was being released. Ms. Oscura had filled her prescription at the hospital pharmacy, and they were on their way back to school. It was quite a whirlwind few hours. From her and Nico's secret tryst to almost losing a toe, Pepper doubted many other students had such an exciting evening.

Pepper was still groggy from the medication she'd been given and dozed lightly in the back seat. As the scenery rushed past,

Pepper pulled the band of her sweatpants up to cover the stiff, scratchy hospital shorts she hadn't returned. For some reason, she found pilfering these dingy blue shorts a source of endless amusement.

"I called your parents to inform them of your accident," Ms. Oscura said when they were turning into Valentina's driveway. Pepper's attention snapped back to the moment. She knew what was coming. "The number I had on file was for a pizza restaurant," Pepper grimaced. "I will need to tell them what happened," the headmistress continued.

"Can you say I dropped a knife on my foot during class, and I'm fine?" Pepper asked.

"Will you tell me exactly what happened?" Ms. Oscura countered.

"I already did," Pepper replied.

"No one steps on a piece of glass and almost severs their toe from the top of their foot down." Pepper looked away, unwilling to reveal the truth. "Very well. I see no harm in a slight fib to your parents." Ms. Oscura handed her the phone.

Pepper entered Margaux's cell number and waited. She handed the phone over to the headmistress as it went to voicemail. Ms. Oscura did as she had promised. She said it was a kitchen accident that injured Pepper's toe but that she had received medical attention and would be fine. Pepper doubted there would be a follow-up call from her stepmother. That suited her.

When they pulled up in front of the school, the pink rays of dawn illuminated the sky over Valentina's. Grateful it was Saturday, Pepper maneuvered herself out of the van. She could stay in bed and sleep for the rest of the weekend. Besides, she was in no hurry to see Cherry or The Fruit Bunch.

Marco offered to carry her up to the cupola, but Pepper refused. She'd need to learn to maneuver this boot eventually, so it was best to start now. They had supplied her with one crutch, which left her feeling unsteady and lopsided, but her foot was beginning to throb, and putting pressure on it sent spikes of pain shooting up her leg. Pepper stared at the steps, then admitted defeat. She'd master the stairs another day and allowed Marco to carry her inside. However, she insisted on being put down once they reached the entryway.

Ms. Oscura held the dusty tapestry aside and punched the code into another hidden keypad. "Just for today," she said as Pepper hobbled inside. "I'll send up some fluids and snacks. Don't forget your pills are to be taken every four hours. Set an alarm."

Pepper nodded and slid the gate closed. It rumbled to life and slowly lifted her to the tower level. She slumped against the wall. She was finally alone, and the weight of the past several hours hit her hard. Instead of feeling scared, Pepper felt a resolve burning at the center of her core. Scare tactics might work on some, but not her. She was not going to be intimidated away from the truth. Then the lift door slid open, and she shuffled out to the gasps of her roommates.

"We thought you were dead," Salty wailed, bounding forward to embrace her in a fierce hug.

"No, we didn't. But I did take bets on your coming back with nine toes," Azucar said, closing the elevator gate for Pepper.

"Sorry to disappoint," Pepper said, "But I still have all ten. Thanks to your quick thinking."

"We changed your sheets," Ginger said, helping Pepper across the room. "Who do you think did this?"

"Cherry, who else?" Salty replied.

"She is vicious," Ginger said, propping pillows at the end of Pepper's bed.

"What are we gonna do to Cherry?" Azucar said, smacking her fist into her palm.

"Nothing," Pepper said, wincing as she maneuvered onto her bed. "I'm acting as if it did not happen."

Salty gingerly placed Pepper's foot on the pillow tower.

"Right, that boot on your foot is a new fashion accessory," Azucar said.

"She wants me to freak out. I won't give her the satisfaction, and neither will you. If we don't do anything, she has no ammunition."

"If you say so," Azucar said, seeming crestfallen. "But I'm not responsible if I accidentally trip her down the stairs."

Pepper chuckled.

"Do you need anything else?" Salty asked.

"Ms. Oscura is sending up some essentials, but right now, I just want to sleep," Pepper said, her eyes fluttering closed.

ODDLY ENOUGH, Pepper's injury didn't deter her bullies. They began bumping her booted foot as they passed her in the hallway on the way to dinner Sunday night. It looked like this was life now, she thought, hobbling into the dining room. She wondered what Cherry would do for a follow-up, then cringed. Pepper didn't want to imagine what she had planned for the encore if a razor-blade-rat-trap was her first attempt.

Other than the icy stares from her peers, things seemed normal until just after dessert. As dinner was winding down, Ms. Oscura cleared her throat and stood. The clattering of utensils against plates and the room's chatter quieted as she stood, waiting for silence.

"It has come to my attention that retribution is being carried out at this school. At first, I was willing to allow you girls to settle your disputes, believing these were internal squabbles. I do not believe that interfering in interpersonal matters helps you learn to resolve your differences. It has come to my attention that this incident is not merely a misunderstanding that can be settled once bruised egos have healed." She stopped and surveyed the room.

Pepper slouched in her seat, praying the headmistress wouldn't call on her by name and make everything ten times worse. "Every one of you took an oath upon arrival. I take that oath seriously and will not tolerate having it broken. We are one family here. No one goes against the family. This code of honor has allowed our people to survive for centuries." She paused for effect before continuing. "The goings on of the outside world do not infiltrate Valentina's Academy. This is the reason for your code names. What happens beyond the grounds of this school is inconsequential to your time here. I will not tolerate any more acts of retaliation upon any student in this institution because of her family, connections, or past. If these incidents continue, the party responsible will be expelled. Am I understood?"

A murmur of "Yes, ma'am" undulated through the dining room.

"Very good. All evening activities are canceled for tonight. If things continue as they have been, the final dance will also be canceled, and you will sit traditional end-of-year exams instead. Please return to your rooms for a contemplative night in."

Pepper did not look up from her dinner plate, but she could feel the angry stares of her classmates attacking her. She picked at her half-eaten pot roast as the other students silently filed out.

"For a school teaching us how to carry out clandestine missions, her announcement is not comforting," Pepper said.

Salty gave her a sympathetic look and slid her untouched brownie sundae across the table.

"Thanks, friend."

"Brownies will make it better," Salty replied, smiling.

If only that were true, Pepper thought, taking a large bite.

# Chapter Thirty-Two

The kitchen was peaceful, with the gentle hum of the refrigerator and the warm afternoon light spilling onto the countertops. Now that almost the entire school was against her, Pepper found solace here most days. She was either researching her grandparents' past in the archives and coming up empty—or testing and perfecting recipes for the cooking final.

They had begun planning for their final project: catering the end-of-year dance. Each group was responsible for a carb, two appetizers, one meat and one vegetarian dish, and two desserts. No two recipes could be alike, so they had to coordinate and cooperate with the other groups. It was not a terribly easy task when Cherry was involved. Salty convinced her that Crostini would be a better choice than Focaccia. Now Pepper's group was free to make focaccia Parmesan eggplant sliders.

Signore Tonelli allowed her access to the pantries since she was the only one interested in working outside of class time. She had spent this Saturday morning amid the dusty pages of the filing room searching in vain for answers to her family's past and was transitioning to the kitchen to try a sausage and sage stuffed mushroom cap recipe. She was loaded with supplies from the pantry and pushed the kitchen door open with her backside.

"I thought you'd be here," someone said.

As she spun around, the spices flew out of the mixing bowl and smashed against the stone floor. She looked up to see Coco seated at the nearest table.

"Damn it, Coco. That was the last bottle of oregano in the pantry," she said, reaching for the broom. "Don't help or anything." Coco stayed where she was across the kitchen as Pepper swept up the glass. "Did you want to test one of your dishes? There's plenty of room for both of us."

"No," she replied.

Pepper dumped the broken spice bottles into the trash. "Mind if I get started? I'm going to the movies later."

"With my brother?" she replied.

"How did you know?" Pepper said.

"We're twins. Don't you think we share everything?"

"I didn't realize he talked to you about me."

"He does. And he likes you."

Pepper dumped the mushrooms in a colander and passed them under the running faucet. "Thank you for telling me. I like him, too."

"I mean it. He likes you enough to jeopardize his future," Coco said.

"What's that supposed to mean?" Pepper asked as she patted the mushrooms dry and began slicing off their stems while attempting to remain calm.

"Someone tipped off our father about your past."

"My family's alleged past, you mean."

"Right," Coco said. "And they also told him about you and Nico."

Her heart hammered in her chest. Pepper knew what was coming, but she couldn't bear to hear it. "He thinks I'm unsuitable."

"Not my words. But there's bad blood between our families."

"What exactly?" Pepper asked, her curiosity outweighing the dread of what Coco would say next. But she only shrugged.

"Don't know. Something bad enough that our father has forbade Nico to continue seeing you."

A wave of dread engulfed her. "Why are you even telling me this?" Pepper asked, laying the knife on the cutting mat.

"Because he's refused."

"For me?" she replied, stunned.

Coco nodded. "Our father doesn't go back on promises. He will choose someone else to run the family."

"You?" Pepper asked.

"I doubt it," Coco said. "Besides, I don't have any interest in running the family business. But it'll ruin Nico's life. He acts like he doesn't want it, that soccer is all he cares about, but it's his birthright, his identity. His destiny."

"And you want me to stop seeing him because he won't," Pepper said, putting the pieces together.

Coco touched the tip of her nose with her finger. "I knew you were sharp."

Pepper's mouth went dry, and her tongue stuck to the roof of her mouth. She tried hard to swallow to find her voice, then dipped her head under the faucet and drank.

"I can't do it. I won't," she said, standing to meet Coco's gaze. "He can certainly make his own decisions. Why pressure me to do something he could do himself? Isn't it enough that we make each other happy?"

"For now, can you guarantee that you guys will last?" Coco asked.

Pepper stared at her hard, wanting to proclaim that they'd be together forever. But if she knew anything about life, it was its unpredictability. No one knew what the future held. The weight of the situation settled around her shoulders.

"Nico becoming the next Don of the Rossetti Family is a certainty. Your relationship's survival is not."

"What would you do? If it was the other way around?" Pepper asked.

"The same thing Nico is doing. As hard as it is, I'd hope that the guy I loved would do what was best for me, which is what I'm asking of you," she replied.

Pepper gripped the edge of the counter as wave upon wave of prickly hot sensations traveled from her armpits through her chest and back. She struggled to maintain her breath, knowing Coco was watching her intently. "But he's one of the only bright spots in my life. I can't just turn off my feelings for him," she replied, just above a whisper.

"If you care about him, you can," Coco said. "Sacrificing for the ones you love is the highest calling?"

"That's a cute saying. Did you read it on a greeting card? Who says I love him?" Pepper shot back, incensed at Coco's bravado, coming here and demanding things of her.

Even in her anger, Pepper's mind returned to her family's past —the one she read about in Maria's book over winter break. Fiammetta Castellano came to America alone with her two sons, leaving behind her family and the world she knew. She had sacrificed everything for the ones she loved. It took courage. Pepper knew she had that in her. To sacrifice for love, what more could someone ask? Even if they didn't ask. She nodded slowly.

"Thank you on behalf of my father, even though he'll never know. It'll be hard right now, but this is the right decision. It's Nico's destiny to lead the family."

Pepper swallowed hard. Her emotions were threatening to overpower her composure. She couldn't stand there another moment longer. "You're wrong about not being good at running the family. You have the makings of a leader," Pepper said.

"You'll end it today," Coco said. Pepper noticed it wasn't posed as a question but as a command.

"Don't worry. I'll do it this afternoon," Pepper replied, turning to the oven. She lit the burner and waited, her back to the door, until she heard the soft click of the latch as Coco left. Then she switched off the stove and threw the mushrooms across the kitchen one at a time.

The sage and sausage stuffed caps would have to wait for another day. If she ever had the desire to try the recipe again. Once she finished crying, Pepper put everything away and shuffled outside. She was early for her meet-up with Nico, but it would give her time to figure out what she had to say. Her mind raced with alternatives. Should she tell him about Coco's request? She couldn't guarantee that Nico and her relationship would last. Sacrificing his future for her was a monumental decision, and she was overwhelmed by what that said about his feelings for her. Could she be responsible for changing the trajectory of his life? How could they hope to have a happy future now, with this hanging over their heads?

PEPPER WAS SO preoccupied that she jumped when Nico revved the engine as he pulled up outside the gate.

"Whoa, sorry. I thought you were waiting for me," he said, hopping out of the car. "When do you get that boot off so we can resume our Wednesday workout sessions? I miss my partner."

She looked up at his carefree, happy face. How could she do this to him? "Next week, I think," she replied, voice trembling. She turned her back to him and leaned against the door.

"Are you okay?" he asked, walking around the car.

"Not great, actually."

"Have they started beating you up again?"

"Nothing like that," she replied, touched by his concern. "It's just ... we're getting our final assignments for algebra in a couple of weeks, and I'm already so overwhelmed by the combined English, history, etiquette, and cooking classes final. I can't juggle everything and us. My schoolwork can't suffer." She lied, hating herself.

"What are you saying?" Nico asked, his face hardening.

"We ... I can't see you anymore," she sputtered.

Nico shook his head and turned away. "To think I was willing ..." he drifted off, but she knew what he was thinking. He had been willing to give up everything for her. "That's it. You have to study, so we're through? That doesn't make any sense."

"Classes are more demanding than I imagined, Nico. I can't juggle everything. I care so deeply for you." She reached for his hand, but Nico snatched it away. "I'm sorry."

He paced around the car and kicked the tires. She silently cursed Coco for interfering and herself for going along with this plan. It was unbearable to be causing Nico so much pain, but she stayed silent, knowing it was for the best.

"Don't do this," he said finally. "School will end. We'll have the summer. We don't have to give up on us."

Shoot, she hadn't considered that argument. "That's true," she conceded. "But..."

It was too late; that was the opening Nico needed. He knelt before her, grasping her hands. "We can take a break if you need time to focus on schoolwork."

"But it's not right now, it's ... finals."

Nico stared at their joined hands for a few moments before looking up. "You're right. School is important and deserves our full attention."

Pepper sighed. He was seeing things her way.

"We won't see each other or have any contact at all. It'll be a clean break until school is over," he offered.

Shoot, this was not going how she had planned. But, if he agreed that a break was the best thing, her heart contracted with delight. Maybe they could work this out. She could figure out a way to prove to Nico's father that her grandfather was not the coward he had been rumored to be. And if not, a small voice of doubt said...she could handle the rest once school was over. Save the heartbreak for later.

"All right, but I mean it. No contact," she said.

"None. I promise," he replied. "We'll start after today and won't see each other until the dance."

"The dance?" she echoed.

"Yeah, that's the day after finals, right?"

"Sure," she said, knowing she couldn't reveal that Valentina's finals were the dance.

"We're going together, aren't we?" he asked.

Pepper's mind was racing. She wanted to say, of course, and throw her arms around him, but a public event together when they were supposed to be broken up wouldn't be wise, especially if she hadn't found the proof she needed to clear her family's name. How was she going to talk her way out of this? Pepper chewed on her bottom lip in concentration until Nico cleared his throat.

"Yes, of course," she replied. "Just don't tell Coco our plans."

I'll figure out what to do about the dance later, she decided.

The worry lines between his eyebrows relaxed. "Coco-nuts?" He laughed. "Why would I tell my sister about us?"

"No reason, I thought twins shared everything," she said, remembering Coco's comments in the kitchen earlier today.

"No. We definitely do not," he said, standing.

"Just don't mention it, okay?"

"Of course." He leaned forward, kissed her forehead, and swung open the passenger door. "Hop in."

NICO TAPPED on his smartwatch before flipping a U-turn and speeding toward town. The last few hours were an emotional roller coaster, and she chastised herself for agreeing to continue their date. She should have opted for a clean break, but it wasn't what she wanted. Not at all. Why add today to the misery she would face tomorrow. She cursed Coco for putting this task before her, sighing heavily as she stared out the window. The scenery rushed past, and she realized they had bypassed the movie theater.

"Where are we going?"

"Surprise," he said, the corner of his mouth turned up mischievously. "If this is our last date for a while, I want it to be amazing." Nico turned off the highway and pulled up to a chain-linked gate. A guard stepped over and glanced at his tablet.

"Rossetti reservation," Nico said.

The guard tapped on his tablet, then scanned the code Nico flashed from his smartwatch. "Have a pleasant flight, Mr. Rossetti. You're in bay twelve." The gate slid open, and Nico drove forward.

"We're flying somewhere?" Pepper exclaimed. Nico grinned.

They pulled up beside a sleek, silver jet. A porter appeared as if by magic and opened her door. The whine of jet engines filled the air.

"Welcome, Miss," the porter said, holding his hand to help her out of the car.

Pepper stared at his open hand, trying to process what was happening. She turned to Nico, who was still in the car beside her.

"Where are you taking me?"

"It's a surprise," he replied.

"But ... I look--"

"Beautiful."

"This is crazy! You are crazy!"

He shrugged. "What good are resources if you can't enjoy them?"

Her heart was racing. She trusted Nico. But this was a lot. She'd miss curfew. Although, she was confident she could sneak back in undetected. She took the porter's hand and marveled at the size of the jet. This was the most unbelievable thing that had happened so far this school year.

"We don't have to go," he said, reaching for her. "But I wanted to do something unforgettable since we won't see each other for months."

Her resolve disintegrated. She was about to tell him she didn't want a break. They could keep on seeing each other from now 'till forever.

"No," she replied. Nico's expression grew solemn. "No, I mean, I want to go."

He picked her up around the waist and twirled her in a circle. Then he carried her up the steps onto the plane.

They were greeted by a woman similarly dressed to the porter who opened the car door. She welcomed them aboard and offered them a selection of refreshments and a mezze platter. Pepper declined, too amazed by her surroundings, to contemplate eating or drinking anything. It was the most luxurious level of transportation she'd ever experienced. And it certainly didn't look anything like the planes she'd seen on television.

"Is this for real?" she whispered. The seating area resembled a regular living room with plush white carpet and low leather sofas.

"Come on, we strap in for takeoff and landing back here." Nico took her by the hand and guided her to a row of captain's chairs toward the rear of the plane.

The intercom crackled, and the pilot informed them they had been cleared for takeoff. The engines revved, and they lurched forward. Pepper sucked in a breath and gripped the armrest. Nico grasped her hand.

"I've never flown before," she confessed.

"The pilot does all the work." He winked. "Sit back and relax."

She tried, but each strange clank and bump made her jump. Soon, they were racing down the runway. Pepper squeezed her eyes closed as the nose of the plane tilted up, and she was pushed back into her seat. Then . . . nothing. It was smooth as if they were suspended in air – which they sort of were.

"We'll be at our destination in approximately one hour. You are free to move about the cabin," the pilot said.

Pepper opened one eye. The view was an endless expanse of sapphire blue. She leaned forward, straining against her seatbelt as they passed through thick, cottony clouds. Pepper turned to Nico, but he wasn't in his seat.

"Psst, over here," he said, leaning out from a doorway she hadn't noticed.

"There's more?" she exclaimed, joining him.

He swung the door open, revealing a bedroom. Her eyes widened. "There's a bathroom back here with a small shower if you want to freshen up."

Relief flooded her. "Yeah, that would be awesome, thanks."

"Mind if I go first?"

"Sure," she said, backing out of the bedroom.

She was just getting sleepy when Nico reappeared. His hair was wet and slicked back; water droplets clung to the ends of his curls. He'd changed out of the tear-away workout pants into cream linen pants and a V-neck, form-fitting black t-shirt. He was breathtakingly handsome. Suddenly, Pepper felt very self-conscious about her unwashed three-day hair.

"Guess I'll shower in the plane before we land," she said, still quite nervous about the entire concept. "How does it work?"

"Like a normal shower," Nico replied. "All the stuff is in there, and there's a closet to the right of the bed with women's clothes. Not sure what's in there, but if you want to change, there should be something you'd like."

SHOWERING IN A PLANE was as strange as she imagined. She was steady on her feet one moment, and the next, she was pressed against the shower wall. Pepper quickly rinsed, wrapped herself in a towel, and entered the bedroom. As she slid the closet door open, she forgot she was in an airplane. It was stocked with anything and everything she could possibly need. Rich people lived far different lives than she ever imagined. Pepper ran her hand over the clothes. Sumptuous, buttery, soft fabric in loud, vibrant prints delighted her fingertips. It wasn't her style, but it was better than staying in her hoodie and jeans.

There was a selection of beautiful dresses, but her boot looked clunky beneath the delicate fabric. Eventually, she selected a pair of wide-legged, black lace pants, a gold chainmail handkerchief top, and a cropped blazer. Even though the pants were lace, they still camouflaged her boot. She looked at herself in the mirror. It felt like playing dress-up. Did these clothes belong to Nico's mom or Coco? Were they just on the plane for whoever wanted to wear them?

By the time the pilot announced they were fifteen minutes from landing, Pepper had just finished blow-drying her hair. She felt a little self-conscious, especially since she was in someone else's clothes. When she emerged from the bedroom, Nico looked up, and the expression on his face dissolved her uneasiness. He whistled.

*"Bella ragazza."*

Like magic, a small, glittering oasis of lights appeared out of the blackness below. She pressed her face against the window. As they got closer famous landmarks came into focus, she gasped.

"Vegas!"

# Chapter Thirty-Three

This was an elite world she neither knew about nor dreamt about accessing. It was as unfathomable as being on the moon. Yet here she was. As the sleek elevator doors slid closed, a thumping bass pushed in on them from all sides, followed by complete darkness and then flashing strobe lights. The elevator shot up like a rocket. It reminded her of the plane taking off. Nico grasped her by the waist, and they danced around the small space, then into the club as the pulsating bass of the elevator was replaced by the same heart-thumping music of the club.

It was too loud to express her happiness, but she beamed at Nico. He smiled back, his teeth glowing otherworldly in the black light. They joined the throngs of bodies jostling on the dance floor. There wasn't one style of dance, and Pepper didn't feel self-conscious, just jumping around and moving to the beat. In the darkness, she felt liberated and whooped in delight at the sense of freedom rushing through her body.

THEY DANCED for what felt like hours, and she loved it. When Nico motioned for her to follow him off the dance floor, she was ready for a break. Pepper collapsed onto a plush red velvet sofa beside a sparkling blue pool. The cool spring air was refreshing. As she looked around, Pepper suddenly felt out of place amid the sophisticated people chatting and cradling cocktails. She pulled her jacket on and zipped in all the way up.

"You okay," Nico asked, languidly stretching his arms across the top of the sofa. Pepper shrugged. "Hungry?"

Pepper nodded as he pulled up the menu on the table-top touchscreen. She didn't consider herself a picky eater, but the concoctions listed were too out there for her, and the prices left her speechless.

"Come on," Nico said, standing. "Let's get out of here." Pepper began to protest, but he kept walking. This time, the elevator was normal and zipped them to the main floor, where the valet had their convertible waiting.

"I'm sorry," she said once they were in the car. "We could have stayed."

"Nah, I saw the look on your face. You weren't into that menu."

"No, it was incredible, really."

Nico shook his head. "It's okay. Besides, I have a better spot in mind." He tore out of the hotel driveway, fishtailing across Las Vegas Boulevard.

The strip's glitz and glamour thinned into non-existence. There were still flashing signs, but these were advertising 24-hour slots or dancing girls. Most people passed darkened storefronts.

When Nico pulled into a gas station, she didn't think anything of it until he bypassed the pumps. A long silver food truck was in the corner of the parking lot. A sign stretching the length of the structure advertised they were open twenty-four hours. There was a line stretching to the curb. Nico hopped out of the car, running around to help Pepper up. Then he offered her his arm, and they bypassed the line, walking around to the open back door. Nico rapped on the side of the truck. The woman taking orders finished scribbling on her pad before looking up. Her exquisite face blossomed into pure joy.

"Nicolito," she exclaimed, tearing the order slip and attaching it above the prep area before rushing over to envelop him in a very long hug.

Pepper nervously shuffled her feet and looked at the gray, pebbled asphalt.

"Maria, this is Pepper."

The woman regarded Pepper critically before smiling warmly. "*Mucho gusto*, Pepper. *Ay*, you like 'em spicy, eh, Nicolito?" She poked him in the ribs, and a blush bloomed over his tan cheeks.

"Where is *Mami*?" she asked.

"Back home. We're just taking a quick break from school. I wanted to show Pepper the town."

"*Ay, que bueno.*" She nodded. "I know, you want the usual. What about you, *mi hija*?" Pepper hadn't seen a menu and had no idea what to order. "You like spicy?" Pepper nodded. "Not a vegetarian." Pepper shook her head no. "*Bueno*, I fix a special for you." Then she whirled around, her caramel ribboned ponytail swishing behind her as she returned to the order window.

"I have a feeling I am in for a real treat," Pepper said. Nico beamed at her. "How do you know Maria," she asked, trying to ignore the twinge of jealousy.

"I've been coming here since I was little. The original owners died, and their kids didn't want to run the business. Maria was working at our hotel. She had always been kind to me. One day, she mentioned that she was graduating culinary school but feared she'd never own a restaurant because of start-up costs. I talked to my father, and he agreed that I could invest in her business by providing the start-up funds for her to get this place."

"How old were you?"

Nico thought for a moment. "Thirteen, I think."

Maria passed them a bag and two cups of white liquid that was definitely not milk. She pinched Nico's cheek and returned to the kitchen. They went back to the car, which was garnering a lot of attention from the patrons in line. Pepper knew nothing about cars, but she imagined everything the Rossetti's owned was top-of-the-line.

"You are so involved in, like, grown-up pursuits," Pepper said, taking a tentative bite. Flavors she hadn't even known existed filled her mouth. "Yum!"

"It was worth every penny." Nico smiled proudly before digging in. Pepper wiped a stray smudge of hot sauce from his cheek. "My father encourages us to get involved in causes that speak to us and better the community. That's what we are, right? Guardians of the people we protect."

Pepper nodded. She didn't know. Mostly, she had very little idea what the mafia did.

"I thought everything happened in New York," she whispered, sipping the white drink. A creamy cinnamon flavor coated her tongue and softened the aftereffects of the spices that had set her mouth on fire.

"Not everything," he replied. "Vegas is a bit of a ... it's like neutral territory. Every high-powered family takes care of the city as a unit. It's where we can get business done and not worry–too much–about trouble."

"I feel like I have so much to learn," she replied, focusing on her food. It was some of the most delicious things she had ever eaten. "Azucar would LOVE it here. She's always complaining about the gross Mexican food in Monterey."

"You up to hit another spot?"

"Sure!"

Pepper felt ready to dance the night away, but instead of heading toward The Strip, Nico drove a block down the road and pulled up in front of the Neon Sign Museum.

"This is one of my favorite places in the entire city," he said as they stepped through the lobby and into another world where vintage marquees and hotel signs loomed like giants.

"I love it because these are our roots. Our people built Vegas from dreams and sand."

"You sound like my Nonnu," she said. "In a good way!"

Holding hands as they walked through the exhibit of larger-than-life, vibrant, buzzing signs. Nico explained the history of the original hotels. She liked those signs the best. They made her feel connected to the past.

"I never figured you for a history buff," she said.

"I'm full of surprises," he replied, leading her to a grouping of individual letters stacked into a mismatched alphabet wall. Suddenly, he reached forward and grasped the M, pulling the entire wall forward. Pepper jumped back. Nico grinned and motioned her forward into the dimly lit space.

"You enjoy shocking me, don't you," she said.

He stepped in after her, the wall sliding back into place behind them. "I love seeing the look on your face."

It felt like they were going downhill, but it was difficult to tell in the darkness of the hallway. "Where are we going now? Secret tunnel to a speakeasy?" Nico abruptly stopped. "Did I guess right?" she squealed.

"Yeah, you kinda did." They reached a dead end, and he turned to her, leaning against the rough stone wall. "The life's-blood of Vegas has always and will always be the mafia," he said simply. "Those hotel slots are for tourists. But this is for us."

He knocked on the wall and reached for her hand. She was growing to love the solid, warm certainty of his palm against hers. The door swung open to reveal a gritty, almost seedy room with a thick layer of smoke hanging in the air. They stepped up to a velvet rope.

"Who's this?" The doorman asked, giving Pepper a look that made her recoil.

"My guest. That's who," Nico replied, a steel edge in his voice.

The doorman pulled the velvet rope aside. "Alright, pup, no need to show your teeth. Come on in, kids."

Pepper felt Nico stiffen at the implied insult. He let go of her and placed his hand on the small of her back, ushering her into the den. Light fixtures hung low over all sorts of gambling tables, from poker to craps. It wasn't just gambling taking place, either, she noticed. Men were huddled together deep in serious conversations along the edge of the frivolity.

"Are we underground?" she whispered.

"Yeah. It's cooler in the summer. Back in the day, this place was impossible for the feds to find."

What at first glance looked like one room grew into a warren of smaller dens connecting to the main playing area. Pepper was conscious of the looks they were receiving and wondered if this had been a good idea. A stocky man with wisps of black hair combed from ear to ear waddled over. He stood on tiptoes and said something to Nico. He grunted in agreement and turned to her.

"What do you want to play?"

Her eyes grew wide. "We're allowed?"

"Of course."

"I don't know how to play . . . any of these games," she said, gesturing to the various tables scattered around the room.

"Let's try roulette. It's pretty straightforward."

Nico fished some gaming tokens from his pocket and handed them to her before explaining the general rules. She watched a few spins before placing her one-hundred-dollar chip on fourteen, red. The croupier turned the roulette wheel and dropped the ball. It spun in dizzying circles until it finally came to rest.

"Fourteen, red," the croupier announced.

Pepper turned to Nico. "I won?"

His face split into a wide grin. "You did! You can keep the bet the same or move your chips to another number."

Pepper opted to stay on fourteen, red. Once again, her lucky number delivered a win. Emboldened by her success, Pepper began to select other number combinations. Every time, the ball on the roulette wheel landed on her number. Soon, she'd attracted the attention of the room—tough guys with cigars and beautiful women in revealing dresses crowded around the table, cheering her on.

"She's a natural!" one man said, the ashes of his cigar falling down the front of his tuxedo like snow.

"I should call you Pepper Roulette," Nico whispered, placing a kiss behind her ear.

She moved the tower of chips once more and was lucky again. The people around the table erupted in cheers of disbelief. Then, the man who had spoken to Nico earlier parted the crowd and leaned heavily on the edge of the roulette table.

"Alright, you've had some fun, kids. Playtime's over. Get outta here."

To her surprise, Nico didn't argue. He kissed the man once on each cheek, then turned to her.

"Let's go."

"Don't forget your winnings, honey," the platinum blond, hanging off the arm of the cigar guy, called.

Pepper collected her chips, spilling some as she gathered them against her torso, and followed Nico to the exit. They stopped at a small window where her winnings were exchanged for more cash than she'd ever seen.

Once they were outside bathed in the soft glowing light of hundreds of neon signs, she handed him the wad of cash. "I can't take this."

"Why not? You won it."

The blinking sign to their right sent shadows across his face. "Did I? Or did the ball just happen to land on all my picks?" She teased. "I'm not stupid, Nico. No one is that lucky." His face grew concerned. "I still had fun, don't worry." Pepper stroked his arm. "I'm just sorry you didn't get a chance to play," she said, walking down the gravel path. "You could have won, too." She turned and winked at him.

Nico closed the distance between them in two long strides and was suddenly behind her. Pepper did not turn around as Nico moved her hair to the side. "I am the biggest winner in all of Vegas." His breath was hot on her neck. Swirls of electricity traveled from her ear down her arm and back. She turned around and noticed the vein throbbing in his neck. "And . . . it's because you're with me."

Nico grasped her around the waist and pulled her tight against him. When their lips met, a fire rivaling their dinner's hot sauce burned through her. Unlike the burrito, Pepper had no desire to extinguish this flame.

NICO CUT the car's engine as they silently rolled up to Valentina's gate.

"Thank you for showing me your Vegas," Pepper said, realizing that tonight wasn't just an excuse to show off. Nico revealed deeper parts of himself to her, and she couldn't even continue seeing him. The realization tore through her, leaving a gaping hole in her heart.

"Hey," Nico said as if he could hear her thoughts. "Three months will go fast. You'll see. Unless. . ."

"No. Don't tempt me," she wailed. "I have to be strong for my grades."

"See you at the dance," he said.

Nico pulled Pepper onto his lap. The steering wheel pressed uncomfortably into her side, and her booted foot rested awkwardly against the gear shift. They clutched at one another, like holding on tighter would make time stand still and reality dissolve. As midnight drew near, they had to admit defeat.

"See you in May," Nico called, giving her that stomach-flipping lopsided smile.

"Can't wait." She climbed out of the car, straightened her hoodie, and hobbled across the lawn.

. . .

As Pepper snuggled into bed just before midnight, her tablet dinged softly. She reached for it, perplexed who would be messaging her now. The rapid beating of her heart gave away the truth. She hoped it was Nico, but not after today. They'd promised. She swiped open the home screen, and his face popped up in a chat bubble.

This goes against our deal. No contact.

Nope, I have two more minutes. We said not after today. It's still today.

Let's keep Vegas on ice.

It'll melt ; )

You know what I mean.

I promised to before. I don't go back on my word.

Right. I forgot.

How's the search about your grandfather coming along?

Not great. I've done some web searches, but I'm stuck without access to the good databases.

You'll figure it out. Maybe this will help.
Username: NRosetti Password: 34D0NYk7kH

What's the login for?

Something to help you find the answers. Use it wisely.

The answers? To my Nonnu's banishment?

I know you'll figure it out. Buona sera, signorina.

Grazie, mio principe. Buona notte.

The hallway clock, normally a muffled and overlooked nuisance at night, clanged its twelve chimes, each one like a dagger in her heart. Nico and Pepper's message profiles hovered on the screen. Neither one typed a letter, but the icons glowed dimly, letting the other know they were still there in silent sentry.

Nico had just given her the login to the secure databases she'd desperately needed. She had three months to figure it out, and now she had the tools. Pepper pulled her bed curtains closed and logged in to the server. It would be a long night, but it was worth it to get started. The sooner she cleared her grandfather's name, the sooner she and Nico could be together—and everything would go back to normal.

# Chapter Thirty-Four

The blatant efforts to make Pepper's life hell ceased. A cool indifference followed, worse than any whispered insult or kick to the shins. It was the void of unbelonging that tortured Pepper over the last three months of the term. When she wasn't in class, Pepper retreated to the cupola to hide away from the frigid glares of her classmates. Instead of wallowing in self-pity, she threw herself into preparations for their final project and, of course, continued her research into Nonnu's guilt or innocence. If their training had taught her anything, and it had taught her plenty, it was that giving up was not an option. Even with the distraction of schoolwork, life would have been intolerable if it weren't for her roommates, who showed a fierce loyalty that, in Pepper's opinion, demonstrated true mob wife character.

Not seeing Nico was probably the greatest torture. He abided by their no-contact rule. But before bed each night, she would pop on the chat, and he would be on, not saying a word, his text bubble just hovering in quiet sentry—letting her know he was there. As the days ticked by and they grew closer to the end-of-year dance, Pepper began to dread and anticipate seeing him again. She had made a few minor gains in discovering some insight into her grandfather's life but nothing about this egregious transgression.

Pepper wasn't sure what she had expected to find online; surely no one was going to publish a *Here's What Really Happened to Vincenzo D'Angelo* article. However, since she didn't know the other family or person involved in the incident, she was still coming up empty-handed and faced with the reality of breaking up with Nico in a month. It was a confusing mixture of emotions that often kept her up at night.

Coco had not said another word to her, so Pepper figured Nico had kept their secret from his twin. She was still unsure about ending their relationship. She thought this break might cool her feelings for him, but it had done the opposite. She craved him like she did the dark chocolate torrone Granny made once a year at Christmas. It was a longing that she ached to satiate.

However, with the dance a month away, she had little time to ponder her dilemma. Mrs. Sabatini wasn't kidding when she said this would take all the skills they'd acquired this year. Months ago, they'd received their assignment but had gotten no further assistance from their instructors. It was entirely up to them. The groups Ms. Powell had placed them in for etiquette class became their final project teammates. Some teams had already learned to work together over the year, naturally falling into their leadership roles, while others were ready to murder each other and continued to struggle. Ms. Powell kept a serene smile on her face as if to say, *you wanted to do this your way. Enjoy.* Luckily, Pepper's group had figured out their strengths early on and were content to remain in their positions of power, as Ms. Powell called it.

Also, luckily for Pepper, Chutney did not seem fazed by her family's past and did not join the masses in the school-wide freeze-out. Something for which Pepper was incredibly grateful. She'd never been popular at school before, but she'd also never been a pariah. The friends who stood by her were solid gold. Olive, their fourth team member, wasn't exactly warm and fuzzy anymore. Still, she wasn't overtly hostile, which meant they could all get on with planning for their final.

After winter break, they'd had a final project reveal with their core teachers. It seemed that this was a first for Valentina's Academy, and even the students who were legacies were stunned to learn their final project would be a Don Academy student. Not kidnapping or anything like that, but they would be assigned a student from the Don Academy and tasked with retrieving specific pieces of information known only to the members of their group. Information that would require them to not only work together but utilize everything they had learned this year. This was the ultimate test of their skills. It made it even more challenging because the Don students were being well-trained, too. It was a daunting task that Pepper threw herself into with gusto. After all, what else did she have to do with most of the school ignoring her and being on a relationship break with Nico? Pepper was determined to complete their assignment and receive high marks.

THE COUNTDOWN to finals was on. They had three weeks to go, and Pepper was busy finalizing plans for the dance when Salty burst into the cupola, startling her.

"We need to plan our dance outfits," Salty proclaimed.

Azucar just groaned and pulled her bed curtains closed.

"Don't you have enough dresses?" Pepper asked, looking up from the diagram she was designing on her tablet. She had the brilliant idea to station her team around the auditorium to best intercept their mark: Mario Testaverde. That way, they could ambush him individually, which would be less conspicuous than together. However, she didn't like the idea of one person being responsible for acquiring the target. Pepper's scheme used each girl's skills to facilitate their assignment easily rather than burdening one person.

Mario was the son of a high-ranking capo in the Mid-Atlantic

Segal family. He had dreams of grandeur, but if the aptitude test Chutney found in the Don's database could be believed, he would be lucky if he became a wiseguy. If things went according to her plan, Mario would have no clue he was being pumped for information. That is precisely how she wanted it.

"Firstly, no. Secondly, I was mostly talking about you," Salty said.

Pepper sat up. "Really, Salty, don't you think I have better things to worry about than what I'm wearing? For one thing, we need to review our strategy at the dance."

"For an undercover operative, being convincing is as important as being stealthy," she replied, quoting Ms. Powell.

"Fine," Pepper replied, putting aside her diagram. "But I'm not wearing a tutu."

Salty rolled her eyes. "That is *my* signature look. Besides, you need to wow your haters with something stunning."

"I don't have the budget for stunning. My funds are more the 'I tried' variety."

"That just won't do. We are going shopping," Salty proclaimed. Pepper made a move to protest, but Salty ignored her. "Relax, we aren't going to Carmel. I think we should hit the boutiques near the wharf. Trust me. We will find you something amazing."

"Make that thrift shop, and you've got a deal, but you also have to help me plan our strategy for the dance."

"Of course, what's a good Beta for?" Salty replied.

"Salty, you aren't my Beta," Pepper replied. "It's just an assignment."

"Of course I am. And with you as the Alpha, it's fun. I don't think I could have stood taking orders from some of the other Alphas, but you are fair, and I like that. Besides, you also don't lord it over us. You're on the team, not just in charge of it."

Pepper was taken aback. She hadn't thought much about the whole "roles of a team" thing since they were assigned early in the year, but Salty was right. Pepper found leading came second nature. She hadn't been able to exhibit it in her father's house, and she was happy that Salty felt she was a good leader.

"That means a lot, thanks," Pepper replied.

"Anytime. Now, can we go shopping? The van is leaving in ten minutes," Salty said.

Pepper hesitated as she was reaching for her shoes. "The van?"

"Yeah, how else did you think we'd get there?"

"Uh…walk?" Pepper replied.

"Not enough time."

"Is anyone else going?" Pepper asked in a small voice that betrayed her vulnerability.

Salty sat beside Pepper on the bed. "You have to stop hiding. I know these last few months have been hell for you, but making this your personal cave of solitude isn't helping at all."

Pepper flopped back against her pillows. "It's just so hard not being able to defend Nonnu. They think he was a rat, and I still don't have any proof he wasn't."

"Hiding up here isn't helping anything. It's just making them feel like they won. Show those witches what a bad babe you are," Salty said.

Pepper chuckled. "I'm not sure about that, but you're right. With just three weeks left of school, I might as well come down from my tower."

"Good," came the muffled reply from behind Azucar's closed bed curtains.

"What was that?" Pepper replied.

Azucar flung the panels aside and swung her legs out. "I was so tired of your moping around up here. It's about time you grew a backbone."

"Is that so?"

"Yes, it is. Now, are we going shopping or what?" Azucar asked.

Salty and Pepper smiled at each other. Since they were in different groups, the girls had been spending less time together as the dance grew closer. This would be a rare moment of togetherness.

"With you two by my side, I can face anything in that van," Pepper said. "Azu, it's a shame you aren't in our group. We'd kill the final assignment."

"Uh, let's hope not," Salty said. "We aren't whacking Mario Testaverde, just finding out...uh, nothing." She quickly stopped speaking when Pepper gave her a deadly look. Their target was supposed to be a secret.

"Don't worry. I won't spill the beans," Azucar said.

Pepper was cautiously optimistic about their shopping trip. She had a few bucks saved and relied on Salty's fashion prowess to create an incredible outfit. Despite her trepidation about the dance, she desperately looked forward to seeing Nico again. Even if she couldn't uncover the truth about Nonnu in these last few days, and had to end things once and for all.

Later that afternoon, laden with packages, mostly all Salty's, the girls trudged up the stairs to the cupola.

"I can't believe they wouldn't let you try this stuff on, not even over your clothes," Salty exclaimed as they reached the door. She had found a wide variety of items in the boutiques they had stopped into "for just a minute," which turned into at least an hour. But Pepper was pleased with the items she'd found in the thrift store. She just hoped they all fit.

When they got inside, Pepper handed Salty her packages and placed her own on the bed. Salty turned over her bags and dumped out her purchases.

"Come on, try on your dress. I'm dying to see it," she demanded.

Pepper pulled the slinky wine-colored sheath from the plastic bag and held it by the thin spaghetti straps. Out of all the formal wear in the thrift store, she liked this one the best. It reminded her of the minimal vibe of the 1990s. She imagined Granny wearing a similar dress to a dance.

"Try on your stuff, too," Pepper said, fishing a pair of black satin gloves from the bag. Her look was simple, which she thought provided a nice contrast to Salty's over-the-top fashion sense. It was also cheaper. She picked up a ribbon from her desk drawer, slipped on the cameo-style button she'd bought at the thrift store for a dollar, and tied it around her neck.

"Understated elegance," Salty said.

Pepper turned and regarded herself in the mirror. The dress skimmed her curves in just the right place. The woman at the thrift store, who wouldn't let her try the dress on, said it was sewn on the bias, and it would fit fine. Pepper still didn't know what that meant, but she was grateful the dress stretched and cinched in all the right places. Her long hair fell past her shoulders, and she gasped at her reflection. Their resemblance was uncanny.

"All right, you're next," Pepper said, crossing the room to assist Salty, whose bangles had gotten snagged in the zipper. Pepper unhooked the metal pieces and pulled the dress over her friend's head. It fluffed out like the top of a cupcake.

"You know what? You could hide some serious equipment up in there," Pepper said, marveling at the skirt's width.

"I could what?" Salty exclaimed.

"Hide stuff, like if we need…I don't know…stuff."

"You are thinking like a Don, not a wife. We don't need to go in guns blazing," Azucar said, smoothing out her skintight body-con mini dress that shimmered, snakelike when it caught the light. To Pepper, it looked more like a fancy workout get-up.

"She's never letting you wear that," Salty said, fluffing her bubble gum pink skirt.

"That's why I got this to go with it," Azucar said, removing the black lace dress she'd bought at the thrift store. It was more grandma-goes-to-a-funeral than high school dance.

"Is that going on top of the dress? You know there are gonna be chaperones. You can't just strip in the bathroom once you get there," Salty said.

"Have you no faith in me?" Azucar replied, reaching for the scissors on the desk. She cut the floor-length skirt from the long-sleeved, shoulder-padded top. Then she ripped the lining free from the lace and slit the skirt up the middle. Pepper was intrigued. This seemed like it could go from masterpiece to DIY hot mess with one wrong snip of the scissors. Then Azucar held it around her waist, letting the sides almost meet. When she stepped forward, there was a flash of leg and a shimmer from the black fabric.

"If you can pull it off, it'll look incredible," Pepper said.

"If? Trust, *chica*. My Abuela taught me to sew by hand, thank you very much. I could whip this up tonight if I had any ribbon." Azucar sighed and put the lace skirt piece aside.

"Here," Pepper said, un-tying the velvet ribbon around her throat. Azucar looked up, eyes shining.

"I can't take that. It's yours."

"I'd rather wear my locket and ring," Pepper said, tugging on the gold chain. "Keeps my family close."

"Thank you. You're the best."

"Anything for a friend," Pepper replied.

Pepper noticed that the three of them made quite the picture—fierce individuals yet still a cohesive unit.

"Hey, are you going to the dance with Dameon?" Pepper asked Azucar.

"Probably," she shrugged.

Salty gasped and looked at Pepper. By this point in the year, they could almost communicate without words, but not quite. Pepper had a feeling she knew what her bestie was excited about.

With a week to go, Pepper and Salty decided on a group meet-up to finalize their assignment. But before the rest of the members arrived, they huddled in the center of the cupola. A rare burst of afternoon sunlight encircled them on the whitewashed wood floor.

"This is madness. How are you going to run two operations at once?" Salty exclaimed, staring at Pepper skeptically.

"Easy, we all have our part, and mine is nearly completed," Pepper replied. "I'll sneak away during the dance."

"But breaking into the Don Academy's archives during the dance," Salty said, "that's insane. It's like you want to get caught."

"Nonsense. Firstly, when else will I have a legitimate reason to be there? Secondly, I can say I got lost if I get caught."

"But the gym isn't even attached to the main school," Salty pointed out.

"Then I'll say my date lured me away from the crowd."

"You are impossible," Salty said. "What about the chaperones?"

"Have some faith," Pepper replied. "I have it all figured out."

"What's in there that you think you so desperately need?"

"Remember when Chutney hacked into Don's main frame so we could research Mario last week?" Salty nodded. "Well, I took some extra time and checked on the archives."

Salty gasped. "I don't know why I'm surprised."

"Me either," Pepper replied.

"Obviously, you didn't find what you needed."

"Not exactly. They haven't digitized their files, but they did make an index, and there is an entire file on Nonnu dated around the time we ended up in Denver."

"What does that prove?"

"That they have some information that I currently don't."

"It seems too risky," Salty said.

"You know how hard I've been searching. There's nothing in the paid online databases, which means it wasn't news or someone worked hard to cover it up. Either way, I have to find out which it is. Come on, Salty. You know this is my last chance. We're leaving in a little over a week, and then it'll be back to suburbia."

Salty sighed dramatically. "I'm in. What do you need me to do?"

"Just have my back at the dance."

"You know I always do," Salty replied.

The door swung open, and Olive stepped inside, ending the debate over Pepper's side mission.

"Come on in," Salty said. "Pepper has a great plan for the dance."

Olive sat at the desk nearest to Salty's bed. Pepper wondered if maybe they should have met in the library, but this was the only place they could be assured of not being overheard.

"How's the toe?" Chutney asked, joining them a moment later.

"Still healing," Pepper replied. "It aches when it's gonna rain, so that's...helpful, I guess?"

"Way to look on the bright side." Chutney smirked, leaning back to stare at the domed ceiling. "I hope I get this room next year."

Pepper and Salty looked up sharply.

"What? You think Ms. Oscura's gonna let you four have it every year until we graduate?" Chutney asked.

"Hadn't given it much thought," Salty replied. "But it certainly feels like home now."

"Since we're all here, let's finalize this plan," Pepper said, reaching for her tablet.

THEY WORKED for the rest of the afternoon, smoothing out the coordination of Pepper's tag-team recon-style operation. Salty would be the decoy, charming Mario. Chutney would act as Salty's wingwoman when, in reality, she would be pairing Mario's phone to her own and downloading more intel. Olive would be the stealthy wallflower waiting to lend a hand if needed.

Thanks to the audio-relay system Chutney had designed, they'd be in constant contact. Pepper would oversee the entire process and make sure it ran smoothly, then slip away when the coast was clear. Of course, Salty was the only one aware of that fact. That way, they'd know when all the information had been retrieved. After it was all over, they would have to present their findings and tactics in a final paper due first thing Monday morning, so the more precise they were now, the easier it would be to write their essay after the dance. Now that the school project was in place, Pepper just had to worry about her side mission—breaking into the world's most prestigious Mafia Boss Academy—without getting caught.

# Chapter Thirty-Five

The afternoon of the dance was devoted to preparing their dishes for their final and getting ready. They had a deadline of four p.m. to give Signore Tonelli their appetizers and dessert before he took everything over to Don's gymnasium. Pepper crossed the small prep kitchen and began slicing the cooled focaccia.

"Too much?" Salty asked, holding a mushroom cap overflowing with sausage meat.

"Uh…yeah, maybe," Pepper said, looking over her shoulder. "Just put about half of that in for the rest."

Salty returned to the counter and continued stuffing the mushroom caps before transferring them to baking sheets.

"How much longer 'till we can go get ready?" Salty asked.

"You said you'd help me cook. Ginger did the prep, and Azu's gonna clean up. Come on, I need you here. We still have the sliders."

"I know, but how much longer?" Salty whined. "I need to wash my hai-ah."

Pepper smirked. Salty's accent thickened when she was stressed. "Should've done it earlier."

"And have my haaai-ahh smell like sausage at the deaance-ahh? Gross."

Pepper checked the timers. "Fine; you can get ready once we assemble the sliders."

Salty powered through assembling the focaccia parmesan eggplant slides, then shot out of the kitchen. Pepper shook her head and sighed. At least everything looked good, and they were running on schedule. She'd still have enough time to get ready. Pepper took the mushroom caps from the oven and set them on the counter to cool before layering the mini tiramisu trifles into delicate dessert cups. She glanced up at the other teams, who were fretting over their cupcakes not cooling in time to apply icing. She was grateful they had decided on a dessert that could be made in advance and assembled quickly.

"TA-DA!" Azucar yelled, bursting through the kitchen door. She twirled in her impossibly high black stiletto heels, the lace overlay skirt fanning out behind her. The other teams were scrambling to finish on time and hardly glanced up as Azucar sauntered into the kitchen.

Pepper applauded her roommate's accomplishment. "You aren't seriously going to clean up dressed like that, are you?"

"Of course. I wouldn't leave you hanging. Besides, I'll just detach my skirt, kick off my shoes, and put on an apron."

"Thank you. Your dress looks great, Azu. I had doubts, but you totally pulled it off," Pepper said.

"What can I help with?" Azucar asked, tying an apron around her waist.

"I still have to get everything in the containers and ready for transportation. Plus, I need to assemble the tasting plate for Signore Tonelli to grade."

"You do that. I'll get everything in the containers," Azucar said.

Pepper nodded, grateful for the support during this last push to finish on time. She had it all under control, but there was a massive amount of food, and this was not a one-woman job.

They worked furiously for the next few minutes, getting everything together. Pepper plated their final dish just as their teacher strode into the kitchen.

"Time is up," he bellowed. "Step away from your dishes. I will taste your creations before transporting the food to the Don's Academy." Pepper and Azucar stood at their station as he approached, a clipboard cradled in his arm. "Where is the rest of your team?" he asked.

"We split up duties, professor," Pepper replied. "They were in charge of prep."

He took one bite of each dish, made a notation on the clipboard, and then moved on to the next station. Pepper let out the breath she had been holding and wiped a drip of sweat from her temple.

"Good job, now get upstairs and get ready," Azucar whispered. "I got it from here."

THE ENTRYWAY WAS PERFUMED with the heady aroma from dozens of arrangements that began arriving the morning of the dance. It looked like a florist shop. Some were from parents eager to celebrate their daughter's end-of-year accomplishments, others from suitors awaiting their partners at the dance. Pepper was surprised when Marco called to her as she emerged from the basement. He passed her a long, slim box. She saw a stunning arrangement of red roses through the clear cellophane panel.

"There was no note," he informed her with a wink.

Pepper smiled and thanked him before continuing to the second floor for a vase. Preparations for the dance were well underway, and she had to squeeze her way into the bathroom to fill the chipped glass vase with water.

"Oh, it looks like someone is popular," Ginger said, adjusting her towel before stopping to push open the box and smell the fragrant blooms. She wrinkled her nose slightly. "Are they from Nico?"

Pepper shook her head, aware of the others in the room. "Doubtful. We aren't together anymore, remember?"

"Yeah, I thought maybe he was trying to be gallant and makeup," Ginger said, sighing.

"Wishful thinking. Besides, there wasn't a note," Pepper said as she finished filling the vase.

"Secret admirer," Ginger replied dreamily. "I'm gonna see if I got anything." She raced out of the bathroom, still clad only in a towel. Pepper could hear her feet slapping down the hallway. She smiled inwardly. Ginger was a hopeless romantic. She, on the other hand, was not, but there was a small part of her that grew giddy at the thought these were from Nico in anticipation of their reunion date tonight.

Pepper pulled off the ribbon and removed the lid to reveal a dozen long-stemmed roses. Mingled with the sweet scent of the roses was a sour note she couldn't identify. It reminded her of the marina at low tide. She shrugged, having never received a bouquet of anything before, and figured it was the container they had been delivered in. Pepper sniffed each flower as she placed them, one at a time, into the chipped, clear glass vase. As she reached for the last rose, she noticed a lump under the green wrapping. Pepper moved aside the filler greenery along with the paper and discovered a slim, soggy, newspaper-wrapped parcel hidden underneath her flowers. She placed the greenery into the water and recoiled as she picked up the stinking parcel. Pepper peeled back the wet newspaper to reveal a dead fish. She shuddered and placed the top back on the box.

"Are you feeling okay? You're white as a sheet," Ginger said as she stepped inside empty-handed.

Ginger's voice sounded like it was underwater. Pepper barely registered her question as she looked up and nodded robotically.

These weren't from Nico, after all. She should have known he wouldn't give up their secret yet. On the afternoon of their last date, she suggested that they make their reunion appear spontaneous. He'd thought it was silly, but she pressed him to agree. At that moment, she probably could have asked him to wear a bow tie and nothing else to the dance, and he would have consented. At least this way, if she found what she needed, it wouldn't look like she had tricked Coco all these months. And if she didn't, no one would have to know, and she'd break up with him as she'd initially promised all those months ago.

Salty slammed the cupola door. Pepper flinched at the noise. "Oh my Gawd, you got flowers!" she squealed, dramatically changing her demeanor. She bounded over to Pepper's bed but recoiled when she went to smell the flowers. "Ugh, the tide must be low," she said, reaching to close the window.

Pepper tugged Salty's sleeve as she reached for the window and motioned to the parcel in her lap. Salty paused as Pepper removed the lid and pulled back a corner of the newspaper to give her a peek at the fish.

Salty let out a strangled cry and blessed herself. Then she quickly wrapped the fish back in the newspaper and replaced the top of the box across Pepper's lap. Salty grasped the parcel and marched to the door.

"Wait," Pepper said. She motioned to the roof door. Salty gave her a confused look, then shrugged and followed Pepper. They stepped outside, leaving Ginger in the room oblivious to their actions as she blew her hair dry.

They'd learned their lesson after Pepper figured out how Cherry had overheard her identity, but this was still the best place to talk privately; they just had to be smart about how they did it. Since covert communications were part of their training, they used the tactics they'd been taught.

"This is bad," Salty whispered, holding up the fish. "Where was it?"

Pepper pointed to the fish parcel and pantomimed where she found it hidden inside the bouquet of roses.

"Who?" Salty replied soundlessly.

Pepper shrugged and shook her head. Salty embraced her friend in a hug that put her close enough to whisper in Pepper's ear. "This is a Sicilian mafia omen of death. You need to tell Ms. Oscura."

Pepper pulled back and shook her head. She looked past her friend to a bird that had alighted on the stone railing. She watched it for a moment. When a large gust of wind blew over the roof, the bird took flight, unperturbed. Pepper realized that the bird put its faith in neither the railing nor fear in the wind but trusted its wings. She needed to find out what was happening, but if she told Ms. Oscura, the dance would surely be canceled, which wouldn't allow her to figure out who wanted her dead and why. She had to be innovative.

She thanked her proactive self for washing her hair yesterday. A spritz of dry shampoo and she'd look presentable enough for the dance without fighting for the showers. Clearly, this was bigger than a petty dispute over a boy; at least, she thought so. Cherry hadn't sneered in her direction since Ms. Oscura's dressing down at the beginning of the term. This was something else. Pepper was going to figure it out. It was time to trust her instincts and fly.

She turned back to Salty and touched her index finger to her heart and then to her head before holding it aloft, meaning she had a plan. Salty pursed her lips but tugged at her right earlobe, signaling she was in. Pepper nodded. It was time to end this.

# Chapter Thirty-Six

The Don Academy gymnasium was a later addition to the original school. It sat adjacent to the soccer and football fields to the right of the main building. The girls were not permitted to be picked up from Valentina's by their dates. They crammed into the van until it was well beyond its seatbelt-approved capacity of twelve. Salty, who refused to be left behind, lay across the laps of the five girls in the back row, her pink skirt enveloping them in a cloud of cotton candy-like fluff. No one wanted to arrive after the festivities had started.

"Why didn't they just hire more buses?" Salty whined.

Pepper tried to shrug her shoulders, but she was hunched between Azucar and Coco. "They're cheap?" she finally replied.

Valentina's van pulled up outside. Searchlights on either side of the entrance sent towers of blood-red light into the sky. Pepper knew it was the Don Academy's school colors, but considering her earlier delivery, it felt ominous. Don's students milled around out front. Some held bouquets or corsages while others were waiting, squinting against the glow from the searchlights as the girls exited the van as elegantly as possible.

"Now, Missy," Marco said, helping the last girl from the third row out of the van. "How you expect to get down now?"

Salty twisted to the side and tried to prop herself up by digging her elbows into the thighs of the girls she was reclining upon.

"Umm..." she said.

"Come on, Salty, we want to get inside," Coco whined.

"Just slide out the way you went in," Azucar offered.

"With my bum in the air?" Salty asked, aghast. "My dress will expose my goodies."

"Whatever works," Azucar replied. "But get going."

"Yeah, my dress is getting wrinkled," Chili said. "Hurry up."

"All right..." Salty sighed, scooting toward the open door. Marco stepped forward to guide her as she began to wiggle backward, kicking her legs into the air. Salty's wedge heel connected with his face. He cried out in pain and dropped to the ground.

Soon, Don students were rushing forward to assist. Before Salty could protest, they grasped her like a rolled-up carpet and heaved her to the sidewalk. Luckily, her dress had so many fluffy layers that her "goodies" were not on display. Half of Salty's dress was over her head, giving her the appearance of a popped wad of bubble gum.

"OH MY GAWED!" Salty exclaimed. "I'm so sorry."

Marco waved her off. "Fuggedaboutit." Blood was dripping from his nose in a steady stream. Dameon, Azucar's date, handed Marco a handkerchief. "Thanks, *paisan*." He pressed the white square to his nose and hobbled back to the van. "Everybody out?" he asked. "Good." Then he slammed the door and drove off.

Pepper had extricated herself from the van and was smoothing her dress down when Nico picked her up around the waist and twirled her in a circle.

They'd never decided on a place to meet, and she was hyper-aware of Coco's presence. He placed her on the ground, and Pepper took a step back. Nico's smile faltered. She put her hand on his bicep and gave it a little squeeze.

"Let me just make sure Salty's okay. See you inside," she said with a quick wink.

Nico's expression relaxed, and he nodded.

Pepper found Salty in the bathroom repairing her eye makeup, which had run down her cheeks in multi-hued drips.

"Nice entrance," Pepper said. If we had planned for you to be the diversion, I would have been ready to slip away when we arrived."

Salty glared at her.

"I'm sorry. Look, not that many people saw. Plus, your dress stayed down. Well, most of it did anyway. It's fine."

Her friend swiped a paper towel angrily across her cheek.

"You brought stuff for touch-ups, right? We'll fix everything good as new."

Salty took a deep breath and nodded, handing over her clutch, which was indeed filled with all the supplies they needed to repair the damage done by her tears of embarrassment.

"So I have an issue," Pepper said, dabbing concealer under Salty's eyes. "Nico's already seen me. I think it's gonna be tough to sneak away."

"Then don't," Salty replied. "Listen, I've been thinking, trying to take this on by yourself is madness."

"It's too late now," Pepper replied.

"Hey, should I maybe tone this down?" Salty asked, gesturing to her eyes.

"Why?"

"Cherry said it looked like a unicorn threw up on my face."

"When was this?"

"Just before I took the last spot in the van."

"*Che vacca!* She's just jealous. You be as colorful and glittery as you want. I think you are a sparkly, fabulous original."

The corners of Salty's pink pout turned up in a smile. Pepper did a quick check of her makeup. Salty had applied smoky maroon eyeshadow that matched the color of Pepper's dress and made her green eyes sparkle like emeralds. She swiped away an errant black smudge of mascara from under her right eye before returning to Salty, who was now mainly composed.

As THEY LEFT THE RESTROOM, the base from the music inside the gymnasium pulsated through the air. Olive was ascending the stairs alone. Pepper was impressed with how committed she was to her role. Usually a bright and cheerful personality, she had donned an unadorned black dress and kept her makeup and hair minimal.

"Olive," Pepper said, waving her over. "I almost didn't see you. Has the second van arrived?"

"I was in the first van," Olive replied.

"With us?" Pepper asked, stunned. "I didn't even see you."

"That's the point, right?" Olive said.

"Exactly. Wow, excellent job. So we know our roles, right?" Both girls nodded. "Chutney is probably on her way in the next van drop-off, so let's get in there and get this party started."

"Remember the school motto," Olive said.

"Never underestimate a lady," Salty replied.

"And don't get caught," Pepper added with a wink.

The three walked into the auditorium and were swallowed by the glittering spectacle. An old-fashioned disco ball that looked like a remnant from the school's attic twirled lazily overhead, sending squares of light across the crowded floor.

"See? You aren't overdressed," Pepper said. Salty gave her a look, then flitted away in search of their target. Pepper turned to make a comment to Olive, but she'd already disappeared. Wow! That girl was good at blending in.

"Ew, it's eau-de-stinky-boy in here," Azucar said, walking up. "Why couldn't we have had this in a hotel ballroom?" She handed Pepper a cup of punch.

"Same reasons we only have one van," Pepper replied, taking a sip. She looked up sharply. "Did you spike this?"

Azucar grinned.

"Where did you get it?"

"I told my date to bring me a flask instead of flowers. Speaking of dates," she said, slinking away.

Nico sidled up to Pepper, sliding his hand along the small of her back. The once familiar but now unexpected gesture caught her off guard, but she leaned into his touch, craving more. "Crisis under control?" he asked.

"Yes, thankfully," Pepper replied. "Want some? I don't care for whiskey."

He took the plastic cup and drained the liquid. "Dance?"

"Wait, follow me," Pepper said, weaving through the crowd to the food station. She searched the trays until she found her appetizers. "Try one." She selected a sausage and sage stuffed mushroom cap from the platter and held it out to Nico. His smile melted, and he shook his head.

"Not good?"

"No, perfection," he replied. "What restaurant catered?"

"We did," she replied proudly. "Part of our culinary final."

"This was you?" he asked, reaching for another. Pepper nodded shyly. "Did you make anything else?" She looked down at the row of appetizers and spotted their focaccia eggplant parmesan sliders. They moved down the row, sampling other teams' appetizers. The canapés were decent, but Cherry's bruschetta was soggy. Pepper smiled inwardly. Serves her right, rat trap setting witch.

Salty was adjacent to Mario Testaverde. He was loading a plate with multiples from each tray and hadn't glanced up at Salty, who looked on the verge of tears once more. Salty gave Pepper a pleading look. Things were not going well. Flirting was a subject they'd only touched upon; it was an advanced class for their later years at Valentina's. From how Salty was floundering,

Pepper sure wished they'd had better training in that department.

Where was Chutney? It wasn't Pepper's assignment to be the wingwoman here. She'd step in, of course, but that wasn't the point. They were a team. Pepper bit into a slider and was momentarily distracted by the burst of flavor. They'd better get an A for their culinary portion, she thought.

Pepper dropped her bag and "accidentally" kicked it under the table. Nico moved to retrieve it, but she dove under the table ahead of him. With Nico so close by, this was the only way to communicate with her team unnoticed—a flaw in the plan she'd need to resolve for future assignments.

"Chutney, where are you?" she whispered, confident the wireless earbuds would transmit her question. There was no reply. Pepper cursed under her breath. She had a moment, maybe less, to come up with something. "Olive, get the DJ to play *Jump Around.*"

"Ick, why?" Olive replied.

"Because it's his favorite song. Salty, get out there and jump around with him on the dance floor."

"Affirmative," Salty replied.

Things were not going according to her plan.

"Hey, you all right?" Nico asked, holding the tablecloth aside as Pepper backed out, clutching the bag.

"Yeah, why?"

"That crease between your eyes tells a different story. Is something wrong? You seem preoccupied."

Pepper opened her mouth to reply when the screeching, siren-like opening of *Jump Around* pealed through the gym. Mario Testaverde stopped mid-bite, fist pumped, then exclaimed: I love this song, before bolting for the dance floor. Salty hurried after.

"Nope. Everything's great," she replied.

Things were back on track—at least the project was. Now, she just had to figure out how to ditch Nico and break into the Don Academy. Like those were small tasks, she chuckled to herself. It would have been easier to loop him in, but she couldn't have taken the risk without Coco seeing.

"I was hoping for a dance where I could hold you close, but this will do," Nico said, offering her his hand. They joined the crowded dance floor, fist-pumping and hopping in a frenzy.

Suddenly, Mario doubled over, and Pepper stopped to search the room for a threat. Nico, she noticed, had done the same. Then, Mario spewed a stream of vomit across the floor. Pepper looked up in horror as Salty was already in mid-jump and descending fast. She landed in the pool of sick, splashing everyone, including herself.

People screamed in horror as the drops of vomit went flying into the crowd. Mario looked up, his face covered in puke. Realizing what had happened, Salty blanched and looked like she would up-chuck in a moment. Pepper rushed forward, fighting the crowd running away from the scene.

"It's fine," she said, reaching her friend, mindful to avoid stepping in the throw-up. "Come on, let's get cleaned up." Pepper guided Salty, like a traumatized child, across the gym floor to the restroom.

The restroom was already packed with girls. But Pepper pushed her way inside, depositing Salty in a rigid plastic chair behind the door.

"Ew, she's tracked puke in here on her shoes," Peach said, making retching noises.

Pepper flung a wad of paper towels to the floor to cover the mess and returned to her best friend. Salty was staring into space, not reacting as Pepper took the wet towel and wiped the splashes of vomit off Salty's ankles and calves one at a time. The stench was overpowering, and it took all of Pepper's willpower not to be sick herself. Then she removed Salty's shoes and ran them under the faucet, grateful that her friend had gone with sparky acrylic wedges that were waterproof.

The crowd inside the bathroom thinned out. Salty was

physically mended, but she still hadn't uttered a word. The door swung open, and in walked Chutney.

"Where have you been?" Pepper snarled. "We are flunking this assignment!"

"Someone broke Marco's nose, and we had to wait for Ms. Powell to get dressed and drive us here. What's wrong with her?"

Pepper sighed and filled in her teammate about the last fifteen minutes.

"That's rough. But you get out of here. I'll take over," Chutney said.

"No. In case you hadn't noticed, she's catatonic. I'm not leaving."

"My assignment is wing-woman, so yes, you will. She'll be fine. They're making everyone go outside while they mop the floor anyway. I'll take her out the back. After some fresh air, she'll be fine."

Pepper hesitated, but she knew Chutney was right. Salty's cheeks had started to regain their color. It was time for Pepper to stick to the plan and go.

"You take care of her," Pepper said. She turned to check her reflection in the mirror, smoothed back a strand of hair, and walked out. Salty would be fine with Chutney, but Pepper still felt awful for walking away from a friend in her time of need. As she stepped back into the gym, the stench of vomit mingled with the aroma of the appetizers. She felt the bile rise in her throat, but Pepper used the last of her self-control to push it aside. The rows of saucer-shaped lights above had been switched on and hummed to life. The disco ball was still lazily rotating above the scene, unfazed by the goings on. It all felt much less magical than it had a few moments ago.

Mrs. Sabatini, one of their chaperones, noticed Pepper and called to her. "This way, all students out through this exit until we get this awful mess cleaned up."

"The dance isn't over?" Pepper asked.

"Gawd, no, it's just a tiny setback. Get going." She shooed her to the exit.

WITH THE DJ still merrily spinning tunes, Pepper pushed against the door, but nothing happened. She turned to see if this was the correct exit, but Mrs. Sabatini was not in sight. She grasped the crossbar with both hands and leaned against it using her full body weight. With a creak, the heavy exit door swung open into the night. Some emergency exit, she thought, stepping outside and promptly wobbling unsteadily as her heel sank slightly into the gravel. The door closed with a whoosh, and she jumped. The only light was over the door, sending a halo of yellow around the exit. Where was everyone else? She squinted into the darkness. Burbling conversations floated in the shadows, but they weren't out here. Chill bumps that had nothing to do with the frigid night air rose along her arms. Her breath came in quick puffs of white mist. She turned and reached for the door handle, only to find it locked.

"Copy. Anyone? Hello," she said into the transmitter on her wrist. Silence.

# Chapter Thirty-Seven

Pepper stared into the abyss of darkness and realized she must be looking at the hedge-covered fence surrounding the tennis courts, which were adjacent to the soccer field. If she were facing the field, outdoor lights from the main school building would be visible, and the only light was behind her around the door. Unsteadily, Pepper inched along the outer wall through the gravel toward what she hoped were the rest of her classmates. The talking grew louder, echoing around her in the darkness.

However, when she turned the corner, the empty field dimly lit by the softly glowing sentry perimeter security lights around the Don Academy greeted her. That was when she remembered the seating area beside the concession window. On several occasions, she'd noticed it during PE class. They must have funneled everyone into that space to keep them together. She shook her head at Mrs. Sabatini's inattention to detail, funneling her out the wrong door. Silly old bat, she mused.

Pepper had been so overcome with worry for Salty and then confused at her surroundings that she had forgotten about slipping away from the dance unnoticed. Until she reached the edge of the field, just before she turned the corner to join everyone else, Pepper realized she was within spitting distance of the boys' locker room. She peered around the corner. The entire dance had been moved outside, well, the students anyway. People were milling around recounting the soon-to-be infamous vomiting incident. There was no sign of her team or Mario, but she couldn't get a clear view of everyone unless she wanted to be seen herself, and she didn't.

Pepper did catch a glimpse of Nico surrounded by Cherry, Honey, and Peach. Cherry was grasping Nico's arm and laughing at something he said. She grimaced, remembering that chart she'd seen on Mrs. Sabatini's computer months ago. So, it hadn't been a matchmaking flow chart but an early draft for their final assignment. Cherry must've been thrilled to have an excuse to mingle with *Il Principe*. Pepper had to fight every instinct not to run over and snatch Nico out of Cherry's red talons. But she pushed her jealousy aside and reminded herself Nico was her date —once she returned to the dance.

Just as Pepper was about to dash across the slim beam of light falling across the track, the gym doors opened, and Coach announced everyone could head back inside. The shuffling of feet and clattering of heels signaled that they were on the move. Pepper removed her shoes and silently slipped onto the track and back into the darkness.

Her pulse quickened as she approached the tunnel to the home team's locker. Pepper dropped her shoes beside the main door, knowing that her heels and the tile flooring would not be a stealthy combination. Besides, she'd exit through these doors on her way back to the gym when she rejoined the dance—hopefully, clutching the file that contained the truth about Nonnu's transgression and subsequent banishment.

She punched in the code Nico had used months ago when she'd been injured during PE. The light flashed green, and she turned the door handle.

"So far so good," she whispered.

Counting the steps along the hall, as she'd done on her last visit, Pepper padded through the darkness into the locker room and made a quick right. The glowing green exit signs were her only guide to the main building. In preparation for the dance, Chutney accessed the Don Academy floor plan, which Pepper had memorized. The archives were unmarked on the blueprint, which was a curious oversight, but from Nico's description, she was positive she knew where to go.

Finally, she reached the door that led into the main building. It should be unlocked. Pepper rested her hand on the door handle and paused. This was it. She said a silent prayer of protection and pressed down, then pulled the door open. The hallway was deserted and dimly lit by a single sconce fixture midway down the hall. If her guess were correct, the archives would be the third door on the right. She tiptoed along the cold tile floor. Sure enough, a small plaque on the door read *archives*, but to the left of the door handle was a keypad, and Pepper didn't have that code.

She held her breath and tried the code that allowed her into the locker room. An angry red light flashed twice. Pepper raised her right wrist to her lips and was about to ask Chutney to break into the mainframe when a hand clamped over her mouth. She let out a muffled scream that still managed to echo down the deserted hallway.

"It's me," Nico hissed. He punched in the code; the latch released with an audible click just as the quick clip of footsteps could be heard on the stairs before they stumbled inside.

"What are you doing here?" he demanded as the door closed behind them.

"How did you find me?" she fired back, completely annoyed at being caught.

"I saw you sneaking away, and I was curious what could be more interesting than a high school dance," he said wryly.

"You thought I was meeting another guy," she accused, jabbing a finger at his chest.

"Maybe. You certainly haven't seemed too interested in reconciling with me tonight. Again, what are you doing here?"

Pepper blew a hot breath of frustration past her lips. "Lookit, now is not a great time to do this. Can we put off our first fight for later?"

"What's the rush?" he asked, folding his arms across his chest.

"Uh, breaking and entering, escaping from the dance, and not least important—finding proof my Nonnu wasn't a rat."

"*Mannaggia!* Pepper, you have a one-track mind."

"I know this all seems silly for *Il Principe*, but unlike yours, my life has been far from perfect. The memory of the one person who was my angel has been irreparably tarnished..." She paused, fighting back angry tears. "And I'm willing to risk everything to put it right, so you can just leave if you want to make this about you."

"How'd you manage to get inside?" he asked.

"I'm a Valentina. We have our ways."

"When I let you into the locker room, you saw."

Pepper nodded.

"So what was this?" He gestured to the space between them. "Just a con?"

"No. And getting in here was an opportunity, not a hustle," she replied. Pepper flipped on her phone's flashlight to study the layout.

"The log-in I gave you for the entire history of knowledge available on the internet couldn't help, but you think the answers you're searching for are in this room?"

She spun around. "Yes. I think there's a cover-up, and of course, it wouldn't be plastered about on a website or in a newspaper. I think Nonnu took the fall for someone else."

"But why would it be here?" he asked.

"It's the only place in the world it could be," she replied, shining the weak beam of light over the dozens of rows of cabinets. "These aren't just filled with decades of immunization cards and final grades. Don's keeps track of their students the way Valentina's does. Except my grandmother's file cuts off just before the incident. There is a file here about Nonnu. I found it when Chutney hacked into the mainframe. I'm hoping they didn't censor the truth here."

"All right, this is your mission. Where do you want to start looking?" he asked.

"Seriously? You aren't leaving?"

"I probably should, but I'm a sucker for a good mystery." Pepper rolled her eyes but smiled. "And in case you haven't realized, I'd do anything for you."

"*Grazie, mio principe*," Pepper replied, cupping his face in her hands before kissing his lips sweetly. "Now, let's figure out if these are organized by date or alphabetized."

"Or none of the above," he added.

"*Basta*. Have some faith."

AFTER PULLING open the first few drawers, they quickly realized that the filing system was arranged alphabetically. Nico and Pepper split up to determine which cabinets held the D section and then which of those cabinets held the D'As. To her utter dismay, the D'A section was extensive, and there was more than one Vincenzo D'Angelo. Nico took the last two cabinets in one row while Pepper searched the next section. Grasping her phone between her teeth to shine the light onto the file tabs, she quickly slid the drawer free, pulled the file up a quarter out of the sleeve, and flipped down the first page to peruse the contents. After a moment of searching, she'd find a date or detail incompatible with Nonnu and start again.

"At this rate, we'll need months to get through them all," Pepper said, the phone still in her mouth.

"What?" Nico called.

"Nothing," she replied, closing the middle drawer with a heavy heart. Maybe they should just go back to the dance. If only these were arranged by date, it would be much easier. They had been filed alphabetically by first letter but then at random. Students stuffed files anywhere with little to no thought about their later retrieval, like it was a detention assignment. She had reached the bottom drawer of the middle cabinet.

Pepper folded her legs under her and reached for the bottom drawer's handle. She prayed that Nonnu would direct her to the truth. But this drawer was the same as the others until the second-to-last file. Pepper pulled it halfway out of the sleeve, as she had done with all the others, and noticed a few dates that matched Nonnu's time at school. She yanked the folder free and scanned the documents.

"Nico, I got him," she called out, forgetting about being quiet for a moment. "Stop looking over there and help me go through his files."

Nonnu's transcripts, sports stats, records, demerit slips, essays, and even an immunization card were included, but the file didn't extend beyond his time at Don's. She set the file aside and reached into the drawer for the last folder. This one was thick, with bits of paper and newspaper print untidily sticking out from the edges.

When she realized Nico hadn't answered, Pepper tucked the new file under her arm and stood. She sensed something in the room, like that feeling you get when someone is staring at you in a crowd. She lifted her phone, but the flashlight was too weak to penetrate the darkness.

"Nico, did you fall asleep on me?" she joked, deciding what to do. Someone was undoubtedly ahead of her. With a wall to her back, Pepper was trapped in this row. Rather than continue to give them the upper hand, she switched off her phone flashlight.

"Ugh, stupid battery," she whined. "Nico, is your phone working?" In the dark, she could hear the intruders' muffled steps. They were coming closer.

Pepper felt for the handles of the cabinets to her right and began pulling drawers open—the more, the better. They would act as a barrier between the assailant and herself.

"Hey, what's going on?" a man shouted. She heard him start to run; then he let out an audible grunt. It sounded like he was knocked to the ground after running into the open file drawers. Pepper stepped onto the edge of a drawer and quickly pushed off to reach the top of the cabinets behind her, where Nico had been. Then she rolled silently along the filing system and dropped to the floor. She landed beside Nico's unresponsive body and reached out, feeling for a pulse. It fluttered steadily against her fingertips, and she said a silent prayer of thanks.

*Now, how am I getting us both out of here?*

Her attackers fumbled with the drawers, searching the empty row for her. Pepper figured she wouldn't be able to drag Nico to safety, but she might be able to make it to the door and call for the security guard. They might hear her if he was on the lower level; then again, they might not.

The lights flashed on, and she recoiled at the brightness. There was shuffling and commotion. Pepper shrank back, pulling Nico along with her against the wall. When her eyes adjusted, one man was approaching. He was in all black, a sinister grin plastered on his lips, but no visible weapons, not that it meant much. Pepper glanced at Nico and saw the gash of red on his forehead for the first time. The first guy reached for her, and she kicked him squarely in the chest, sending him spiraling backward, which allowed her a moment to stand and take a defensive position. Then, she was plunged again into darkness as a bag was placed over her head. The second guy must have used her over-the-cabinet tactic to get the drop on her. Suddenly, two sets of hands were on her, grasping her legs and torso as she bucked and clawed at her attackers.

"What do you want to do with him?" one of them, nearest to her head, asked. His breath was putrid, and Pepper pulled away or tried to anyway. After the vomit incident earlier and now this,

Pepper pushed down the bile rising in her throat with a few hard swallows. She had no intention of hurling with a bag over her head.

"Leave him," the other replied. "I'm not catching no heat for roughing up *Il Principe*. Besides, it's her they want."

"What about that scrape on his head? They'll think we did it."

"Kid hit his head when we gassed him, happens all the time. It'll toughen him up."

The smelly-breath guy grunted in agreement.

At least Nico was safe, she thought, as they bundled her out of the archives.

"Where are you taking me?" she demanded when they reached the hallway. There was no reply. Pepper repeated her question, but this time, she shouted.

The point of a knife poked in her side.

"Listen, girly, another outburst like that, and we go back for lover boy and finish him off when we're done with you."

"Unlikely, you seem unwilling to harm your boss' son," she shot back.

"Our boss…yeah, aren't you the smart little lady."

Pepper rolled her eyes.

"Called our bluff, hey Chris?"

"Sure did. But here's a promise," he said, pressing the tip of the knife deeper. She hoped he wasn't making a hole in her dress. "We won't hurt *Il Principe*, but we'll get our friends in CIM Mojave to ensure your daddy won't be coming home again."

She stopped squirming.

"That's what I thought."

"What's the code?"

"Did you forget already?" smelly breath replied.

"298714," Pepper offered.

"Hey, look who's being cooperative. Thanks, little lady."

Pepper's mind was racing. They were taking her through the locker room, which meant that they were going to kill her there or take her across the field to the dark and craggy coastline. If this were her mission, she'd choose the coastline: less cleanup, fewer questions, easier getaway.

After a few moments, the outside door creaked open, and the fresh scent of dewy grass and briny ocean reached her nostrils. Pepper took a refreshing gulp of air. Already, she could feel her pulse settling and her mind snapping into focus. If she were getting out of this, it wouldn't be in a state of panic. The music from the dance could be heard in the distance, but it became fainter with each step and then grew nonexistent as the constant crash of the waves replaced it.

Inside Don's, she couldn't hear anything her team was transmitting from the dance, but she should have been able to pick up the ambient noise from inside the gym, which meant her earpiece had fallen out at some point. Her phone was back in the archives room, but she still had on the transmitter bracelet. It was a long shot, but maybe…

"Are you drowning me or shooting me and then sending me over the side of the cliff?" she asked conversationally. The men ignored her. She was disappointed they weren't confessing. "You could remove this bag. It's not like I don't know we're going to the bluff."

When they stopped walking, Pepper's heart began to race. It was now or never. The men set her down on the scrubby rough brush adjacent to the bluff trail. Pepper immediately kicked out, connecting with the man's torso, then she hooked her leg around his and twisted herself around, toppling him to the ground. Since her hands were unbound, Pepper pulled off the bag and jumped up. The other kidnapper grasped her around the waist. Pepper pulled her knees to her chest, then, through the momentum of her body weight, brought herself forward and flipped the man ass over end. The other man had already recovered and was on his feet. They tousled for a minute as Pepper worked her arm free of his hold and elbowed him in the solar plexus. Just as she stepped out of his grasp, he got ahold of her necklace and pulled it taut against her throat.

Pepper clawed at her neck, trying to work her fingers under the gold chain cutting into her flesh, but it was impossible. She sucked in ragged breaths as her air supply was slowly being cut off. The sounds of the ocean grew faint, and Pepper knew she was close to losing consciousness. Her hands grasped her neck in one final attempt to dislodge the thin chain, but it was useless. Then she felt the signet ring at the base of her throat. Pepper worked her middle finger into the ring and pulled the necklace down with every fiber of strength she possessed. The force broke the clasp open, propelling her forward. Pepper sucked in the cool salty air before spinning around and socking the man in the jaw. The solid gold ring packed a brutal punch, and the man dropped to the ground. A slow, methodical clap broke her concentration.

"Very good, dear," a woman said. Pepper gasped. She knew that voice. "You should get extra credit for ingenuity. Unfortunately, you won't live long enough to receive your final grade." Mrs. Sabatini stepped out from behind the soccer field fence, the dim light from Don's illuminating her face.

# Chapter Thirty-Eight

"You..." Pepper croaked, her voice hoarse from the attempted strangulation. She swallowed hard, wincing in pain. "No. This is wrong. It's supposed to be..."

"Cherry?" Mrs. Sabatini laughed. "Witless girl. I'm almost ashamed we're related. But you know our code...family first."

The two men were writhing on the ground in pain. However, they quickly jumped to attention once they realized Mrs. Sabatini had appeared. She waved them off with a flick of her wrist.

"Stand down, morons," she ordered, moving closer. "I knew I should've taken you out in your sleep."

Pepper surveyed the scene, cataloging her best means of escape. Even though they were out in the open, she could, if she had wanted, bolt in any number of directions and would likely be able to get away. But looking into Mrs. Sabatini's serene face, it was clear that Pepper wasn't going to budge until she knew the truth.

"Are you working for the Rossetti family?" Pepper asked, still trying to grasp the history teacher's part in all of this.

The woman laughed. It was a mirthless sound devoid of any joy. "Girls are so easy to manipulate when there's a boy involved," Mrs. Sabatini said. "That was a ruse, stupid girl. And a clever one, if I'm not being too arrogant. Cherry convinced Coco that breaking you two up would save her mother the embarrassment of having it exposed to the world that her famous cannoli were from Contino's bakery."

Pepper gasped. "So that's why you had me find out their family bakery."

"I told you it was clever."

"That means Nico's father doesn't think I'm unsuitable for his son?"

"I don't know the inner workings of Don Rossetti's thoughts, but I doubt you are what he has in mind for his son. However, as far as I am aware, he doesn't have a clue about your relationship."

"Then why?" Pepper asked, twisting the signet ring around her finger.

Mrs. Sabatini clasped her hands together. "I guess you deserve to know before you die. One reason is on your finger right now," she said, stepping forward.

"My father's ring?" Pepper said, inspecting the signet on her right hand.

"That wasn't your father's," she replied. "That ring is the signet of the Salvatores, a Sicilian club for elite mafia bosses. That ring is why your grandfather was exiled."

Her chest constricted. It was difficult to draw a deep breath. "How did my father have it?" she asked softly, afraid of the answer.

"Who knows how your weasel of a father got ahold of it after it served its purpose? Maybe he felt guilty. Maybe he was planning to sell it. He was always had a get-rich-quick-scheme."

"How do you know so much about my family's past?"

"I am a history teacher, but to be blunt, we're the reason you were in exile. Until you arrived at school, I'd almost forgotten all about your family. Of course, I didn't know who you were at first. Your names are hidden from staff, too, but you slipped that necklace out of your shirt and played with the ring one morning, and I knew instantly who you were. It didn't take much digging. Ms. Powell, the old bat, let it slip that you were having trouble with that ridiculous natal chart assignment. She told me all I needed to know to confirm you were Enzo D'Angelo's granddaughter and thus a threat to our legacy and future."

Mrs. Sabatini's words stung as if she had slapped Pepper across the face. "Our? You mean Cherry," Pepper said. "But she's a Bianchi."

"I am, too, honey. Sabatini is my married name. My father was Bruno Bianchi. I lived there until my husband died. Then I decided to start fresh and teach out here for a change of scenery."

The pieces were falling into place, but not quickly enough. The two goons looked restless, and Pepper wasn't sure how long she could keep her teacher talking.

"Then it was you, not Cherry. You're the one behind all of it. The rat trap and the fish in the bouquet, it was all you."

"I gotta give you credit, honey. You are clever and remarkably well-suited to the Cosa Nostra lifestyle. It's a pity you won't live long enough to become a mob wife." She turned, and Pepper's breath caught in her throat, thinking this was the signal. However, Mrs. Sabatini continued. "My original plan was to keep an eye on you and just make sure you really had no idea about your past, but your inquisitive nature couldn't leave well enough alone. You had to go and research your grandparents' past. I removed the files from Valentina's archives, but that wasn't going to deter you." She chuckled bitterly. "With each barricade I erected, I was sure I'd deter you or, as time progressed, scare you off, and you'd back down, but not even the threat of death stopped you."

"Couldn't you have just gotten the files from Don's yourself?" Pepper asked.

"Sweet, naive child, life isn't as simple as that. Besides, it would have meant tipping my hand. And after all, I know the truth. I was trying to keep you from finding it." With a sneer and a flick of her head, Mrs. Sabatini signaled to her two goons. They grasped Pepper by both arms before she had time to react.

"No," Pepper screeched. "I deserve to know the truth, all of it." She kicked her legs wildly as the two men carried her to the edge of the cliff. Neither her scissor kick takedown nor her body weight slam would cut it right now.

"Please, it's like you said, I was never going to give up. You've won. Just tell me what happened," Pepper pleaded.

"Hold her," Mrs. Sabatini ordered, coming closer. The strands of beads edging her decorative kimono wrap glinted in the dim light. "You've been a tougher adversary than I had anticipated. I suppose you deserve to know the whole truth." She stepped before Pepper, a look of complete self-satisfaction on her face. "Bruno Bianchi, my father, rolled for the Feds. He turned Fat Louie, Carmine Guillespe, and Paulie DeSanto in for racketeering and collusion. In the early days of the *After Times*, when the world was still rebuilding after the reset, it was a huge get for the Feds. They were trying to regain power and authority in the public eye. The fools. As if that was going to stop us." She laughed mirthlessly. "My father helped them appear to once again be in control. But my father wasn't going to roll for a life in exile. He wanted to move from underboss to boss. The deal he cut with the Feds planted evidence, your grandfather's signet ring, to suggest D'Angelo was the rat. The Feds went along with it, taking your grandfather and family into custody the way they would for any informant, which allowed my father to move from number two to the Don. No one was the wiser until you came along."

"Nonnu was framed by his BETA! His birthright—was stolen from him!" Pepper exclaimed.

"Your grandfather didn't inherit his territory; he worked for it. Makes it that much more bitter, huh?" she said, dragging her nail through the tears cascading down Pepper's cheek.

"You're horrid, and your family is horrid," Pepper spat.

"That's Cosa Nostra, honey, not a double-blind taste test. If you haven't figured out it's not fair by now, maybe I am doing you a favor because the meek do not inherit anything in our world. Throw her over the side."

Pepper dug her heels into the soft earth and braced herself. A commotion from behind gave her the distraction she needed to drop to her knees and slip out of her captor's grasp. Three figures rushed forward. At their appearance, the two men bolted down the trail to the beach.

"I got 'em," Nico said, running after the two who went down the embankment.

Pepper spun around, shocked to see him. In the darkness, she was only aware of three people. Who were the others?

"I'm so relieved you're here!" Mrs. Sabatini exclaimed, reverting to helpless teacher mode. "They're getting away."

"Shut it," Salty said, approaching their teacher. "We heard it all, and so did Ms. Oscura. You're done."

"Did you? Clever." The history teacher lunged forward, grasping Salty's long black hair before pressing a small switchblade against Salty's neck. "Now, I'll leave this party with this young lady as my protection." She backed away toward Valentina's, dragging Salty with her. "Do not be a hero," Mrs. Sabatini warned. "Or she dies. But I'll let her go once I reach the airport unfollowed. Just back away."

"You don't think we came without backup?" Azucar said, stepping forward.

Thank goodness, Pepper thought, releasing the breath she was holding. The two of them could certainly handle this situation.

"I can tell when a student is bluffing," Mrs. Sabatini said, turning to address Azucar. It was the opening Pepper needed to drop and roll. She was betting this abrupt movement wouldn't be noticeable in the darkness. She popped up beside the history teacher, startling her into dropping the knife. At that point, Salty elbowed the woman in the ribs. Pepper grabbed both of Mrs. Sabatini's arms and forced her to the ground.

"Quick, Azu, your skirt," Pepper said.

"Why?" she asked aghast.

"I need the ribbon to tie her hands."

"Ugh, fine," she replied, untying the bow and tossing the lacy wad to Pepper.

"You won't get away with this," Mrs. Sabatini sputtered, her face in the dirt. "I haven't done anything wrong, and you can't prove a thing."

"We have it all recorded, thanks to our tech support for the final assignment. And I'm fairly sure attempted murder is illegal, even in Monterey," Salty replied.

"Besides, no family will stand by a teacher who put their daughters' lives in danger," Pepper said. "Hey, way to stand up for yourself, Salty, you're doing your name proud."

Salty curtseyed and promptly erased whatever gains she'd made in the last few minutes.

"Should we cart her back to the dance?" Pepper asked, just as the roar of voices and the glare of lights broke the darkness apart.

Ms. Oscura jumped from the golf cart, her hair a wild tangle of curls. "Is everyone unharmed?" she asked, running up.

"We are," Pepper said.

"You heard everything?" Salty asked.

"I heard enough," she replied. "Marco, take over," she ordered.

"*Pronto.*" Marco stepped forward, pieces of white tissue fluttering from his nostrils. Salty groaned. He expertly zip-tied Mrs. Sabatini's wrists together and hauled her to her feet.

"Take her back to Don's," Ms. Oscura said. "We'll be interrogating her there."

Marco nodded and shoved the woman into the golf cart. Azucar's lace skirt turned wrist restraints, trailing in the dirt.

"Hold up," Nico yelled, somewhat out of breath. "Two more for you." He prodded the men forward. They stumbled up the embankment and willingly got into the cart.

"Impressive, young man. I'll be sure to tell your Headmaster of your bravery."

"Thank you, ma'am," he replied. Then he turned to Pepper and pulled her to him, planting a fierce kiss on her lips. She was dizzy and breathless when they broke apart. Still, he didn't loosen his grasp. He held her tight. She nuzzled into the soft spot where his shoulder and neck met, a refuge. They stayed like that for some time. Everyone went about securing the suspects, giving the pair their private moment.

"How did you catch those guys?" Pepper whispered.

"I told them that whatever punishment was waiting for them up here, it would pale by comparison to what my father would dole out for going after my girlfriend. They were smart enough to see things my way." He leaned back and kissed the top of her head. "Thank God you're unharmed."

"Attention, ladies," Ms. Oscura said, breaking in on Pepper's respite with Nico. "I won't be able to take your statements for some time, but you might as well go on back to school. We'll debrief in the morning. And don't worry about your assignment. I think you've amply demonstrated mastery of the skills from your first year."

"Headmistress," Pepper said, pulling away from Nico, "I'd like to complete our assignment and turn in the final."

"You what?" Salty exclaimed.

"No special favors. I don't want anyone thinking we got an easy pass."

"You astound me, Pepper. But I see your point. Your assignment will be due Monday morning, as scheduled. And I won't be pulling any punches. You'll be graded the same as everyone else."

Salty groaned.

"And one more thing," Pepper said. "If it's all the same to you, could we return to the dance? That is if it isn't already over."

"You want to go back?" Nico asked, shocked.

"We never got our dance," she replied.

"As you wish, but allow the security guard to escort you back. You certainly deserve to have a little fun tonight." She hopped into the golf cart, and they sped away, Mrs. Sabatini's sobs trailing behind them.

"We were so worried," Salty exclaimed, launching herself at Pepper.

She was almost thrown off balance, but Pepper laughed and hugged her best friend back, relieved they had come to her aid. "I'm so happy you aren't catatonic anymore."

"Do not remind me of that nightmare," Salty replied. "I get nauseous whenever I think about it."

"How did you guys know where I was? Did the transmission work?" Pepper asked.

"Yes!" Salty exclaimed.

"Wait, it'll take her ten years to explain it. *Vámanos*, to the dance," Azucar said.

The wet grass tickled Pepper's bare feet, but she didn't care about getting muddy or wet. She was grateful to be alive and surrounded by people who risked their lives for hers. She reached for Nico. He shrugged off his jacket and placed it around her shoulders before grasping her hand and placing a tender kiss on her knuckles. Then he slipped his arm under the coat, around her waist, and they followed the two girls. Pepper allowed her head to rest against his shoulder. For the first time in maybe forever, she felt safe, not just because of Nico, Salty, and Azucar or the bodyguard discreetly trailing them, but because Pepper knew she could trust the strength of her wings.

"It was crazy. The dance music was blaring, and to be honest, we totally lost track of Mario—thanks for insisting we complete our assignment. We are totally failing, by the way—but suddenly, your voice came through loud and clear. It wasn't immediately obvious what was happening. Then, I heard these unfamiliar male voices and knew you were in trouble. Chutney heard it too, so she went to get Ms. Oscura while I grabbed Azu right off the dance floor and raced to the bluff."

"You guys are amazing," Pepper said. "But, Nico, how did *you* know where I was?"

"When I regained consciousness, the archives were in shambles. It was clear something bad had happened. I ran into the hallway and noticed these long red marks along the wall. They stopped at the locker room door. I figured whoever took you had gone through there. Very clever to scuff the walls like that."

Pepper flashed her nails. Stripes of wine-red were worn away in long streaks across several fingers. "They should have tied my hands together." She glanced down at her hand and realized how swollen it had become from punching one of Mrs. Sabatini's goons. She grasped the signet ring, but it wouldn't budge. *Oh well, at least I won't lose it*, she thought.

"They definitely underestimated you," he replied. "When I ran onto the field, I saw your friends, and we headed to the bluff together."

They reached the gym's door. The sweet, upbeat melody of Louis Prima's *Buona Sera* wafted through the open door.

"Looks like they're wrapping things up," Nico said. "Still want to dance?"

Pepper looked into his deep brown eyes, so full of concern for her wellbeing, and she nodded. Now that she knew Coco's tactics had been a lie, Pepper was more confident than ever that nothing could separate her and Nico.

They walked onto the dance floor hand in hand, turned toward one another, and began to sway with the music. Weary from the evening's antics, Pepper maybe leaned a little too hard against Nico, but he stayed sturdy, supporting her.

"I'm confused about one thing," Nico said. "Did our break have something to do with all this?"

"Mmmhmmm," Pepper replied, snuggling against his chest. She told him the whole complicated mess, figuring it best to come clean now rather than have him find out from Coco. The final song ended, and the chaperones began ushering everyone through the front of the gym. But Nico grasped Pepper's hand and pulled her outside to the concession courtyard.

At first, she thought maybe he wanted privacy for a goodnight kiss, but she realized something was wrong when she saw the lines between his eyes and the frown turning down his full lips.

"How could you?" he demanded.

"What?" she replied, caught off guard.

"Exclude me from literally the biggest thing in your life? Someone was trying to kill you!"

"I told you. Your sister said you were losing your birthright. I was doing it for you." The cement ground was cold on her bare feet. Pepper slid onto the metal picnic table, which wasn't much of an improvement, and hugged her knees to chest.

"But it was a complete lie," he said.

"I didn't know that," she replied, clutching Nico's jacket tightly. "Coco is a very convincing liar. Why don't you go yell at her?"

"I'll be speaking to her, don't worry," he replied, pacing before her. Suddenly, he seemed much older than his sixteen years. "But you just cut me loose like it was nothing."

"You have a short memory. That afternoon was torture, and if you recall, we did not break up, but we took a break until today," she fired back.

"And after today? What if it had been true? Would you have ended it tonight?" he asked, stopping before her.

Pepper shrugged. "I hadn't decided."

Nico laughed bitterly. "Damn it, Pepper. How could you be so cold?"

"Me? That was the toughest thing I have ever had to do. And I couldn't even fully commit to it. I care for you so deeply I couldn't stand to think that your future was in jeopardy because of me," she said, jumping down from the table and crossing the courtyard to reach him. "The time apart has been hell, but I put aside my happiness so you would have the future you deserve. Why can't you understand that?"

"Because you still lied to me."

Pepper had no reply. She had lied. Was a lie to protect the person you loved just as wrong as one used to protect selfish interests? "I had no choice," she said.

"In our world, trust is the solid foundation on which we build our business, family, and relationships." He paced along the chain link fence for a few silent moments. "I ... don't think I can trust you anymore."

"What are you saying?" she asked.

"I can't be with someone I don't trust. I'm sorry." His dark eyes held hers, the pain of this decision a living thing between them. "It's over."

"This is a mistake."

"I have to stand firm in my decision." Nico turned for the field.

"Wait!" she called. Pepper removed his jacket, balled it up, and threw it at him. "Thanks for the rescue."

He gave her a sad smile, then walked beyond the courtyard and was enveloped by the darkness overshadowing the soccer field.

Pepper was dumbfounded, replaying the last few moments over and over. What could she have said or done differently? Each time, the answer was the same: nothing. She would have had to act differently months ago. It was far too late now. TCN, she thought bitterly.

# *Chapter Thirty-Nine*

Tuesday morning, all the Valentina students gathered in the dining room to receive their final grades. Pepper's group had worked diligently all Sunday to complete their assignment, thanks to Olive, who had sought out Mario to console him after the vomit incident and was able to retrieve all the information necessary to complete their final. The dining room was buzzing with frantic chatter only experienced at the end of a school term.

Ms. Oscura stood, and silence descended over the room. "On the table before you are your final assignments, graded by Ms. Powell and me. Mrs. Sabatini has had to leave us unexpectedly and will not be returning next year. I want to say how extremely proud I am of each one of you. Over the school year, you have shown yourselves to be ladies of quality with an aptitude for the curriculum. You deserve a round of applause." She clapped, and slowly, the other teachers awkwardly joined in. "I will have one final announcement regarding room assignments, but that can wait while you review your final grades. You may turn over your packet."

Pepper flipped her paper over and gasped. *We got a B minus!* She turned to the last page and read the notes. Her abandoning the group to pursue her mission seemed to lose them the most points, followed by not having contingency plans in case of…well, all the things that went wrong that night. But underneath the assessment was an addendum. Ms. Oscura awarded her ample extra credit points for thwarting Mrs. Sabatini, bringing her total grade to a perfect score.

"Now for next year's room assignment announcement. Those with the highest grades can select their room next year. I have marked the top right corner of your final with a small asterisk if you have been selected."

"Not fair!" Cherry exclaimed from across the dining room.

"Silence, dear. No one enjoys a sore loser," the headmistress said.

Pepper flipped her booklet closed. Sure enough, a small red starburst was in the top right corner. She looked up and caught Azucar's eye—since everyone was graded with her group, that meant Azucar did not receive the highest marks. She would not get the first choice. Then, to her delight, Azu gave her a wink and flashed the corner of her paper where a red star was visible. Ms. Oscura must have also given her extra credit for foiling their evil history teacher. Good, that was as it should be, Pepper thought. Salty was bouncing in her seat, a clear sign she had received the sign. Pepper searched the room for Chutney and Olive. Only Chutney wore a stunned expression on her face.

"Please let me know your selection before the end of today. You are all dismissed."

The scraping of chairs signaled the girls' mass exodus from the dining room. Chutney approached Ms. Oscura, and Pepper wondered if she was asking for the last spot in the cupola since Salty, Azucar, and herself would not be vacating. Pepper pushed her chair back and gathered her things, still watching the exchange.

Coco paused beside Pepper's table and cleared her throat. "Listen, I'm sorry for all the trouble I caused. You didn't deserve it."

"That's big of you. Thanks."

"Have you heard from my brother?" she asked.

Pepper shook her head.

"He told me off good. I've never seen him so mad. He must care about you a lot."

"Come on, Coco, I still have to pack," Cherry whined.

"That can wait. Do what we talked about," Coco ordered, stepping aside. Cherry gave her a pleading look, but Coco was not messing around.

Cherry turned to Pepper. "Sorry for leaking the info about your grandfather. I wouldn't have, but my great-aunt made me."

"Sure you would have," Pepper replied, "if it meant getting what you wanted. No hard feelings. I'm not sure what I'd do if the guy I had my heart set on were with someone else."

"By the looks of things, you'll find out," Cherry replied. I'm spending the summer with the Rossettis in Capri, and I'll do my best to help Nico forget all about you."

An electric shock of fear coursed through Pepper's body. Instead of lashing out, she took a deep breath. Cherry was all talk, after all. "Listen, even though our grandfathers were rivals, we don't have to be," Pepper said, extending her hand.

"Don't count on it, Pepperoncini," Cherry replied, striding off.

"She is the absolute worst," Salty commented. "I hope Ms. Oscura expels her."

"We can only hope," Pepper replied.

"I guess this means we're getting a new history teacher," Azucar said. "I hope it's a hot guy."

The girls laughed. "Always thinking of the important things," Salty replied.

THE LAST FORTY-EIGHT hours at Valentina's were a whirlwind of packing and bittersweet goodbyes. As Pepper closed her backpack, she looked around the empty room. Never would she have imagined she'd become so attached to this place or the people. It had been an escape from the suffocation of her stepmother's house, and it had ended up truly being an oasis where she'd thrived. Pepper patted the space in her bra that held the signet ring. She hadn't had a chance to replace the necklace that was broken during the fight. She had, however, lost the locket. Pepper had returned to the bluff over the weekend when she realized the loss but could not locate the trinket.

"You ready?" Salty said, returning with a final piece of clothing she stuffed into the nearest bag. "Vito's downstairs, and he said if we don't leave soon, you and Azu will miss your bus in Salinas."

Pepper took one final look and nodded. "Yeah, I'm ready." She heaved the pack over her shoulder and followed Salty.

"I'm going to work all summer designing a whole new decor for the cupola," Salty said, bounding down the stairs.

"But why? It's great as it is, isn't it?" Pepper replied, trying to keep up, which wasn't easy with her heavy pack weighing her down.

"What we have now are band-aids. What we need is a comprehensive design."

Pepper sighed, knowing it was no use arguing. "Fine, but you better clear it with Azucar and Chutney first."

"I liked having her in the group," Salty said. "I think she'll be a good addition to the cupola, but I'll miss Ginger."

"Me too, but she said she really bonded with her etiquette group and was excited to share a suite with them next year."

"I can't believe she wanted to switch rooms."

"Those stairs could make anyone think twice. How often have you almost bit it trying to get to the bathroom in the middle of the night?"

"Ugh, don't remind me. I still have the scars. Hey, would everyone be agreeable to a discreet chamber pot?"

"Ew, no," Pepper replied.

As Vito heaved Salty's suitcases into the van, the girls waited on the patio, reluctant to get into the SUV. It had been a rollercoaster year, but Pepper didn't want it to end.

"I'm going to grab some grub for the long bus trip," Azucar said, turning for the door. "Do you want anything?"

"Something that will survive being in my hoodie pocket for a few hours," Pepper replied.

"I'm good," Salty said before gasping. "Oh no! I forgot to clean out my bathroom cubby," she exclaimed, trailing Azucar back inside.

Pepper shook her head. She didn't see a reason to move all their belongings out only to bring them back in three months, but Ms. Oscura was firm. All possessions had to be gone, or they would be disposed of. Pepper closed her eyes and inhaled deeply. She was going to miss this old place. The crisp, salty air was tinged with pine and citrus. Pepper spun around. Ms. Oscura was standing just behind her.

"Headmistress, you startled me," she said.

Ms. Oscura smirked. "If you have a minute, please step into my office."

"We're catching a bus soon-"

"It'll just take a moment. I don't want to be overheard." Pepper followed the headmistress across the sun-dappled patio through her office French doors.

"Out of curiosity, how did you know I was there?"

"Your citrus perfume," Pepper replied.

Ms. Oscura nodded. "Very astute." She gestured to a pair of armchairs on either side of the fireplace. "Please sit."

Pepper plopped down into the chair, her knee bouncing nervously. "Am I in trouble?"

"Not at all, but I wanted to speak privately before you head home. This year has undoubtedly been a bit more challenging for you than the other girls. The incident at the dance is not something I would ever put a student through. However, you showed real Valentina gumption and proved yourself to be a lady of quality. If you have any doubt about belonging in our world, I hope it has disappeared. Because you very much do. I wanted to say that I'm proud of you, Pepper."

Heat flooded her cheeks. "I don't know what to say. Thank you?"

"Thank yourself, my dear. But now that people know Vincenzo D'Angelo's granddaughter is back in our world, your life will get more complicated."

"TCN. I mean, it's part of the deal, right."

"Just stay on your toes. Ah, I see your classmates are ready to go. Have a nice summer." Ms. Oscura shook Pepper's hand.

"I don't know how nice it will be," Pepper replied, crossing for the door. "I'm looking forward to being back here in the Fall."

"Try to have some fun," Ms. Oscura replied as Pepper stepped onto the patio.

"There you are!" Salty exclaimed. "We have to go if you want to get lunch."

Pepper bounded down the stairs, Ms. Oscura's words still echoing in her mind.

*Vincenzo D'Angelo's granddaughter is back in our world.*

SALTY HAD Vito stop at their favorite taco place in Monterey for one last farewell meal before going through the lush, hilly countryside, which gradually turned more arid and brown as they drove farther inland.

Salty deposited the girls at the depot. There were tears, hugs, and promises to keep in contact over the break. Then she was gone. Pepper and Azucar took a seat on their luggage and waited for the bus to board in fifteen minutes when suddenly, a sporty Lamborghini roared around the corner.

"Here comes Ratboy now. I'll watch your stuff. Don't go easy on him," Azucar said, pushing Pepper toward the red sports car.

Nico pulled up in the loading zone and hopped out, leaving the engine running. The fancy car was drawing the glances of people passing by. He didn't seem to care.

"There you are," he said, striding up.

"How did you find me?" she replied. "Never mind, Coco, right?"

Nico nodded. "Why are you taking a bus?"

"Because no one knows I attend Valentina's. And they would never have allowed it if they had known. So, I lied." She let the words hang in the air between them. "It was the only way to get away from my horrid stepmom and try for a better life instead of being stuck at the public school. But that part doesn't matter, does it? Because lying makes me untrustworthy, right? It's a character flaw in your book."

"Pepper, I'm sorry. I overreacted."

She gave him her iciest stare and raised one eyebrow, challenging him to continue.

"I deserve that," he said.

Why did guys always show up at the worst possible moment? Right when you've convinced yourself that you're better off alone, wham, they are all puppy dog eyes and pouting lips.

"I have something of yours," he said, reaching into the car.

Pepper gasped. "Did you find my locket?"

Nico pulled out her heels. "Locket? No. I found your shoes after the dance."

"Oh. Thanks," she said, reaching for the pair.

"Your locket went missing?"

"Yeah, the one that used to have a picture of my mom—my only picture of her—when the battery worked anyway."

"Boarding for the Southbound Inter-County number twelve," the intercom blared.

"That's me. I have to go."

"Wait. I could … drive you," he offered.

"Right, and getting dropped off by a Lamborghini wouldn't look strange. Too many questions, Nico. You don't know my family. It's better if I get on that bus." She glanced to her right. Azucar was motioning for her to get going. "Besides, I hear you're going to have a great summer in Capri with Cherry."

Nico rolled his eyes. "Longest summer ever, especially if I can't at least talk to you."

At war with herself because of the duality she'd have to inhabit once she returned to Irvine, Pepper groaned.

"I'm sorry. This isn't fair to you," Nico said, misreading her frustration.

"I don't know the right thing to do," she said finally. "But I tried to rationalize away our relationship as just friends, even when I knew it was something so much more. Then, I thought I was doing the right thing by breaking up with you. And finally, I tried to forget you, but it was impossible. After the dance, you made me so angry with your comments that I tried simply hating you."

"I know. I'm sorry. I was terrified of losing you, too, but I was so hurt. I realized what a terrible position you were in and how, faced with the same choices, I'd have done the same thing. Forgive me." He stepped forward and gingerly placed his hand on her arm. "*Per favore, mia principessa.*"

"It seems that staying angry with you is impossible, too, *mio principe.*" Pepper jumped into his arms and wrapped her legs around his torso, kissing him with all her might.

"Ew, get a room, you two," Azucar teased from the bus's steps.

"Last call, Southbound number twelve, departing."

Nico carried Pepper to the bus, a few feet away, and placed her on the first step.

"Son, you need to move that sports job," the ticket taker said.

"Yes, sir, just making sure my…girlfriend got aboard okay." He beamed at her and leaned in for one final sweet kiss before the doors slid closed.

THE MILES FLASHED by outside the window as they traversed the southland. This time, the journey wasn't nearly as tiresome as it had been in the fall. Azucar and Pepper kept each other entertained and watched the other's stuff when they dozed off, lulled by the constant motion of the bus. Pepper's mind was filled with the goings on of the last several days. There had been a lot to digest, and she hadn't had time, not with their final and packing up for home. Of course, Nico showing up before she departed Monterey County was another surprise to process. They didn't have time to figure out how they'd handle the future. All she knew was that she wanted him in it.

Chutney had sent her a file with the recording from the night of the dance. Pepper downloaded it onto her phone. For that reason alone, she was glad Chutney would be their newest roommate in the fall. She'd proven to be a loyal friend and confidant, plus it was always handy to have a techie on board. Pepper pressed play and skipped ahead. She did not need to relive the vomit incident ever again. Pepper's blood boiled with each replaying of Mrs. Sabatini's confession about Bruno Bianchi's transgression. How dare someone steal Nonnu's territory in a double-crossing scheme. But the part about the signet ring being used to place Nonnu at the scene bothered her the most. How had Dad ended up with the ring? She didn't want to consider the possibility that her father was involved in framing Nonnu.

By the time they passed through the smoggy Los Angeles basin, Pepper knew what she needed to do. This was no longer about getting an education or becoming a mob wife. Pepper was determined to regain Nonnu's territory from the Bianchi's. This was why Nonnu had set her name down sixteen years ago. To take her rightful place as head of the D'Angelo Family. It was her birthright. She was not going to disappoint him.

WHEN THEY PULLED off the freeway, the driver shouted: "Next stop, Irvine Spectrum."

"Look, I know it's gonna be tough for you to get away. Come by for a visit if you can. The train goes all the way into SD. It's like forty minutes from here. We'll go watch the surfers at Pacific Beach and drink *cervezas*," Azucar said, winking.

"I'll try," she replied.

"Evil step-monster picking you up?"

"Not a chance. Ethan said he would swing by after school."

"That gonna be weird?" Azucar asked.

Pepper shrugged. She wasn't looking forward to telling Ethan their friendship would remain just a friendship.

"I mean, after your make-out sesh with Il Principe, I figured you two are back together. *Si?*"

She smiled shyly. "Yes, we are figuring it out. But Ethan and me … I think our friendship can move beyond this without too much heartache." The bus slowed as it pulled up to the curb. Pepper pulled her backpack down from the overhead bin.

Azucar gave her a skeptical look. "Take care of yourself, Pepper."

"You too," she replied, hugging Azucar before lifting her backpack onto her shoulders.

The doors folded open with a hiss. Pepper paused at the bottom step. The dry, scorching summer air pressed against her face. She took a breath and stepped onto the sidewalk. The doors closed with a puff of cool A/C that ruffled her hair before the bus rumbled down the street.

"Stella, hey Stella," someone called in the distance.

It took her a moment before realizing they were calling to her. She turned, and Ethan was crossing the street, a bright, welcoming smile on his face. She waved. It felt surreal to hear her real name. It was as if she was waking up from a dream where she had been Pepper, and now she was back in reality. Just as she was about to step forward, a black SUV with dark-tinted windows skidded around the corner on two wheels, sending a cloud of nauseating burned rubber smoke into the air. The engine revved, but instead of racing by, the SUV screeched to a halt between her and Ethan, pulling so close to the curb Stella was forced to take a step back to avoid the SUV grazing her thighs.

As the rear passenger door opened, two large hands grasped her shoulders, propelling her forward into the SUV. Stella dropped her phone as she reached out to keep from falling, her right foot landing in the gutter, twisting painfully. Then, someone grasped her under the arms and pulled her inside. The car door slammed shut behind her as the engine roared to life. Ethan banged on the window and screamed her name as they sped away. Then everything went dark.

**Scan the code to see the cover for Mafiella: Never Betray The Family - coming soon!**

Dear Reader,

Welcome to The Family. I hope Valentina's Academy Year 1 captured your imagination because this is just the beginning…

What happens next? A Mafiella doesn't snitch, but I can reveal that book two will be available soon!

Did you scan the code to sign up for alerts? You'll be the first to see book two's cover and receive a surprise excerpt from the first chapter.

Did you enjoy Mafiella? Don't keep your opinion on ice. Let other readers know. Written and video reviews are great ways to spread the word about what you're enjoying. Plus, you'll have my utmost gratitude.

*Alla prossima,*
RosaLinda Diaz

facebook.com/rosalindasidiaz
instagram.com/authorrosalinda
bookbub.com/authors/rosalinda-diaz
tiktok.com/@authorrosalinda
goodreads.com/rosalindadiaz

# *With Gratitude*

When a writer is actively writing, they exist in a vacuum - when they aren't scrolling social media, that is. ; )

However, writers need a community where they can lament about a story not behaving, figure out plot holes, or receive encouragement to keep going.

A HUGE thank you to my own *Mafiella* squad (you know who you are), who championed this story when it was just an idea, helped me flesh out the plot, read early drafts, and encouraged me to reach the finish line.

To my CVHS Dragon kiddos, thank you for being excited about this novel and asking me often when it would be finished. Your enthusiasm lit a fire under me to get this novel into the hands of readers just like you.

The biggest thank you goes to my mom, whose unwavering belief in me is the kindling that keeps me going. Thank you for introducing me to *The Godfather*.

www.ingramcontent.com/pod-product-compliance
Lightning Source LLC
Chambersburg PA
CBHW011549190726

48287CB00010B/2813